ENCHANTRESS

The Evermen Saga, Book 1

OTHER TITLES IN THE EVERMEN SAGA:

ENCHANTRESS

The Evermen Saga, Book 1

JAMES MAXWELL

47N◉RTH

This is a work of fiction. Names, characters, organizations, places, events, and incidents are either products of the author's imagination or are used fictitiously.

Text copyright © 2014 James Maxwell
All rights reserved.

No part of this book may be reproduced, or stored in a retrieval system, or transmitted in any form or by any means, electronic, mechanical, photocopying, recording, or otherwise, without express written permission of the publisher.

Published by 47North, Seattle

www.apub.com

Amazon, the Amazon logo, and 47North are trademarks of Amazon.com, Inc., or its affiliates.

ISBN-13: 9781477823521
ISBN-10: 1477823522

Cover design by Mecob

Library of Congress Control Number: 2014930141

Printed in the United States of America

This book is for my wife,
Alicia,
with all my love and gratitude
for our enchanted years together.

THE TINGARAN EMPIRE

IN THE YEAR OF THE EVERMEN 541

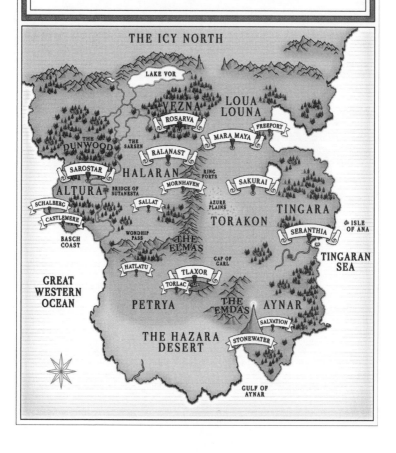

PROLOGUE

The great war that destroyed Lady Katherine's life was a seventeen-year-old memory. The emperor crushed Altura, and the hope of the Western Rebellion ended with the bitter taste of betrayal. Yet on this day, Katherine would join the ranks of the traitors. Only the Lord of the Sky could forgive her, for she would never forgive herself.

Katherine navigated the sprawling market, a veil clutched below her eyes. She felt naked without her guards, yet she was terrified she would turn a corner and there they would be—come to escort her back to the palace and end it now, before it even began.

A man bumped into her, turning and mumbling an apology. He stopped mid-sentence as he saw the face of the woman he had just knocked into.

"I'm sorry, my Lady, I didn't recognize . . ."

Katherine whirled past him. Alone and unprotected, she had never realized before how frantic the market could be. An old woman hurried by, a steaming pot in her hands. Liquid sloshed and spilled onto the ground.

Katherine's husband was Tessolar, High Lord of Altura. She had servants and lived in a palace. She wore fine garments of silk, and jewelry of gold set with emeralds. At state dinners she sat at her husband's left hand, and people of all ages and stations sought her ear, begging her to speak with the high lord on their behalf. When she walked into a room, conversation halted and people stood, touching their fingers to their lips and forehead with respect. Women were envious of her, jealous of her beauty and the prestige her position brought her.

Yet what if the people in this market—her people—could look into her heart, and see how easily she had been manipulated? Katherine's betrayal wasn't of her own making, but it was a task she knew she would carry out. The thought of what she planned to do caused a part of her to recoil, not because of any feelings for her husband, but because of her people. She knew she had no choice.

Katherine tried to calm her breathing. Her reddened eyes darted to the left and right, and her ivory skin was grayed and drawn. She had known this day would come, but she had never expected it to be like this.

It began with a nightmare.

Katherine always slept soundly and alone, yet this last night she had felt a presence beside her. It was there in her dreams, full of menace, and she fought to tear herself from slumber's grip. She woke gasping for breath, her heart beating in her ears, and the blindness was finally banished when she opened her eyes.

Crisp morning sunlight poured through a barred window. The bed linen was soft and luxurious, and Katherine stretched, feeling the blood flow through her body. She pushed the nightmare to the back of her mind and inhaled, slow as a summer breeze, catching the scent of flowers in the air.

Her breath stopped. There was something next to her head on the pillow.

It was a rolled piece of paper, sealed with black wax, resting atop the silk like a lover's note. But Katherine had no secret lover, and she froze as she realized whom it must be from.

She stayed motionless for several slow heartbeats, looking at the message as if it were a coiled viper. She willed her limbs to take her body closer, but simply couldn't summon the courage to reach forward. A maid could walk in at any moment—or even Katherine's husband. The fear of discovery finally overcame the fear of what she would read, and Katherine sat up, snatching the paper and breaking the seal with shaking hands.

You must go today to the Poloplats market and visit the girl's stall. Do not do anything out of the usual. I will be watching you. You must buy a single nightbloom from the girl to indicate you understand what you must do and that you know what will happen if you do not do it. If you need reminding . . .

Katherine read on in horror. Shaken and terrified, she dressed and summoned her guards. Instead, to her shock and surprise, her husband entered the room.

Katherine's arm whisked behind her back, hiding the message behind her body.

"Where are you going?" Tessolar demanded, his face curled into a scowl. "You are not going to the market."

Katherine took a slow, deep breath before answering. Her heart raced, and beads of sweat formed at her brow. "I won't be long." She stepped toward Tessolar, hoping to distract him from the hand behind her back.

"No, Katherine." He lifted his chin. "Enough. Your visits are becoming an embarrassment to me."

"Husband, please," Katherine implored. "Just this once . . ."

"Husband?" Tessolar raised an eyebrow. "You must really want to go this time. No, Katherine, I forbid it. The high lord's wife is not some simple woman of the fields who can associate with all manner of folk."

"This is about the girl, isn't it?"

"Of course it's about the girl!" Tessolar snapped.

Katherine realized with a sense of dread that Tessolar wasn't going to relent. To have him forbid her today, of all days! The thought of what would happen if she didn't follow the instructions in the message sickened her. He was fully capable of carrying out every threat he had listed.

"I understand," Katherine nodded. Moisture burned behind her eyes. "You don't want me to see her anymore. I will go, just this once, and say good-bye."

"No," Tessolar said. "Obey me in this, and I will see that you prosper in the position you have. You have a life of comfort, Katherine, and I know you do not wish to have the court know that you are out of my favor. Do you understand what I am saying? As the high lord's wife you have access to privilege, but only at my discretion. Do you wish to lose that access?"

Katherine looked down at the ground. "No."

"Good," Tessolar nodded. "Spend the day in your chambers, and I will see you at dinner."

Katherine looked at Tessolar with despair. "Yes, my Lord."

As soon as he left the room, Katherine threw a maid's winter coat over her dress. She knew secret routes out of the Crystal Palace, ways that even Tessolar didn't know. Less than an hour later, Katherine had left the palace and crossed the river, walking in the direction of the Poloplats.

"Excuse me?" It was a woman's voice, bringing her back to the bustling market. "Are you well?"

The merchant, a seller of elegant enchanted jewelry, had one hand hesitantly resting on Katherine's shoulder. The human gesture touched something inside Katherine, and she almost broke down then and there.

"I'm fine," Katherine said.

The merchant drew back. "Of course, my Lady." She removed her hand as if she'd burned it. "My apologies for being so forward."

"Please,"—Katherine softened her tone—"what is the fastest route to the flower market?"

"Why, you're not far, it's just another two blocks ahead, out in the open square. Through the restricted section."

"Thank you." Katherine pressed a coin into the woman's palm. The merchant looked at it and frowned, but she put the coin away.

Katherine followed a short alley to the market's heart. Bright colors were everywhere. Richly patterned cloth vied with multihued spices from Halaran, and a stocky man lifted the lid of a huge blue pot, creating a cloud of rising steam. He ladled a yellow liquid into a bowl and handed it to a customer, taking two copper cendeens in return. An old man belched, clinking his mug with a fellow. A woman cried out the latest prices for summer fruits. Boot heels rang out on the cobbled stones as a group of soldiers in Alturan green marched in formation. Katherine pretended to examine a silver kettle, setting it down when they passed.

Ahead she could see the tiered tables, lined with velvet, that were the market's main attraction. The enchanted items were artfully displayed, carefully spaced and with tiny white cards showing their prices. The most expensive pieces weren't available for general view, but those in sight were nevertheless fascinating. Silver igniters etched with tiny symbols covered one table, and nightlamps glowed in an array of colors on another. An entire aisle was devoted to necklaces, rings, and bracelets. Locks that would open with a spoken word. Knives and swords. Shields and armor. Altura was the land of enchanters, and here were the finest items Katherine's homeland produced. It was a feast for the eyes.

Katherine barely noticed. In her mind, present at all times, was the text of the message. Written with such a steady hand, it was all the more chilling for its clarity. This man had left her to her own devices for well over a decade, but deep down she had always known that one day he would make good on the infiltrator he had placed in the highest circles of the nation of Altura.

The restricted section was barred by two grim-faced guards, their spears held at angles. Katherine straightened her back and smoothed her face. She wouldn't be allowed to cover her face here, but she was so close that it would be worth the risk. The guards dipped their spears as she approached, and Katherine's heart squeezed in her chest. Then she realized they were merely bowing before her as she entered.

"My Lady," one of the men said.

Katherine's legs felt suddenly heavy, but she nodded in return and passed between their broad shoulders.

The market here was covered by a wide dome. Intricate designs and fluted stonework decorated the heights, where below, a more somber and well-dressed crowd browsed the stalls and spoke to the vendors in hushed tones.

Katherine passed a bold sign: "Strictly No Activations." The first word had been underscored.

This was where the more dangerous enchantments were bought and sold: forges and industrial heatplates, sound-and-light security devices for the wealthy, and razor-sharp weapons covered with arcane symbols.

Katherine tore her gaze from the costly array.

Her eyes met the stony gaze of Tessolar's personal guard and five of his fellows.

It was over. It was all over.

"My Lady," the guard spoke, his voice a deep baritone. "The high lord requests your immediate presence. Please come with us."

Katherine closed her eyes.

You must buy a single nightbloom from the girl to indicate you understand what you must do and that you know what will happen if you do not do it.

She opened her eyes as the guards began to encircle her, and then it came to her. Katherine looked down at the display table next to her, her fingers alighting on a cube-shaped sentry device. She traced the symbols with her fingertips, and the activation sequence came to her mind.

"*Ohr-ahn. Tal-ihn. Tal-seh,*" she whispered.

As Katherine spoke, the object came to life.

Bright colors flashed, and a sound like a thousand birds screeching rang through the market. The guards put their hands to their ears, grimacing in pain. There was a huge crash as fleeing shoppers struggled to escape the cacophony.

Katherine quickly ducked under an awning and pushed through a tented area, surprising a stunned merchant. The sound of raised voices and panicked townsfolk followed her as she searched for a way out, eventually spying a vertical split in the rear of the tent. She pushed through to where a narrow space opened up and a glimmer of light could be seen in the distance. Katherine squeezed her slim figure through the gap and shuffled along the wall behind the tents.

Gasping, she came to where the tents ended and joined the throng of the crowd as they fled the area. Katherine stopped for a moment and leaned against the wall, but the sense of urgency made her look up. She was moments from her destination.

Ahead the market opened up onto a small square. Rays of sunlight shone down on a central fountain, scattered by the spray. Some vendors had stalls here selling simple food, and the aroma wafted toward Katherine as she approached.

Slightly away from the other stalls, a young woman had set up a stand selling flowers. A smiling man walked away as Katherine approached. In his hands he held a bunch of beautiful summerglens, their delicate petals drawing the eye to the rainbow of colors. Amid such turmoil in her mind, the arrangements of flowers displayed at the girl's market stall were suddenly captivating, and Katherine couldn't look away. Some bold bunches stood as tall as a boy, whereas others were tiny and looked terribly fragile.

Katherine felt her back itch—he would be watching; she had no doubt of that. It sickened her that such an evil man would be sitting by, watching the girl's every move.

Ella's face lit up when she saw Katherine, and the noblewoman felt her own spirits rise in sympathy.

"Hello, Ella," Katherine smiled down at the young woman.

"My Lady," Ella touched her fingers to her lips and then her forehead, but her eyes were sparkling.

"Could I . . . could I buy a single nightbloom?"

"Of course. Is there one in particular? Are you sure you wouldn't like one of these beautiful . . ." Ella said.

"No, no. Just a nightbloom—any. Please, quickly, Ella," Katherine said.

"Of course, my Lady," Ella handed Katherine a flower, her expression puzzled.

Katherine breathed a sigh of relief when the flower was in her hand. There, it was done.

She handed Ella a gold coin.

"No, Lady Katherine, it's too much," Ella said.

"Please, Ella. Just take it. Please, I insist."

Ella hesitated, evidently torn between disagreeing with the noblewoman and her desire to take only what was fair. "I'll buy something for my uncle," she promised, putting the coin into a pocket in her tunic.

Lady Katherine smiled. "How is he? And your brother?"

"They're both well. They still think I'm mad, but Uncle Brandon generally lets me do what I like. He's more interested in Miro, anyway. I've started to sell gift cards too. Have you seen?"

Katherine nodded. "They're beautiful."

"I think I'm really going to do it. In two years I'll have enough money to sit the entrance examinations at the Academy of Enchanters."

"I'm so proud, Ella. You're so close to realizing your dream."

"I couldn't have done it without your help. I still sell most of my flowers to your friends, and all the books you've given me . . ."

Some men in dark clothing entered the square, and for a moment Katherine's heart stopped, but these laborers weren't her husband's men.

Ella looked at her with concern.

"Lady Katherine, is something wrong?"

"Yes . . . no . . ." Katherine struggled to pull herself together. She was conscious of eyes watching her. She had accomplished her goal, she had to remind herself.

"Ella, I . . . I'm not going to be able to see you for a while."

"What do you mean?"

"I'm sorry, Ella. You don't know how sorry I am."

A huge hand clapped onto Katherine's shoulder, holding her in a grip of iron. Katherine turned to once again face Tessolar's personal guard. He wasn't pleased.

James Maxwell

"I . . . I have to go now. Trust in yourself. You will do well."

As the young woman looked on with an expression of confusion, the guards led Katherine away.

1

In the beginning, the world was empty. There were trees and plains
of grass. Birds flew through the sky. The oceans teemed with fish.
But the world was empty. And then the Evermen came.

The Evermen Cycles, 1:1

Fergus the ferryman had always been told that one day his curiosity
would get him into trouble.

His wife was someone who "knew how to mind her own business." She told Fergus he ought to keep his opinions to himself, and
more importantly, keep his questions locked up in his head.

He'd never seen the harm—being a ferryman could get tedious
at times, and his customers always seemed to respond well to his
questioning. At times Fergus felt he knew more about the hap-
penings of Sarostar than did the high lord himself. It was amazing
how sometimes all it took were a few questions to get the most
guarded tongue wagging. A few words of praise or an insightful
remark, and it didn't matter who he was talking to—from soldiers
to farmers, priests to court officials—they all opened up in the end.
Why should Fergus change the way he was? Especially when he had
the tips to show for it.

The wife simply tut-tutted and shook her head.

The second Evensday of spring began well. The ice had thawed, and the people of Sarostar were again traveling the river. It had been a cruel winter, and the children had grown tired of root vegetables and old apples.

Fergus plied his trade from one side of the Sarsen to the other, his breath steaming in the chill air. He knew all of the best places to find a customer and quickly picked up three young women in green woolen dresses. There were a growing number of new students at the Academy of Enchanters, and for many it was faster to take a boat across the river than to cross at one of Sarostar's nine bridges.

Fergus had one eye on the river while the other regarded the girls. The students looked so young, yet he knew they had learned more in their short lives than Fergus would learn in whatever time the Skylord gave him. They seemed eager to talk, but some of the things they spoke about made no sense to him. Apparently, they were very lucky to be studying at the Academy.

Each student gave him two copper cendeens, and by mid-morning Fergus was pleased with the amount of gilden jingling in his purse. People who had gone to the Poloplats market early then began to return home, and Fergus was suddenly so busy that he had to put his talk aside while he navigated the river's hazards—mainly other ferryboats, for the Sarsen was a gentle mistress.

The wind picked up in the afternoon, and Fergus put his back into the oars and pushed hard against it, spying an older man waving at him. The man thanked him profusely as he settled into the boat. It seemed the other ferrymen had neglected him, upriver as he was. Fergus felt a momentary surge of pride, and not for the first time he thanked the Lord of the Sky that he was a ferryman.

The day passed swiftly, and almost before he knew it, Fergus found himself wiping his brow as he dropped off his last customer. He sighed, but it was a pleasant sigh—his purse was half full, and his family would be pleased when he was able to return home the next day with a boat full of fresh food.

Pushing off, he felt the river breeze blow gently on his cheek and heard the gurgle of the water as it splashed against the sides of the boat. The setting sun was silhouetted against the graceful arches of the Winebridge in the distance. Farther still, the Crystal Palace began its evening display, cycling through a multitude of colors—emerald, turquoise, crimson, and gold.

This was Fergus's favorite time of day, when the world seemed to take a short rest, a time for reflection on the day's achievements and preparation for a night with family and friends.

Fergus was a clever ferryman, and unlike many of his fellows, his small house was located downriver rather than upriver. This meant that at the end of the day he could make his way by steerage only, gently nudging the boat to the left or the right as the current took him along. Tired as he always was, he could enjoy a pipe and watch the sun as it sank below the horizon.

He leaned back against the gunwale and took an igniter from a trouser pocket. Its runes were a little faded, but it was Fergus's most treasured possession, worth an entire month's gilden. From another pocket he withdrew a wooden pipe and a pouch of redleaf. He tapped some of the hairy leaf into the bowl of the pipe and then carefully put the pouch away. Fergus named the activation rune, and the symbols etched into the igniter suddenly lit up with power; he felt the heat radiating from its tip. Touching the igniter to the bowl of the pipe, Fergus inhaled, exhaling a cloud of sweet smoke.

The river widened, and the boat's stately progress slowed, but Fergus decided against hurrying. He'd had a good day, and he deserved this quiet time. He watched the banks of the river change from cultivated land to wilderness. Tree-covered hills rose on both sides, and birds cawed as they flitted from one branch to another. Fergus sighed with contentment, and stretching out on the boat, he began to dream.

It was still light enough to see, but even so he wouldn't have noticed the length of cloth twisted among the reeds of the riverbank, except for the color—deep orange. Fergus thought it a strange color to be seeing with the greens and browns. Still, it was just some cloth that had made its way downriver, so why should he investigate?

He drew on his pipe and blew out a trail of smoke. It wasn't just a piece of orange cloth; he could see that now. The cloth was wrapped around something. Fergus looked up at the sky; there certainly wasn't much light left in the day. The sun was a red ball on the horizon, and slanted rays reflected from the river in a golden shimmer. However, his curiosity was nagging him like an old woman, and if he wanted to find out what it was, he needed to do it now.

Finally, it was the fact that he was upstream of the object that won the argument. It took only a light sweep of the oars to get him steering in the right direction.

Fergus let the river take him closer. He would wait until he was nearly on top of the object before he tried to take a proper look. If it was something worth salvaging—perhaps some goods had slipped off a trading barge—he wanted to know for certain.

The ferryboat bumped gently into the riverbank. The boat was flat bottomed, and the sure-footed Fergus had no difficulty walking to the front.

Fergus leaned out. The orange material was just out of reach. Whatever the cloth was wrapped around, it was submerged beneath the reeds. He stretched and stretched, one hand holding to the gunwale and the other clutching in vain at the material. He was so close—barely a hands-breadth away. He took the igniter from his pocket and tried again. With the extra length provided by its long stem, he could nearly touch the cloth.

He almost lost his balance, then regained his footing, his breath heaving. He tried again. Finally he caught hold of it with the end of the igniter, pulling the cloth close enough to grasp with his finger-tips. What in the Skylord's name was it?

He could see now that the cloth was silk—expensive and unaffected by the water. Fergus tried pulling on the orange material but it was caught, weighed down by whatever it covered. He took it in a firm grip and leaned back, careless of how his balance was affected. With a sucking sound the cloth moved, tearing from the reeds the thing from below.

Fergus cried out and fell back into the boat. His eyes went wide with shock, and the igniter fell out of his fingers, landing in the river with a plop. He clutched the sides of the boat with both hands, his fingers painfully gripping the wood, as if to wake him up from a horrible dream.

The body was that of a woman, middle-aged and beautiful. She was clothed in the most expensive of garments and wore dainty bedroom slippers on her feet. There was no color in her skin, and her hands were wrinkled from the water. She could have been asleep except for her eyes. She stared at Fergus with a far-off look that spoke of terrible pain.

Fergus's chest heaved; his breath became ragged. His mind whirled while he tried to decide what to do. He knew what he was supposed to do, but the thought filled him with fear.

He knew who the woman was. Lord of the Sky—everyone knew who she was.

He cursed his curiosity. What should he do?

Morning dawned over Sarostar, grand capital of Altura.

The city rested snugly in a low valley, surrounded on all sides by green hills. The River Sarsen entered the valley through a gap between the hills, passing untamed wilds. It wound its way through the city's heart before exiting the great basin at the other side. The river felt the light first and carried it sedately in, a golden saddle on its green back.

The sun rose ponderously at first, its light touching each of Sarostar's nine bridges in turn. It lit the Crystal Palace, instantly diffusing with a sparkle. The markets of the Poloplats woke and shook off the night's chill. The wealthier districts of the Woltenplats basked in its glory, while the outlying farms and hamlets soaked it up with joy. It touched on the lawns and buildings of the Academy of Enchanters, and for an instant the Green Tower was silhouetted against the sky.

The farmers always woke first, then the market vendors and craftsmen, and finally the lords and wealthy merchants. And so the city came alive from its rim to its heart—the outlying areas were a flurry of activity long before any movement was spied at the Crystal Palace.

A lone figure walked on the Tenbridge, tallest of the nine bridges. She was a young woman, carrying a basket of flowers in her arms.

A passerby would have assumed she was older than she was—it was something about the depths in her emerald-green eyes. But if she smiled, then they would have seen her youth. She was slight of build and clad in a simple tunic, such as a farmer's daughter might wear. She wore her pale blonde hair long.

However, at this early hour there were few passersby, and Ella had the entire bridge to herself. She shivered in the crisp morning air and looked forward to summer.

The basket was uncomfortable in her arms, and she shifted it to her other hip. She had a hard day ahead of her, and she quickened her pace when she saw the length of the shadows cast by the buildings.

Before long Ella reached the waking markets of the Poloplats. Vendors were drinking coffee and speaking quietly—something about early mornings always made them speak in softened tones. She knew how loud they could be, though, hawking their wares when the market opened in earnest.

A few men and women nodded to Ella as she walked past with her basket of flowers, wondering where she would set up today. She'd been coming to the market for so long that it was as familiar to her as the house she lived in, yet it never stayed the same from one day to another.

Ella's home was close to the Dunwood, far from the center of Sarostar. She woke every morning while it was still dark, and hunted for flowers, and she knew all of the best places to find them. Sometimes she found few, and her takings were meager. Other times she was lucky, and she was able to return home with a handful of copper cendeens.

Winter was always the hardest. Ella hunted for pretty mosses and winter blooms, but she was never able to gather many, and people were unwilling to pay good gilden in hard times. In addition to rising early, she stayed awake long into the night, trudging through the dark forest, seeing by the runes of a faded pathfinder.

The sun shone in Ella's face as she exited a narrow lane, and she smiled. Winter was over now, and she had a good feeling about the day.

Please, Ella thought, *let her come today.*

Nearly two years had passed since Ella last spoke with Lady Katherine. She had replayed that encounter again and again in her mind. What had really happened that day? Why hadn't Lady Katherine come to see her anymore?

Some of the market girls had laughed when Ella told them Lady Katherine used to visit her. Why would the high lord's wife visit a flower girl? They called her a liar, saying she just wanted to make up for the mother she never had.

Please, let her come today.

Ella's dream was to study at the Academy of Enchanters and to one day become an enchantress. Uncle Brandon couldn't understand it, and although her brother, Miro, tried, he was too busy learning to be a soldier to really help. The only person who had ever encouraged Ella was Lady Katherine.

For some reason the high lord's wife had shown an interest in her. Lady Katherine loaned Ella books, and when Ella returned them, the noblewoman always took them back with a soft smile. Lady Katherine brought some of her friends from court to Ella's market stall, and with them came their friends. The high lord's wife was always different when her friends were around, and Ella guessed this must have to do with the difference in their stations, and acted especially deferential. Ella owed much of her success to Lady Katherine.

Please, she thought, willing it to become true, *let her come today.*

Ella thought about the time her brother almost died.

When Ella was young, there had been a bitterly cold winter, and the Sarsen froze from one bank to the other. A group of boys had gathered on the bank and were throwing stones at the river, trying to break through the ice. Each boy tried to pick up a heavier stone than the other boys and to throw his stone farther. Ella and Miro watched them for a time. Though Miro would never leave his younger sister's side, as small as she was, Ella could still see the desire in her brother's eyes.

"It's all right. Go and play with them," she said.

Miro left without another word, running over to the group of boys and trying to join their game. His face set with determination, he had picked up a gray boulder, bigger than any of the others.

As Ella looked on, Miro tried to make his throw but slipped on the treacherous ground, his feet scrabbling before he fell heavily over. The boys laughed.

Expecting Miro to run away or burst into tears, Ella was instead surprised to see him pick himself up off the ground, his face red with anger, hands held in fists at his sides.

Without another word, Miro ran out onto the ice. His footsteps left cracks behind him, each wider than those before. The other boys stopped everything, dropping their stones to the earth with a series of thuds. Before long they were calling out encouragement, as Miro did what none of them had the nerve to do.

He reached the far bank, and raised his arms in the air triumphantly while the boys cheered. Then on the way back to where Ella stood watching, her fingers twisting nervously, the icy surface of the river broke.

It didn't happen slowly; it happened all at once. Miro plunged through the ice, his body vanishing in moments. Ella screamed, a piercing, little girl's scream, but ear-splitting none-theless. She frantically looked around her, trying to find some kind of rope, or a long stick. There was nothing that would come close to being long enough to reach the place where Miro had fallen through.

Miro struggled, desperately trying to find some purchase. All Ella could see was the occasional flash of his arm, or his white eyes, wide with fear. There was nothing for it. Ella took a step out onto the ice.

"I wouldn't do that, young lady," a booming voice rang out.

A hand grabbed Ella by the arm in an unbreakable grip.

"Let me go!" Ella screamed, watching her brother's movements weaken.

"If you want to save him, you will need to stop struggling," the man said in a steady voice. "I need both hands for this."

Ella looked at the newcomer for the first time. He was dressed in the green robes of an enchanter. At his side he held a stout length of wood, inscribed with arcane symbols—runes, Ella knew they were called. He had a crisp white beard, gentle brown eyes, and a long face.

He let go of Ella and she stilled, suddenly transfixed, watching the thrashing of her brother and then looking at the enchanter, wondering what he would do, praying it would be something to save Miro.

The enchanter took his staff in both hands and moved it to a horizontal position, his body sideways so that his left shoulder pointed toward the river. He began to chant in a sonorous voice, strange syllables coming from his mouth in a lilting rhythm. The symbols on the staff lit up as the man chanted, bright colors in silvery lines running up and down its length.

Ella gaped as the staff began to grow. The man grunted with effort as he angled its increasing length in the direction of Miro's twisting form. The end of the staff reached the crack in the ice and stopped there.

"Grab hold!" Ella cried. "Miro, grab hold! Please!"

There was nothing but stillness. The group on the riverbank— the young boys, Ella, and the green-robed enchanter—cried and bellowed, but there was no activity.

Then an arm thrust out of the water and took hold of the staff. When his second hand also took hold, Miro shakily pulled his body out of the water. The enchanter began to speak the words again, and the staff began to shorten, bringing Miro with it. Ella's brother was saved.

From that day Ella wanted nothing more than to become an enchantress. The young girl spoke of nothing else. It hadn't taken Uncle Brandon long to shatter her hopes.

It cost nearly five thousand silver deens to study at the Academy of Enchanters. Aspiring students sat a grueling examination, and the knowledge that was tested was more than just what was taught at the temple school. No, it was better that she learn the skills they taught at the sky temple: weaving, sewing, numbers, and letters. If she was lucky, she could get a position as a maid or a nanny. Without gilden she would never be able to become an enchantress.

Ella had thought about it long and hard. She didn't make the decision rashly, whatever Uncle Brandon said.

At fourteen, the earliest age it was allowed, Ella left the temple school altogether. Her mind set on the five thousand silver deens, she started a stall, selling flowers in the Poloplats market. The arguments with Uncle Brandon were long and bitter, but Ella could not be dissuaded. She worked from early in the morning until late at night, and she began to save. It was difficult at first, and business was slow, but Ella applied herself, and soon the copper cendeens began to trickle in.

She put most of the gilden aside in a cache that grew slowly but steadily. With some of it she bought books from the market. Any book she could lay her hands on, provided the price was right—books about history, books about language, and books about the laws of nature. Most of all Ella kept up with what she was supposed to be learning at the temple school. And Ella read books about enchantment.

If any were too difficult—and initially that applied to most of them—Ella put it to the side and kept it for another day. Over the years it constantly amazed her how a book that once had made little sense to her could be comprehensible at a later date.

She thought about all she had learned as she set up her stall and arranged the flowers in attractive formations. *Please,* she thought again desperately, *let Lady Katherine come today!*

For the last four years Ella had worked at the market day after day, and finally the time approached when young men and women of Ella's age would have their one opportunity to sit the entrance examinations at the Academy of Enchanters. Enchantment was serious business, and there were few places for the multitude of applicants, so only at the first spring after the age of eighteen could an aspiring student have this one chance. For Ella that time was now at hand, but she'd done it—she'd saved her five thousand deens, and she'd taken every spare moment when she wasn't selling flowers to study.

And so a week ago Ella had taken her gilden to the Academy and lined up with the finely dressed merchants' sons and noblemen's daughters. They sent her strange looks, dressed as she was in her simple tunic and holding a bulging sack in both hands. Ella tried not to show her feelings, but she was terrified.

Suddenly she was the next in line, and then she was walking toward the huge wooden desk, where a fussily dressed man with shaggy eyebrows frowned as she approached.

Grunting with effort, Ella planted her gilden on the desk with a mighty clunk. She heard snickers from behind her but didn't turn around.

"And what have you got there?" the clerk said, pursing his lips.

"It's . . . it's the gilden for the fees," Ella said.

The snickers grew louder.

"My dear," said the clerk, shaking his head, "I'm afraid it doesn't work like that. First, what were your parents thinking, allowing you to walk about town with that much gilden? It should be on account with one of the lenders. And don't you think it's a little presumptuous to arrive with your fees when you have yet to sit your entrance examinations?"

Ella heard laughter behind her and turned a deep shade of red.

"However, never fear, we can still get you enrolled to sit your turn. May I have your letter of recommendation?"

A chill ran through Ella's heart. "Letter of recommendation?"

"Yes," the clerk said; his patience was obviously being tested. "From a member of the court, to say you are of good character; or from a priest at the sky temple, to say you completed your studies." He looked Ella up and down. "I'm guessing in your case it will be the latter. At which temple did you complete your studies?"

Ella had left the sky temple years before. She'd never finished her studies and would never get a letter to say she had. How could she have let this happen? Why hadn't anyone told her?

"I . . . I don't have my letter with me," Ella said.

"Well, you had better go and get it then. Perhaps you should return home and come back tomorrow. Enrolments close in a week, so you have plenty of time to deposit your gilden with one of the lenders and come back a little more prepared, eh?"

Ella nodded and turned away. It didn't take her long to realize there was only one chance left to her. A member of the court, the clerk had said. Lady Katherine!

A woman entered the market square where Ella was searching every face in hope. The woman looked up, and Ella's breath caught. Then she slowly released it. It wasn't Lady Katherine.

For the last six days, Ella had waited in hope, searching the market for Lady Katherine from morning to night. And now the week was nearly up. Tomorrow, enrolments would close. Her opportunity would soon be over.

If Ella didn't see Lady Katherine today, she decided, she would go to the Crystal Palace, no matter what trouble it got her into.

With a letter of introduction from the high lord's wife in hand, Ella would at least get her chance to sit the entrance examinations.

Nevertheless, the idea of presenting herself at the Crystal Palace and demanding to see the high lord's wife filled her with dread. *Please, let her come today!*

A thin man with a ragged beard and a hooked nose came up, pawing through Ella's flowers with one hand while the other held a mug of steaming brown liquid. His name was Harry Maloney, and he was a buyer—someone who didn't hold any of his own stock but sourced stock when other merchants had particularly large orders come in. He was a notorious gossip and seemed to spend as much time in taverns as he did working in the market.

"Ho there, Ella. Anything good today? You'll need to step up, I should say, what with the funeral. Let me add that I'll buy all you've got and all you can get." He put down his mug, examining Ella's wares with both hands now. "I'm sure you've heard the news. Good for the flower business, funerals are," he chortled.

"News?" Ella interrupted. "What news? What funeral?"

"You haven't heard? The high lord's wife, Lady Katherine. A ferryman found her body in the Sarsen late yesterday evening. She drowned, still in her bedroom slippers. The funeral's tomorrow. It's a big job, but there's going to be plenty of gilden in it."

Ella didn't hear Harry's next words. She sat down heavily on a crate. Lady Katherine wouldn't be coming today—or any other day.

2

The artificers use lenses of curved glass in their work.
This enables them to draw runes so tiny they can hardly be read.
—Diary of High Enchantress Maya Pallandor,
page 372, 411 y.e.

Ella stood high on the Tenbridge, leaning out over the water. She stared into the turbulent river far below and imagined the sensation of falling, flying through the air, as light as a bird for an instant, before the icy water slammed into her body and drove the air out of her lungs.

She caught a strange look from a passing man and, realizing how she must look, straightened, looking away from the river and up at the rising sun, amazed that such a sad day could seem so full of promise. She considered her options. She needed a letter from a priest or a noble, but she didn't know any nobles, and Father Morton would never help her. They hadn't parted on the best of terms. He'd thought she was foolish to give up her studies, and it seemed he was right.

Looking down at the Sarsen one final time, she saw the water splash against the ferryboats, knocking them against each other. She wanted to talk to someone—anyone—who knew what had happened and could give her some reason as to why her friend and only supporter had died.

Ella's brow furrowed. Fergus—that's what Harry had said the ferryman's name was.

She turned and descended the bridge the way she had come, where a narrow staircase led from the foot of the bridge to the dock. By the time she reached the waterside, she was out of breath, but she had met a ferryman on the way who described Fergus to her and told her where she could wait for him.

Huddled against a low wall to escape the biting wind that came off the river, Ella finally saw a thick man with a bald pate help an older couple disembark from his rocking boat. He fit the description, so she walked over before her courage could fail her.

"Excuse me," Ella said.

"Where will it be, lass?" the ferryman said, holding out his hand. "Here, jump on."

Ella stepped down into his boat, and before she knew it, he had pushed off, and they were heading out into the river.

"Well?" The ferryman glanced at her as he gave a few sweeps at the oars.

"I'm sorry. I don't want to go anywhere. I just want to talk to you."

He snorted. "You can talk to me all you like, provided you pay the fare. You want a tour of the river then? It'll be two copper cendeens for a start. I know all about the city, the palace, the bridges. No one knows Sarostar better than me."

"Here." Ella handed him two copper coins. "Is your name Fergus?"

He froze and then began to row furiously, turning the boat around. "I think I know what this is about. Here, take your money, young lady." He returned the coins. "I don't want any of your questions." The oars churned the water into foam, and Ella was almost thrown out when the boat hit the dock with a clunk.

"Please, she was my friend. Won't you at least talk to me?" Ella pleaded.

"There's nothing to say." He held the boat fast to the dock. "She must've fallen into the river. It's a sad story. On your way then."

"Harry Maloney said she was in her bedclothes," Ella persisted.

Fergus put a hand to his temple. "Harry Maloney says a lot of things."

"Is it true?" Ella still hadn't stood up from her seat in the boat.

Fergus blew out of his nostrils. "Yes, it's true. Now, will you leave me alone? Do you understand the position I'm in? The high lord's men made it clear I wasn't to say anything to anyone." He shuddered. "She fell in the river and drowned—that's the story. Me and my big mouth. Harry got the truth out of me. I'm going to go and see him now and tell him . . ."

Fergus stopped talking; he was looking over Ella's shoulder. Ella followed his gaze, and a chill ran through her spine.

The first thing she noticed about the man on the Tenbridge was that he was wearing a sword. She'd never seen someone who wasn't a soldier or a palace guard with a sword. He wore it comfortably and walked with a smooth grace. He was tall and lean, with dark hair and a wide scar on his cheek, and his eyes were on them. He was clearly heading in their direction.

Fergus pushed away from the dock and began to row. The ferryman was looking anywhere but at the swordsman, and Ella could almost believe Fergus hadn't seen him. The swordsman held up his hand for them to stop, but his words were lost in the wind.

"Who is he?" Ella asked. Fergus's face had paled. "Aren't you going to stop?"

Fergus put his back into the oars, staying silent until some distance had grown. "His name's Jarvish. Rogan Jarvish," he spoke in between strokes. "He's one of the high lord's men, and let's just say he's not the man you send to have a polite conversation."

"Aren't you going to talk to him?"

"No, I'm going to pretend I didn't see him." Fergus grimaced. "I think I'm overdue to visit some family in Halaran. Long overdue."

Ella watched as Rogan came to the dock, dropped his arms, and stood watching them silently. For some reason she thought it was she he was watching, rather than Fergus. The swordsman finally disappeared from view as they rounded a bend. Ella shivered in the chill air and tried to think of something to say to Fergus, but no words came to mind.

Ella felt she was losing control of events. Her whole life, there had always been something she could do, some path she could take. Just this morning she'd had a plan. Now what should she do? She was even being warned not to ask about what happened to Lady Katherine.

She should go home and stop wondering. The funeral would be tomorrow, and Lady Katherine deserved something special. Whatever had happened, it was none of her business.

"Whatever happened to the high lord's wife, I'm going to stay quiet," Fergus said, echoing her thoughts. "I promise you that." He pulled up at a narrow pier and helped Ella disembark, refusing her money. "Young lady, I would advise you to do the same."

———•———

It was the morning of the funeral, and the last day of enrolments at the Academy of Enchanters. As the sky grew lighter, the clouds parted, and the sun burst over the horizon. Alturan funerals were always held early, when the Lord of the Sky touched the world with his majestic palette. Rather than death being an end of things, it was seen as a beginning.

Townsfolk gathered on the banks of the Sarsen, walking singly and in pairs, groups, and families. Their mood was somber—children stayed close to their parents, and husbands and wives held hands. Many of the men had doffed their hats, and the women carried symbolic green branches. From the variety of clothing and badges, it was clear that every kind of resident was represented, from craftsmen to lords, farmers to priests.

They lined both sides of the river and crowded on Sarostar's closest bridges. At the appointed hour a clear note sounded, and the shining walls of the Crystal Palace lit up with colors of emerald. In the palace grounds the fountains burst their boundaries to rise ever higher, and the crowd gasped at the fleeting beauty of the moment.

Tied at a small pier and hidden from the townsfolk, a stately barge of pale wood bobbed on the water. Ella touched a finger to her flower arrangement. There—it was perfect.

The palace guards had been reluctant to let Ella through, but one of them had convinced his fellows to relent. The young woman with the beautiful flowers just wanted to leave something special for Lady Katherine. It would be cruel to turn her away.

Looking at the barge, Ella thought about the woman who would soon be placed among the flowers, ready to drift down the Sarsen on her final journey. Again and again she remembered the conversation from two years before. Why had Lady Katherine said good-bye to her that day? What had really happened?

The sound of voices broke the stillness of the setting, and Ella suddenly had a strong feeling that she didn't belong here, coupled with an urge to flee. The sound of two men talking grew louder. Ella desperately looked around for somewhere to hide. She heard footsteps and the rustle of clothing, and in a flurry Ella climbed onto the barge and hid under a rail.

Ella's heart raced in her chest, and her breath came short. What was she thinking? If the guards caught her here, they wouldn't just be angry; they would see it as a violation, and she would be severely punished. Terrified of any sound she might make, she put her hand over her mouth to quiet her breathing. She peeked out from her hiding place through a crack, hoping the men were just passing through.

A man was looking right at her, only paces away! No, he was looking at the barge. He wasn't a guard either; he was a noble—that much was certain—with a patrician nose and tailored dark clothing to suit the occasion. He was old, but not as old as Uncle Brandon, and he looked sad.

A second man had his back to her but then he turned, and suddenly Ella couldn't look away. This man was smaller, and his features were lined with age. His hair stuck out in tufts, and a green ceremonial cloak covered his clothing, the Alturan *raj hada*—a sword and flower—prominent on the breast. An immense collar framed his head. It was the High Lord Tessolar.

Ella felt an overwhelming urge to run, even if it meant them seeing her for the briefest instant. She didn't belong here.

Then the man in dark clothing spoke. "'Tis better this way. I know that isn't what you want to hear right now, but it is better for you and better for Altura."

Ella froze.

Tessolar sighed. "I suppose you're right, Devon."

"We would have had to put Katherine on trial. The people would have been devastated."

Ella couldn't believe what she was hearing. On trial? For what?

"Why, Devon? Why did she do it?" Tessolar clenched his hands into fists.

"I cannot say," Devon said, shaking his head.

"She was not happy—no, don't tell me otherwise; I know. There was little love between us," said Tessolar. "But this?"

"I don't know what I can say, High Lord. At least let it be finished, here, today."

Tessolar nodded decisively. "Promise me, Devon. Promise me this will stay secret between us. I want the people to remember her the way she was."

Ella's cramped foot was growing numb. She moved slightly and brushed against a piece of wood holding a latch open. The latch began to swing closed but she placed her foot in the way, and instead it crashed onto her foot.

"Did you hear something?" Lord Devon said. "It came from the barge."

He began to walk toward where Ella hid. Her protection was scant at best; if he took one more step, he would see her.

A new voice spoke. "My Lords, please, they are bringing her down."

"We should take our places," Lord Devon said, turning.

Tessolar assented, and they departed the area.

Ella sighed with relief and hopped out of the barge. She ran until she found a guard, telling him she was lost. Grumbling, he let her out, and she rejoined the townspeople on the bank of the Sarsen.

Ella's heart raced, more from fear than exertion, but she felt safe in the crowd. She looked on as eight soldiers carried a cushioned litter on their shoulders. They walked down to the grassy bank below the palace, taking perfectly synchronized steps. High Lord Tessolar walked beside them. His face was bowed, the great collar of his robe masking his expression.

Lady Katherine's body lay on the litter, and as she came closer, the crowd sighed again. She looked more beautiful than ever, and a sob was heard from more than one quarter.

The white barge drifted to where the solemn litter bearers silently waited, and Lady Katherine's body was placed carefully on it. When the bearers had again resumed their places by the river, the barge left the bank, glowing symbols on its decks giving the vessel the ability to move under its own power.

Ella stood with the crowd and watched the barge slide past. Flowers covered the vessel from one end to the other. Her eyes misted as it came ever closer, and she squinted against the strong morning light, trying to find the special arrangement she'd made. There it was!

Ella wondered what terrible secret it was that Lady Katherine had taken with her, what crime it was she had committed. The vessel passed from view, and Ella turned away. It was done; she could go home now. She would keep the secret. No one would know.

As she moved through the crowd, Ella's skin prickled, and she felt the horrible sensation of being watched. Then she saw him. It was the swordsman from the river, Rogan Jarvish; he stood motionless, staring directly at her. Then he began to push through the crowd, moving toward her.

Fergus's warning still fresh in her mind, Ella turned and ran, weaving through the crowd. She glanced over her shoulder. He was catching up to her!

People grumbled indignantly, but they got out of her way. With a burst of cool air, Ella was suddenly out of the crowd while he was still tangled in the mass of people. She began to run in earnest now, ignoring the startled looks of the townsfolk. She darted down an alley and then popped out in the Poloplats, and soon she was among the maze of market stalls and tented areas.

Ella risked a backward glance. She couldn't see him anymore, but just to be safe, she entered a cloth seller's display and remained there until the merchant saw she wasn't going to buy anything and sent her on her way.

Ella's mind whirled. She needed to talk to her brother, but the morning was passing, and with her home far from Sarostar's center, she would need to hurry.

She crossed the Sarsen at the Winebridge and passed through the city's outskirts. Soon patches of grass began to show through the stones, the large houses of craftsmen and landowners replaced by simple cottages on farmland, and the street became a road. When the pasture turned into rugged grassland, and the massive trees of the Dunwood grew closer, she knew she was nearly home.

Ella's path followed the stony stream and took her to the little bridge. She caught the stench of burning coal long before seeing the small house. Ella hated the smell, and one day she promised herself she'd buy a set of heating stones. Still, the price of essence had gone up again. Every runic symbol that filled objects with life was drawn with the precious liquid; enchanted items were more expensive than ever.

Ella found the old pail lying on its side and took it down to the stream. The rope tied to the handle was broken, so she was forced to wet her tunic in the process, but she filled the bucket with clear water and struggled with it to the door of her home.

A sign over the door proclaimed the house "Mallorin," a name that meant "forest home." It was still early, so she opened the door quietly, but even so Uncle Brandon was sitting by the open stove, toying with something in the light cast by the burning coals. There was no other light in the room—it was still too cool to open the wooden shutters—and he appeared to be in another world. Ella set down the pail.

"Uncle!"

Brandon started. He was an old man now, but then again, he'd always been old, for as long as Ella could remember. His eyes were rheumy, and the skin on his hands was dry. Ella couldn't imagine him as a soldier, but that's what he had been, a sergeant in the

Alturan army. She called him "Uncle," but she knew they weren't really related.

"Shut the door, Ella. You're letting the heat out." Then he looked at the bucket in her hands. "Don't worry—I'll shut it."

Ella was careful to avoid sloshing water all over the floor. She filled the heavy iron pot with water and added oats and a sprinkling of salt from their meager store. Brandon took the pot from her hands, carefully resting it over the coals. Ella's eyes smarted from the acrid smoke.

"What were you doing when I came in?" she whispered, in case Miro was still sleeping. Ella's older brother usually slept at his lodgings at the Pens but he'd spent the last night at home. "You need more light—you'll strain your eyes."

Brandon held up their nightlamp. "It doesn't work anymore. The runes have faded."

"It was working before . . ."

"Well it isn't now—" Brandon broke off, coughing. The winter had been hard on him, and he'd picked up a chill he couldn't seem to shake.

Ella reached over and took the nightlamp—a carved piece of marble the size of a man's fist. With her fingertip, she traced the silver symbols that covered its surface, mouthing the names of the runes.

"*Tish-tassine,*" she spoke softly. The nightlamp lit up with a wan, gentle glow.

Brandon started. "How did you . . . ?"

Ella smiled. "When they start to get depleted, they become a bit less forgiving with the way you activate them. The inflection has to be just right. Still, it probably won't last another week. We'll need to buy another."

"More gilden," Brandon grumbled. "So you went to the funeral then?"

Ella nodded. "They let me put my arrangement on the barge."

"That's good." He nodded. "Poor woman—she deserved better than to die like that."

Ella turned her head. There was something strange in the way he said it. "What do you mean?"

Brandon coughed. "Forget I said anything, lass. I merely meant that drowning's not a good way to die."

"Where's Miro?" she asked.

"The boy's still sleeping." Brandon grunted. "They're working him hard at the Pens. Poor lad's chest is blue with bruises—he needs armor and a sword. Each year without his own arms holds him back." He looked up at Ella, and she thought of all the money she'd saved.

Ella realized with a sense of dejection that there was no reason for her to work so hard anymore. At that moment she acknowledged the truth: She would never be an enchantress.

"Uncle?"

"What is it?"

"The gilden I've saved. I want you to use it to buy Miro the things he needs. Get us a new nightlamp too—and a coat for you."

There was a long pause. Finally Brandon spoke. "No, Ella. You've worked hard for it, and it's yours."

"Please, it's what I want." Ella looked away so Brandon wouldn't see the tears in her eyes.

"Are you sure?"

"Yes, I'm sure."

Brandon gripped Ella's hand, surprising her—it was rare for him to show affection. "Thank you, lass. The boy won't know it, but this is what he needs. They say he's got real talent. Don't worry—we'll find you work. Or you could keep working at the market—perhaps a merchant will take you on as an apprentice. Maybe we'll even find you a husband, eh?"

Ella couldn't trust herself to speak, so she simply nodded.

At that moment a cry came from Miro's room. Ella glanced at her uncle. "I'll go and see."

Miro tossed in his bed. Sweat glistened on his skin. He rolled first one way, then another, fighting with unseen enemies.

Ella crouched next to her brother. For temple records they said he was two years older than Ella, but no one was really sure how much older he was. She wasn't surprised to see him still sleeping; it was early, and his training was hard.

"Miro!" Ella gently shook his shoulders. He lashed out, and she barely missed being hit. Ella shook him harder, calling his name. He fought like a demon, but suddenly his eyes were open and wide with confusion.

"Wh-What is it?"

"You were having a nightmare."

Miro blinked. He took a deep breath and looked away. "It was nothing."

Ella pitched her voice low, so it wouldn't carry to the next room. "You were crying out. It was the same dream, wasn't it?"

"It's always the same." His voice shook. "I never see his face properly—only reflected in his dagger. And I can't fight back."

Miro had been having the same nightmare since childhood. Ella tried to brighten. "Well, it's daytime now. Get up."

Miro sat up and rubbed his eyes. He studied her. "What is it? Something's wrong."

Ella smiled, though it was hard. "Come on, sleepy. I've got some oats on."

She returned to where Brandon still sat, watching the pot about to boil over.

"Uncle!" Ella quickly grabbed a cloth and lifted the pot from the heat. Had he been asleep? It was fearful how old he was getting.

"Sorry, lass, I didn't notice. Smells good," he said.

Ella filled three bowls, Brandon taking his and digging in with a metal spoon. She took the other bowls out to the raised front porch, where a pair of wooden chairs slumped near a small table. Ella looked out over the trees and shrubs that surrounded their forest home. She could hear the woods come alive. Birds and insects formed a buzzing music. She heard Miro's footsteps, and soon he was sitting across from her.

Ella looked at her older brother. His dark eyes regarded her with concern.

Miro had always watched over Ella. He had his own pains, though, and behind his confidence was an inner turmoil she thought only she could see. He was tall and lanky, and this morning he'd neglected to brush his unruly black hair.

"Ella, tell me. What is it?" Realization dawned in his eyes. "Of course—the funeral. I'm sorry. I know you were close. Was it sad?"

Ella took a deep breath. She needed to speak to someone. "Yesterday a man from the market told me that Lady Katherine was discovered in her bedclothes. Why would she drown in her bedclothes?"

"They're just rumors, Ella. You shouldn't listen to them."

"I went and found the man who discovered her body, Miro, and he confirmed it."

Miro frowned. "Why are you asking all these questions?"

Now that she'd started, Ella couldn't stop talking. "Then I overheard the high lord speaking with another lord. They said she committed some kind of crime and that it's for the best that's she's dead." She stopped, out of breath, waiting for Miro's reaction.

"You were spying on the high lord? Ella, what were you thinking?"

"It was an accident . . ." Ella pleaded.

Miro hesitated before speaking with authority. "Ella, I don't think you should say anything to anyone. Someone just died—the wife of our high lord. I think you should leave it at that."

"Don't you care what happened to her?"

"Just let it be. Think about what you're saying. What do you think you'll find out? It wouldn't be anything good, would it?" A temple bell sounded in the distance, striking the hour. "I need to get going now."

Miro stood and stretched, his shirt rising, and Ella blanched when she saw the black and purple bruises on his back. She was glad he would soon have the armor he needed.

Uncle Brandon came out to the deck, wearing his patched overcoat. "Hold on, lad. I'm going to go to the market. I'll walk with you."

Brandon and Miro descended the rickety steps, and Ella's brother turned and waved as they disappeared into the trees, leaving Ella on the deck, listening to the sounds of the forest. Sighing, she entered the house and cleaned up the breakfast dishes with the last of the water. She took the pail outside to fetch more.

Rogan Jarvish stood at the foot of the steps, looking up at her, his hand on his sword and the gray cloak billowing around him.

Ella screamed, and the sound of the pail clattering against the steps rang through the morning air.

3

You can learn more about people from their instruments of torture than you can from their works of beauty.

—Louan saying

Ella spun on her heel and grabbed one of the chairs. She would hurl the chair at the swordsman and dash into the small house, slamming the door shut behind her. In the confusion she would be able to escape through a window.

"Stop, lass." Rogan's voice sounded like gravel. He was suddenly next to her; he'd moved so quickly, she could hardly believe it. He held her by the arm, gently but firmly. The chair fell out of her hand.

"Please, I mean you no harm." He took his hands off her and spread them.

Ella was overwhelmingly conscious of how alone she was. No one would come to investigate her scream.

"Ella, listen to me. I was a friend to Lady Katherine."

She stood, her chest heaving, before turning to face him. He didn't seem so fearsome all of a sudden, with his arms imploring and his expression earnest. Rogan took two steps back to open some space between them.

"You knew her?"

Rogan chuckled ruefully, shaking his head. "Sometimes I wish I'd killed the Petryan who gave me this scar twice over. Once I was thought handsome. You don't need to be frightened, lass. You're a difficult girl to find, did you know that? I was told I could find you at the market, but you weren't there. And then at the river, I was certain you'd seen me. I don't know what you think it is I want from you, but it's nothing sinister, I assure you."

"I was told you were dangerous."

"Only to Altura's enemies," he said. "My name is Jarvish, Rogan Jarvish. I'm here to deliver a message."

"What message?"

"I can't tell you that, because I haven't read it—it's for you, Ella. I do, however, have an idea what it says, and I have one simple piece of advice. Read it quickly, for you don't have much time—not much at all."

With that he handed her a scroll, sealed with green wax and the imprint of a flower. Rogan nodded to her and met her gaze for a moment, then departed quickly, leaving Ella standing on the porch, her mouth open.

Ella promptly broke the seal and began to read. Something fluttered to the floor, two smaller sheets rolled inside the larger, but Ella ignored them, her pulse racing.

Dear Ella,
I have left this legacy with a friend, to be given to you in the unlikely event of my not being able to give it to you myself.
In the time that I have known you, I have come to be so proud of all you have achieved, and with no help from anyone except yourself.

I have made many mistakes in my life, and I cannot express how pleased I am that you dream of becoming your own person, and not beholden to anyone else.
Please think of me kindly.

There was no signature. Ella's hand trembled, and her knees went weak. She sank down to the floor, where she became aware of the two pieces of paper resting next to her hand.

She picked the first up. It was bordered with glossy black lines, and the text was in the legalese of the moneylenders. All she caught were the words "on account" and "tuition." With wide eyes and shaking hands, Ella picked up the next sheet.

It was a letter of recommendation to the Academy of Enchanters.

Enrolments closed this morning, and examinations finished today. She might already be too late.

Ella had always promised herself she wouldn't be afraid, no matter what life threw at her, yet here she was. If she hadn't been afraid of Rogan, she wouldn't be in this situation.

Adrenalin surged through Ella's body.

She began to run.

Someone different sat behind the desk when Ella arrived, flushed with exertion, at the Academy of Enchanters. She was a pretty girl Ella's age, with waves of auburn hair tucked behind her ears, full lips, and soft brown eyes.

"Hello, can I help?" the girl said.

Ella looked around her, disconcerted to see there was no queue and the paved footpaths were uncannily quiet. "I'm here for the examination," she said, holding the letter of introduction and lender's draft out for perusal.

"Don't worry," the girl smiled, "you're here early. There's plenty of time."

Ella breathed a sigh of relief. She knew the examination involved hours studying specific texts before being verbally tested on their contents, as well as other things. As today was the last day, she didn't know when the masters would be finishing up—but she'd made it in time.

"Madam Foley, our administrator, will be here to take you shortly." The girl paused. "I think I've seen you before. Do you have a brother who trains at the Pens? Miro, I think that's his name."

"How did you know?" Ella's heart was still racing, but she began to calm herself.

The girl blushed. "I watch the boys train sometimes, after classes. He's very good, you know. Oh, sorry, I haven't given you my name. I'm Amber."

"I'm Ella."

"Nice to meet you, Ella. Is Miro your older brother, or younger?"

"He's the older, but I'm not sure by how much. Can I just ask—how does the test work?"

"Don't worry," Amber said. "Madam Foley will interview you. How could you not know how much older he is?" she asked with open curiosity. "When's your birthday?"

"I don't know. Miro doesn't either. My parents . . . they died. Another man raised us."

"Oh." Amber looked down. "Sometimes I don't know when to keep my mouth shut."

They spoke while Ella waited, and Ella soon found herself warming to Amber. Even as they were talking, though, Ella wondered what the examination would be like. She'd heard it was difficult. What would they ask her?

Eventually, an older woman came over, her face stern and her hair coiled in a tight bun.

"Ah, there she is," Amber said as the woman approached. "Madam Foley, this is Ella. She's here for the staff position."

Ella looked at Amber with shock. "No, I'm not. I've got my letter of recommendation here and a lender's draft for the fees. I'm here to enroll and sit the entrance examinations. I want to study at the Academy."

"Amber?" Madam Foley said. "What have you done?"

Amber turned white. "Ella, your clothes . . . I didn't realize. There's not even ten minutes to go before the masters close the examination room. Lord of the Sky, what have I done?"

"Please just tell me where to go," Ella said.

"Here," Madam Foley said. "I'll take you. Quickly, come with me. Amber, take her letters, and perhaps next time don't be so swift to come to conclusions, dear. I'll see if I can reason with the masters."

"Yes, Madam Foley," said Amber morosely.

Madam Foley took Ella by the hand and half-led, half-dragged her through a series of twists and turns, down alleys and narrow footpaths, obviously taking a shortcut to the examination room.

"Here," the woman said, opening a door for Ella. "Go inside and take a seat. There's no one in there but the masters, and I'm guessing they'll be surprised to see you. I'll speak to Master Lodley for you, but I'm sorry, dear, I can't guarantee they'll show any sympathy. Normally, each student gets six hours."

Ella nodded, entered the cavernous room, and took a seat.

Five minutes passed before Ella gave up. The books stacked on the desk were each as thick as her finger; she simply wouldn't have time to read any of them.

She looked up. The three masters sat along one side of a long desk, each with a similar stack of books piled high in front of him. The centermost glanced at the glowing timepiece on the wall and then frowned at Ella. Each man wore the green robes of an enchanter, but because these were masters, their sword and flower *raj hada* was lined with gold. Master Lodley, on the left, had sad eyes and a drooping mouth, and though they all had graying hair, he seemed older than the other two. The man in the middle was slim with sharp, hawkish features; dark eyes; and frown lines. He wasn't someone, Ella thought, she would like to see angry. In contrast to the other two, the man on the right was younger and a little overweight, with a round face, shaggy eyebrows, and an absent expression.

"Excuse me?" Ella said.

Master Lodley's sorrowful eyes opened with surprise, and he leaned back a little. "What is it, young lady?"

"I don't have time to read these texts."

The frown on the face of the slim master in the center deepened. "Yes, I think that's quite clear. Master Lodley, would you agree with the girl's estimation?"

"Now, Master Goss," Master Lodley said, "no need to ridicule the girl."

"I can do this," Ella said. "Can you just ask me the questions? This is my only chance—you all know that. Please." Ella felt her eyes burning and struggled to hold back the tears.

"I'm sorry, young lady." The younger master on the right spoke for the first time. "I'm afraid it doesn't work like that. We've been here all day, and I'm sure you'd agree we've had nothing to do with your tardiness. Without having read the texts, asking you would waste all of our time."

Ella fought to hold back tears. "Just let me try?"

Master Lodley looked at Master Goss. "What harm could it do? Perhaps we should let her try. We don't have to focus on the texts."

Master Goss snorted. "It's ridiculous. I don't know how you can even suggest it."

Master Lodley fixed his gaze on the younger master. "Master Samson?"

Ella held her breath. If Master Samson agreed, her intuition told her Master Goss would have to accept.

Master Samson thought about it for a moment. Ella looked again at the timepiece on the wall. She had minutes left.

"I'm sorry, young lady, but I have to agree with Master Goss," Master Samson said.

Ella felt her heart sink. To have come so close, that was worst of all.

A shadow moved in the mezzanine above the desk where the masters sat. Ella realized someone had been watching. A moment later there was a knock at the door. Master Goss's expression grew even more irritated as he stood and opened the door abruptly, his mouth open to let whoever it was know they were not to be disturbed.

Ella couldn't see whom it was Master Goss spoke to, but his attitude changed dramatically.

"Of course," she heard him say. "Yes. I understand."

He closed the door and walked back to his chair, seating himself with a sigh of exasperation.

"Looks like you have your chance, young lady. Don't think we'll make this easy—enchantment is dangerous, and we can't afford fools." Ella gulped and nodded. "Stand up and come closer would you? Yes, stand there. Now, Master Lodley, Master Samson? We've each been tasked with testing Ella's knowledge of the material, the mental, and the magical. Master Lodley, for the material, perhaps you'd like to start your verbal examination? Let's get this over with."

Master Lodley nodded, and was pensive for the briefest moment. With a shiver of fear, Ella realized the formidable intellect that hid behind his drooping eyes.

45

"What is the composition of bronze?" he asked without pre-amble.

"Bronze is an alloy of copper and tin. No more than one-third tin," Ella said.

"And steel?"

"An alloy of iron and carbon."

"How much carbon?"

Ella hesitated. "A very small percentage."

Master Lodley's response didn't tell her what he thought of her answer. "Order these by weight. A Petryan ounce of copper. A fifth-thimble of silver. An imperial dram of sulfur. A jeweler's droplet of gold. A regular ounce of iron. An alchemist's ounce of phosphorus."

Ella thought for a moment. "Well, imperial drams are the same as ounces, and as far as I know there's no difference between a Petryan ounce and an ounce anywhere else in the empire. You would know that, and I've never heard of a jeweler's droplet in all my time working in the market." Her gaze met Master Lodley's gray eyes. "I think all the measurements are the same." Her mind worked furiously. "But also they're all elements. So I think you're asking me which element has a greater elemic weight. In order from lightest to heaviest, they are phosphorus, sulfur, iron, silver, and gold."

Master Lodley sat back in his chair. She couldn't tell whether he was impressed or not. Ella's heart was racing. She had worked so hard to be here. She couldn't afford to fail, not once.

"How would you measure the weight of a mountain if you only knew its height?" Master Lodley said. He may have supported her earlier, but he wasn't letting her off easy now.

Ella felt a pressure grow behind her temple. "If I only knew the height? I would measure the circumference of the mountain by walking around it and calculate its volume using the circumference and height. I would weigh a smaller volume of the mountain to estimate the density. Finally, I would multiply density by volume to calculate the weight."

Master Lodley nodded. "Master Samson, would you like to go next?"

"Yes, of course," Master Samson said. His eyes regarded her under heavy eyebrows. "How can you throw a ball as hard as you can and have it come back to you, even if it doesn't bounce off anything? There is nothing attached to it, and no one else catches or throws it back to you."

Ella thought furiously. "Throw it up in the air?"

"Next question. You are in a room with no metal objects except for two iron rods. Only one of them has been given a magnetic charge. How can you tell which one of them is magnetic?"

Ella's headache grew in intensity. She tried to work it out in her mind. If she brought the two iron rods close, they would both move together. So how would she know which one of them had the magnetic charge? Master Samson already said there were no other metal objects in the room. What other properties did magnets have? She suddenly remembered reading a book called *A Brief Cartographical Analysis of Merralya*, which described a mechanical device called a compass. Modern travelers generally used a seeker to help find their way, but long ago an alternative to lore was found.

"I know. Hang them both from a piece of string. Whichever points in a north–south direction is the magnet. Is that it?"

Master Samson simply nodded. "My final question: How do moneylenders create gilden from nothing?"

Ella's brow furrowed. She felt the headache grow until it was a pulsing pain that increased with each beating of her heart. "If I give one silver deen to a moneylender, and he promises to give me five cendeens every year as interest, then I still think I have one silver deen. But if someone else then comes and borrows my silver deen, then we both believe we have a deen, and there are two deens where before there were one."

Master Samson looked at the timepiece on the wall. "I am finished. Master Goss?"

Master Goss sat up in his chair. He looked down his nose at Ella. She was suddenly very worried about what he was going to ask her. "I am going to test you on your knowledge of lore, young lady. First,"—he quickly drew something on a sheet of paper—"what is this rune?"

Ella could barely see the symbol. She started to step forward.

"No, don't come any closer."

Ella's head pounded. *"Asta?"*

"You may come closer now."

Ella walked toward Master Goss and looked down at the symbol. She could see her guess was correct, and silently breathed a sigh of relief.

"Now, point to the whorl," Master Goss said. Ella pointed. "The bridge?" Ella circled it with her finger. "Mark out the hollow."

Ella looked up. "There are two hollows." She ran her finger along the dip on the left of the rune, then on the slight curve at the bottom."

"You may step back now. What is the rune for?" Master Goss said.

"I . . . I think it's a rune for color," Ella said.

"What activation would you ascribe if you wanted to use this rune in the creation of a nightlamp?" Master Goss asked.

"Tish-suka."

Master Goss looked satisfied.

Ella continued. "But you wouldn't use *asta* without a tertiary chain. You'd end up having to darken the lamp by activating a sequence for darkness, which doesn't make sense. One would instead include a sequence to deactivate the lamp."

Ella saw Master Lodley smile and then attempt to cover it up.

"My final question," Master Goss said. "When will the Evermen return?"

Master Lodley coughed and choked. Ella opened her mouth and then closed it again. How was she supposed to answer? Did they want the kind of response a priest might give? Or was it another mental challenge?"

"Your time is up," said Master Goss. He smiled, but it wasn't a friendly smile. "You may have some knowledge, young lady, but don't forget that you also need faith."

Master Lodley glanced up, evidently aware that the hidden figure in the mezzanine was listening. "You may go now, Ella. You can speak with Madam Foley regarding your tuition."

Ella's eyes widened. "My tuition?"

"Yes, Ella, your tuition. Classes start on Lordsday."

Ella felt a thrill run through her. "Thank you," she said to the masters. She beamed up at the mezzanine. One day she would learn who could tell a man like Master Goss what to do. "Thank you," she said to the hidden heights.

Master Lodley gave her a hint of a smile in return. As the timepiece struck the hour, Ella left the room.

4

*Possessing essence doesn't lead to wealth, else the Assembly of
Templars would be preeminent. It's what we do with
essence that leads to power.*
—Memoirs of Emperor Xenovere I, page 205, 381 Y.E.

The sun beat down mercilessly. Miro blinked sweat out of his eyes,
then ducked as one of his opponents took advantage of his lapse.
The sword came close. He felt the nick as the razor-sharp steel sliced
into his temple. A small amount of blood welled out, but the flow
was small.

"Fight on," said Blademaster Rogan.

If Miro had a cendeen for every time he'd heard those words he
would be a rich man.

"Concentrate!" his teacher called, though whether the advice
was intended for him or his opponents, he wasn't sure.

Saporo and Rimor gathered themselves. Saporo looked
proud for scoring a hit. Still, Miro knew he was the less dangerous of the two, and kept an eye on Rimor. His two opponents
spread apart, forcing Miro to take two steps back lest they outflank him.

Ringed around them, fifty novice swordsmen watched closely.

"Notice how Miro watches the eyes and the legs, not the hands or the arms. The eyes tell you what your enemy intends, while the legs tell you how he will do it," said Rogan.

Rimor's eyes flickered, but Miro didn't take the bait. Saporo waited, following his ally's lead.

Miro didn't know how he knew it, but he suddenly sensed that Rimor was about to step to the right. He waited for the first signs of Rimor's movement. Then, with reflexes like an adder, Miro was there to meet him. Saporo was behind Rimor for a split second, and Miro seized his opportunity, ramming the hilt of his sword savagely into Rimor's face and breaking his nose. Blood sprayed over the young man's face, blinding him.

"Always use every part of your body, every part of your weapon. Miro is an adept at this; he uses his blade like an extension of his body."

Faster than the eye, Miro's sword flashed at Rimor's neck.

"Hold!" shouted Rogan Jarvish.

The sword touched the young man's neck with the lightest of kisses, the razor-sharp steel leaving a faint line on Rimor's neck. What did Rogan think—that Miro was going to kill him? No. But Rimor's mocking words hadn't been forgotten, and this was Miro's chance to strike on a level playing field.

"Come on! What if Miro were holding a zenblade? Rimor, you're out," said the instructor. "Saporo, let's see you get another hit."

With a grimace and his hands clutched to his face, Rimor left the field, throwing Miro a hateful glare. Miro knew he would pay for that later. He didn't regret it. Away from supervision, with his friends to back him up, Rimor had left worse scars on Miro's own tender flesh.

With the better opponent out, Miro grew more confident. He lunged, forcing Saporo back. He feinted right but instead spun to the left. Saporo caught himself and tried to lift his sword in warding. The steel tip of Miro's blade lanced at Saporo's face; the youth fell away from Miro's onslaught. Miro kicked out with his leg, landing a painful blow to his opponent's ankle. Saporo stumbled and lost his balance, falling backward into the dust. Rather than pushing farther, Miro waited, allowing his opponent to rise.

"Did you see that coming?" the instructor asked. "Saporo should have. If he'd been watching Miro's eyes, it was clear. Well done, Miro; now finish him."

Miro could have done without the praise. From the sidelines he caught several resentful glances from the watching young men.

Saporo threw himself at Miro, his sword twisting and thrusting. It came straight at the center of Miro's chest. Miro went to turn—too late! The steel was going to skewer him. At the last moment he arched himself backward. Confident of a hit, Saporo overextended. Miro pirouetted, resting the point of his sword over Saporo's collar.

"Excellent, Miro," Blademaster Rogan called. "Now bow." The two standing fighters did so, absent Rimor, who'd been taken to the infirmary. "All gather."

Saporo joined his fellows. Blademaster Rogan came to stand beside Miro. Slightly taller than the lanky youth, he casually placed his hand on Miro's shoulder. The gesture wasn't lost on many. Miro heard snickers and groaned inwardly. Why did he have to get so much attention?

"You use steel swords. You hone them until they are sharp enough to cut a falling leaf. You wear no armor. You fight daily, in deadly combat. Someone, tell me why this is so?"

A student answered, "To make us better fighters."

"Correct, but there is more to it. Miro?"

Miro knew the answer Rogan was looking for. "Because combat without real fear teaches nothing."

"That's right. There is more to being a bladesinger than carrying a zenblade, just as there is more to being an enchanter than possessing a vial of essence. A zenblade is to a normal sword what an ocean is to a gentle stream. The lightest touch from a zenblade will cut through anything. Anything!" he growled. "It will cut through armorsilk, and armorsilk is the strongest armor our enchanters know how to make. And if we can't make it—then who can?"

"No one!" the young men said in unison.

"So do yourselves a favor. Sharpen your steel sword, cut down your opponents, and keep your eyes sharp, for one day you might be facing someone with an enchanted blade." He gazed around him. "I see close to fifty of you here. No more than three of you will become bladesingers, the elite of our swordsmen, given the most powerful of our enchanted weapons. Some will become soldiers in our army. Some are here to learn the military arts and prepare for a political career. But some will become cripples, here in the Pens, and some will die. That is all."

Blademaster Rogan strode away, leaving the young men standing pensively, uncertain for a moment.

Saporo came over with two of his friends. "That was a dirty piece of work. Rimor was going to a pageant tonight, and you broke his nose. I know you, Miro. I know you're good enough that you didn't have to."

Miro frowned. Saporo wasn't close to Rimor, and Miro didn't need another enemy. Saporo probably didn't know about the ambush on the Tenbridge two nights ago.

"Leave him," said another of the youths. "He's got no father, so he never learned any manners."

Some of the regular troublemakers gathered. Miro knew he could never take them all. And if he drew his sword, outside of the arena and unsupervised, he would get kicked out of the Pens altogether. It was the first rule they were taught, a rule that was rigidly enforced.

"Maybe his father was a pig, and his mother was a goat, and he's what you get when you breed the two," one of the youths, a lord's son named Gordin, said. It was a feeble joke, but it still raised a few laughs.

Miro had nothing to say. He'd never had the courage to ask Brandon about his parents. They were dead; he knew that much. What if there was some dirty secret? Perhaps he'd be better off not knowing.

"Maybe his mother couldn't bear the thought of looking at Miro all day, so she left. I know I would!"

"Maybe she was a whore!" said Gordin.

Flushing, Miro turned away. If he provoked them, he'd get more than bruises. He could sense that after the thrashing he'd given Rimor, they were looking for vengeance.

Miro walked away with his head down, his eyes burning.

The taunting stopped. "Who's that?" one of the youths asked.

Miro looked up and saw Ella. She stood transfixed, staring at him with a strange expression on her face. He realized she must have been there for some time, long enough to hear at least. His sister looked clean and sweet in her green woolen dress, the garb of a student at the Academy. Ella was already a year into her studies, but Miro still felt proud every time he saw her in green.

"That's Miro's sister. Lord of the Sky, how did such an ugly sod end up with a sister like that!"

The youths laughed.

"I wouldn't mind slicing off that dress and seeing what's underneath."

"Let another part of your body do the talking," said Gordin. "You'd probably slip and cut something off."

Miro didn't consciously move. In the blink of an eye his sword had slipped out of the leather scabbard at his side and he'd lunged forward. Fast. The point of his sword was suddenly pressed up against Gordin's throat. The lord's son gulped. A thin rivulet of blood trickled down from the tip of the razor-sharp steel. Miro's muscles bulged, tensed to the breaking point with the effort of restraining himself.

"Miro, please. Don't kill me."

"Miro?" It was Ella's voice. "Stop it, please."

Ever so slowly, Miro removed the sword, his eyes never leaving the youth's. Finally, he turned. The shame he felt at seeing Ella's face was painful. He wished she never saw this side of him.

Their goading had a purpose, Miro realized suddenly; they knew the rules as well as he did, and as soon as he left, they would be speaking with Blademaster Rogan.

Miro threw his sword on the ground and walked away from the crowd, leaving Ella staring after her brother and the marks his boots left in the dust.

"Blademaster? I'm sorry to bother you," Ella said as she caught up to the striding figure.

"Yes?" the blademaster turned, and instantly Ella realized that Miro's teacher and the man who'd given her Lady Katherine's legacy were one and the same. His dark eyes went wide with surprise. "What are you doing here?"

Tall and lithe, Blademaster Rogan cut an imposing figure. Ella wondered how old he really was; it was hard to tell.

Ella was nervous. Rogan Jarvish definitely did not seem pleased to see her. "When I met you, I didn't realize you were one of my brother's teachers. I don't want to trouble you."

"Something tells me that's exactly what you're going to do," Rogan said. "I heard about what Miro did. If he wants to apologize, he can come himself; much good it will do him."

"They made him do it. The other boys—they goaded him. He drew his sword, but it wasn't his fault. It was mine. I wanted to tell you . . ."

Rogan towered over her. "He's just lucky no one was hurt. Just exactly what happened?"

Ella looked down at the floor, uncertain what to say. She blushed. "I came to see Miro fight. The other boys saw me. They said some things."

Rogan drew back. "Ah. I see." He surprised her by looking uncomfortable. "What did Miro do?"

"I . . . I think he threatened one of the boys with his sword. He . . . he touched it to his throat. There may have been blood. Lord of the Sky, I know it sounds terrible. No one's hurt."

Rogan shook his head. "I won't be able to protect your brother, Ella. Word of this is going to get out. Those boys talk, and many of them have powerful parents."

"It was my fault. There must be something you can do," Ella pleaded.

Blademaster Rogan shook his head from side to side. "I'm sorry. He shows a great deal of promise, and I don't want to lose him. But they are going to want to see him punished."

"Can you punish him in some other way? Anything other than throwing him out?"

Rogan's brow furrowed before he looked up. "Three months in the salt mines. It's the only thing strong enough."

Ella blanched. She'd heard about the salt mines. The workers lived completely underground, huddled in caves and passages half a man's height. The salt was rough enough to cause cuts and abrasions from mistakes made in the constant darkness, and when the salt got into the wounds, which it always did, it burned like a scorching flame.

"Bring him here," said Rogan Jarvish. "I'll tell him about his punishment, and let's see what he says."

———◆———

Ella walked with her brother, taking a longer route than was necessary. She stayed quiet, giving Miro time to calm down. She supposed that what he had done was only beginning to sink in. She had decided not to say anything to him besides that the blademaster wanted to see him. She had the feeling he wouldn't appreciate her speaking up on his behalf.

Miro had settled by the time they reached the Pens. "I'm sorry you had to see that," he finally said. "Lord of the Sky, what have I done?"

He frightened her sometimes. He had such pain in him, and also such strength. It was times like these that she forgave him his absences and the way she bore most of the burden taking care of Uncle Brandon. He had always protected her and cared for her. She wasn't the only one who struggled.

"I saw you fight in the arena," she said. "I was frightened—do you really have to use real swords? You could have been killed." She touched the thin line of dried blood on his forehead.

"I let him do it." He shrugged. "If I showed them how good I really am, they'd just hate me for it all the more."

"Are you really that good?"

The blademaster's voice sounded from behind them. "Yes, he's good. And he could have been better. Perhaps even a bladesinger one day."

Ella frowned. "What do you mean, 'could have'?"

"I hear you drew a sword outside the arena, Miro."

Miro met Rogan's stare. "I did."

"He was only trying to . . ." Ella spoke up.

"Quiet, young lady," said Rogan. "Well, what of it? Why did you do it?"

Miro stayed silent.

"You do know word of this is going to get out, don't you? Do you want to be thrown out of the Pens?"

Miro still said nothing. His expression was black.

"Look at me, Miro. Listen; I have an idea. Contrary to what you may think, I have no wish to lose another promising boy. But if I don't punish you, they'll punish you themselves. That's right, don't think I haven't seen it. This time you might not survive the experience." He turned to Ella. "Can you keep a secret?" Ella nodded, and Rogan continued. "I thought so. Miro, there's a salt mine in the north, and for the next three months you're going to be working in it."

Miro took a deep breath. "When do I leave?"

For a long moment, Rogan stared at Miro. "You do want to stay, don't you?" he finally said. "Miro, you wouldn't last a week in the salt mines. Our worst criminals go there and come out broken men. But it's good for me to know that under that stubborn surface you're willing to do what it takes. Sending you to the salt mines is the word I'm going to put around." Ella breathed a sigh of relief but waited for the catch. "In reality, I'm giving you a choice. Either leave the Pens today, or I'm sending you to Tingara as a guard with our delegation to the Imperial Chorum. Who knows? You might learn something."

Miro's face showed cautious hope. "I'm going to Tingara?"

"What will he have to do?" Ella asked.

Rogan grinned at her. "Looks like you're the one with the questions. He'll be gone for at least three months. He'll need to serve and protect—and fight if need be, although that's unlikely. And most of all, he'll need to do what his officers tell him. Miro, if I get a bad report about you, there'll be nothing I can do. You'll be out."

"I understand." Miro nodded.

"Just keep with the story. You're going to the salt mines for three months. I can place you as a normal guard with the other Alturan soldiers. They'll just assume you're a new recruit. Keep your wits about you, and you'll do fine."

Ella couldn't decide how to feel. Three months! She felt happy for Miro. Becoming a soldier had always been his dream, but she couldn't imagine being away from her brother for such a long time, with only Brandon for company.

She looked at his face. She could tell he was happy that he would be taking a sword into the field, even if it was largely ceremonial.

"Thank you," said Miro.

"Just see that I don't regret it," Rogan said. "When you leave today, take your things with you. We won't be seeing each other for quite a while.

"You won't regret it. I promise."

Blademaster Rogan grunted and left.

Ella helped Miro gather his few possessions.

"What's the Imperial Chorum?" Ella asked. "It's like a big meeting of the houses, isn't it?"

"When something important is happening and requires a meeting of the high lords, either the houses or the Imperial House can call the Chorum. It's held in Tingara, in the Imperial capital, Seranthia. The primate of the Assembly of Templars mediates."

"Why has this one been called?"

"No one knows."

"Do you have to go? Actually, don't answer that."

He looked at her. "You know I do. If I had to leave the Pens, then what would I do? When I'm a soldier and you're an enchantress, we'll be able to move out of that tiny hut in the woods."

"I like Mallorin," Ella said.

"It's not enough," Miro whispered. Ella held her breath. It was so seldom that he spoke like this. Sometimes she thought he'd buried his feelings so deeply that she'd never penetrate the wall he'd built around himself.

"We're happy, Miro, and that's the important thing isn't it?"

"Happy?" Miro was pensive for a moment. "I'll be happy when I'm a soldier and can hold my head high."

5

The idea is not to create the tallest, thinnest turrets. Nor is it to raise walls that will withstand the mightiest foe. It is to build structures that will inspire the world with their beauty for a thousand years.
—Lore of the Builder, 14:12

It was the time of the rains.

The sky opened and water came out. The Sarsen grew dramatically high, its banks near bursting. It became impossible to move on the roads; only transport by ferry was possible.

"Tish-tassine." Ella spoke the rune, and feeble light glowed from the nightlamp. It barely provided enough light for her to see. Their old heatplate was little better; water took over an hour to boil. They'd run out of coal long ago.

Ella carefully spooned a measure of cherl into the mug, following it with hot water, filling the mug to the top. She added a dash of redspice to mask the fact that she was rationing the cherl.

She walked carefully so as not to spill any. "Here you go, Uncle," she said.

Brandon was sitting on the porch, looking out at the rains. The sound was soothing, and the air was warm.

"Thank you, lass," he said hoarsely, taking the mug.

"Careful, or you'll burn yourself," she cautioned.

He had a small sip. "It's good. Aren't you going to have some yourself?"

"No, Uncle, I'm fine. I had a few cups of wine with Amber, a friend from the Academy," she lied.

"That's good," he said. "Make sure you don't drink too much. A lady never lets too much wine go to her head." He broke off, coughing.

"Yes, Uncle."

Ella missed Miro terribly. It didn't help that Amber kept bringing his name up, talking about him incessantly. He'd been gone for over a month. Didn't Amber have anything better to talk about? Every time they studied together she'd ask Ella new questions about him.

Thinking about her studies made Ella frown. Over a year at the Academy, and she still had to learn anything meaningful about enchantment. Amber told her she was being impatient. Ella was certainly learning, but her dreams of glowing swords and shimmering robes had yet to be realized.

"Is Miro still at the Pens?" Brandon said.

Ella sighed. "Miro's on his way to Tingara, Uncle. He's part of our delegation to the Imperial Chorum."

"The emperor," Brandon growled. "Skylord scratch his name from the heavens."

"Uncle!"

Brandon said nothing more, gazing without seeing at the rain. Ella had rarely seen him in this mood.

"Uncle?" she ventured.

"Hmpf?"

"I need to ask you about something. I once heard the boys at the Pens taunting Miro."

"It's nothing the boy can't handle, lass. He's tough, that one. The Pens can be hard, though, I have to say. I trained there briefly. Got into my own share of trouble, I did."

"The boys at the Pens said some things about my parents. I need to know. What really happened to them?"

"Hmpf."

For a long time he didn't respond and they both sat in silence. Ella held her breath. She'd never asked him so directly before—Brandon wasn't the easiest man to talk to at the best of times.

"Better not to talk about these things, girl. Is there any more of that cherl about? How about we both have a mug and talk about what we're going to do about this leaking roof."

"We fixed the roof last spring. Tell me. I don't think even Miro knows. Tell me about my parents."

He sighed. "It's not a happy tale. Another time, Ella."

"Please." Ella held her breath.

Brandon put down his mug. He seemed to be gathering his thoughts.

"Your parents were good people, Ella. Your father—he was a soldier. Well-born and educated, trained as an officer, but a soldier nonetheless." He wet his lips. "Your mother was the daughter of a minor lord. Your father was fifteen years her senior, but they were married, and you and Miro were the result."

Ella held her breath, willing Brandon to continue. He paused again for a long moment. His eyes were half shut, and she thought he might have fallen asleep, but he suddenly opened them again.

"I fought with your father nearly twenty years ago—not long after you were born. I was his sergeant in the war they now call the Western Rebellion. We just called it the War.

"The Tingarans have dominated the other houses for hundreds of years. They call themselves the Imperial House, and they call their ruler emperor, but really they're no better—just bigger and more powerful. The Rebellion started when High Lord Peragion Telmarran of House Halaran gave his daughter to the emperor in marriage. Emperor Xenovere had a reputation for dark deeds—still does—but Peragion was eager to curry favor with the emperor and see Halaran grow under his reign.

"Our last emperor, Xenovere IV, was a man of peace, dedicated to preserving the balance of the houses under a fair essence agreement. Xenovere V is different. He is a ruthless, cruel man.

"A year after the marriage, High Lord Peragion stopped receiving word from his daughter. When he inquired about her, the emperor initially lied to him. The truth was that he had beaten her in a sudden rage. She died."

Ella put her hand to her mouth. "How could he kill his wife?"

Brandon shrugged. "The truth came out. Peragion couldn't forgive himself. Our High Lord Serosa answered our ally's call, and Altura and Halaran went to war against the emperor."

"What happened to my father? What about my mother?" Ella tried to conjure an image, but there was nothing. She felt remote from it, like she was hearing about someone in a history class.

Brandon took another sip of cherl and swallowed before continuing. "The war was long and bitter, and Serosa and Peragion would never have surrendered. But back here in Sarostar, a lord named Tessolar managed to convince the other lords that the war was futile and it was better to surrender sooner while we still had some strength.

"Serosa was betrayed by Tessolar, and both he and Peragion were captured. Tessolar made himself High Lord of Altura and immediately initiated peace talks. The emperor demanded a group of Alturan and Halrana officers as a bond before negotiations could begin."

Ella felt a shiver run up her spine. She almost wanted him to stop.

"The officers were captured at Mornhaven, in eastern Halaran, as part of the negotiations. Your father was one of them. Your mother heard about your father and came to try to free him. She was unable to. I won't tell you what happened, but he was killed by the emperor's executioner, Moragon, along with many other brave fighters. Tessolar still proceeded with negotiations. Your mother . . . she became ill. She died of grief."

"Was I there?" Ella said in a small voice.

"Yes, my dear, you were there. You were just a baby. Miro was a tiny boy. I'm sorry, my little one. It was so hard on the both of you, Miro especially. He still has those nightmares."

The intensity of the rain grew. Puddles grew into pools. Ripples collided into each other with each drop that fell.

"You were a sergeant?" Ella couldn't picture the aged figure before her holding a sword or facing armies in battle.

Brandon smiled. "An old sergeant, even then. Hard to picture? Brandon Goodwin was my name. Old Brandon, they call me now." He sighed, and Ella could hear the rattling in his chest.

"The way they say it now, the Rebellion was a lost cause. Tessolar came to power amid growing fear of the outcome of the war and worry about the emperor's retribution if we lost. Tessolar helped to end it quickly, and now they praise him as a peacemaker. They now call the old high lord 'Serosa the Dark' and say he was a warmonger."

Brandon coughed, and when he resumed, his voice was hoarse. "That's not how I remember it. Not at all. We were so close to having all of the houses united against the emperor. So close! Serosa kept saying that all we needed was one decisive battle. And it all came to nothing. The emperor punished us, killed our soldiers, rationed our essence, and now Altura is a shadow of her former self."

Brandon's mind was obviously reliving those days, nearly twenty years ago. His lips smacked on dry gums, and he fell silent. Fearing he'd fallen asleep, Ella rose and used what was left of the hot water and the last teaspoon of cherl to make a mug, taking it quickly over.

"Here, Uncle. Please tell me more about my mother."

Brandon took a slow sip, sighing in pleasure. "She was a beautiful woman like you, lass. Her hair was darker, but just as long as yours. She was clever and resourceful, and you probably get your intelligence from her."

Ella tried to picture her. She closed her eyes. There was a fragment at the edge of her memory. Then it passed.

Brandon's head fell down. Ella thought for a moment that he might have fallen asleep, until she saw a tear trickling down his cheek.

"I don't know if I can blame Tessolar. War is a terrible thing, and no one in living memory had seen a war to rival this one, a major war of the houses. It was just minor disputes before, with the Imperial Legion sorting matters out, and the primate of the Assembly of Templars mediating a peaceful solution. The templars control the essence, after all, as well as being the natural go-betweens with priests in every capital. But this time was different."

Thunder boomed out. Ella shivered.

"War on this scale was devastating. Plains flooded. Peasants dying by the tens of thousands. Famine and disease running wild. Dead bodies bloating in the sun. Whole divisions consumed by the worst weapons our lore could devise.

"I once came across a town, a small village really, on the edge of Torakon, the land of the builders. There were tall cathedrals devoted to the Lord of the Earth, impossibly high, House Torakon's lore allowing them to build taller than you or I would think possible.

"A brigade of elementalists had been routed. Though Torakon was their ally, they had passed through this town before us."

Brandon paused, and tilted his mug to his mouth, but it was empty.

"They played with the townsfolk, Ella. Tortured them. At first we thought it had been to find the essence, but that was when we found the children."

Ella wished he would stop.

"Scores of children. They are mad in the head, those Petryans. They used the elements on them. I saw a girl—she couldn't have been older than five—taken by elemental water—drowned on land. Another child had been filled with elemental air like a balloon until he exploded into tiny pieces. His head stayed intact. Another child had been burnt to a pile of ash. Such a tiny pile."

Ella thought she would be sick. "Please, Uncle, don't tell me these things. I just want to know who killed my parents."

"Your parents were killed by the emperor." Brandon gestured around at the weak light cast by the nightlamp. "And here we are. We've been on essence rationing ever since. Now the emperor's called a Chorum, and who knows what evil we can expect next."

Ella entered the small house, closing the thin door behind her. Brandon still sat on the wooden porch; he'd asked her to leave him there, alone in the darkness.

Ella leaned heavily against the wall and slid slowly down until she rested on the floor, her head on her knees.

Her mind was in turmoil, thoughts running back and forth in her head. On the one hand she felt guilty for dredging up such painful memories, but on the other she felt angry with Brandon for holding so much back for so long.

It was a comfort to know that her father had been a man of honor, a man who had fought for a cause. Brandon hadn't said, but she sensed that her mother had loved her father and that she had been loved in return.

Who knew what would have happened if Tessolar had never betrayed High Lord Serosa; if Serosa had forced his decisive battle?

Perhaps the other houses would have joined them in rebellion against the emperor, and she would now be laughing with her parents, Brandon promoted to some comfortable position.

It was pointless to worry about what could have been.

Ella's thoughts turned to Miro. She didn't know how she was going to do it, but she would force a confrontation between him and Brandon. Miro needed to hear what she had just heard for himself. He thought his parents had some guilty secret and didn't have the courage to ask and find out the truth.

Sitting against the wall, emotionally exhausted, Ella began to slip into sleep, thinking about her parents, about the past.

In that stage between wakefulness and sleep, Ella's memory cleared for the briefest instant. She felt the soft touch of her mother, heard a gentle lullaby.

Ella woke from horrible dreams. Men with faces of fire were throwing children about Sarostar. The Sarsen in her dream had been replaced with a river of molten rock, the fiery lava overflowing the banks and burning its way through the town, buildings and people exploding in its wake, sounds of screaming.

The rain had stopped some time in the last few hours. She had fallen asleep leaning against the wall. Her back ached from sleeping in such an uncomfortable position. As Ella stood, it made a sound like a cracking whip.

Stretching, she looked about. She had forgotten to deactivate the nightlamp, and if anything it looked fainter than ever.

Ella went to the door and peered through the window. She could see Brandon still sitting motionless in his wooden chair, the empty mug beside him.

"Uncle Brandon," she muttered, opening the door.

Ella stooped to shake him awake. There was something strange about his body and the stillness of his form.

"Uncle Brandon?" Ella shook him, first gently, then with insistence. "Uncle Brandon!"

The old man stayed seated, motionless.

Brandon Goodwin, soldier of Altura, who had fought his way from one end of the Azure Plains to the other, was dead.

The rain started again.

Ella's sobs were inaudible above its patter.

6

People are changed not by coercion or intimidation, but by example.
                    —Sermons of Primate Melovar Aspen, 538 Y.E.

The trader ship yawed in the strong wind, thrusting her great weight over the crests before plunging again into the troughs.

High above the decks, in the area the sailors called the crow's nest, Miro gazed out at the sea, enjoying the thrill of the ship listing first one way and then another. Here at the very top of the mast, any movement was exaggerated. Miro felt like a bird caught in an unpredictable air current, tossed back and forth in the stiff ocean breeze.

The ship was what the sailors called a storm rider—an armed cruiser with a long range and enough firepower to hold her own against most enemies. Her name was the *Infinity*.

Two months ago, Miro could never have imagined life aboard the trader ship. It was like a complete community on the water, more than a house, something like a moving fortress.

As a vessel of House Buchalantas, nearly every square inch of the *Infinity* was covered with runes, the structures among the most complex Miro had ever seen, particularly on the sails. They buzzed and glowed as they were activated by the sailmaster, an imposing man named Scherlic. His calls as he activated and deactivated the runes were heard night and day; his voice had become so familiar on the journey that Miro no longer even noticed it.

So much had changed in the last two months. Miro almost felt like a different person—with the Pens, Sarostar, Brandon, and Ella part of another life. He had now seen High Lord Tessolar in the flesh, along with several other members of the Alturan elite. It seemed everyone who was a name in Altura was a part of this delegation.

There were even ten bladesingers included in the group. They kept largely to themselves, but Miro yearned to catch a glimpse of their zenblades: single-edged swords of shining steel, slightly curved and covered in runes. With long hilts, they could be wielded with one hand but generally required two, and were the most powerful blades Altura's enchanters produced. The series of activation sequences to control a bladesinger's arms was complex and required continuous chanting, giving bladesingers their name. Miro had thought they might participate in the regular sword practice on the listing deck of the ship, but they spent their time below decks in each other's company, deep in discussion or reading books.

There had been some argument among the delegation's leadership over the decision to make the journey to Seranthia by ship. Miro had only heard it secondhand, of course, from the other guards.

Lord Marshal Devon was the named leader of the contingent. A stately, serious man with an impeccable dress sense, Devon was a noble in every degree.

Captain Sloan was in charge of the men-at-arms, and he and Lord Devon were as different as two men could be. Gray-haired, rough-voiced, and made as if hewn from a block of granite, Sloan was a veteran of the Rebellion.

Lord Devon had argued for the journey to be made by sea and, in particular, with the sailors of House Buchalantas. Not to insult Captain Sloan, he'd said, but the Buchalanti sailmasters held undisputed sway over the oceans, and to them a deal, once made, was unbreakable.

Captain Sloan had nodded politely at Lord Devon's assertion and then made the point that on land they passed through predominantly friendly territory and had the protection of many swords, whereas if something went wrong at sea, they lost the entire leadership of Altura at a single blow.

Lord Devon had made a brief comment about Captain Sloan's description of the Azure Plains as being "friendly lands" and won the argument.

Miro seemed to get along well with the older soldiers. For some reason he was able to avoid the sea sickness that affected many of his fellows, and his willing attitude even made him a few friends.

It had been a long and eventful journey, filled with storms and clear days, arguments and late-night discussions. As they traveled south, it had grown hotter, and many of the men, Miro included, had doffed their tunics to be bare chested in the sun. At first the sailors had stared at Miro's milk-white skin, but after a few weeks he'd developed a deep tan.

Seeing the life of the Buchalanti sailors, he sometimes wished he could be one and leave his cares behind as he spent his life aboard ship, spurning land to sail the length and breadth of the world. He was amazed to see that many of the sailors were women. They looked similar to the men, wearing canvas coveralls much as the men did, and they had low, gruff voices.

One night he had asked a one-eyed soldier named Tuok where they were. Tuok shrugged. "We've gone beyond the limits of our maps, young lord." Miro frowned. He had no idea where the nickname had originated, but some of the men had started calling him "young lord," and it had stuck. He sensed no malice in it and so let it stay. "Only the sailors know where we are now," Tuok finished.

Miro couldn't believe people wouldn't want to map these uncharted lands, or at least purchase a map made by famous explorers like Toro Marossa. Surely, perhaps in the libraries of the Academy, they must have maps of these lands?

He resolved to ask one of the Buchalanti where they were. It was going to be difficult, though; the Buchalanti sailors deferred to the sailmaster, even to the point of fear. Miro tried striking up a conversation with one of the sailors, but the man just looked at him blankly.

Then, without any action on Miro's part, an opportunity came. It was early dawn, a time when most of the other members of the Alturan delegation were still asleep, and Miro could walk freely around the deck without fear of getting in the way or overstepping his bounds.

Miro was at the ship's port rail, gazing out at the strange landscape to the north. They had been following the yellow coast of this land for week upon week. The terrain was barren and devoid of all life. Not a single tree or even a plant could be seen. Heat waves rolled off the ground.

A man came up to stand next to him.

"The land of the desert tribes," said the man in a deep, heavily accented voice.

Miro turned slightly so as not to break the spell. It was the sailmaster, Scherlic. He knew he had to say something.

"Such a barren land," he ventured.

Sailmaster Scherlic smiled. "They do not think so."

"You've met them?"

"Few people have, but yes, I have. A harsh people living a harsh existence. They fight each other, valuing strength above all else.

Survival is the word in these parts. But they love their land, much as I'm sure you love yours."

Miro had never thought about it before, but now that he was here, farther from his homeland than he had ever been in his life, he knew he missed the rivers and lush forests of Altura terribly. He missed Ella and the way Brandon always grumbled when Ella gave him his cherl, but smiled with love to her departing back.

"Where is your land?" Miro said.

"My land is here." The sailmaster gestured to the ocean. "Of course, we spend some time in cities, but never too long."

"Aren't cities like Schalberg and Castlemere trader cities?"

The sailmaster looked surprised. "No, they are not. We spend time there, and many of the inhabitants are descended from Buchalanti stock, but they are not of House Buchalantas. They administer themselves and earn their income from trade. A Buchalanti's place is here, on the sea."

Miro wasn't sure whether he'd insulted the sailmaster. "I'm sorry."

"Nothing to be sorry about, young man. I might add that you handle yourself well on the sails. If you are looking to join us, the only requisite is a love for the sea."

With a broad smile, the sailmaster left Miro gaping on the deck.

It was a good memory, one of many that he would take away from this trip. Miro hoped he would be sailing with the Buchalanti again on the return journey. In the time since he'd spoken to the sailmaster, he'd saved up many more questions.

The swaying of the mast brought Miro back to the present. Looking behind the ship, he saw a piece of wood in the ship's wake. Over time he noticed more flotsam start to appear. Then he noticed a low form in the cloudless sky.

He knew what he was supposed to do but bided his time, waiting until he was certain.

"Land ho!" Miro bellowed with all his might. A great whoop came up from the deck, and Miro grinned down at the men below.

The men excitedly gathered themselves at the rail, waiting until land came into sight. They would be looking forward to a hot meal, a warm bed, and plenty of time away from the sonorous chanting of the sailmaster as he activated the runes. Their luck had proven true, and they were about to visit a strange land far from home.

Over the course of the journey, Miro had heard a lot about the land of Tingara, homeland of the emperor, and its capital, Seranthia—some of it fanciful, some of it downright bizarre.

It was said to be the biggest city in the world, bigger than a hundred Sarostars laid side by side. One of the men said it was so big that new professions had been created just to administer the city. Miro wasn't sure if the man was telling the truth. Perhaps the roles were something like those of the lords and marshals of Altura—men who were responsible for trade and deciding on military matters.

A small island barred the way to the massive harbor. Barely an outcrop, it jutted out only a few feet above the deep blue ocean. Miro's breath caught when he saw the great stone statue of a man standing astride the island, as tall as five ships like the *Infinity*, one on top of the other. The huge figure appeared to be bursting out of the water.

The Sentinel, it was called, famous throughout Merralya. As the *Infinity* drew closer, Miro could make out more detail. The man wore a strange headpiece like a raised crown, with a rune decorating its front. The man's expression was stern, but noble. His hair beneath the headpiece flowed down to his shoulders, and his features were soft, almost female. He had one arm raised, pointing slightly upward, as if at the stars or the setting sun. Miro didn't know what the man was supposed to be trying to say. The other soldiers said he was ancient, old when Seranthia was just a small fishing town. Once again, Miro didn't know what to believe.

He saw more ships ahead and behind them, and even a few Buchalanti ships, notable by the glow of runes on their decks and sails. Seranthia was a busy trade port, with countless mouths to feed and a population hungry for exotic goods.

Passing the Sentinel, they entered the great harbor, with rocky headlands to either side. Instantly, the ocean smoothed, the ship's motion grew calmer, and the *Infinity* slowed. Miro heard the chant of the sailmaster increase in volume, and some of the runes on the sails shifted hue as they responded. Whatever the sailmaster was doing, it was working. They soon overtook the ship in front of them; the high lord was paying the Buchalanti well for speed.

A straight gray line stretched from one end of the horizon to the other. Miro frowned, squinting and trying to focus his eyes. What was it? Then he drew back as he realized what it was: the Wall.

He saw the soldier Tuok moving about down below, carrying crates up from the hold. "Ho, Tuok! Is that really the Wall?"

"Sure is, lad. Soon you'll be seeing much more than that. Now get down here and give us a hand."

Grinning, Miro gathered himself and leapt from the crow's nest, catching hold of a spar as he fell.

Tuok winced. The sailors, men and women both, barely looked up from what they were doing.

Miro swung off the spar and slid down a yard, burning his hands slightly from the friction, before landing on the deck triumphantly.

"Well done," Tuok said. "Now get to work."

7

I blame the Alturans for all the death. If they hadn't
come to their Halrana allies' aid, this rebellion
would have been crushed long ago.
—Emperor Xenovere V at the surrender of Altura, 524 Y.E.

There were so many new sights that Miro was constantly turning his head, first one way and then the other. Tuok said Miro was making him dizzy and to please stop before he put his fist in Miro's ear.

The harbor formalities had been lengthy. At one point Miro saw Captain Sloan discretely hand over some money to the harbormaster as if he didn't want to be seen doing so. Miro decided to ask Tuok, who was busy hauling crates.

"It's the way they are here in Tingara," Tuok grunted. "Everything comes at a price."

"But we're an official delegation. Our high lord is with us. Why do we pay?"

"We pay so the harbormaster does a good job and promptly gives us our papers so that we can be on our way."

"But . . ."

"Enough, Miro. You'll find out soon enough."

Now they were being led through the streets of the port district and into the city proper. Word of House Altura's arrival had quickly reached the emperor, and an escort soon arrived.

Miro didn't like the look of the Imperial Legion.

The legionnaires were huge men with uniformly shaved heads, and rather than wearing their *raj hada* on their clothing, the sun and star of House Tingara was tattooed somewhere on their skin.

A few carried pikes, twelve feet long and razor sharp. These were Alturan made, the runes familiar to Miro's eyes. Their armor was also enchanted—heavy steel covered with arcane symbols, glowing softly even though it was standard practice in Altura to leave enchanted armor deactivated unless actually in combat. Either the emperor was flush with essence, or he was showing off his power for the Alturans' benefit. Perhaps it was both.

Each legionnaire carried a few prismatic orbs at his waist—fist-sized magical spheres designed for throwing or launching and made to detonate on contact—and one even had a mortar strapped to his back. These weapons were all made and sold by the artificers of Loua Louna.

They were hard men, trained since birth and armed with the best weapons money could buy. Miro felt vaguely resentful that some of his house's finest work had ended up here for the emperor's men. But then he looked at the bladesingers bringing up the rear and chatting quietly. Their armorsilk, blazoned with the Alturan sword and flower, was light, and all they carried were their zenblades, yet they radiated power, deadly beyond belief. Miro noticed the way the legionnaires' gaze kept moving warily to the bladesingers and felt his pride return.

Miro forgot about the legionnaires among the sights, sounds, and smells of this fantastic city. The buildings were old and grand, tall and intricately carved with fanciful figures. The streets twisted and turned haphazardly so that Miro was soon lost. For once he couldn't simply climb a bridge and see for a good distance in all directions. The structures were so tall and close together that he couldn't even see the sun.

The Wall stood above it all. Miro could see it close behind them and followed it with his eyes. It curved away into the distance until it became a gray blur, but it was so high that it never left his vision completely.

Miro couldn't believe such a city could ever come into being.

The delegation passed through market after market, so that Miro wondered if the entire city was made up of markets. How could there be so many people, willing to buy so many goods?

The legionnaires led them through food markets with strange vegetables and fruits Miro had never seen before. A man held a pumpkin half his size above his head, testing its weight. Not only was it the biggest pumpkin Miro had ever seen, it was bright yellow.

They passed through fish markets, where the fruits of the sea were lined up and sorted by size, color, and type, from the smallest red shrimp to the most fearsome blue shark. Hanging from a balcony was a strange creature with dozens of tentacles, each covered in round suckers. The tentacles were so long they touched the ground three stories below.

As he walked, Miro began to notice other facets of life in Seranthia. Groups of youths were begging on the street, fighting each other for the gilden thrown their way. An old man slept in an alley next to a pile of garbage—at least, Miro hoped he was sleeping.

A ragged woman came up to Miro, ignoring the legionnaires as she tugged on his clothing. "Please, young sir, I have no job, no money; my daughter is ill."

Miro didn't know how to respond. "What of your family?"

"My family is dead, killed by the Imperials. For speaking out, for nothing!" She spat at the closest of the legionnaires.

"Get gone, hag!" the legionnaire growled, kicking at her.

She scurried away.

They passed through spice markets and gem markets, and a section of moneychangers. For four blocks Miro saw only carpet sellers. Then it was tinkers, selling pots and pans, tools and knives. A vendor held up an old enchanted knife; Miro could tell it had once been a valuable piece, but it was scratched and the runes were fading.

"Please, only two deens!" the vendor called after them.

"Not so pretty after a while, is it?" Tuok said.

A litter jostled past, borne by eight swarthy men. Through the gauze of the litter Miro could make out a female silhouette. She spoke to an attendant, who, at her request, brought back items for her to inspect. When one took her fancy, the attendant handed over gilden without even haggling. The market vendors bowed and scraped as the litter swept past.

"Seranthia, capital of the world," said Tuok.

"It's a beautiful city, but why are there so many begging? Isn't there enough food?"

"There's enough food, but you have to pay for it. If you've got money you can buy anything in Seranthia. Anything. Trust me—you don't want to know some of the things for sale here. On the other hand, if you've got no money, you're out. The emperor routinely rounds up vagrants and throws them over the walls." He looked at Miro with meaning. "It's a long way down. But still people keep coming, looking for something, I'm not sure what. It's often I'm glad to be Alturan."

Hearing music, Miro turned.

A woman danced on top of a small stage. Men stood around, clapping and cheering, drinking and laughing.

She was the most beautiful woman Miro had ever seen, with long flowing hair the color of gold and shimmering blue eyes rimmed with a dark paste. She smiled as she danced, her body curving and writhing with her movements.

She wore a small skirt, ending high above her knees, almost at the tops of her thighs. A tiny piece of silk was crossed in front of her breasts, and as Miro watched, she removed the silk, throwing it out into the crowd.

The men yelled raucously as her breasts were revealed, and she began to play with the material of her skirt.

Then Miro noticed she never moved far from a particular part of the stage she was dancing on. Looking down, he saw her ankle was chained to the stage, a heavy manacle around her delicate foot.

"Tuok! Lord of the Sky! Look . . ."

Miro started to run toward the stage.

Tuok grabbed Miro and dragged him away. They both had to move quickly to push through the crowd and rejoin the delegation. Fortunately, Captain Sloan hadn't noticed their absence. Some of the soldiers smirked.

"Take care, Miro," Tuok said. "You're a stranger here. Do nothing except what you are told." He roughly pushed Miro away, his one eye blazing. Miro had never seen him so angry.

Finally, the group entered the district of market houses, the financial center of the Tingaran Empire. Each nation of the empire had its own market house: great square structures where the distinct goods manufactured by each were bought and sold. Services could also be bought; for the right price even elementalists from Petrya could be hired.

Tuok's good humor returned. "Want to buy a magic sword, build a big glowing fortress, blow it up with prismatic orbs, and have little wooden men put it back together? This is where you come."

Miro also knew that the market houses were diplomatic centers, where information was worth good gilden. They'd all been told to be on the lookout for spies.

Some said that the origin of the term "house" being used for the individual nations, each with their own customs and distinct flavor of lore, came from these buildings.

Miro saw the *raj hada* of House Torakon on the huge building they were currently passing. Then it was the *raj hada* for Loua Louna, the land of the artificers. The Veznan market house, whose people were called cultivators, was on the other side of the street. Then, next to the building of House Halaran, they came to the Alturan market house.

The delegation from Altura, the land of enchanters, had arrived.

***

The men quickly settled into their new lodgings. Miro, Tuok, and two others shared a room in the east wing. They'd barely been sitting still for five minutes when Captain Sloan called the soldiers out.

After they lined up in front of him, he regarded them for a moment and then assigned various guard duties. "Remember, men, we're far from home. Keep your wits about you, and don't trust anyone."

He signaled Tuok and four other soldiers, ignoring Miro. "You're on special duty; come with me."

"And Miro?" Tuok ventured.

Captain Sloan regarded Tuok with a level gaze. "All right, and Miro."

Miro looked over at Tuok, who grinned at him and nodded.

***

The streets were quieter in the district of market houses than in the rest of Seranthia, populated with a less lively crowd. The men wore golden rings on their fingers, and some had their noses or ears pierced. Many openly displayed an affiliation with a particular house, and Miro saw emerald for the green of Altura, amber for the brown of Halaran, and turquoise for the blue of Loua Louna. Many, perhaps prudently, wore imperial purple or showed no affiliation at all.

One of the bladesingers spoke briefly with Captain Sloan, then was followed a moment later by the other nine bladesingers and High Lord Tessolar himself. Lord Marshal Devon said something to High Lord Tessolar, who nodded.

It was the first time Miro had seen the high lord up close. Tessolar was even older than he looked from a distance. His eyes were sunken, and what was left of his hair tufted out in wisps. Miro wondered if Lady Katherine's death had affected him badly.

Tessolar wore a flowing green cloak with an immense collar, the sword and flower *raj hada* woven into the fabric on his chest. The cloak was covered in runes; Miro assumed they gave the cloak properties similar to the armorsilk worn by the bladesingers.

The soldiers fanned out, with the bladesingers occupying the inner circle, close to the high lord.

Miro was surprised to see that they were only taking a short journey to the market house of Halaran. The Halrana *raj hada* was displayed proudly above the formal entrance—an open hand with an eye in the center.

The heavy doors opened, and a tall man stood regally in the center of a crowd, his arms open with welcome. Miro realized this must be Legasa Telmarran, High Lord of House Halaran.

The Halrana high lord wore a brown robe, his *raj hada* on a torc around his neck. Miro realized with a start that this was the man whose sister had been married to the emperor and whose father, along with Serosa the Dark, was killed in the aftermath of the Rebellion.

High Lord Legasa's hair was stiffly erect in the formal Halrana style. In contrast, High Lord Tessolar cut a less imposing figure, but seemed wiser in his years.

High Lord Tessolar touched his fingers to his lips and then his forehead, and then High Lord Legasa touched his breast and swept back a leg, looking briefly at the ground before meeting High Lord Tessolar's eyes.

"Halaran welcomes Altura to our house," the Halrana high lord called loudly. "I, Legasa Telmarran, High Lord of House Halaran, give welcome."

In a thinner voice, but audible to all, High Lord Tessolar responded. "I, Tessolar Mandragore, High Lord of House Altura, accept the welcome of our traditional allies. We thank the Lord of the Sky for bringing us together."

"We thank the Lord of the Earth for bringing us together," said High Lord Legasa.

The Alturan lords and soldiers entered the Halrana market house and were led down a corridor to a reception chamber, decorated with Halrana art: paintings of the land and the harvest, with colors of brown and red. The lords took seats around a stone table, and the heavy chamber door closed with a boom.

A bladesinger stood behind each Alturan lord, and the Alturan soldiers lined up against the wall. Behind each Halrana lord stood a black figure, polished to a high gloss and standing motionless. Beautifully crafted, perfectly in proportion, Miro thought they could only be iron golems. He measured one against his height and realized they were nearly seven feet tall. Symbols covered the golems, the runes glowing red, indicating they had been activated. The constructs, creations of the Halrana animators, were alive.

Halrana in brown robes lined the wall behind the golems. Each wore a torc around his neck and carried a small tablet in his hands. These were the men who controlled the golems.

Then Miro forgot everything when High Lord Legasa spoke his first words, staring directly at High Lord Tessolar.

"Our Lexicon has been stolen. We need to know, what do you know of this?"

All in the room tensed.

Miro glanced at the closed door.

8

Do you know what the problem with the world is? Too many houses open their doors to unwelcome guests.

—Emperor Xenovere V, 532 Y.E.

Students at the Pens were given only a basic class in lore before their abilities in swordsmanship were developed, honed, and tested.

Those who proved themselves at the Pens, the fastest and deadliest swordsmen, were accepted into bladesinger training. Miro assumed this was when a bladesinger's knowledge of the runes was taught.

Yet even accomplished bladesingers knew only enough lore to control their weaponry. It was enchanters who held the knowledge, and in matters of lore, out of the two siblings, Ella was the real expert. Sometimes Miro felt she knew things he wouldn't understand if she spent a lifetime trying to explain them.

He pictured her now, her eyes lit up with excitement, explaining to Miro what only an enchanter knew about Lexicons.

"Each house has its own lore," Ella explained. "Halrana animators bring golems of wood and bone to life, while Alturan enchanters make the sharpest swords and the toughest armor. Builders from Torakon construct the tallest towers and strongest fortresses. Petryan elementalists can heat the air or draw moisture from it. Louan artificers use their skills to create everything from timepieces to mortars. A Lexicon is the key to all of a house's lore."

"So everything an enchanter needs to know is in our Lexicon?" Miro had asked. If this was the case, why were there so many books on enchantment?

"No, there's more to it than that. In the pages of the Lexicon are the perfect representations of the rune structures. Something like an alphabet combined with a dictionary."

Miro nodded slowly. He hadn't particularly enjoyed grammar.

"At places like the Academy of Enchanters in Sarostar, new methods and techniques are always being created—ways of arranging runes into matrices for stronger steel, for example—but the runes themselves, drawn by hand by a fallible human—well, they can only approximate the perfection of the Lexicon."

"Is that all?"

Ella sighed in exasperation. "No, that's not all. Each Lexicon is a relic of the Evermen—they weren't created by human hands—and from a Lexicon stems the power that allows the lore to function. Our Lexicon must be hidden and protected at all costs, not only for the knowledge but also so it can be renewed. Just like enchanted items fade and need renewal, so does a Lexicon. Our high enchantress wouldn't be able to renew our Lexicon if it were lost, which means the runes would fade, and the magic would no longer work."

"All magic?"

"Everything that was made with those rune structures. In our case that means all of our enchantments: zenblades, armorsilk, nightlamps, pathfinders, heatplates—everything."

"So it needs to be protected."

"That's right. Each house appoints one individual above all whose responsibility it is to maintain and protect their Lexicon.

Unlike the lords, whose position is hereditary, it's a position that can only be reached with intelligence, skill, and dedication."

Miro nodded. From what he'd heard, even High Lord Tessolar deferred to High Enchantress Evora Guinestor.

───────◆◆───────

Lord Marshal Devon was the first to speak. "You have lost your Lexicon? But how?"

Next to him, High Lord Tessolar placed a hand on Devon's arm. "This is a grave and serious matter. We offer our sympathies and our full support. This is the first occasion we have had to know about this."

High Lord Legasa nodded, as if confirming something.

The Alturan high lord continued, "But I have to agree with Lord Devon. This comes as a shock. How did you lose your Lexicon? What of the high animator? Were there safeguards in place?"

High Lord Legasa motioned; there was a creak, and the heavy chamber door opened. A newcomer entered, a man wearing a brown robe similar to High Lord Legasa's, but where Legasa's was plain, the newcomer's robe shimmered with runes, and the torc around his neck glowed with flickering lights. As he stepped forward, he rested his weight on a thin wooden cane, and when he reached the table, he released the cane and placed his hands on the stone, peering at each face in turn, his gaze strangely intense.

Miro gaped in astonishment as the cane sprouted tiny wooden legs and walked into the corner, resting itself against the wall.

"I think I am best suited to answer your questions, High Lord," the newcomer said.

"May I introduce High Animator Gazzio Marcado," said High Lord Legasa.

To a man, all of the Alturans stood and touched their fingers to their lips and forehead, even High Lord Tessolar.

"It is an honor, High Animator," said High Lord Tessolar. Miro understood that it was rare for a man in his position to leave his homeland.

"High Lord," said High Animator Gazzio. "Please sit down. You asked how our Lexicon was stolen. My answer is that I do not know. I personally administered the safeguards, the traps and wards. The thief went through them like they did not exist."

Legasa took up the dialogue. "We tracked the thief for a time before he vanished completely. He went east."

"To Torakon?" asked Tessolar.

"That way, yes. But he could have been heading for Tingara. As we speak, our Lexicon could be somewhere in Seranthia. The high animator is investigating."

"How long has it been?" Devon spoke.

"Over a week," said the high animator. There were gasps from around the chamber. "I renewed our Lexicon not long before the theft, but in time our lore will fade, seriously weakening us until our Lexicon is recovered."

"May I offer you the support of some of our men—perhaps a few of our bladesingers could help get some tongues moving?" Tessolar suggested.

"Your offer is appreciated. However, we will not require your assistance at this stage."

"Money," said Captain Sloan.

All eyes turned to the reticent guard captain. "I'm sorry, Captain?" said Tessolar.

Captain Sloan faltered and then spoke up. "Fear will only get you so far in Seranthia. You need plenty of money. Offer the right sum for knowledge leading to the whereabouts of the Halrana Lexicon, and word will get out. There's a chance you'll get your results."

"I don't think . . ." Devon began.

Legasa held up his hand. "An excellent piece of advice, Captain. We will see to it."

"Do you think this is in any way connected to Emperor Xenovere's reasons for calling the Chorum?" Tessolar said.

Legasa nodded. "It could be. At any rate, we will know tomorrow."

"What of the primate? Have you spoken with him, or anyone else for that matter from the Assembly of Templars? The templars may not have any lore, but they are the custodians of essence, and their priests give them access to every nation in the Tingaran Empire."

Legasa shook his head. "Primate Melovar Aspen seems too interested in his relics of late. He declined a meeting."

"High Lord Legasa, I need to know," Tessolar said delicately. "Does this affect our stance?"

"I'm afraid it does. We need to swiftly increase our presence before the runes fade along with our military strength."

The Alturan leader's eyes darkened, and Miro felt the tension in the room grow. He became very aware of the glistening black golems, still motionless but coiled with pent-up power. "I fear we might be taking actions that offend . . ."

"We are dealing with uncertainty, High Lord Tessolar, but above all we must be decisive. We once said that with the Ring Forts again under our control, we could build alliances and do something about our pitiful essence ration. With this setback, we need to move faster than we might wish. The emperor needs to be challenged, and the other houses are looking to us for leadership. I have assurances from High Lord Vladimir of Vezna, and although the Petryans, as always, are an unknown, I believe the Louans and the primate will support us against House Tingara's growing power."

Tessolar licked his lips. "Yes, but we must be careful to avoid confrontation."

Legasa's eyebrows drew closer. "*You* want to avoid confrontation? What about *us*? We lost more blood than you in the Rebellion!"

"It was your war!" said Devon.

Tessolar silenced Devon with an angry glare. "It was a just war," he said. "You called and we supported you. And some still say the day may have been ours. I am not one of those people."

Miro grew cold. He avoided sharing glances with the other soldiers.

"We have been biding our time at your request, gathering our strength," said Legasa. "Now the emperor has called a Chorum. We cannot afford to let him grow in power."

"We will fight." Tessolar bit the words off. "But first you need to find your Lexicon."

"This discussion is over," said High Lord Legasa, standing up. His lords stood beside him, the Alturan lords reluctantly following suit. "We will reconvene after the Chorum."

Shaking his head, High Lord Tessolar led his men from the room.

9

Pray for the return of the Evermen. Pray with all your heart,
for glory and life everlasting will follow.
                                        —*The Evermen Cycles*, 19:12

Tuok found Miro preparing for bed.

"We've got the night off," said Tuok with a wicked grin.

Miro paused in the middle of pulling off his boots.

"But if you'd rather stay here with the merchants, that's fine with me. Perhaps you can find some work selling nightlamps to old women, young lord."

Miro grinned back. "The whole night?"

"The whole night. And most of tomorrow too."

"Doesn't the high lord need us?"

"Tomorrow's the Chorum, lad. The Chorum is under the primate's protection, and so are the market houses; it's the one thing that remains inviolate."

Miro frowned. "Tuok, what's going to happen? You heard what they said. What's the emperor going to announce at the Chorum?"

"Miro, when you've been a soldier as long as I have, you learn two things. Want to know what they are?"

Miro smiled and shook his head ruefully. "You're going to tell me anyway, aren't you?"

"The first thing you learn is, someone is always talking about war, whether it's the last great war or a potential war to come. There's no use worrying about it—not until it actually happens. The emperor probably just wants to announce a new event at the next Imperial Games. The second thing is, never turn down a night off, and especially not in Seranthia. Now, your chance has come. Good news for us?"

"Good news for us," Miro echoed, punching Tuok in the arm.

Tuok punched him back. Miro chuckled, unable to hold back a grimace of pain.

Tuok left the room, laughing. When he was sure Miro wasn't watching, he rubbed at his arm. Lord of the Sky, the lad didn't know his own strength!

Tuok took Miro to an area called the Tenamet, assuring Miro it would be the best place to see what he called "the real Seranthia."

They first passed through a wealthy neighborhood called Fortune, where the merchants who worked at the market houses had their manses. Miro couldn't believe the size of the manors. Nothing like the Crystal Palace, of course. But these weren't even lords—they were just men who sold wares in markets!

The distance from Fortune to the Tenamet was surprisingly short. The manses gave way to a sparse area, spotted here and there with rectangular storage buildings. There were few people walking the streets here, and those there were seemed like the kind Miro was in no hurry to meet. At one point Tuok grabbed Miro by the shoulder and forcibly crossed him to the other side of the road.

"What—?" Miro began. He then noticed the twisted expression of the man who'd been walking toward them. The man held a stick he was using as a club and was cursing as he strode on the path, beating the walls with his club as he went.

His cursing rose in intensity as he passed Miro and Tuok on the other side of the road.

"Ignore him," Tuok muttered.

The man shook his fist at them and continued walking.

"Redberry," said Tuok. "Never cross a man on redberry."

"Was he in pain?" Miro said.

"Far from it. In his own mind he was probably having the time of his life."

Miro shook his head.

The frequency of other passersby began to increase.

"Are we late?" Miro asked. "I'm guessing most people will have gone home, given the hour."

Tuok snorted. "In Seranthia the celebrations don't really kick off until after midnight."

"After midnight? When do they finish?"

"Dawn. Sometimes after dawn. Sometimes through the next day. And because tomorrow is the Chorum and there are newcomers in the city, I'm thinking there'll be more revelers out than usual."

A party of young men walked past, swaggering and pointing things out to each other, laughing raucously. They seemed to find Miro hilarious. One of them tugged on his simple jerkin. Miro frowned.

"Don't worry about them," Tuok said.

Miro turned toward a scuffle in an alleyway nearby. A fat man had a young woman by the hair, pulling her down to the ground.

She screamed as he twisted her arm behind her back and lifted her skirt above her waist, displaying a pair of white buttocks.

"Help! Please help!" she cried.

Before Miro could react, Tuok gripped him by the arm and marched him away from the alley. The woman's cries followed them.

Miro pulled away from Tuok angrily. "What? You can't tell me you didn't see that! He was—"

"Miro, you take one step into that alleyway, and four of his mates will step out of the shadows and you'll be dead. It's one of the oldest tricks in the book."

"You can't be serious."

"I am serious. She'd probably be the first to slit your throat. It was a setup, lad."

"You think . . ." Miro said.

"I'm sure of it."

"But what if it wasn't? What if we just walked away from someone in trouble, serious trouble?"

"Trust me, Miro. It was a setup."

"But what if it wasn't!"

Tuok sighed. "If it wasn't, then she should have known better than to get herself into that situation. A woman shouldn't be out without company, not in Seranthia, and especially not anywhere near the Tenamet. Miro, if I were in Altura or Halaran or any of a number of other nations, I would be there in a flash. But not in Tingara. And especially not in Seranthia."

"I don't understand. Why doesn't the emperor do something?"

"It's the way of the people here. What would you advise the emperor to do?"

Tuok stepped over a comatose body on the ground. Miro put his hand to his nose as the smell of vomit rose from the prone figure.

"Make some laws!" retorted Miro.

They entered the Tenamet proper. Miro had never seen so many bars, saloons, taverns, gambling houses, food stalls, beer halls, and other places less readily categorized. The sounds, sights, and smells were an assault on the senses. Music, singing, talking, and cheering echoed around the streets.

"What kind of laws?" Tuok continued.

"I don't know. What kind of laws do they have now?"

Tuok chuckled. "In Tingara? None really. It's punishable by death to insult the emperor or the primate. Denigrating the Evermen on one of the holy days results in a public flogging. All business with the houses must be conducted in the market buildings—it's illegal to sell goods or services involving lore anywhere else in Seranthia. Possession of essence will see all your possessions taken and have you thrown out of the city. Distribution of essence will see you and your entire family executed. Other than that, no laws."

"What about murder?"

"If the person murdered had rich or powerful friends or family, one of the streetclans will see justice done. If not, nothing."

"The streetclans?"

"They act for the businesses that can't afford their own guards. They provide a loose set of rules and protect those too small to protect themselves. They charge for the service, of course. The number of clans changes all the time, but last I heard, the Melin Tortho were dominant."

"At least there's someone to keep order," Miro grumbled.

Tuok barked a laugh. "Sometimes the streetclans are worst of all. They're a law unto themselves. The emperor lets them be so long as they don't interfere with areas like Fortune or the Imperial Quarter. They have terrible wars when one clan seeks expansion into another's territory. The winner wins protection rights for all the businesses in the new area; the losing clan is broken up and absorbed by the other clans—the survivors at least."

Miro frowned for a minute.

"So why does the emperor let the clans run things?"

"How would you do it?"

"Well, to start with, I would make new laws to make crimes like murder illegal."

"And how would you enforce the laws?"

"With soldiers like you and me."

"And who would pay the soldiers?"

"The emperor, of course."

"And where would the money come from?"

"From taxes."

"I see. And who would you tax?"

"People like the merchants who had those great houses in Fortune. Anyone wishing to do business in Seranthia would have to pay a tax."

"And what if the merchants decided they would simply do business outside Seranthia? Put up stalls outside the walls?"

"I wouldn't let them."

"So you would make that against the law? And enforce this law also with your new soldiers?"

"I guess," said Miro.

"And if they left Tingara altogether? Would you go to war against the country that harbors the merchants who used to live so happily in your city?"

"Hmm. I see what you mean," Miro sighed.

"Don't worry, Miro. To me, you're making sense. But the people here have a great distrust in what they see as intervention from the emperor—new taxes, more soldiers, trade laws."

"Even if the laws are protecting people? Stopping people from getting murdered or swindled?"

"That's right."

"It's a strange place."

"That it is, young lord. That it is."

They rounded a corner, past a motley group of women who called out and tugged on the clothes of whoever passed by. One of the women tried encircling Miro in her arms. Close up, he could see she had a nasty rash on her neck. Another of the women scratched incessantly.

"Get away!" Miro pushed the woman.

"You're catching on," Tuok chuckled. "Don't ever touch one of the street whores, not if you've spent the last five years at sea with only fish for company. No, there are far finer establishments where the company of a beautiful woman can be had for the right price. Or even just a refreshing beverage after a hard day's work."

Tuok stopped to sweep his arms grandly at the building in front of them. A hanging wooden sign proclaimed it "The Gilded Remedy." An attempt at the fluted and intricate style of Seranthia's classical architecture had been badly botched, with pockmarked columns and an upper level that leaned heavily on the building beside it. The second "e" in "Remedy" was missing.

Miro grinned. "A mug or two of cherl could definitely be in order."

"Cherl! We can do better than that."

Miro followed Tuok into the bar, where he could barely see through the smoke. The bar was crowded, the combined body heat hitting him like a fist. The gentle murmur of conversation he'd heard from outside became a roaring din as he passed through the swinging door, and the acrid stench of sweat and stale beer nearly made him put a hand to his nose.

Miro followed Tuok through the crowd and over to the bar, thankful for his own lanky height as he looked over a man's shoulder at the bartender, a young girl perhaps his age, with brown hair curling past her shoulders. Her bodice was laced up tightly over her breasts, and her pleated skirt showed the swelling rise of her hips and stopped well above her knees.

Tuok yelled something at her—Miro didn't hear what—and in a moment Tuok turned to Miro, grinning and holding two tiny glasses.

Miro remembered one of the few pieces of advice Brandon had given him: "The smaller the glass, the stronger the drink."

He skeptically took the glass from the bigger man. Tuok clinked his glass against Miro's and yelled, "To your health!" into Miro's ear.

"To yours!" Miro yelled back, following Tuok's lead by tipping the glass into the back of his throat.

It was like fire, burning acid that tore at Miro's throat as it wound its way painfully into his chest.

"Ahh," Tuok's mouth moved in obvious satisfaction, as if sipping from a cold stream after a week in the desert.

Miro began to choke but managed to refrain from spluttering. He kept his face carefully calm as sweat beaded at his forehead.

"Very nice!" he shouted at Tuok.

"Well done, young lord." Tuok grinned back.

Then he leaned in to speak into Miro's ear. "How much money do you have?"

Miro felt into the pocket inside his jerkin and carefully counted. "Three deens and fifty-two cendeens."

"Good! Your round—ask for two large measures of Whitehaven."

Beginning to feel the effects of the drink, Miro grinned and turned to the bar, pleased to have another opportunity to look at the serving girl.

The first few drinks passed pleasurably. Tuok and Miro withdrew further into the back of the bar, where they could speak more easily. It took some time, but they were eventually able to beg two stools and seat themselves up against the wall, where there was a thin shelf.

When it was Tuok's turn to buy a round, Miro asked for a mug of cherl. Tuok laughed and came back with two tankards of a dark, almost black beer with a crest of white foam.

"Try it. It's called Rootslinger."

It looked and smelled awful.

Miro cautiously took a sip. It actually wasn't bad. The white foam tasted creamy, almost milky, and the dark liquid was surprisingly sweet.

"Not bad," Miro said.

"Get caught drinking cherl around these parts, and you'll be called a woodskin or worse."

Miro laughed. He had no idea what it meant to be a woodskin, but his head was buzzing and he felt warm.

The next drink was another beer, much lighter in color and with a bitter, slightly sour taste. It was served with a rough chunk of lemon in the tankard.

They then drank a thin fluted glass of honeywine, sparkling like the foam churned up by the crystal clear waters of the Sarsen.

Three big men, who obviously worked at the Gilded Remedy, cleared a patch of floor raised slightly higher than the rest. Presently, two sober-faced men arrived, bowed from the waist in the eastern manner, and sat down on two squat stools, facing the crowd. One of the men carried an immensely long flute whose base rested on the ground, and the other carried an instrument with a single string. He lengthened and shortened the string, using a series of clamps and levers, causing it to emit a high-pitched warble.

The crowd seemed to know many of the tunes, almost all the people making an effort to tap along to the beat, whether it was by stamping their feet on the ground, clapping their hands together, or thumping their tankards on the bar.

Miro smiled and clapped along with the rest, often missing the beat but laughing his way through the songs. He particularly enjoyed the trills and low notes of the flute, so different from the chiming music of Altura.

He noticed Tuok chatting amicably to a Tingaran, the man's broad face and shaved head giving away his identity. Tuok seemed to be telling a story, both men pausing occasionally to laugh uproariously.

Then Miro's attention was completely refocused when a weight landed on his lap. It was the brown-haired barmaid, undeniably pretty, with a twinkle in her eyes.

"Oh, my pardon, young sir."

"Quite all right," Miro said with an attempt to sound gallant.

"I seem to have slipped. Hmm, it is comfortable here, though; am I bothering you?"

Miro fought to keep his voice casual. "No, not at all."

She snuggled further into his lap, her round bottom resting close to his body. "Perhaps a drink then?"

"Ah, of course. A glass of honeywine would be nice."

She laughed—a soft, girlish, tinkling sound. Miro had never been happier. "No, silly. A drink for me?"

"Oh, I'm sorry."

She laughed again, leaning in to speak close to his ear, her sweet breath tickling him. "How much money do you have?"

He felt around in the inner pocket of his jerkin. "Umm. At least two deens."

"Good." She smiled. "My name's Esmara."

"Esmara," said Miro. It was the loveliest name he had ever heard.

She waved at someone, Miro didn't see whom. Presently, a thin man arrived, with white hair and a hooked nose. He looked Miro up and down before handing Esmara two glasses of honeywine.

"Mmm," she said, taking a sip. "Aren't you drinking yours?"

He hadn't realized he was holding a glass. "Oh, of course." He took a sip, hardly tasting the drink. It felt warm in the bar, almost too warm. He felt like he needed fresh air; the smoke was irritating his eyes, but he didn't want to move. Not with this wonderful creature so close.

"It's good, isn't it?" she said, smiling up at him. She leaned back into him as she watched the musicians. Cautiously, Miro lifted his arm and awkwardly placed it over her lap. She smiled and firmly grabbed his arm, putting it around her waist. He could feel the curve of her hip, the softness of her skin beneath the thin material. Her bodice rose and fell with every breath. Miro's heart raced, his own breath growing short.

"You are not from around here?" Esmara said.

"Umm, no," said Miro. "I'm from Altura."

"An enchanter! How exciting!"

"No, no—nothing like that. I'm a soldier, here for the Chorum."

"Such a strong soldier too," she murmured, running her hand idly over his bicep. He blushed.

"I hope to become a bladesinger one day," Miro said. "I'm actually very good with a sword."

"I'm sure you are." She looked up at him, her lips parted. They were as red as rubies, glistening with moisture. He badly wanted to kiss her. What if he was a bad kisser?

"Ooh, tell me," she said. "Have you ever seen a zenblade? I hear they're deadly."

"I've seen one, yes," he said. "I've never held one, though."

"Oh, that's a shame."

Esmara took his hand and surreptitiously slid it onto the skin of her stomach, under the material of her bodice. Miro thought every person at the bar must be able to see what his hand was doing. He waited a moment and then began to softly caress her bare skin. It was the smoothest thing he had ever felt. Esmara continued chatting pleasantly as if nothing was happening. Miro wondered how she could keep her composure.

"Our people think very favorably of Altura," she said.

He tried to concentrate on what she was saying rather than the feel of her skin.

"Really?"

"Of course, what would we do without nightlamps and heatplates? Prices are always high, though. I hope whatever is happening at the Chorum makes prices go down. The emperor said he was going to try to stop the other houses from charging so much."

"Mmm," said Miro. His hand started to work its way higher. He could feel the underside of her breast, round and soft.

Suddenly, Esmara sat up, and Miro's hand left the confines of her bodice. He tried not to show his disappointment.

Esmara turned so that she sat astride him, facing him now. She raised herself and leaned in to him, presenting her neck. Miro took the offer, kissing her gently on the neck. Her hair cascaded over his own neck as he moved in close to her. She raised his face up, gently pressing her fingers under his chin.

Ever so slowly, Esmara moved in close, her lips parted, hungry. Miro could wait no longer and moved forward to close the distance, his lips finally touching hers.

The contact sent a jolt of pleasure through him. Their lips parted and then touched again. This time her mouth opened, and he felt her tongue probing gently, trying to enter his mouth.

The sounds of the raucous music, the drink, the crowd, the smell of the girl, all combined headily. Miro felt dizzy, intoxicated.

Esmara leaned in to whisper in Miro's ear.

"We need to go upstairs. I have a room."

"Yes," he croaked.

She gathered herself and then slid off his lap. He quickly sat up, not willing to glance around the crowded room for fear someone would meet his gaze. Esmara took Miro's hand and led him to the very back of the room, where a small set of stairs led upward.

He watched the swing of her skirt, the curve of her round bottom as she walked up the stairs, thanking the Lord of the Sky, or whoever would listen, for his luck.

Esmara turned when she was at the top of the stairs and offered him a wicked grin, taking his hand and holding it tightly. He boldly wrapped his other arm around her waist, giving her a kiss on the neck. She squealed with pleasure.

"It's this room here," she said.

He followed her into a sparse room, furnished only with a nightlamp on a small stand and a large bed.

No sooner had he entered the room than she closed the door behind him and pushed him, hard. Miro fell onto the bed, laughing and turning over. His laughter stopped dead when she began to untie the cords holding her bodice, tied at the front. She loosed the strings one by one and then untied the cords at the back.

Miro watched, transfixed. In one move Esmara slipped the garment up and over her head and was standing in front of him, wearing only a skirt. Her breasts were young and firm, smaller than he had thought, while her long brown hair curled down to spill over her nipples. She cupped her hands under her breasts, smiling suggestively.

"Do you like them?" she said.

"Yes," Miro whispered. He cleared his throat. "Yes. Very much."

Esmara began to sway her hips to unheard music. Miro watched, mesmerized by the movement of her body.

Esmara's skirt fastened at the side, and Miro's breath caught as she undid the buttons.

The skirt fell to the floor.

10

There's more to the truth than just the facts.
—Louan saying

Miro frowned when Tuok started clapping. He couldn't blame the man; he must look a sight—still in last night's clothing, arriving back to the market house after noon.

A few of the other soldiers cheered too. Miro guessed Tuok hadn't been reticent when asked about the whereabouts of the "young lord." Miro only hoped Captain Sloan hadn't found out about his disappearing act.

"Don't worry, lad. I covered for you while the captain was so caught up with worry about the Chorum that he never thought to ask why we were one man down at breakfast. Now come, why the black expression?"

"Sounds to me like you should have a smile on your face bigger than a Louan's love for money!" one of the guards joked.

"So what's the story?" asked Tuok.

"Nothing."

Tuok glanced around the room. He tactfully led Miro into their quarters, looking like he had an idea about what was going to happen next.

Miro sat on the bunk and put his head in his hands.

"She get a better offer, is that it?" said Tuok.

"No, nothing like that. Tuok, she took my money and left me."

Tuok looked confused for a moment and then burst out laughing. "Miro, she's a whore!"

One minute Tuok was sitting on the bunk next to Miro, and the next he was pressed up against the wall, Miro's hand tight like a vise around his throat.

"She is not a whore," Miro said in a voice like ice.

Tuok struggled to get the words out, his breath wheezing. "Miro, you must have known . . ."

"She is not a whore!"

Tuok got the words out with the last of his breath. "Not . . . a . . . whore . . ."

Miro let go and Tuok fell to the floor gasping, his face purple. Tuok began to cough in fits.

The strength went out of Miro. He fell to the floor beside the older man.

Tuok coughed for a moment, gathering his breath. Color started to even out on his face. His breathing slowed. "Miro, only once before have I seen a man move faster. I saw two bladesingers at practice in the Pens." Tuok shook his head. "You move like they do."

Miro groaned.

Tuok's tone softened. "Why don't you tell me about it?"

Miro stared at the wall for a moment, desolate. Then he started to speak.

"We went to her room. It was . . . amazing. We talked afterward. She asked me all about Altura; I asked her about Tingara. She said her father had been accused of stealing and mutilated by the streetclans, his hands cut off. Then we did it again. It was . . . different the second time. We talked some more. She said she thought the emperor was going to try to bring the houses together in friendship. That's why he called the Chorum, she said. Then we did it again." Miro noticed a small smile creeping on Tuok's face.

Tuok calmed. "And then what?"

"And then I woke in the morning with a head the size of a house. A house with a thousand prismatic orbs exploding inside it."

"Sounds something like my morning," said Tuok with a wry smile.

"She was gone. And so was all my money. She didn't leave a note—nothing. Tuok, that was all my money in the world. I went downstairs to the bar and asked about her. A big man came up to me and told me to leave. We had some words."

"Words?"

Miro held up a fist, the knuckles scratched.

Tuok chuckled. "I'm guessing the man won't be having words with you again any time soon? Be careful, boy; the streetclans don't mess about, and the whores . . . I mean, some of the girls . . . they belong to the clans."

Miro sighed. "I guessed something like that."

"I'm sorry, lad. Seranthia's a tough city. You either leave out the gate with nothing but the shirt on your back, or you leave over the gate with only your shirt to cushion your fall."

Miro nodded.

One of the soldiers poked his head around the wall. "The Chorum's over," he said.

Exchanging glances, Miro and Tuok followed him out.

High Lord Tessolar and the other Alturan lords had sequestered themselves in their quarters. The market house was rife with rumor. The Chorum had not gone well.

Miro asked around, but different soldiers knew different things. Many said it was something to do with House Torakon. Others said it was the Halrana who were angry about something. No one knew for certain.

Then Captain Sloan moved from group to group, gathering the men. "The high lord has requested a gathering of everyone in the market house. Assemble immediately."

Whispering to one another, they followed the captain. Everyone in the market house gathered—it was a surprising number of people. Merchants with emerald earrings stood side by side with soldiers in green uniforms. Pageboys and couriers vied for space with administrators and emissaries.

High Lord Tessolar stood on a podium, deep in discussion with Lord Marshal Devon. He nodded in response to something Devon said and then gazed about the room.

Miro looked around him. There must have been two thousand people in the room, crowded up against the podium and heads tilted back as they gazed at the high lord expectantly.

"Altura overcomes!" the high lord began. He stood stiffly, one hand over his heart. His other hand touched first his lips and then his forehead.

Everyone in the room followed suit.

Miro shouted it along with the rest of them. Momentous events were taking place, and he felt proud to be here, sharing them with these people.

"Greetings, my countrymen, members of my house. Many of you are wondering what has transpired at the Chorum. I wish to inform you—you are my people and you have a right to know. However, the tidings are grave and a sign of dark days to come."

High Lord Tessolar paused, his hawklike gaze sweeping the room. As his eyes moved past where Miro stood with Tuok, Miro was sure the high lord was looking right at him.

"First, let me tell you something you will soon hear from others: House Torakon is no more. The builders as we know them are no more."

A sense of shock flowed through the room. Confusion.

"*How*, you are wondering. No, they weren't killed or conquered. The Toraks have volunteered to join House Tingara. They have surrendered their identity as a house and given their Lexicon over to the emperor."

The confusion grew stronger, tainted with anger.

"I know," said Tessolar simply, "I know." He took a deep breath. "I saw High Lord Koraku with my own eyes as he gave his assurance that he was voluntarily joining his house to the emperor's. If he was acting, it was an excellent performance."

"What does this mean?" someone called.

Lord Devon frowned, but High Lord Tessolar regarded the man gravely. "What does it mean? It means a great increase in the emperor's power, both economic and military." Tessolar did little to disguise his anger. "It will be impossible for any house to improve their fortifications or build new defenses without the express permission of the emperor. The Toraks will now take on imperial purple and the sun and star of Tingara. Torakon will become a land within Xenovere's borders."

"What about the primate?" someone called. "Surely, he must have said something."

"Yes, the leader of the Assembly of Templars mediates the Chorum, but what could he say?" Lord Devon replied for the high lord. "High Lord Koraku's move was voluntary. The primate said he can only interfere if there is a threat to the peace. He says there is currently no threat to the peace."

Everyone started to speak at once. High Lord Tessolar held up his hand. "I go now to consult with our allies, House Halaran. Perhaps they can shed some light on this new order. Be wary of who you speak to, as Altura has few friends here. Go in peace."

Once more the high lord touched his fingers to his lips and forehead and then stepped off the podium.

Miro was as shocked as anyone. It was an unexpected move, coming from nowhere. What house would voluntarily give up its traditions, its color, its lore, its Lexicon?

He felt a hand on his shoulder and jumped. It was Tuok.

"Guard duty. Your head still troubling you?"

Miro shook his head. "No."

"Come on."

Once more the Alturans paid a visit to the Halrana market house. Miro wondered if there was some subtle political nuance here, why High Lord Tessolar was always visiting Halrana home territory.

He entered the strange room and again lined up against the far wall with the other Alturan soldiers. The tension was higher than ever before. Without fanfare the lords took their seats.

"First, so I know. Have you found your Lexicon?" High Lord Tessolar began.

High Lord Legasa sighed. The Halrana high lord wiped a hand over his forehead, looking older. "No. The high animator says he has made some small progress. That is all I know."

"I am sorry," said Tessolar.

Legasa spoke, "This makes it even more imperative that we plot a course of action. The emperor is moving. He consolidates his power as we speak. Lord of the Earth, what was Koraku thinking? House Torakon has always been fiercely independent. Allies of the emperor, yes—it would be hard not to be when they share such a large border. But merging with Tingara? It's unthinkable!"

"Well the unthinkable has happened," Lord Marshal Devon said.

Legasa put his head in his hands and then looked up. "Tessolar—let me speak plainly."

Miro was surprised to hear the high lord addressed by his first name.

"Our every bone screams against this move of the emperor's, but we are weak. We need to combine our forces, for Altura to send her men to stand by our side. Together we will be stronger. We have the Ring Forts, but we need your men. He is going to attack; I can feel it."

Miro's blood went cold. Two rulers were here in front of him, plainly discussing war. War between his nation and the nation he was presently in.

"I agree with you," Tessolar said. He licked his lips. "Something is happening here that we're only just coming to terms with. This is the biggest threat we've faced since the Rebellion."

"I agree, so let us be ready! Let us make the first move! We cannot take the defensive like we did last time. With the lands of Torakon at his disposal, Xenovere will simply continue to build his forces on the Azure Plains until we are forced to surrender due to lack of supplies, lack of essence, and lack of men."

"We need time!"

"We cannot afford it!" said High Lord Legasa.

"As old as our alliance is, you must give us time. In the name of the men who died in the Rebellion, both Alturan and Halrana, you must give us time. If we provoke the emperor now, we don't have a chance."

"Think about what you are saying, Tessolar. The emperor will attack, you agree, but you don't want to deploy your men to the Ring Forts because you think it will provoke him. We need to take the initiative! Honor our alliance, Tessolar."

Captain Sloan spoke up, "High Lord, I believe . . ."

"Silence," Tessolar snapped.

Devon took a breath. "High Lord Tessolar, the Halrana speak sense."

Tessolar sighed and put his head in his hands. For the first time, Miro thought long and hard about how old the high lord was. He looked every day of his age.

As the chamber fell into silence, finally, Tessolar spoke. "So be it. We will honor the alliance. We will send our men to the Ring Forts. We will send our enchanters to help arm them. We will send our bladesingers to combat the Imperial Legion. We will bring down this tyrant once and for all."

High Lord Legasa placed his hand over his heart. "House Halaran thanks you for honoring the alliance."

The Alturan high lord nodded. "What of your border with Loua Louna?"

"The one place Xenovere would never dare attack. Without artificers his war machine grinds to a halt—no one to repair his dirigibles, replace his mortars, or supply him with prismatic orbs."

"These days are uncertain."

"Not one house has ever survived an attack on the artificers. 'Those who hold the tools of war hold the keys to victory,' as my father used to say. No, they stand to make too much profit, as always, supplying both sides."

High Lord Tessolar nodded. "We will send our men to the Ring Forts, and we will get back your Lexicon."

11

I wonder how many houses vanished from Merralya simply because
their Lexicons were lost and the magic was never renewed.
—Diary of High Enchantress Maya Pallandor, page 514, 411 Y.E.

Miro retired early but couldn't quiet his mind. His thoughts kept turning to Esmara. She'd liked him, hadn't she? Why had she left? Would his house and hers be at war soon? Was this how the emperor promised his people lower prices from the other houses?

Miro slept fitfully. The dream came to him again. An old man held a shining knife close to Miro's eye. Miro was powerless; there was no strength in his arms, like when he was a young child. At first when he heard the screams, he thought they were part of his dreams. His eyelids fluttered, and a low sound escaped his lips.

A commotion woke everyone in the chamber at the same time. A thudding boom.

Miro leapt out of bed, reaching for his sword. Men were yelling and calling to one another. A woman screamed. Miro realized the noise was coming from somewhere outside. Bare chested and wearing only coarse trousers, Miro ran into the street.

He stopped and stared at the Halrana market house. Flames were pouring from the side of the building. Black billowing smoke clouded the night sky.

Soldiers in Halrana brown were running and calling out. In the distance Miro saw an iron golem leap out of a window, barely pausing as it landed with surprising agility and scanned the street, searching, its skin glowing silver.

"We've been attacked! The high animator has been assassinated!" a Halrana soldier cried. Other soldiers took up the call.

A warrior in brown came bursting out of the shadows, crashing into Miro. They both fell down in a tangle.

"Sorry," Miro said, standing and extending his hand.

The soldier glared up at Miro. His head was shaved, and Miro drew back as he recognized the round features of a Tingaran.

"Over here!" he yelled.

Something dropped into the impostor's hand.

"Shekular!" the man named an activation sequence and lunged at Miro, who barely leapt out of the way. Miro saw he held a small knife.

The assassin's lunge hit the wall behind Miro instead. Sparks instantly shot in a fountain as the enchanted blade tore a deep gouge into the solid stone.

The assassin lunged at Miro again, his body twisting with the movement. Remembering his training, Miro slipped deftly around the assassin's body. The knife glowed intensely, brighter than the brightest nightlamp. Once again the assassin swung, this time directly at Miro's face. Miro saw the deadly point, bursting with energy, coming toward his eyes, blinding him as he ducked. Miro sensed the blade making contact with his hair, felt the breath of its passage, heard the buzz and hum as its runes seethed.

Another Alturan soldier burst out of the market house. The newcomer instantly grasped the situation and drew his sword, hanging back, looking for an opening. Miro shifted around, allowing the soldier to come forward.

The Alturan executed a classic attack, feinting the razor-sharp steel at the assassin's legs, then making a pass at the head, before thrusting at his chest.

Miro saw the assassin's counter coming, but there was nothing he could do.

"Shekular-astassine-shekular." The assassin hummed the activation runes. The runes on the blade glowed first silver, then pure white. The assassin ducked under the Alturan's sword and thrust at his chest.

Miro saw his countryman's body explode as the knife hit his abdomen. Blood poured out in a torrent, instantly coating both Miro and the assassin.

Miro saw his opportunity. His steel sword shot out at the assassin's head, an attack meant more to delay than to score a hit. Yet instead of blocking, the assassin ducked out of the way and began to run.

"Over here!" Miro called again. He began to chase the man, hoping more soldiers would follow.

Miro wished he were wearing armor, but it was too late for wishes. At any rate, only enchanted armor stood a chance at stopping the blade.

Glancing behind him, the assassin saw he was being pursued and spurred on extra speed. Miro put all his strength into running, his strides lengthening and his breath coming deep and even.

Yet the disguised assassin was fast, and Miro soon found he was racing from street to street, quickly becoming lost, and the assassin was still drawing away.

The assassin ducked and weaved behind a series of containers. Miro followed, the awful smell meaning they could only contain rotting garbage. The assassin swerved to the side, taking an unexpected turn. Momentarily thrown, Miro stopped, then saw the brown of the man's clothing as he escaped into yet another side street. Miro ran, twisting and weaving, and then the assassin was again just ahead of him.

The assassin jumped a steel fence taller than his height, placing only the palm of his hand on the top and leaping over with extraordinary agility.

As Miro approached, he realized he needed to make a difficult choice. There was no support—he could hear no one coming behind him.

He threw his sword aside.

With a burst of speed Miro leapt the tall fence, barely touching the top with three of his fingers.

Looking over his shoulder, the running man turned, and seeing Miro gaining on him, put down his head.

Completely unarmed now, Miro increased his speed to the limit. He was gaining on the assassin, but what would he do if the man forced an encounter?

They had by now followed so many turns that Miro knew he was lost. The only familiar landmark was the Wall, visible in all directions, staring down at him.

Then Miro rounded a large building, and a new vista was revealed in the half-light just before dawn. He realized they were back in the port district. Fishing boats were unloading at the dock, and the ground was slippery with tiny baitfish and scales. Larger fish were being sorted in containers.

The assassin jumped a huge wooden bucket. Intentionally or not, his foot kicked the side of the bucket as he leapt, spilling the contents. Fish splattered over the ground, and unable to stop himself, Miro slipped and tumbled, falling among the slippery fish, their sharp fins cutting into his unprotected skin.

Miro rolled and leapt up again. The assassin glanced back and saw his pursuer still following.

He then noticed for the first time that Miro was without a weapon.

The assassin grinned and paused, turning and then walking toward Miro, taking his time.

Miro looked frantically around for a weapon. Fifty paces away he saw a cleaver lying next to a tray of spindly green fish.

Miro ran for it, just as the assassin leapt for him.

Something threw him to the ground, a blast of hot air punching into the very center of his back. Miro's wind was taken from him; he couldn't breathe, couldn't move. His vision blacked out for a moment, clarity only returning slowly.

He reached around to feel his back. It was sore, but there was no blood. He was alive.

Miro turned, wincing. With movements like those of an old man, he raised himself onto his knees.

Where the assassin had been was now only a pile of burnt flesh. Miro was staring into the dark, blank eyes of four legionnaires. Lord of the Sky, they were huge men—bigger than the heaviest wrestler Miro had seen back in Altura. They wore armor with bands of imperial purple, and all sported the sun and star of Tingara tattooed somewhere on their faces. One of them casually tossed a prismatic orb from one hand to the other, glancing at the double-banded leader, questioning.

The leader waited a moment, and Miro knew his life hung in the balance. The legionnaire shrugged. "Leave him," he said.

The legionnaires walked away, striding purposefully, their challenging stares intimidating all around them. The fishermen and other pedestrians studiously looked in any other direction, wanting no involvement with whatever was happening here.

Miro looked down at the ground. The enchanted knife lay paces away, its runes still glowing softly but fading as he watched.

Gingerly picking it up, he began his long journey back to the Alturan market house.

Things had settled somewhat in the financial district, yet smoke still poured from the Halrana market house, and soldiers still ran from one place to another.

The day was beginning to dawn, the sky a menacing red above the imposing gray of the Wall.

An Alturan soldier saw Miro and immediately called for the captain.

Captain Sloan came striding up, his face grim. For once, his gray hair wasn't brushed. "Well, what happened?"

"He carried an enchanted knife . . ."

"Yes, yes, I know. What happened to the assassin? Did you see where he went?"

"I chased him to the port district."

One of the soldiers whistled. "All the way there? You ran all that way?"

Captain Sloan silenced him with a glare.

"I lost my sword. I'm sorry, I had to leave it. I caught up with the assassin. He looked Tingaran."

Captain Sloan snorted. "Anyone can look Tingaran. Shave my head and I'd look like a Tingaran."

"Yes, but he had that look. The same features—you know what I mean?"

"So what happened?"

"Four men of the Imperial Legion. They blew him to pieces. They left me."

"Skylord scratch the emperor's name! We have nothing."

"I'm sorry."

"Never mind . . . Miro, isn't it? Never mind, Miro. Once again the emperor has covered his tracks. We have a great deal of suspicion, but no proof we could take to the other houses. Get to the infirmary, and have yourself looked at."

Captain Sloan turned to go.

"Captain?" said Miro.

"Yes? What is it?"

"It's probably not much use, but I picked this up." Miro opened his hands, showing the knife. The symbols etched into it still faintly glowed. "It's the assassin's weapon."

Captain Sloan's face lit up. "No, Miro, this is good. This is one of ours. When we get home, we'll start looking into how it came into the possession of this assassin right away."

"We're leaving, Captain?" Miro asked.

"We certainly are. The protection of the Chorum is obviously meaningless. It's not safe for us here, and it's only going to get worse."

One of the bladesingers came forward, a slim man with gray eyes, his manner friendly enough. He deftly took the knife from Miro's hands, holding it carefully. *"Shant-lurada,"* he said softly. The runes deactivated. It was an ordinary knife again.

The bladesinger spoke softly. "He was a dangerous man, young soldier. You did well. Miro, is it? My name is Huron Gower."

Exhausted, Miro simply nodded. He turned and left for the Alturan market house, his back stiff so he wouldn't show how much pain he was really in.

12

Our strategic alliances and proximity to Stonewater, yes, these were advantages. The superior tactics of our legionnaires also cannot be underestimated. But let us not forget House Tingara's lore. It was our meldings that gave us the strength to form an empire. Before I was proclaimed emperor, wars among the houses were common. Now, we have peace.

—Memoirs of Emperor Xenovere I, page 121, 381 Y.E.

Ella basked in the afternoon sunlight, enjoying its warmth on her skin.

With the ending of the rains, the Alturan summer had begun the gradual decline into autumn. The centurion trees at the Academy of Enchanters had turned first dark green, then deep gold, the leaves falling softly to the ground before they were raked into piles by the groundskeepers.

Ella sat on the grass of the Great Court, the Academy's central feature, in the shade of a centurion tree, a yellowed book in her lap, oblivious to the other students around her. Occasionally, she took a bite from a sourmelon, first making a face at its acidity before the underlying sweetness came through.

She heard giggling and looked up to see a boy and girl holding each other close. The boy leaned forward to whisper something in the girl's ear. She laughed and kissed him on the lips.

Autumn's arrival reminded Ella that she would be graduating in winter. With their studies soon over, many of the students were pairing up. A season of dances awaited them after graduation, before their hard work began in earnest.

"Good reading?" Talwin asked, grinning down at her. He was one of the students in Ella's naming class, not a close friend like Amber, who shared most of Ella's classes, but a friend nonetheless. His sandy hair was always unruly, and he constantly fidgeted, as if unable to keep still. But he had a wicked sense of humor and often made Ella laugh.

She looked up at him, smiling as she closed her book. She'd have to read about Saimon Bower's strength matrices later.

"Do you mind if I sit down?" Talwin asked, wringing his hands.

"Got a new joke?" Ella grinned.

Talwin sat down, a little too close for Ella's liking. "I thought you finished early on Evendays? This is the first time I've seen you still around."

"I usually do. I guess I just thought I'd stay here for a bit. I love the autumn, the reds and the golds, the chill in the night and warm in the morning."

He shuddered. "It's getting too cold for me already. I was just going to head home." He took a deep breath. "Ella . . . Would you like to come and have dinner with my family?"

Ella blinked. She liked Talwin; he made her laugh, but they were friends and he made Amber laugh too. He'd never given her any indication he felt anything more for her. "I . . ." she started.

"Ella, it must be terribly lonely out there in that shack."

"It's not a shack. It's Mallorin. And it's my home."

"Come on, Ella. Everyone is talking about it. With your brother gone and uncle passed, you need to spend some time with other people."

"Everyone? Who's everyone? Miro will be back any day now. What would be the point of going to live somewhere else? Where would we go? It's our home. We grew up there."

Talwin shuffled himself forward, moving still closer. He picked up one of Ella's hands in his own. She froze, not knowing what to do, her hand limply grasped in his.

"Ella, I . . . I think you're beautiful." He gazed into her eyes, evidently waiting for her to say something. "You could meet my mother—she makes the best country pie in the world. She's really sweet—you'd really like her."

Talwin stared up at her, searching for a response.

Ella looked down at her hand, wondering what she should do.

Mildly encouraged, Talwin reached forward and ran his fingers over a lock of blonde hair that had fallen loose.

Ella tensed.

"Please say something," Talwin said.

Ella gently removed her hand from his grasp. Talwin gulped.

"Talwin," Ella spoke slowly, softly. She wanted to choose her words carefully. "I care about you. You and Amber, you are both my friends. I . . . I'm still trying to discover who I am. What I want from life."

There was a long pause. Talwin looked down at the ground. "Is it another?"

Ella sighed. "It's no one."

"Then why not me?"

"We're friends. For now, can we just let it stay that way?"

He glanced up at her. "Are you sure . . . ?"

"I am sure. Talwin, I—"

Talwin was cut off by the sound of a girl's voice screaming Ella's name. She turned to see Amber running toward her. Ella turned back to Talwin, in that moment catching what she thought was a tear in his eye. Without a word Talwin stood up and left.

Amber was obviously in trouble. Tears streamed down her face. Ella watched Talwin's departing back. Had she said the right thing?

"Oh, Ella," Amber threw herself down next to Ella and cried without any sign of stopping.

There was nothing Ella could do except hug her friend and murmur sweet platitudes.

Finally Amber pulled herself together. "My parents told me they've chosen someone for me to . . . to marry." Her voice choked at the last.

It wasn't unusual for parents to choose a suitable husband for their daughter, depending on how old-fashioned the parents were. It was the only thing Ella could say she was glad about concerning her upbringing. No one would ever choose whom she married.

"And . . . ?"

"At first I was happy when they told me. They'd asked me what I wanted in a husband. I said I enjoyed the Academy, my friends here, the books, the learning. Spending time with you and your brother." Amber started to choke again. "So they picked me a husband, here at the Academy. They listened to me, Ella!"

Amber broke down in sobs, sounding like she would drown in her own tears. Her face was red, her hair tangled, and her nose running. Some girls looked pretty and delicate when they cried. Amber was definitely not one of those girls.

"I don't understand. They picked one of the students? Who was it? Warren? Jorge?"

Amber whispered something, as if to say it louder would make it all the more true.

"What? Amber, I can't hear you."

"Master Samson," Amber said.

Ella pulled back in shock. "Did you just say Master Samson?"

"Y-Yes!" Amber cried. Her sobs grew louder. She howled. The other students in the Court looked at Ella in consternation. Ella shook her head, patting Amber on the back.

Ella couldn't believe Amber's parents had chosen the dour teacher as a match for their young daughter.

"I know you love your parents, but don't you have any say in the matter?" Ella asked.

Amber shook her head. "They say it's time I'm married, and my mother thinks Master Samson is a good match. When I said I wanted more time, my mother said she's already invited him to dinner and he has accepted. She says I'm not being practical." Amber drew a shaky breath. "He accepted, Ella, which means he'll agree. I don't know what to do. I can't reason with my mother. The only one who can stop this is Igor Samson."

"He's not a young man," Ella said, frowning. "Why hasn't he found someone before now?"

"You know what he's like. He never leaves his workroom unless it's to teach classes."

Ella didn't say it out loud, but marrying her daughter to a master of the Academy would enhance Amber's mother's status. Amber was young and attractive. It seemed Amber's mother had found an opportunity and taken it.

"I suppose one of his students makes sense," Ella said.

"Everyone says Madame Foley is in love with him. Surely she's more suitable," Amber said.

"She is?" Ella's eyebrows went up.

"It's common knowledge. Everyone must know it but him."

Ella had an idea. Madame Foley wasn't an unattractive woman. Most likely, Igor Samson hadn't looked up from his books to notice her. "How do you feel about playing matchmaker?"

"What do you mean?"

"All we need to do is get Master Samson to notice her. He's not the type to approach a woman on his own, and your mother made it easy for him. We just need to show him someone else."

"How can we do that?"

"First, all we need to do is get Master Samson and Madame Foley talking. Let me think on it."

Her mouth set in a line, Ella determined to find a solution. Ella knew Amber loved Miro, who obviously felt at least some affection for her. Miro would return soon. The best way to help Amber would be to help Master Samson find love with another.

The first class of the next day was lore, taught by the sharp-featured Master Goss. Usually attentive, Ella found herself more concerned by her distraught friend sitting next to her.

Master Goss's voice droned. Ella didn't even hear the words coming from his mouth.

"As Ella here knows, there is a limit, depending on the matrix and its purpose." Master Goss looked at her expectantly.

Ella looked up. "I'm sorry?"

"Essence, Ella, essence. Also known as *raj ichor*. The cornerstone of our lore."

Ella was quick to recover. "The limit is proportional to the activation cost; more energy requires more essence."

Master Goss harrumphed. "Correct. Now, I'd like everyone to draw the rune for the color green on their deskpad."

It was one of the most familiar runes, being the color of their house.

Master Goss turned to the wallpad and, taking his glowing pen, started to draw with slow, even strokes. The rune was near perfect, the tiny circle above the cleft in exact proportion to the curve of the arch. Ella wondered if only she could see the minor flaw in the upper crest.

Master Goss waited while the class followed suit, drawing the rune on their deskpads. He walked down the front row, looking down at the busy young men and women, frowning at some, praising others.

Master Goss frowned as he passed Ella and saw she'd already finished, but he nodded.

He returned to face the students.

"Good. All done? Now, what would I need if I wanted to make this into a matrix for something simple, say . . . a nightlamp?"

A tall boy in the middle of the room raised his hand. Master Goss nodded. "The activation runes?" the tall boy said.

"Correct." Master Goss added a basic activation sequence to the rune for green.

Ella wondered why he was going over such elementary material. They'd created far more complex matrices than those for nightlamps.

"What else?" said Master Goss.

Ella didn't even raise her hand. A girl near her spoke up. "The deactivation sequence?"

"Correct." Master Goss added a simple deactivation sequence. "What else? Ella?"

Ella tried not to speak in a bored tone. "The time sequence."

"That's correct—otherwise we might have a flare on our hands, rather than a gently glowing nightlamp."

Master Goss added a time delay to the matrix. Reading the runes, Ella could see no problems—when activated, the rune for green would cause the enchanted object to glow at the rate and brightness specified in the time sequence.

A few of Ella's classmates stirred, evidently also confused by the step down to basic lore.

As the class muttered, Master Goss put on a pair of silver gloves. He then reached into a cabinet and withdrew a tiny vial. Suddenly the atmosphere in the theater changed, and the students leaned forward, trying to get a glimpse.

Ella's breath caught. It couldn't be. For all the learning, the practice, copying the runes again and again, day after day, she had never actually seen it. Real essence.

There were no more yawns, no signs of tiredness. The students were sitting up straight, their expressions expectant.

"What do I have here?" murmured Master Goss.

"Essence," several of the students whispered, the one word holding infinite import.

"No!" Master Goss yelled, shocking them out of their reverie. "What do I have here?" he asked again, looking around the room, challenging. This time no one answered.

"Poison," said Master Goss. "The deadliest poison in existence. The most vicious substance you will ever encounter." He bit the words off, gazing intently from face to face. "Essence—or *raj ichor*—is black, slick, odorless . . ."

"Tasteless?" Trellon, the class clown ventured.

"Would you like to find out?" Master Goss held the vial up.

"Umm, no . . ." Trellon said, at a loss for once.

Ella had heard this all before, but somehow, with the actual substance held up before her eyes, it was all the more real.

"No, seriously, Trellon. Come here. There's something I'd like your help with."

Trellon stood up and walked down to where Master Goss faced the class.

"Wait here a moment," Master Goss said.

Master Goss left the room, taking the vial with him. Instantly murmurs rose up from the students. Even Amber seemed drawn out of her melancholy.

Master Goss reentered the room. He still carried the vial in one hand. In the other he carried a large white cat, probably a stray from the Poloplats, brought up scratching a living from the scraps of the food markets.

The cat mewled.

"Here," said Master Goss. Without ceremony he handed the cat to Trellon.

The youth struggled for a moment before the cat settled in his arms. Its eyes closed contentedly as it began to purr.

"Many of you are going to object to this. In fact, probably most of you. However, the high enchantress not only permits me to give these demonstrations, she approves."

Remembering everything she had been taught about essence, Ella began to feel sick.

"I take no pleasure in this, but I would rather a stray animal than one of my students whom I have spent so long teaching. Better the lesson be learned now, an unpleasant memory, than become a grim reality some time in the future. You may put the cat down, Trellon."

The boy put the cat down. It looked up at him in surprise and then began to rub against his leg.

Master Goss separated the cat from Trellon with his boot. "Now stand back, Trellon. Farther. Right back, by the door there. Good."

All eyes were on the cat. Ella heard a gasp from next to her and looked quickly at Amber. Ella's friend had her hands over her eyes, allowing just a crack to peek through.

Master Goss leaned down and ever so carefully allowed a single drop from the vial to fall from the tiny bottle. The entire class watched the black drop plummet through the air before landing on the skin just behind the cat's head.

"I have heard that many of the other houses perform similar demonstrations," Master Goss said, keeping a careful eye on the cat. "I have even heard that the elementalists of Petrya use a human, a half-wit or other type incapable of surviving without care. Here it goes."

The cat's back began to arch, and a soft whining sound came from its throat. It clacked its jaws together, twisting its head from side to side. It stopped and rolled over twice, three times, before leaping up again, its mewling getting louder.

Suddenly it squawked. Its back arched further and further, impossibly bent, like a whipcord mid-flight about to release pent-up energy. A keening started from its throat, a howling screech that grew louder and louder. Ella put her hands over her ears. The cat was in such terrible pain.

"Stop it!" she heard Amber cry. "Please just stop it!"

Master Goss stood back, watching impassively. He had seen it before.

The cat's jaws opened wide, wider, as if trying to vertically line one jaw up with the other. It twisted, screaming, screeching. Its tongue was black.

The cat's back was arched too far now. Everyone in the class heard a massive crack, as the stray's back eventually broke.

Ella thought it would be over now, but it wasn't. It was horrific, yet she couldn't look away.

A rumbling sound came from the cat's throat. In an instant the liquefied contents of its body erupted from its throat. Its eyes burst, dripping down its ruined face. Finally, it stopped moving. The cat was dead.

Ella could hear Amber sobbing to herself now, and felt the bile in the back of her own throat rise. She swallowed, trying to keep it down.

"I will give you all a short recess. I expect you all back in here once you have had a chance to think about what you've seen."

Once more the theater was filled with students—a sober, white-faced bunch. A few of the seats were empty, but Master Goss nodded in satisfaction. There was a tall metal stand placed beside the teacher, a set of strange objects resting on it.

Ella looked with concern at Amber. Her friend's face was pale. Amber had been sick during the break, Ella holding her hair back from her face as she retched.

Ella reached across and gave Amber's hand a quick squeeze. Amber rewarded her with a brave smile in return.

She grew even more determined to help her friend.

"Now that you've seen my demonstration, I hope you will all give essence the proper respect it deserves," said Master Goss. "It requires less than a drop on bare skin to elicit the type of reaction you've just seen." He gazed about the room, pausing to make his point. "Now, back to our green-hued nightlamp." He pointed at the matrix of runes he'd drawn on the wallpad. "You are going to see your first enchantment."

Some excitement came back into the class, although Ella noticed many angry eyes directed at the teacher.

The teacher again put on the silver gloves. With exaggerated care, Master Goss took an incredibly thin metal rod from its holder. He then dipped the end of the rod into the tiny vial.

"As you know, the rod is hollow, to draw up a small amount of the liquid. It is important to draw just the right amount of essence into the scrill. I find that dipping the rod and counting two short breaths gives just the right amount to aid decent rune-making and minimize waste."

A small block of polished wood rested on the stand. Master Goss carefully withdrew the scrill and began to inscribe the rune matrix that was up on the wallpad.

As the rod moved against the wood, Ella heard a hissing sound. Smoke rose into the air as the teacher drew the symbols onto the surface of the block.

"The essence will write on any surface, any at all. Choosing the correct tool for the job is critical—we have scrills for inscribing on cloth, scrills for delicate work, scrills that take two hands to hold . . . The list goes on. Keep your face away from the smoke. It won't kill you, but it can make you quite ill."

Master Goss spoke as he worked, his hands moving deftly with sure movements. Presently he stood back, regarding his work proudly.

"Trellon, do you want to do the honors?"

"Tish-tassine," called Trellon.

The runes lit up as the nightlamp was activated, glowing brightly with a steady green light.

"And then all you need is a material such as paper or cloth placed over the runes to diffuse the light, and you have a nightlamp! A very good one, I must say."

Ella suddenly felt reckless. She was angry that Master Goss could be so cruel one moment, so proud and arrogant the next.

"There's a flaw in the upper crest," said Ella.

"What?" Master Goss said, interrupted.

Ella knew she was probably making a mistake, but she couldn't stop herself. "The upper crest—there's a flaw."

"Oh, really?" said Master Goss. "Well, perhaps you would like to show the class how you would do it?"

"I will," said Ella.

She stepped forward and walked down to the floor, going straight to the stand. Of course, she had been introduced to these tools before, but never had she stood so close to real essence. Ella thought again of the cat.

Before she could change her mind, Ella deftly put on a pair of the gloves and took a new scrill from its holder. The green light from Master Goss's matrix was in her eyes. *"Tish-toklur,"* she muttered. Instantly, the nightlamp deactivated.

Master Goss stood back, a look of surprise on his face.

Ella gingerly took the vial of essence off the workbench. She placed another small wooden block in front of her, dipped the steel rod in the vial, and began to draw.

The smoke drifting up from her steady hand smelled surprisingly pleasant, but Ella kept her head turned to the side. She had practiced the runes so many times that, if anything, she kept her eyes away from the wallpad, afraid she would copy Master Goss's mistake.

It took her a little longer than Master Goss, but then Ella was done. Remembering her training, she carefully put the stand back to its original state, double-checking all of the seals and ensuring everything was in its proper place.

"It's done," she said. "I used a slightly different activation sequence to distinguish the two."

"Well?" said Master Goss. "Let's have it. I think you'll see that—"

"Tish-tassine," said Ella.

Master Goss's nightlamp lit up brightly, filling the room with a green glow.

Pausing for dramatic effect, Ella spoke again. *"Tish-tassun,"* she said with a different inflection. Her nightlamp flared brightly.

There was no doubt. Ella's nightlamp was the brighter of the two. Its light was clearer, yet softer, a richer shade of green.

The class erupted in applause.

13

It is better to negotiate standing on two feet compared to when a foot is on your chest.
—High Lord Tessolar Mandragore to
Lord Marshal Devon, 524 Y.E.

Outside, in the Great Court, students kept rushing over to congratulate Ella. She felt slightly foolish. They assured her it was the greatest moment in their entire time at the Academy. Master Goss didn't have a lot of adoring students, it seemed.

The two girls sat underneath one of the centurion trees, Amber sprawled next to Ella, with an envious expression on her face—especially when young men kept approaching Ella.

"Ella, the students are going to be talking about that for the next ten years!"

Ella blushed.

"I swear, you're going to make high enchantress one day. Imagine all the lords bowing to you, Ella. You!"

Amber enthused as Ella sat, lost in thought. "And Miro will be a famous bladesinger. We'll all travel far and wide together, our enchantments known for their quality and beauty." Amber's face suddenly fell. "Only . . ."

Ella looked up. "What?"

"Only I'll be married to some old man." Amber burst into tears.

"Don't worry, Amber. I have an idea. I know how to get Master Samson to notice Madame Foley."

She'd help her friend yet.

———————◆———————

Ella crept through the Academy halls, so empty at this time of night, when most people were fast asleep and alertness was at its ebb.

She couldn't believe she was doing this, but then she couldn't believe she'd stood up to Master Goss. She was going to help her friend, and that was all there was to it.

Master Samson's work area was located in the east wing, at the far end of Graven Building. Without difficulty, Ella located the entrance and crept down the set of sandstone stairs. A small pathfinder rested in the pocket of her dress, but she refrained from using it yet, the moon providing more than enough light to see by.

Ella came to a locked door. She tried a trick Master Merlon had shown her, a naming technique used more for remembering common activation sequences than anything else. Some enterprising students had found it worked for testing locks or other devices with encrypted activation sequences. Word had got out.

Whispering softly, Ella ran through a series of activation sequences. Nothing. She tried another. Nothing. Hearing a noise behind her, she started to panic. She quickly tried a third series. *"Torn-aloa!"* As she spoke the words, the door popped open.

Ella dashed inside and closed the door behind her, her heart pounding. Perhaps this was a bad idea. What if someone caught her?

Ella waited for a moment, but whoever was moving outside eventually passed. Feeling more confident, she rose from a crouch and regarded the room.

Some runes on a mysterious cube were activated in the corner, bathing the room in a soft glow. Master Samson's various enchantment projects were situated around the room: a sword, exceptionally large and slightly curved; a set of armor made with heavy steel—if the runes ever faded the wearer would still have a good degree of protection; and a set of two deskpads, linked with a slim fabric.

Ella walked to one of several benches lining the wall. Scanning each in turn, she finally found what she was looking for—a worn book, conveniently located: *Advanced Techniques for Heat Generation*. Flicking through the pages, she saw that the margins were filled with notes in Master Samson's spidery handwriting.

Ella smiled.

This first part of her plan to bring the two faculty members together was simple. Master Samson no doubt referred to this book frequently. Ella would remove it from his workroom and get Amber to put it someplace where Madame Foley would find it. Madame Foley would return the volume, and the mystery of its disappearance would get them talking as they tried to figure it out.

Ella placed the book inside the satchel she'd brought with her for the purpose.

As she began to exit the room, weaving around Master Samson's strange projects, Ella suddenly stopped. Her breath caught.

There, on a central workbench, was a tiny vial filled with black liquid. It could only be essence.

Even as Ella stood mesmerized by the world's most valuable resource, she frowned. It was a serious breach of discipline for a master or his apprentices to leave essence out in the open like this. She shook her head; it wasn't like she could report it.

Ella tore her eyes away from the precious liquid. She instead pictured Master Samson and Madame Foley's perplexity as they discussed the book's mysterious change in location. With her and Amber's hidden assistance, Ella was sure Madame Foley could do the rest.

Ella quietly exited Master Samson's workroom, deep in thought.

Only later, much later, did she realize that she'd forgotten to lock the door behind her.

———————

Talwin arrived at the Academy early, hoping to have a word with Master Samson. He'd never had the courage to speak privately with the imposing master before, but after his father had seen his last grade report for naming, Talwin had decided to see if he could get some private instruction, perhaps from one of the master's apprentices.

Talwin stood outside the door, summoning the nerve to knock.

Ever since Ella had turned him down in the Great Court, it seemed life couldn't go right. Talwin was sure Amber saw him cry too. He had avoided both girls, unwilling to face the humiliation.

Why did he have to say something? He'd been so sure. Ella had started spending more time with him after her brother left, and Talwin had felt proud to have such a beautiful young woman at his side. She laughed at his jokes and poked fun at his dress sense. He watched her when he knew she couldn't see, his eyes running over her figure. Aching for her.

Now she thought he was a fool.

Talwin sighed. The Academy was everything to him and everything to his family. His parents expected a lot of him as the first son. He was expected to be at the top of his class, not dragging up the bottom.

With trepidation, Talwin knocked on the door to Master Samson's workroom.

He waited. Knocked again.

"Ho, is anyone there?" he called.

Talwin pushed gently on the door. It fell open in front of him.

In awe, Talwin ran his gaze over the master's workroom. He knew he was overstepping, but he couldn't look away. He took a step inside.

All manner of strange and fantastic equipment was spread around. He couldn't believe his eyes when he saw a set of enchanted armor covered with matrices of runes, too many for his mind to encompass.

Talwin took a few steps farther inside, running his hand over the armor. It was deactivated, he was sure of that. There was no harm in touching, was there?

Growing bolder, he moved deeper into the workroom. Talwin stopped, staring.

It was a special zenblade, he was sure of it. The sword was massive, bigger even than the swords he'd seen at the sides of the bladesingers. Whoever wore this sword would be a powerful man.

Talwin ran his eyes down the length of the blade, trying to decipher each rune as he came across it, but giving up. Then he saw it. His heart stopped.

It had to be. It shouldn't be. But it had to be. Essence.

Talwin stepped closer and looked at the tiny vial in awe. He wondered why it wasn't in one of the cupboards. Talwin moved slowly forward, not taking his eyes off the vial. Yes, there was liquid inside it.

Wasn't essence supposed to be kept locked away? It was terribly dangerous, leaving a bottle of essence on the workbench like this. What was Master Samson thinking?

Talwin saw an opportunity to do a good deed. He would put the vial away in a cupboard, where it should be.

He picked up the small vial.

Talwin's hand shook. The lid wasn't on properly, and a droplet, the smallest amount of moisture, slipped out of the bottle and onto the bare skin of his hand.

Sweat broke out on Talwin's brow. The bottle dropped out of his hand, smashing on the floor. He screamed.

14

If the builders ever get as greedy as the artificers,
wars will take a good sight longer.
—Tingaran legionnaire, date unknown

Ella strolled along the familiar path to the Academy, crossing the Sarsen at the Tenbridge and admiring the immaculate surrounds. There was a morning chill to the air, not enough to be uncomfortable, but crisp and fresh. Ella coughed, feeling the beginnings of a cold. For once she was glad of the thick green wool of her student's gown.

She passed an elderly couple, not talking but sharing the view from the bridge, and smiled at them. Maybe one day she would find someone to grow old with.

The previous night's adventure seemed far away now, banished by the light of day. Ella had Master Samson's book with her. It only remained now to come up with the next step in the plan, and get Amber to place the book somewhere Madame Foley would find it. Once again she pictured Master Samson's perplexity, and Ella grinned.

A passing groundskeeper—several years older than Ella—smiled in response and touched his fingers to his forehead in greeting. Ella's smile grew broader as she nodded to him. The groundskeeper's gaze followed Ella as she walked past, and she could feel his eyes on her back. In a moment of mischievousness Ella increased the roll of her walk, her hips curving first one way, then the other.

Ella turned suddenly and caught the almost docile expression on the groundskeeper's face as he watched her body. His face turned red, and he quickly looked away.

Finally arriving at the Academy, Ella walked through the archway leading to the Great Court. She could see an astonishing number of people in the Court, milling around, expressions of consternation on their faces. It seemed everyone shared some momentous piece of news.

Students gathered beside the sandstone walls, deep in discussion. As she drew closer to the throng, Ella realized the largest crowd was near the east wing. She heard a sound coming from beside her as she passed a couple of students sitting in the shade of a centurion tree. Looking over, Ella realized a girl was crying, the tears rolling down her cheeks. The girl looked up at Ella as she passed, her expression desolate.

Starting to feel concerned, Ella decided to walk straight toward the crowd loitering outside the corner of the east wing. A peal sounded, and she jumped. It was the great timepiece on the face of Green Tower, calling the start of classes. Not one student moved.

She passed a youth from her naming class. His eyes were red rimmed. He walked past Ella without saying a word.

Directly outside Graven Building was a small group of teachers. Expressions of sorrow marked their words to each other.

Master Samson shook his head as Master Lodley said something. The usually jovial Master Merlon kept running his hands through his hair. Two of Master Samson's apprentices sat on a wall close to the teachers, murmuring to each other.

Master Goss was absent. Ella looked around for him and saw his familiar figure in the distance under one of the arches, talking to a tall woman in green silk.

Suddenly realizing where she was, Ella stopped dead in her tracks. It was so different in the light. Graven Building. The stairs were right there, leading down to Master Samson's workroom.

Ella started to walk again, faster this time. She heard Master Lodley say a name—Talwin?

". . . the boy's family," Master Lodley was saying. "They should not see him like this."

"And you are certain you locked the door?" Master Merlon asked Master Samson.

"Completely."

"Then how did the boy get in?"

Had Ella locked the workroom door behind her? Essence had been in there in plain sight, and essence was dangerous. It hit her in the pit of her stomach, like a heavy stone being dropped from a height. Ella felt her face drain of all blood as she realized she'd left the door unlocked.

"No . . ." she said.

Master Lodley turned, noticing Ella for the first time. "My dear, you should not be here."

"No . . ."

"It's a terrible tragedy. I'm so sorry, my dear. He was a friend of yours, was he not?"

"No!" she screamed. Ella ran for the workroom stairs. Master Samson grabbed hold of her tightly, his grip like iron, the pain almost welcome. She twisted savagely and kicked out. He let go, stunned.

"Ella!"

Ella ran clear of the teachers and threw her body down the stairs. The door was ajar. She thrust it to the side and entered the workroom.

A terrible smell assaulted her, the most dreadful smell she had ever encountered. It was every bad, noxious odor combined into one. It was so thick, it was almost tangible, like a wall of evil.

What was left of the boy who had loved her lay on the floor. The mat of his sandy hair was his most recognizable feature, tousled, with the front hurriedly combed in the way he always did it. She could look no farther, could go no farther.

Ella fell down. She was sick, retching painfully, her entire body rejecting the sight in front of her. Her stomach cramped again and again; she curled up on her side. It was impossible to look away.

The masters came for her.

Back outside, Ella told them she was to blame, between sobs and gasps. When they probed, she said she'd broken into Master Samson's workroom to borrow one of the books she wasn't yet allowed to study. Ella knew that if she said more, she'd bring Amber's engagement into the situation.

They were shocked when Ella produced the book and the proof was there for all to see. Ella had stolen from a master's workroom and now Talwin was dead. Was she responsible?

Huddled on the ground, Ella still couldn't stop the cramps in her stomach, the convulsions of her body. Goose bumps rose on her arms. She shivered. Her mind kept returning to the sight of Talwin's broken body.

As Ella listened to the masters make plans to call an emergency session of the faculty, Amber arrived to take her home.

Ella's dreams were filled with eyes: Amber's eyes, accusing; Master Goss's eyes, staring into her without pity. He held up a vial of essence above Ella's head. "It's for your own good," he kept saying. The eyes of the students bored into her.

She dreamed that she stood outside a window, where a cold pie lay on the sill, untouched. She couldn't see inside the window; it was hazy. All she could hear were a woman's sobs, a man's attempts to comfort her. Suddenly a face burst from the window—Talwin's face, but his eyes had melted away, running down his face.

His hands burst forth from the window, grabbing at her. Ella screamed.

"She's ill," a calm voice said. Miro's voice. Ella was dreaming of her brother. "Here, help me with her."

Amber's voice murmured a reply.

Ella fought back at them, pushing at the hands that grabbed at her, painfully clutching, their touch searing her skin.

She fell once more into darkness.

Miro sat beside his younger sister, his hand gently smoothing the hair back from her brow. She lay sprawled on the bed, sometimes drawing the covers close to her, other times throwing them away, fighting when he or Amber tried to replace them. Her skin was hot, and sweat coated her body. Yet her face was white, set in a grimace, an expression it hurt him to see on her.

The guilt Miro felt was terrible. If he hadn't left, none of this would have ever happened.

"It's all my fault," Amber said, standing by the door. She began to cry again.

Miro continued to sit on the bed. He took one of his sister's hands. It felt clammy. A draught from outside carried in the chill autumn air.

"Please. Come in and shut the door," Miro said.

Amber turned and instead left the bedroom, shutting the door behind her. Miro heard sobbing from the next room.

Miro continued to hold Ella's hand, occasionally patting her brow with a damp cloth. Some terrible sickness had gripped her, something dark from inside. He didn't know if she wanted to live, and without the will, she would surely fade away.

She had grown in the months he had been away, blossoming into a young woman. If she could only take her eyes from her books for a moment and see the way people responded to her bright and bold nature, her sunny smile.

Miro leaned forward and kissed her brow. "Be well, my sister. Know that I love you."

He entered the next room and took a seat next to where Amber sat, staring at nothing, morose and red-eyed.

"I'm so sorry, Miro. It's all my fault." She had explained to Miro about her mother's overtures to Master Samson and told him that the book Ella stole could only have been part of her plan; Ella was no thief.

"It was an accident," Miro said. "If Talwin hadn't gone in and played with the essence he would still be alive. It isn't your fault and it isn't hers." Stealing a book and leaving a door unlocked isn't the same as murder."

Miro paused to regard his sister's dependable friend. He'd always seen Amber as a child, but Ella wasn't the only young woman to have blossomed in the last few months.

"You said you thought she was acting as part of a plan to free you from marrying Master Samson. Is marriage such a bad thing, Amber?"

"I don't love him."

"Have you said as much to your parents?"

"Yes, I have!"

"Shh," Miro soothed. "I meant no offense." He looked back at the doorway to Ella's room, stopping to listen. He paused to think for a moment. "In life there are some things you can change and other things you have no control over." His gaze was far away. "Ella and I, we didn't choose to grow up without our parents. It was something that was thrust upon us. What you need to do is to decide what this is and to act accordingly. It's always better to take an uncertain step than to have the same step thrust upon you through inaction."

"It's easy enough to say."

Miro took Amber's hand. "Amber, you're kind and compassionate, and you're growing into a beautiful young woman. Any man will see these qualities in you."

"But I love someone else," Amber said softly. She looked down and then glanced up at Miro, her gaze intent.

Miro suddenly realized what Amber's eyes were trying to say. He opened his mouth and then closed it.

Amber was beautiful, but she was his sister's childhood friend, and they were both so young. She hadn't even graduated from the Academy, and Miro's own future was uncertain.

Miro thought about the events in Seranthia—events Amber was still unaware of—and the dark days he knew were coming. He thought about the simple home he shared with Ella in the city's outskirts, and his status as a training swordsman.

Who was he to get between Amber's marriage to a master of the Academy, a man of means, when Miro himself planned to become a warrior, fighting far from home?

Miro didn't want to hurt her. He pretended not to see the meaning in Amber's gaze.

"Does he love you in return?" he said.

"I . . . I don't think so."

"Then forget about him. He doesn't deserve you. There's no use pining for water in the desert; sometimes you have to pick a direction and start walking."

Amber nodded and looked away.

Miro finally stood and went to check on Ella once more, leaving Amber alone with her thoughts.

When he returned, Amber started when she saw his face; the concern must have been written across it.

"She has a fever. It's rising fast. Amber, do you know where Dunholme is?"

"Dunholme? You want me to go to Dunholme? In the Dunwood?"

"Yes."

"Why?"

"When Ella and I were young, a woman looked after us for a time. Brandon said she was a friend of my mother. Her name was Alarana. She was one of the Dunfolk."

"Really?" Amber's eyes lit up with interest. Miro might have smiled if the situation weren't so grave; he was always amazed at the way Amber could be crying one minute, laughing the next.

"She raised us in the old ways, keeping it secret from Brandon. For a time we worshipped the Eternal like one of the Dunfolk. She knew about the leaves and the plants, about medicine—magic that can be used on the body."

"On the body? Everyone knows lore can never be applied to the living."

Amber's voice fell when she realized what she was discussing.

Miro spoke before she had a chance to dwell. "Not lore; this uses no essence, no runes or enchantment."

"What magic are you talking about then?"

"Medicine, herbs that help the healing processes of the body."

"Is such a thing possible?"

"Alarana was sure of it, and I believed her. As children, whenever we were sick, she would make a special brew of plant extracts, mosses, and fungi. We always got better much more quickly than the other children."

"It's a lot to place our hopes on."

"Amber, listen to me! It's all we have. Whatever this sickness is, in a day, perhaps two, Ella could be dead. I've given her some of a root that I remember Alarana using. It seems to be doing something, but not enough. I need one of the Dunfolk."

Amber took a deep breath. "What do you need me to do?"

15

The Lore of the Enchanter is the precursor to them all.
Study it well.
—*The Lore of the Enchanter*, 12:56

Amber stepped lightly through the trees, barely able to make her way in the dim light. The thick forest canopy closed in on her. She had no idea what time of day it was, but she seemed to have been walking forever. Miro had told her it would take half a day to walk to Dunholme, home of the Dunfolk, deep in the forest, and half a day to walk back. She hoped she would return soon enough.

The trees were ancient, tangled creatures, crowded close together, fighting for the scattered rays of sunlight that filtered through the tallest tops. The farther Amber traveled from Sarostar, the darker the leaves became, and the more vibrant and abrasive the sounds of the forest. The air was redolent with the scent of damp. Somewhere she could hear the tinkle of flowing water, a hidden sound amid the cries of the forest creatures and the buzz of the insects.

A branch crackled under her thin shoe, breaking completely. Amber's foot sank down into something wet and soft.

Ugh, she thought, pulling her now wet shoe out with a grimace. *That makes both of them now.* She wasn't sure which of her feet was wetter.

She reached a patch of open ground, littered with twigs and dead leaves. Some animal had made a nest in the fork of a branch above her head. Whatever it was, it was big.

Amber reached into a pocket in the folds of her brown dress and withdrew the seeker Miro had given her. *"Skut-tsee,"* she said, activating it.

The runes glowed softly, the colors arranging themselves in a pattern. Amber lined the pattern up with the arrows and turned slightly to the left.

Miro's directions had been imprecise at best. "Just keep heading due north from Mallorin. Don't worry—they will find you."

A bird with a red crest burst from the bushes in front her, shrieking. Amber screamed, her hand clutched to her breast. After a moment, realizing she was in no danger, she calmed herself.

With her thoughts fixed on her ailing friend, Amber deactivated the seeker and put it away, setting as fast a pace as she could through the heavy undergrowth.

Something in the character of the forest had changed. If anything, it felt even more ancient, wilder. The trees were much bigger, their trunks so massive that a single slice from them would make a round table big enough for a hundred men. A hundred big men, Amber estimated, walking past a particularly large specimen.

The sheer immensity of the growth around her was startling. Even frightening. At least there was less moisture and thick undergrowth to push through. The trees were spaced far apart, and Amber was able to make much better headway, her posture more erect as she forged her way ahead, occasionally checking her direction with the seeker.

Amber saw a game trail to her left running in the same direction that she wanted to go. With a shrug she joined the trail. It grew larger, more defined as she walked. About the same time she realized she was on a path made by humans, she heard a voice behind her.

"Holy Eternal, what do we have here? Are you lost, young lady?"

Amber jumped and yelped, whirling about, holding her hands before her mouth. She saw nothing but the rich dark green of the forest.

"The little deer startles easily," another voice spoke, this time from her left.

The voices sounded close, but she couldn't see their owners.

"Where are you? Come out."

"Why should we, my deer?" the first voice spoke.

"A fine jest," said the second one. "Dear deer. Why are you not laughing, my doe-eyed beauty?"

"Show yourselves!" Amber said, stamping her foot.

"My dear, you have a temper," laughed the first voice.

"Do you bring a gift, little doe?" said the second.

"I . . . I don't know anything about a gift."

"Then we will have to shoot you full of arrows!" the first voice said, still light and playful.

Amber thought of what she knew about the Dunfolk. Some boys at the Academy had told her stories of the primitive people who lived in the forest and kept to themselves so long as they were left alone.

She hadn't believed the stories at the time. They said the Dunfolk tied a piece of string to a flexible stick. They put sharp sticks against the string, and when pulled back, the string released the sharp stick to penetrate and hopefully kill an animal. It had seemed strange and far-fetched; she had been sure the boys had been laughing at her.

"Arrows? What are arrows?" she said, hoping to bring them out.

She heard a sharp twang. Something whistled past her ear, so fast it was just a blur. The breath of it startled her; she flinched, closing her eyes. Amber heard a thunk behind her.

Opening her eyes, Amber turned and looked. A crafted piece of wood, perfectly straight, stood quivering in the trunk of one of the great trees. It was spliced with small red feathers at its base, and she could just make out the steel of its sharpened head, stuck deep into the tree.

"That, little doe, is an arrow," the second voice said.

Amber reached up and touched a finger to her ear. She felt wetness, and inspecting her finger, saw blood.

"Just a little nick," the first voice said. "I take it you have not been invited to Loralayalana?"

"If she had, she would have said," the second voice responded. "She does not bring a gift; she has not been invited. We should kill her now."

"Wait!" said Amber. "I . . . I did bring a gift."

Amber thought frantically. What did she carry on her?

"Here!" she said. She reached under the neck of her dress, withdrawing an emerald pendant. It sparkled on its silver chain.

There was a rustle in the undergrowth; then, one moment there was nobody there, and the next a small man stood in front of her, facing Amber with a look of suspicion on his face.

He was perhaps a foot shorter than Amber, with a ruddy glow to his cheeks and small, wizened features. Amber's breath caught; it was the first time she had seen one of the elusive Dunfolk.

He wore clothing of brown and green, dark like the forest they were in, and soft shoes of deerskin.

And he carried a bent weapon—a bow, Amber remembered it was called. It was arched with restrained power, an arrow fitted to the string, pointed at her. Her breath quickened; Amber hoped he wouldn't release the string, either by accident or intent.

"What is it?" he said. He was the owner of the first voice.

"It's a necklace."

"What does it do?"

Amber thought she had best get creative. "Well, it shines in sunlight, starlight, or moonlight. Given as a gift to a woman, it can cause her to fall in love with you."

"Good, good," the hunter said. He relaxed his pressure on the string, and walking forward, he took the necklace from her hands.

"What about my gift!" cried the second hunter, still concealed.

"I don't have another gift," Amber started to say.

Another arrow whistled past Amber's other ear. It was a harder nick this time, and she yelped with pain, jumping and clutching her hand to her ear.

"He would like a gift too." The first hunter shrugged.

Amber's ear throbbed; she could feel the blood dripping onto her neck and shoulder and hoped it wasn't a deep wound. What could she do? Then it came to her.

"I do have a gift! I was only joking."

The second voice spoke again, "You were joking?"

"I was. Here."

Amber reached into her dress and took out the seeker. A second man was suddenly at her shoulder, reaching around. He looked much like the first man but had a tattoo of a bird on his cheek. Amber let him touch the seeker, but kept it in her hands.

"What is it? What does it do?"

"It's called a seeker. It helps you find your way," she said. Who knew how she would find her way home now?

"How?"

"Well, first you need to activate it."

Amber spoke and the runes on the seeker were instantly suffused with a silver glow.

The two Dunfolk hunters leapt back in surprise.

"It won't hurt you," Amber said, keeping her voice even. "See? You line the colors up with the arrows, and you can make sure you're always walking in the same direction. You activate it by saying *skuttsee* and you deactivate it by saying *sku-lara*." The seeker lost its glow when she spoke, and the hunters looked on curiously.

"It will do," the second man grumbled, taking the seeker.

Amber took a deep breath. "I'm here because I need your help. A friend of mine is sick, and we need a healer."

"A healer? An apolaranasan you mean?"

"I . . . I think so."

"Hmm," the first hunter said. He glanced at his fellow. "I think we should take you to Loralayalana."

His friend didn't even respond. He was too busy trying to say the words to activate the seeker, every inflection but the correct one coming out of his lips.

<hr />

The small group walked swiftly through the trees, the Dunfolk hunters somehow picking an easier path than Amber ever would have herself. They seemed perfectly comfortable in the woods, two of the creatures that inhabited this wild place.

Occasionally, one stopped to make an idle joke to his fellow, to which they inevitably responded with uproarious laughter.

"Will you not try your necklace on that wood hen yonder? If she falls in love with you, we will dine on her eggs whenever it takes our fancy."

Amber looked up as the hunters laughed. She still couldn't see the sky, but something about the way the light refracted through the immense canopy above her head made her think it was some time around noon.

"Hello, the trees!" the first hunter suddenly called out.

"Hello, the birds!" a voice in the distance replied.

Amber saw more shapes moving in the trees, their forms difficult to distinguish, perfectly blending with their surroundings.

A small party of Dunfolk hunters came into view, a deer held on a pole between two of them, its eyes rolled back into its head.

They stared curiously at Amber while she regarded them back. They appeared to be quite alike. The easiest way to distinguish one from the other was by the style of feathering on their arrows and the tattoo pattern on their cheeks.

Amber saw more of the Dunfolk ahead, and suddenly they emerged from the trees into an immense clearing. For the first time in what seemed like an eternity, Amber could see the sky. The sun beamed down warmly from above; she instantly felt a brightening of her spirits.

Dunfolk were everywhere. Many were busying about, preparing food, fletching arrows, grinding roots, scraping skins, or repairing their tiny huts. Yet many were also sleeping in hammocks slung between two saplings, snoring with expressions of contentment.

They continued through what Amber now realized was a village, then after a short path in the denser forest they entered another clearing. Taking stock, Amber saw clearing after clearing, all filled with the Dunfolk, laughing as they worked. There were so many of them!

"Welcome to Loralayalana!" the hunter with the bird on his cheek called out, jumping and capering in the air, while the first man laughed.

Amber had always pictured them mysteriously nestled in the undergrowth. She couldn't believe this vibrant, pulsing culture was hidden away on the very doorstep of Sarostar, nestled in the Dunwood.

"It's . . . It's amazing . . ." she breathed.

The two hunters with her grinned, appearing pleased with her reaction.

"We will take you to the Tartana now," the first said.

"No, no. I just want to go to a healer. My friend is sick."

He frowned. "We are taking you to the Tartana."

Amber sighed. "I guess we're going to the Tartana then."

After passing village after village, they entered a clearing that was even bigger than the others. Five of the great trees stood evenly around a large hut, the walls of which were decorated with animal drawings and scenes of the forest.

"Is this the Tartana?" Amber said.

The first man looked at her sideways. "Did that arrow hit your head? The Tartana is inside."

"Hello, the trees!" the man with the bird tattoo called.

"Hello, the birds!" a voice replied from within the hut.

Without further ceremony, they entered, drawing aside a thin curtain. Amber stooped to avoid hitting her head on the low doorframe.

"What have we here?" a tiny man sitting up on a chair said, peering down at them. He finished picking at some kind of bird, chomping his gums and throwing the bones aside.

He was withered beyond belief, seeming like a bag of meat and bones, but he had a devilish twinkle to his eyes, which were overhung by immense white eyebrows.

"Tartana, this is a young deer we found in the forest," the man with the bird tattoo said seriously.

"A young deer?" The Tartana frowned.

"Well," the man said, also frowning, "I am sure she is dear to someone."

Instantly, everyone in the room burst into fits of laughter. Amber saw tears coming out of the Tartana's eyes.

Amber began to feel frustrated, waiting here while Ella was sick, close to dying.

"Tartana," Amber said. Instantly all of the faces in the room sobered. She faltered under the Tartana's gaze, disturbed by the quick change in the mood. "My friend is sick, near to death. She grows closer as we speak."

"I have never heard of a plant called 'closer,'" the Tartana said. "And how can she be growing this plant if she is near to death?"

The hunter with the bird tattoo stifled a laugh.

"Tartana, I respectfully request the assistance of a healer. Please, I need a healer. Now."

"A healer? You mean an apolaranasan?"

"Yes!" Amber eventually cried. "Yes, if that's what you call it. I need a healer."

The Tartana made a soothing motion with his hands. "Do not get angry, young one. But you should leave this place and tend to your friend, for I cannot help you."

"Lord of the Sky! I was told by Miro—he said you could help me, that you could provide a healer who could help my friend."

"That name means nothing to me," the Tartana said.

"Skylord scratch you! He would not have sent me here for nothing, and I will not leave without a healer."

A slow change came over the Tartana. His countenance grew dark, the wrinkles getting deeper in his forehead, his eyes sinking, giving him a ferocious glare.

"You make demands on me? You, young girl of the Alturans or the Halrana or wherever you are from? You, who came here and called the Eternal false, who scratched his countenance from our temples? Be gone from here, foolish girl, and be lucky to take your life with you."

Amber cowered beneath his glare, the terrible tirade coming from such a small figure. "Please . . ." was all she could say.

"I said, be gone with you," said the Tartana.

"He said you would help. Their nurse, she was one of you."

The two hunters began to drag Amber from the hut.

"Their nurse . . . her name was . . . her name was . . . Alarana!"

The Tartana waved the two men to a stop. "Alarana?"

"Yes, Alarana."

"Alarana," the Tartana said. "Little Alarana. She left Dunholme in my seventieth year, and she returned, speaking of two children. She is no longer with us."

Amber realized the Tartana must be incredibly old. "Yes, that's right. Two children, Miro and Ella. Tartana, please, Ella is gravely ill. Can you help?"

The Tartana paused, thinking for a moment. He finally nodded. "We will help."

16

The Lord of the Sun said, "Let Stonewater be marked with my favor. It is a holy place, and special to me. Let the greatest of our relics reside here. Let the shape of the mountain guide the people's gaze to the heavens. For one day, we shall return."
—*The Evermen Cycles*, 9:14

Miro lifted Ella's head and rearranged the pillow. She had grown cold now; the illness had worsened. At one stage she had become so hot the skin on her shoulders had blistered, bright red and fiery. She had screamed with the pain of it, clutching at Miro, unseeing.

Even so, the cold was worse. The ravages of her sickness cut him deeply.

The day came and went. Miro hadn't once left her side, bathing his sister's head with cool cloths when she needed it, willing her to be strong.

Ella now lay still. Miro almost preferred it when she was writhing, for at least then she was noticeably alive. Now he had to rest his ear against her mouth to hear and feel the softness of her breath.

He sat on the floor beside the bed.

Miro remembered much more than Ella. He remembered Alarana talking about the Eternal, teaching him the prayers. He wished that Ella remembered more. She said much of her childhood was just a blur, a scent that stirred a vague feeling. When she tried to grab hold of the memory, it was gone.

Miro prayed. It was a prayer Alarana had taught him, from his childhood.

"Eternal. One who watches and waits. Lead us forward; protect us and shelter us. Shelter us from our failings. Shelter us from the failings of others. Show us the way. Shelter this one who is given into your care." He thought he heard a soft voice join with his. "Shelter the body, mind, and soul. May our fathers and their fathers watch us from your embrace."

Miro looked up. Amber stood watching silently. A small, determined-looking woman waited at her side; it was her voice he had heard. The woman wore a soft mantle of precious fur, the garb of a Dunfolk healer.

Miro looked up at Amber. She looked awful, her dress torn, strands of shrub in her hair, her breathing heavy, her knees buckling with exhaustion. She looked beautiful. "Thank you," he whispered.

"Her spirit is broken," the healer said.

Her name was Layla. She was actually quite young, almost pretty, her small features youthful and innocent, yet her mouth set with resolve.

"What do you mean?"

"Simply, she does not want to live."

"What can you do?"

"Me? I can do nothing."

Miro's shoulders slumped. Amber put her arm around his shoulders.

Layla continued, "It is what you can do."

Miro looked up. "What can I do?"

"You can bring her back. Both of you. You can convince her to live. Before I can mend her body, I need you to help mend her soul."

"How?"

"I will show you." Layla moved to stand behind Miro and Amber. With gentle pressure on their shoulders, she pushed them down until they were kneeling beside Ella's bed.

Ella was still. Her lips had turned blue, and her face was as white as death.

"She is close now, so very close."

"Please," Miro said, "help her."

In a small clay bowl, the healer ground together some powders with a little water, to form a thick liquid.

"Do you want her to live? Think long and hard about your reasons for wanting her to live. You will not have long."

Miro drew in a shaky breath. "I do."

"I do," Amber echoed.

"Be ready," Layla said. She leaned forward and deftly dripped a small amount of the liquid into Ella's mouth.

Ella whimpered. Miro held his breath, and then she opened her eyes and parted her dry lips. "Miro? What . . . ? What is it? Where am I?"

"Ella," Miro said, his voice ragged; he knew he had little time. "You're ill. Very ill. I need you to live. Please. I need you to live, because . . ." A tear rolled down his cheek. "Because, without you I have no one else."

Amber spoke, "Ella. Please listen to me. I need you to live. Talwin's death—it wasn't your fault."

Amber broke down, crying. Ella's eyes closed.

Layla said nothing. She reached for a mug she had prepared, an amber-colored liquid filling it to the brim.

Little by little, Layla dripped the liquid into Ella's mouth, moistening the parched lips, wetting her dry throat.

Layla took Miro's and Amber's hands in hers and led them from the room.

"She will sleep now, and let us hope the will to live reasserts itself. I have prepared herbs that will help her rest and recover," she said, handing Miro a pouch, "and other herbs that will need to be mixed with water and slowly fed to her continuously." She handed Miro a second pouch. "I'm sure you did your best, Alturan, but she has been days without food or water, and needs her body to rebuild its strength."

Layla left without another word.

"Thank you," Amber called after her.

It was a slow and steady process, but eventually Ella's color started to improve and her strength began to return.

Amber and Miro alternated periods of caring for her so that she could continue with her studies at the Academy and he with his at the Pens.

Life continued in Sarostar, but it was a different life from the one Miro had left. Miro asked Amber what would happen to Ella's studies, and Amber said she didn't know, that they just had to do their best to see her recovered. Miro stayed silent about his experiences in Seranthia, not mentioning the war Blademaster Rogan said was coming. Amber had enough to worry about.

The two spoke little to each other, their energies focused on caring for Ella. Occasionally Amber's hand would brush across Miro's, or she would catch him looking at her. But neither acknowledged any feeling for the other. Amber's plans to marry Igor Samson progressed, while Miro sought to become the warrior he knew he could be.

Then one day Miro returned from the Pens, a nasty cut under his arm where an opponent had scored him, his body bruised and battered from fighting in the dust. At first he didn't believe it, but then he was certain; he could hear voices.

Creeping forward, Miro kept as silent as he could. He climbed carefully up the stairs to the wooden porch, looking through the open window straight into Ella's room.

Ella sat up in the bed, her face pale but otherwise looking well. Amber was telling her a funny story about one of the class clowns at the Academy. Occasionally, Ella smiled a little and spoke softly.

Miro's heart leapt.

Ella looked up and met his eyes. Amber stopped and turned, her smile growing when she saw Miro's face.

"I'll leave you now," Amber said.

Amber left Miro standing on the porch without saying a word. He thanked her with his eyes, entering the small house and replacing Amber at his sister's bedside.

Not for the first time, Miro thought about his relationship with his sister. They had their own lives to lead, but they shared a bond, something that had kept them sane through the travails of their childhood.

"How are you?"

"I dreamt about you. Somehow I knew you were there with me."

"I'm sorry I wasn't here, Ella. I'm sorry I left."

"No, don't be sorry. I . . . I made some mistakes."

"We all make mistakes, and we all learn from them."

Ella looked away. "Do we really?"

"We do. We feel pain so that we learn. It's only when we stop feeling pain that we should worry."

"Have you spoken to Amber? How does she feel, really?"

"Don't worry, Ella. She doesn't blame you."

"I didn't want to ask, but is she going ahead with the marriage to Igor Samson?"

"She is." Miro's expression grew pensive.

"But she's already in love . . ."

Miro let out his breath. "I know, but she's going ahead with the marriage. How could I get in the way of it? Look at where we live."

"You know?"

"Please don't say anything to her."

"Do you . . . ?"

"It doesn't matter," Miro said flatly. He visibly shook himself. "She wants you to stand with her at the wedding."

"Me? No. No, Miro, not that. Never."

"Ella, she's your friend. She went to Dunholme, alone, to get a healer for you. She was almost killed by a couple of hunters who made sport with her. You know how she got that mark on her right ear? You must stand with her; it is an honor."

"No, Miro. How could I? No."

Miro decided to leave it alone for now. "I heard you did some amazing things at the Academy. They say you're the next high enchantress."

"I'll never go there again," Ella said firmly. She wouldn't meet Miro's eyes.

Miro sighed.

"It must have been tough here. I expected to return to a warm welcome and an order for more cherl for Brandon. Instead, I returned to find he was gone. And you were so sick. You terrified me, Ella. You were so fragile, like when you were younger. I never told you, but Brandon said you were sick for months after our parents died. Please don't do that again."

"I . . . I don't know what to say. I'm sorry."

For a moment they sat silent. Miro could tell Ella was drawing away, the way she sometimes did. Putting that solid wall up again, where he couldn't get in.

"But tell me, how was the journey? What happened?" she said.

"It was . . . eventful." Miro remembered again the grim talk, the fear, the blood, and the aftermath.

"You can tell me more than that. The ship, what was it like?"

Miro took a breath. "It was beautiful, the most graceful ship I have ever seen. I can honestly say that—nothing like our little river boats. The Buchalanti . . ."

"The Buchalanti? Are you telling me you sailed on one of their ships?"

Miro grinned. "Yes. A storm rider called the *Infinity*."

"What were the Buchalanti like?"

"They were like the sea—solid, yet fluid and graceful. The men and women look a great deal alike. The sailmaster told me . . ."

"You spoke with the sailmaster?"

"Ella, please. I'm trying to tell you . . ."

They spoke for a long time, Miro telling Ella a more or less complete version of events, keeping it light, leaving out the darker details. If there was going to be war, she would find out soon enough.

He wasn't sure what to say about the Chorum, so he glossed over it. Yet his mind wandered, his eyes saying more than his words.

With the emperor's peace broken, the primate's protection meaningless, most of the delegations had left the city with alarming speed, seeking the safety of their own borders. With their Lexicon lost and their high animator killed, House Halaran was seriously weakened.

High Lord Tessolar had offered the Halrana lords passage on the Buchalanti ship, but the proud Legasa had politely declined. Tessolar reaffirmed the Alturan commitment to the Ring Forts, while High Lord Legasa again pushed for more decisive action.

Lord Marshal Devon, the commander of Altura's forces, had stayed in Tingara. His task was to buy the allied houses the time they needed to prepare for any coming confrontation.

"Do the men really all have their heads shaved in Seranthia?"

"Not all of them; only the most patriotic Tingarans."

"But isn't everyone in Seranthia a Tingaran?"

Miro paused, unsure of how to explain it to someone who only really knew Sarostar.

"Not really, no. There are people from all over the world, Builders from Torakon. Veznans, even many Alturans, although you wouldn't know it to speak to them. They've spent so long in Seranthia, even their accent has changed."

"What are they doing in Seranthia?"

Miro wondered how to explain the sheer volume of goods passing through the ports and trade routes of Seranthia, the immense wealth of the merchants. "Buying and selling goods, negotiating for services. Administering the city and the realm."

"It sounds amazing. I wish I could go there and see it for myself."

"It is amazing. It's also sad, though."

"Sad? What do you mean?"

Miro thought of the beggars and the desperate hawkers. The slum neighborhoods and the old men and young children sleeping on the street. The streetclans whose only law was violence.

"I don't know. I can't really explain it."

Autumn slipped steadily into winter. At the Academy of Enchanters, the centurion trees in the Great Court lost more and more of their leaves, until they took on a skeletal appearance. Boaters on the Sarsen became rare as people traveled the river less—only as a means to hurriedly get from one place to another. The lights of the

Crystal Palace came on earlier as nightfall moved forward in the day. The chill night air lost the heady scent of flowers and trees, becoming crisp and odorless.

Ella was preparing a mug of cherl from the package Miro had brought earlier. She knew he would be home at any moment, and wanted it to be ready for his arrival, so he could quickly wash after the day's exertions and spend time with her, talking on the porch.

Amber hadn't been able to spend as much time with Ella lately. She never spoke about the wedding preparations, but Ella found out from Miro that the wedding was scheduled for the next month. Several times Ella had caught Amber about to speak, but her friend had swallowed and said nothing, instead talking about the markets or the change of the season.

Looking out into the forest, Ella saw Miro climbing up the last few steps onto the porch. He looked exhausted, covered with sweat and grime. He stopped to lean for a moment on a railing, taking a deep breath before smoothing his face and putting on a forced smile.

"Ho, Ella," he said. Sometimes she waited, but he never asked her about her day.

"Ho, Miro," she smiled.

Rather than entering the house, he stood silently for a moment on the porch, quietly regarding her.

"What is it?" she said.

Ella handed him the mug. Miro put it straight down without even realizing he had done so. He just stood there, looking at her.

"What? Why are you looking at me like that?"

"Ella, I've brought someone to talk to you."

"You haven't. Miro, what are you . . ."

Ella broke off when a tall, willowy figure emerged from the darkness. It was a woman, her steps stately, her manner accepting deference without question. She wasn't old, but her age was high enough to be indeterminate. Her skin was unlined, but the penetrating gray eyes had seen much, experienced much.

The woman wore a shimmering green silk dress, with a hood over her hair. The fabric was covered with arcane symbols, so tiny they were almost indistinguishable from one another, the matrices the most complex Ella had ever seen. The runes glowed softly silver, giving the woman an ethereal, ghostly presence.

As the woman stepped from the shadows, she pulled back her hood. Long silver hair spilled down to her waist like flowing water, straight and lustrous.

Ella gasped. There was only one person this could be. She had never met her, never seen her, had only ever heard her name discussed in hushed tones. Even the masters altered their voices when they said her name, as if to say it in a rough tone would indicate disrespect.

"High Enchantress Evora Guinestor," Ella breathed. She dropped to one knee and touched her lips with her fingertips, resting them there for a full breath, before touching them again to her forehead.

"Rise, child," said the woman, with gravity.

Ella slowly stood. The high enchantress looked carefully about. Miro deferentially offered her a chair. She sat, the folds of her dress flowing to the floor, her hands in her lap.

"I will leave you," Miro said. With a final glance he turned away, slipping into darkness.

"You have not been attending your classes, Ella," the regal figure spoke, her voice precise.

Ella said nothing. She didn't know what to say.

"Do you think you have learned all the Academy of Enchanters has to teach you? You are skilled enough—is that it?"

Sitting here, looking at this woman, whose dress bore more skill than Ella believed possible, she felt nothing but shame.

"No, no, High Enchantress. Nothing like that."

"Knowledge is dangerous, Ella. I think you, more than anyone, should be aware of this. The knowledge you possess now is dangerous. You are an incomplete instrument. Is that the way you wish to be?"

"No, High Enchantress."

High Enchantress Evora shook her head. "Actions can have unintended consequences, as you have learned. Seeking knowledge, you did a dishonorable thing, but now you must return to show yourself to the world and acknowledge, 'Yes, I did this thing. It was foolish. I am sorry.'"

"Talwin is dead. How can I continue to live the same life? My presence alone must be a pain to everyone."

"That's what you tell yourself. But breaking into a workroom and stealing a book does not make you responsible for his death. Don't make his tragedy become your own." The woman's glare was like a razor. "I've been watching you, Ella. Who do you think it was who helped you at the examinations? You are the young woman who stood in front of the final year's lore students, the brightest young minds in Altura, and showed them that you were the best of them all. You are the young woman who has the most potential I have ever seen."

Ella blushed, caught somewhere between pleasure and shame.

"Yet you sit out here on the edge of Sarostar in self-imposed exile. Why? Your house needs good enchanters, the best enchanters, but you don't want to help your house. Your brother needs you. People need someone to lean on sometimes. But you don't want to help him."

Ella hung her head.

"Is something I am saying incorrect? I don't believe anything I am saying is untrue—do you?"

"Please don't make me go back there," Ella whispered.

169

"Make you? Girl, we have better things to do than force students to learn what we have to teach. The life of an enchantress is a life of discipline. You have one final chance. The Academy leaders will allow you one more opportunity to join your fellows, finish your studies, and graduate in a month along with the rest of your peers. I think you have been punished enough. You still have a chance to learn the joys of real enchantment. Of creation. Do you want that chance?"

"I . . . I think I do." Ella met the woman's gaze. "I do."

"Good." High Enchantress Evora rose. "You will be expected at class the day after the morrow."

"Not tomorrow?"

"No, I'm afraid not. I believe the death of your friend was punishment enough, but that doesn't satisfy everyone, for you still stole from a master. Tomorrow you will present yourself at the Great Court at noon. The entire staff and student body will be present to witness your punishment. Tomorrow, you are to be wracked."

Ella held her head high and her back erect. She was terrified. Every part of her being wanted to leave this terrible business behind. Instead she'd put on her green woolen student's gown, a familiar weight about her body, and presented herself at the Academy of Enchanters at the appointed hour.

Even at previous graduation ceremonies she hadn't seen so many Academy staff and students in one place before. The masters sat in a row, a long table of redwood planks in front of them, while the students congregated, standing in rows and columns, a somber mass of youth. The high enchantress was not present. She was rarely seen outside the Crystal Palace or the Green Tower.

Ella had never seen an actual wracking before and couldn't believe it was her being wracked. She still felt like she must be in the midst of some nightmare from which she would wake at any moment.

To the side of the masters stood the Block—a massive square of black iron, stern and unyielding. It was about three feet in height and each side was twice the length of a man. Ella tried not to look at it, but couldn't help herself. She could see the faint outlines of runes on its surface.

Ella now stood in front of the masters. Their expressions were grave.

"Ella," began Master Merlon, the most senior. "For breaking into a master's workroom, and for theft, you are summoned here this day."

Ella, her eyes downcast, stood firm, her heart racing.

"We, the masters of the Academy of Enchanters, have decided your sentence, to be carried out immediately." He paused, looking around at the students. "For misconduct leading to the death of Talwin Horstan, you are sentenced to be wracked."

Master Merlon placed two wooden cuffs on the table in front of him. "It is to be a full wracking." He placed two more wooden cuffs on the table. "May the pain you feel this day lead you away from future misdeeds. May the Lord of the Sky guide your path away from error."

Ella knew what was expected of her. She walked forward and took the first manacle—an ancient loop of wood engraved with runes.

"*Sum-pu-nala,*" she said. The loop sprang open along a previously invisible seam. Ella put the loop around her ankle. "*Sum-sun.*" The loop closed.

After her ankles Ella locked the loops around her wrists. They felt heavy. Her breath started to deepen, and her heart raced. She tried to show nothing and to face her punishment with honor.

In unison, the masters nodded. It was part of the process. Ella had to commence the punishment herself; they were only spectators.

With determined steps, Ella walked over to the Block. She could see the runes more clearly now; they hadn't been activated yet, but the places where she was to put her wrists and ankles were clearly marked.

Taking a deep breath, Ella slowly lay on her back on the Block, gazing up at the blue sky, watching the soft wisps of cloud move in a gentle breeze. The students and faculty looked on as Ella prepared herself, her chest rising and falling rapidly.

"Ak-kara," she cried.

The Block flared to life, the runes glowing red, blue, silver, and green. The cuffs lit up in sympathy, flaring red. The link was made with the cuffs and suddenly it began. Ella's body was now under the Block's control.

At first it was just an uncomfortable sensation of being stretched. Then Ella felt her back start to twist, her bones close to being pulled out of their sockets. Sweat broke out on her brow as her limbs felt near their breaking point.

They said that even Stormhand, the bladesinger traitor, had screamed after two minutes of full wracking.

Not a sound came out of Ella's mouth. Her flared nostrils and wide eyes were the only sign she showed of the pain she was in. She figured she owed that much, to bear the pain in silence.

17

*How far we travel in life matters far less than
those we meet along the way.*
—Toro Marossa, "Explorations," page 51, 423 Y.E.

"It's your turn to bring up the water," Miro said.

Ella had just been thinking the same thing about him. It was tough with just the two of them.

"My turn? It's your turn."

Miro sighed. "Ella, I do enough around here. Don't make this into an issue."

He twisted and turned in his wooden chair, stretching, arching his back. Miro grimaced as it made a painful cracking sound. He hadn't spoken much of his training lately, but he had been finding less and less time to spend at home. His body was changing dramatically—he was always tall and lean, but now his shoulders had grown; the muscles in his chest were rigidly defined.

"You think things are tough for you? I've had so much work to catch up these past weeks I'm drawing runes in my sleep."

"Just get the water, Ella."

"No, you get the water."

Miro took a deep breath. "It doesn't matter anyway. I'll get the water."

Miro stood up. He looked tired. There were lines under his eyes. Blademaster Rogan must be pushing him hard.

Ella stood also. "No, you sit down. I'll get the water."

When she returned, making her way through the forested path with two brimming buckets of fresh water, Ella saw her older brother had fallen asleep in his chair.

Without knowing where the idea came from, Ella upended one of the buckets over his head.

Miro yelped like a dog in a catfight, caught completely unaware. He blinked up at her, shaking droplets from his dark hair while Ella stood over him, bent with laughter.

Quicker than the eye, Miro leapt forward, grabbing the second bucket from her hand. Completely surprised, Ella didn't stand a chance. Soon they were both standing on the porch, laughing and dripping wet.

Ella tilted her head as she looked at her brother. "I can't believe how quickly you can move," she said. His gentle, protective nature belied such ferocious strength. Such speed.

"Miro, I have an idea," she said seriously.

He sobered. "What is it?"

"Next week, maybe we could take a day, hire one of the riverboats? It's their quiet period now, so we could get one for a good price. I know; I've checked."

Miro's face fell.

"We could see if Amber's free. We could spend the whole day together, the three of us."

"Ella, I'm leaving."

"We could visit the Poloplats early in the day, while the best produce is still available—get some sourmelons, maybe a bottle of honeywine, if we have the gilden."

Suddenly Ella realized what Miro was saying.

"What?"

"Ella, one of the bladesingers with us at Seranthia spoke up on my behalf. Huron Gower, his name is. I've been accepted into bladesinger training."

For a moment Ella was too stunned to speak. She fought to make the correct response. "Miro, I'm so happy for you. You, a bladesinger—it's what you've always wanted."

Ella could tell her brother could see right through her.

"I won't be around for a long time. I'll be gone for at least three months. Maybe a lot longer."

"Of course." Ella tried hard to keep her expression happy. It was good news, it was. "Have they told you anything about the training? It's so mysterious—all I've heard are rumors."

"I don't know where I'm going or what I'll be doing really . . . All I know is the training takes place somewhere in the Dunwood. They don't talk about it much. I'm a bit scared, to be honest."

Ella waved her hand. Her smiled was forced. "I'm sure you'll be fine. Maybe one day, when you're a bladesinger, and I'm an enchantress, I can make your zenblade."

Miro smiled. "That would be . . . wonderful."

They sat in silence for a moment. A wind blew up from the trees, a cold winter breeze—a sign of things to come. Ella shivered; she needed to get out of the wet clothes.

"Ella, you should think about moving closer to town. Maybe you could move in with a friend."

"Don't worry about me. I'll be fine."

"I don't like you being here by yourself."

"I'll be fine," Ella repeated.

It was still some time before they left the porch and retired, cold and wet. Throwing the water didn't seem so funny to Ella now.

Amber's mother fussed with her hair once more before stepping back, an appraising look on her face.

"There, that's it," she said.

Amber stood nervously on the bank of the Sarsen, where a colorful bower of trees and flowers had been constructed. With her as the centerpiece, she thought wryly. The water flowed sluggishly past, tranquil and emerald green. Amber kept a close eye on the sky, but the unseasonable weather seemed to be holding up—the sky a clear blue, the sun's rays warm on her skin. When she inhaled, Amber could smell the sweet scent of the roses and the freshness of the leaves. A light breeze blew gently, rustling the leaves around her, causing her green dress to flutter. Graduation was still a week away, but Amber had been allowed to wear silk just this once. She loved the feel of it on her skin, so soft and supple.

"Remember, my dear, this is the best day of your life."

Amber wished her mother would stop saying that. A hand reached yet again for her hair; Amber caught it this time. "Enough, Mother."

"Hmpf," Amber's mother said before planting a beaming smile on her face and directing it at some newly arrived guests.

Amber could see more of her relatives standing under the line of trees. They were all smiling. It seemed like a strange role reversal; everyone kept telling her how happy she must be, but they were the ones smiling.

Not for the first time, Amber wondered if she'd done the right thing. She kept imagining Miro appearing at the wedding, a fiery sword in his hand, cutting the flowers up and threatening the shocked relatives before he picked her up on his shoulder and carried her away.

"Don't look so sad, Amber. Smile. Everyone is watching you," her mother admonished.

Amber grimaced.

"No, I said smile. Smile. There, that's better, isn't it?"

Amber felt like she might cry.

By now all of the guests had arrived. Amber could see her entire family arrayed before her, along with many of the teachers and Academy staff. Suddenly there was a commotion in the distance, and Amber heard raised voices. One voice rose above them all—a strong, female voice.

A figure pushed through restraining hands: a young woman in a green woolen Academy gown. Ella strode with purpose past the relatives, ignoring their disapproving expressions.

"I hope I'm not too late?" Ella smiled up at Amber.

Amber just nodded. Ella took a place between Amber and her mother. She took her friend's hand.

In that moment, Amber did cry.

Ella looked on as Igor took Amber away, amid the cheers and whistles of his fellows. Everyone had said it was a beautiful wedding. No one commented on the bride's tears. They probably put it down to nerves, or tears of happiness.

Ella left the wedding and followed the riverbank, gazing into its depths and thinking about the future. She was glad she had her work. Working with essence, real enchantment, was the great joy of her life. Some of the masters had now begun to let her borrow a few of their texts. Ella read them by the dim light of her nightlamp, sitting and rocking on the porch, with the calls of the forest animals for company.

Master Merlon had told Ella she'd been recommended for the Academy honor list. Ella didn't feel the surge of pride she had expected. Instead, she was simply happy to be finding her place in the world.

Thinking of life and weddings, Ella realized she had walked quite a long way, almost to the Tenbridge. She could see the Crystal Palace, and as she watched, she was lucky enough to see the palace colors begin to glow as the sun set behind her.

"That's the first time I've seen them come on like that," an admiring voice said beside her.

He was a young man, his blue eyes sparkling as he joined Ella's idle walk along the riverbank. He did it with such assurance that it didn't seem rude, but only confident.

He was taller than Ella, perhaps one or two years older, with long, unruly hair tumbling to his collar. It was hair the color of fire—a wild red. His accent didn't sound Alturan. Ella couldn't quite place it. Perhaps it was just the way he spoke. He was undeniably handsome.

"I've always loved the palace lights," Ella said. "Did you know that from inside the palace the lights shine through the crystal walls?"

"Really?"

"The servants have almost an entire language of lore, just to control the lights. It's beautiful."

"You've been inside the palace?"

Ella didn't know why she kept talking. "No, of course not. I would never be invited. I do know some of the lords' children, though."

His eyes grew round. "That's still something most people can't say. What about your family? Have they been inside? Your father, perhaps your mother?"

"No, nothing like that. My parents died when I was young."

There was a long pause. "I'm sorry," he said. "That must have been hard."

Turning, Ella looked at him. He said it with such sincerity, she knew he meant it.

"How old were you?" he said.

"I don't know—only a babe, I suppose. I'm not sure. My father was killed in the Rebellion. My mother died too. We managed to survive. A man, loyal to my father—he raised us."

"He must have been a good man."

"He was, I guess. He was very old. He died not long ago."

"It sounds like you've had a tough time."

Ella shrugged. "Life, I guess. As my brother says, you learn and you move on."

Ella didn't know why she was opening up to this stranger. He just seemed interested. He seemed to care.

"What's your name?" she said.

"Killian."

"Killian. That's a strange name." Ella put her hand to her lips. "Sorry, I don't mean to be rude."

He smiled. "It's the only one I have."

For some reason, Ella smiled along with him, lost in his eyes for a moment. Killian's smile grew broader. "And your name is . . . ?"

She blushed, breaking eye contact. "I'm Ella."

"Ella," he said. "That's a beautiful name. It suits you."

Ella changed the subject. "What do you do, Killian?"

"Do?"

"For work or study. Are you a student at the Academy? I don't think I've seen you before."

"Me? I represent a wealthy merchant from outside Altura. He seeks goods from far lands to trade in his own land. I find them for him. But enough about me. You said you had a brother?"

Killian asked Ella more questions. She found herself talking more than she had in a long time.

With winter fully settling in, it grew dark earlier, and Ella knew she should head home. It was good to talk to someone, though, someone who really listened.

Ella chose the path, picking some of the most elaborate river gardens to walk past, pointing out some of Sarostar's more impressive features. The pair drew closer to the Crystal Palace as they chatted. Ella intended for the palace to be the final piece on her spontaneous tour.

"Do you know the names of the nine bridges?" Killian asked.

"Of course. We just passed the Tenbridge. I don't know why it's called that. Back downriver are the Singer's Bridge, Lord's Bridge, Skyway, and the Winebridge. Ahead we have the Long Bridge, Saimon's Bridge, the Runebridge, and Victory Bridge."

Ella gestured to each in turn, although she could only see the Tenbridge behind her and the Long Bridge coming up ahead—a massive span seemingly of one block.

"The Long Bridge was built by the builders from House Torakon, years ago. That was before the Rebellion, of course. We had to study the bridge from a mathematical point of view. It would never stand without the runes."

It seemed dangerously thin, which gave it an otherworldly aura. Ella could only imagine what the cities in Torakon must look like.

They then passed Saimon's Bridge, a sturdy construction of stone, lined on either side with statues of scholarly-looking men.

The river glistened in the afternoon sunlight. It gurgled and splashed beside them, gentle but with enough of a current that Ella wouldn't have wanted to fall in.

Occasionally, boats passed them, graceful vessels constructed of pale wood. They bobbed in the water, now and then turned deftly by the oar strokes of their operators. So absorbed was Ella that it took a moment for her to realize that Killian had stopped when she began to climb some steps. She glanced back down and laughed at Killian's expression. He stared ahead with an incredulous gaze.

The steps climbed up and up and then abruptly terminated—vanished into thin air. Killian looked on in disbelief as Ella smiled and took another step into nothingness. He winced. Obviously, at any moment he expected to see Ella fall through the air, to hear the splash as she smacked the water from such a height.

Instead, Ella took another step and looked back at him. "Come on, this is the way to the Crystal Palace. If we take much longer, the people on the boats will laugh at us." She smiled to take any sting out of her words.

Killian stood on the last of the stone blocks. Ella looked down at her own feet. She could see the water far beneath her, could make out every crest and foam. While she watched, concentrating, looking for something to mark out the bridge, she suddenly saw the glowing runes. They appeared, and then disappeared, so that she wondered if she had really seen them at all. Then she saw them again, faint symbols that glowed one moment and vanished the next.

Ella smiled encouragement. Taking a deep breath, Killian took a step onto the Runebridge. He half-stumbled, so prepared had he been to fall down to the deep water below. He looked up at Ella in astonishment.

"How . . . ?"

"How does it work? No one knows for sure. It's from an era in the past, when our understanding of enchantment must have been better than it is today. It's something to do with bending the light and giving the air form. The Long Bridge was built by House Torakon, but only we could build something like the Runebridge. Only House Altura could do such a thing. They say it's a last measure of security for the Crystal Palace."

The pair crossed the Runebridge, Killian taking each step gingerly but slowly becoming accustomed. They descended to the opposite bank, where the fountains of the Crystal Palace formed fanciful shapes.

They were now at the palace gate, looking into the grounds, the huge doors close, but separated from them by scores of soldiers in green.

Killian asked Ella question after question about the Crystal Palace; he seemed quite interested.

As they walked away from the palace, there was a sudden commotion behind them. Killian and Ella both turned.

Soldiers were pouring out of the palace, surrounding a cowering man with a circle of bristling weapons.

The man was some kind of merchant—Alturan by his looks. His ear was red where an earring must have been torn from his head by force, and his face was bruised and bloody. The merchant's once fine clothes showed the marks of a long and difficult journey.

"Please, he made me do it. He made me do it," the merchant repeated, over and over.

He carried a wooden box.

"There's something in there!" one of the guards called.

"Open it!" said the leader.

"Please, he made me do it."

"I said, open it!"

The merchant opened the lid of the box.

"What's in there? Take it out. I said take it out!"

The merchant lifted something out of the box with both hands.

Ella recoiled in horror. It was a human head. The hair had been shaved and a message tattooed into the scalp.

"It's Lord Devon!" a soldier cried. "Someone tell the high lord!"

Ella could read the message in the lights of the Crystal Palace.

"War," it read.

Ella turned to Killian, but he was gone.

18

We always prefer war on our terms to peace on someone else's.
—Memoirs of Emperor Xenovere I, page 312, 381 Y.E.

Ella and Amber ran up to each other, laughing and hugging, pointing to their green silk dresses in excitement.

Green bunting decorated the Great Court, running among the sparse branches of the centurion trees. A group of musicians played, the tinkling, chiming music lending to the festive mood. Parents and graduates stood in small groups, smiling and chatting. The smell of cooking food wafted through the air, glasses clinked together, a man laughed.

Ella had seen her friend only a couple of times since the wedding; Amber had seemed different, more subdued. Ella hoped she would find happiness. Maybe it just took time.

"Lord of the Sky, Ella. I swear you look more and more gorgeous every time I see you. The way you fill out that dress is almost scandalous."

Ella blushed. "It's just the material." She pointed at the badge on Amber's dress. "Has anyone used your title yet, Enchantress Amber?"

Each girl wore her *raj hada* on the breast of her dress, the sword and flower of Altura lined with silver.

Amber laughed. "Someone has now. I can't believe we're finally graduating. After all this time, all that work. Do you know what?" Amber said. "I'm going to get drunk."

She ran over to a table where glasses of honeywine sparkled in neat rows, returning quickly and handing one to Ella.

"To enchantment."

"To enchantment," Ella echoed.

Amber took a big draught of her wine. Ella sipped a smaller amount, careful not to appear too frivolous. She couldn't help thinking about Talwin. About his parents. What were they doing on this day?

"It's a shame Miro couldn't be here," said Amber.

"I know," said Ella. There were too many people who should have been here. Talwin. Miro. Brandon. Her parents.

"I still can't believe he's going to be a bladesinger. They've always looked so terrifying. I can't believe I'll know one."

"I can't believe it myself sometimes. My brother, a bladesinger."

"Some of the men look so handsome in their silk robes, don't you think?"

Ella chuckled. "I guess." For some reason Killian's face came to mind. Why had he left so suddenly that day?

"Stop looking so pensive—you've done enough thinking. Enough reading, enough study, enough practice."

Ella saw some of the masters gather on the podium nearby. She began to feel nervous.

"Do you think my armorsilk was any good? What if I made a mistake?"

"Stop it, Ella. It'll be fine. Here, they're about to announce it."

Amber took Ella by the hand and led her to where the crowd gathered expectantly.

Master Merlon stood up and faced the crowd. "Congratulations once again to this year's graduates, one of the brightest sets I have seen come out of this Academy, I must say."

"Get on with it!" someone yelled.

The crowd laughed. Master Merlon frowned down at the students.

"As we all know, this has been a difficult year, with many trials for all of us." The students sobered. "The decision process to select this year's Lorenames, the two outstanding students in a year of exceptional talent, has been terribly hard. I have seen intricate enchantments, works of art, the sharpest zenblade, the strongest armorsilk." He paused for dramatic effect. "Finally, though, we have come to a conclusion."

The graduates hushed in expectation. Amber squeezed Ella's hand.

"This year's Golden Lorename is . . ." Master Merlon paused, enjoying the suspense. "Torsten Alfoll!"

The graduates cheered. A blushing Torsten ascended the steps to the podium. Master Merlon shook his hand and gave him a silver scrill, beautifully worked. "Congratulations, Torsten. May this scrill aid the working of your enchantments."

The graduates clapped, a group of Torsten's friends whooping loudly, causing him some embarrassment. Torsten shook hands with each of the masters in turn and then descended the podium to resounding applause.

"Which makes this year's Emerald Lorename, our top graduate . . ."—Master Merlon drew it out, and then smiled down at her—"Ella Goodwin."

It was Brandon's last name. The graduates clapped all the louder. They had seen her best Master Goss. They had seen her take the pain of the Block.

Amber looked on with undisguised envy, smiling and clapping. "Go on—go up!"

Ella ascended the podium, a shocked expression on her face. Master Merlon smiled, and as he shook her hand, the crowd roared.

Master Merlon then gave her a sealed crystal bottle, half the size of her hand, intricately designed. Ella couldn't believe it when she saw the black liquid inside. Essence.

Ella shook hands with each of the masters in turn. As she shook Master Goss's hand, he leaned forward to speak into her ear.

"That armorsilk, I have never . . ." He shook his head, momentarily at a loss for words, finally saying only, "We expect great things of you, young lady."

The day was finally complete when Ella, descending the steps of the podium, saw a tall figure with dark hair at the back of the crowd, a wide smile on his face. Miro.

Ella smiled broadly, just for him.

It was the first time the three of them had been together in what felt like an age. As they sat under the shade of a centurion tree, Ella realized it was probably the last time she would sit like this, a student of the Academy taking ease in the Great Court. She felt a strange feeling of sadness overcome her.

"I can't believe they let you get away," Amber was saying. She sat close to Miro, their legs touching. He didn't move away.

"I can be pretty persuasive when I need to be." He grinned. There was no mention of Amber's wedding.

They shared each other's company for the entire afternoon. Drinking honeywine. Laughing together. It was the happiest day of Ella's life.

The winter sun started to drift down toward the horizon, and as the day grew dim, the talk turned dark. It was on everyone's mind.

The war.

The emperor had acted with unbelievable speed, surprising everyone. Miro said High Lord Legasa of Halaran had predicted it. In waiting, they had lost the initiative.

The combined forces of Tingara and Torakon had occupied the Azure Plains. This new force was coming to be called the Black Army. Rumors about its nature were in abundance. They said it was devoid of the usual imperial pomp, that the legionnaires had doffed their purple for black and that the Toraks in the army also wore black in a new display of unity and force.

They marched under a new standard, a white sun on a black background. The sun was the symbol of the Evermen, and people wondered what the primate thought of the use of the holy symbol, and waited for the leader of the Assembly of Templars, whose role was to help maintain the peace, to speak out against the emperor's growing evil.

The builders of Torakon set up defenses on the plains, looking up at the Ring Forts, which were steadily filling with Alturan and Halrana soldiers. The Toraks assembled great bastions: spiked barricades and impossibly tall watchtowers, reinforced with lore. They dug tunnels and trenches, and every day the Toraks could be seen assessing the fortresses above them, analyzing their weaknesses, looking for where they could exploit any flaws.

The Imperial Legion numbered in the ten of thousands, the strongest specimens in a race known for its strength, equipped with swords and spears, shields and heavy armor—much of it enchanted.

Greedily taking the emperor's money, the artificers of Loua Louna supplied the legion with their most vicious tools of war: prismatic orbs, mortars to launch them, runebombs, and other explosive devices. Dirigibles floated above the Azure Plains, ready to rain death down on any enemy.

Then there were the regular soldiers, armed with a wide range of weapons, from the rare enchanted blades hoarded by the generals to the meanest club. In their teeming numbers, like ants buzzing on the plains, the only thing uniting them was the color black.

With their fortresses firmly sealed, the occupants of the Ring Forts—Manrith, Penton, Ramrar, Charing, and Sark—gazed grimly down at their doom, feeling thin in numbers and exposed up on the heights.

"I can't believe they killed poor Lord Devon like that," Amber said.

"Did anyone escape?" Ella asked Miro.

Miro took a breath. "They burned the Alturan market house to the ground. Killed everyone inside: soldiers, merchants, women, and children. I met many of those people. They were kind people, just bystanders really. That could have been me."

"It's so awful," said Amber.

"Apparently, the emperor gave Lord Devon a written ultimatum—give up the Alturan Lexicon, or it would be war. The high lord was given the same message shortly after we returned from Tingara. They didn't even wait for High Lord Tessolar's response before they killed Lord Devon and sent his head back to Sarostar."

Ella shuddered. "Well at least we have the Ring Forts," she said.

"With Prince Leopold leading our forces, though."

Ella could tell Miro wasn't impressed. "Prince Leopold?"

"It was to be Lord Devon's son, Rorelan, but he hasn't been himself since the death of his father. There are few lords with the political connections to lead our forces. With Rorelan out of the picture, that means Prince Leopold, High Lord Tessolar's nephew."

"Can he command?" Ella asked.

"The bladesingers say he's intelligent, but they're not sure about his judgment. He's perhaps trying too hard to prove himself."

"To who?"

Miro shrugged. "To his uncle? To people like you and me?"

"Miro, what's the training like?" Amber asked.

"Hard," Miro said flatly.

He looked into the distance. He was growing up so fast that Ella felt she was losing the brother she knew. He seemed like he had the weight of the world on his shoulders.

"It will soon get difficult for you both here," Miro said. "We'll need a constant supply of weapons and armor. They'll work you both hard. Lord Devon was clever. He knew this war was coming and stockpiled essence illegally, without the knowledge of either the emperor or the primate. But it will be a grim struggle, most likely decided by the actions of the undeclared houses."

At the mention of essence, Ella fingered the crystal bottle she had been given. She still couldn't believe she had her own essence, to do with as she wanted. She could walk into the Poloplats right now and exchange the tiny amount of liquid she held in her hand for any single product in sight. Not that she would ever do that, of course. Still, holding such wealth in her hand was a heady feeling.

"I heard some of the townsfolk say it's just bluster, that the emperor doesn't want an all-out war with the houses," Amber said. "That if we all joined against him we would be more than a match for him, so why would he want war?"

"That's what they say, yes." He regarded the two girls gravely. "But they're wrong about it being a show. I don't know why, but the emperor wants war; he's actively pushing for it. Politically, it makes no sense. If anything, the last war did nothing for the emperor's cause. The high lord believes many of the houses will stand together."

"What of the primate? Who is he siding with?"

"High Lord Tessolar says the primate is angry with the emperor, that the emperor is mocking the Evermen and their legacy by war-mongering. The primate is praying to the Evermen to help him choose a course of action. Likely, he will cut off the emperor's essence—the primate controls the relics that produce the essence, and it's perhaps the quickest and cleanest way to end the war. I pray to the Lord of the Sky that he does." Miro's face grew determined. "But if the war continues, I'm ready to fight."

"As am I," Amber said with determination.

A voice called out Amber's name. A figure drew closer: Igor Samson.

"Amber, there you are," he said. "Ella"—he nodded—"and Miro, isn't it?"

"Igor," the siblings said in greeting. It felt strange to use the master's first name, but Ella supposed she needed to become used to it.

"Amber, my dear, it's growing late. We should be going home."

"Yes, Igor, just a moment, and I'll say good-bye," Amber said.

Master Samson walked away to give her privacy, taking out a notebook and flicking through the pages.

"I have to go. I'm sure everything will be fine. Ella, take care, will you?" Amber gave Ella a tight hug. "And Miro . . ." She looked back at Igor Samson. He seemed busy with his notes. She quickly gave Miro a soft kiss on the cheek. "Please be safe."

Then Amber was gone.

Ella and Miro sat in silence for a moment. Ella only now realized how much she had missed her brother.

"I . . . I just wanted to say thank you for coming here today. It can't have been easy."

"No, it wasn't. Given the circumstances, though, they permitted me to leave, to see you."

"Circumstances?"

"My only sister's graduation!" He smiled. Then his smile fell. Ella knew him; she knew there was more. "Ella, they're sending us all to the front, even those who haven't finished their training, like me. I'm to finish my training in the field."

"The front? What do you mean?"

"The Ring Forts. The emperor is going to strike at any moment, and when he does, it's going to be with all his strength. The Halrana high lord has finally convinced High Lord Tessolar to send every last man we have to the Ring Forts."

"Miro, no . . ."

"Listen to me. You be careful—do you hear me? The Skylord only knows what's going to come of all this. It could get bad. War does strange things to people's minds, and it's not only in the battlefield. With most of the soldiers gone, people will test the high lord's strength, here in Altura, in Sarostar."

"What do you mean?"

"I don't know. Looting stores, theft, hunting for food. A pretty young girl like you, alone on the edge of town." He grimaced. "I don't like thinking about it."

Ella smiled. "Don't worry about me. I can take care of myself."

He looked at her, angry. "You think this is a game? How? How can you take care of yourself?" He tensed, the muscles in his arms rippling. "Just try to stop me. Go on, show me."

Miro lunged at her and grabbed at her arm. Ella murmured a short syllable as his hand touched her long-sleeved enchantress's dress.

Bright sparks sprayed out where Miro's hand made contact. "Ahh!" Miro cried, pulling back and wringing his hand. "Lord of the Sky, that hurts."

Ella smiled again. "I told you."

"A real silk enchantress's dress. I should have known." He shook his head. "Just be careful."

"You're the one who needs to be careful. How can I stay here, safe in Sarostar, while you fight for your life?"

"You stay because you're what we're fighting to protect."

"Just come back alive."

"I'll do my best. I assure you of that."

Some time later, he left her.

19

Our final gift to you is your soul. Although your flesh is corporal,
your soul is eternal. It was here before your body came into being,
and you will live when your bones are dust. The soul is for you alone.
It is not for the creatures of the forest. It is not for the fishes of the sea.
It is not for the people of the duns.
                —*The Evermen Cycles*, 15:43

It was as if he were waiting for her, standing by the side of the river, skipping stones across its smooth surface.

Ella was taking one of her regular walks by the waterfront. It grew dark early now. Few other people were about, most seeking the warmth of their homes, trying to keep the winter chill at bay.

This was an especially quiet place, where spindle trees lined the riverbank and an entire section of the land had been devoted to parks and gardens. Across the Sarsen Ella could see the lights of the Woltenplats, the lively arts district, and occasionally she could hear the sounds of tinkling Alturan music wafting over the water.

It had been a season of occasions and celebrations. Ella had been surprised to receive several invitations to dances and parties. Some of the young men had been very forward. It seemed each thought she had spurned the offers of his fellows because she was waiting for him.

Ella recognized Killian immediately by his red hair. She thought to surprise him, but he knew she was there, turning as she approached, a broad, welcoming smile on his face.

She was still angry with him for leaving her so suddenly that day. One moment he had been there—they had shared something; she wasn't sure what, but she was sure there was a connection—the next moment he was gone.

"It's good to see you in something other than green," Killian said with a grin.

Ella looked self-consciously down at herself. With the tiniest amount of her essence, she'd made and sold several simple enchanted pieces, earning enough so she could finally buy some new clothes.

It was only when she had new dresses that she realized how poorly her old Academy gown fit her. It had been so tight around her breasts and hips that she couldn't believe Miro had allowed her to be seen wearing it in public.

Tonight she wore blue with a hem of yellow, a simple but elegant dress that fit her figure—almost too revealingly, she'd thought. The seamstress had assured her it was the latest fashion and that men would be falling over themselves to pay court to her. Ella wasn't sure about that, but it did set off her eyes nicely.

"You look lovely," Killian said. "I hear you graduated from the Academy. Congratulations. What are your plans now?"

He was so direct, so confident—so different from the young men she knew. Ella wanted to ask him where he had disappeared to, but she didn't want to break the mood.

The pair stood side by side, looking over the river at the Woltenplats.

"I don't know," Ella said. "With the war, I suppose I'll help out: enchanting shields and the like."

"The most gifted young enchantress, working on shields? Surely, there'll be more exciting work out there for someone like you."

Ella wasn't sure if Killian was mocking her. She looked over at him, but his expression was earnest, his eyes sincere.

"I guess I'll work on what's needed most."

"Is that all you do—work?"

Ella had a flippant response prepared, but she faltered. "I suppose it is." She shrugged. "What else is there?"

Killian inclined his head. "Walk with me. Let's find out."

They crossed the Singer's Bridge, a thin arch of stones leading from the area just north of the parks and over the river. Ella found herself side by side with Killian, pressed close to him as they made their way across the narrow bridge. She was uncomfortably aware of his presence. The heat from his body.

"It was terrible, what happened at the palace," he said.

Ella felt relieved that he was the one bringing it up. "It was."

Killian thought for a moment. "That was a pretty grim way to send a message. It was good to see how well protected the Crystal Palace was. Did you see how many soldiers came out? A small army."

It wasn't the conversation Ella had been expecting. Why had he left so suddenly?

"I suppose they have to protect the palace. Is it just the high lord that lives there?"

"Well, the high lord, his staff, and his closest advisers live there with their families. The high enchantress has some of her most powerful artifacts in the palace. I suppose it's better protected than the Green Tower. She spends a lot of time there when she's not administering the Academy. It's where she has her personal quarters too."

"Really? You've met her, haven't you?"

"How do you know that?"

Killian looked at her quizzically. "You're an enchantress. I just assumed you would have."

"Oh," she said. "Yes, I've met her. She's . . . strong. She helped me with something. I wouldn't have graduated without her."

"What did she help you with?"

Ella didn't know why, but she found herself telling Killian everything. About Talwin. About the wracking. About Miro and Amber.

They stood at the apex of the Singer's Bridge, their heads close together. Ella spoke softly, but Killian never once asked her to repeat herself, nor did he interrupt her.

"Your brother will be fine. It sounds to me like the Imperials should be the ones afraid."

"I hope you're right."

Killian gestured to the other side of the river, in the direction they were headed. The multihued lights of the Woltenplats winked suggestively.

"They say in times of trouble, when people are afraid, they come together. Come now, a little wine and company is good for the soul, what do you say?"

Ella smiled, and he took her by the hand. Killian's hand was much larger, dry and warm, and enveloped hers completely. Ella felt safe in his company.

They laughed as they ran recklessly down the far side of Singer's Bridge.

———————

"No, this one!" Ella laughed.

"How about this one?"

"No, I want to go to this one!"

Killian grinned. "We'll have it your way then. For tonight's entertainment, venue number five is . . ."—he paused dramatically—"The Prey Turned Hunter!"

"I love the name," Ella said as they entered their fifth tavern for the night. They had made it a game, drinking a different drink at each tavern as they walked south along the river, until they found what Killian called "the perfect tavern."

More of a music hall than an eating establishment, the entrance of The Prey Turned Hunter bore a hand-drawn sign of a deer stalking a terrified man. Ella laughed again as Killian pointed at the expression on the hunter's face.

Inside, a group of five musicians played together on a raised stage. Three played the traditional Alturan metal-keyed instruments, the largest as tall as the man who played it, the smallest barely two feet high, while the other two tapped chimes and drums. Ella had never seen so many musicians play in unison—it made the sound much fuller, more raucous. She found herself tapping along without even meaning to.

Some young women were dancing, their skirts swirling around their legs. There were a far greater number of women than men on the dance floor. Not that the hall was empty of men—far from it. They sat against the walls, smiling and nodding along to the chiming music, barely taking their eyes off the girls.

It was a casual place, where drinks were ordered at the bar.

"What will it be this time?" Killian said.

"I don't know. I don't know any of these drinks, really. You choose."

"How about . . . have you tried coulna?"

"I've got no idea what that is." She smiled up at him.

"Two coulnas it is, then." He smiled back.

Ella stood close by Killian as he ordered the drink. A warm feeling was coming over her. She still held his hand, and leaning, she snuggled into his body. He looked over at her and smiled.

"Lord of the Sun, you have an eye for a good tavern."

Killian placed his arm around her. Ella tensed a little and then relaxed. There was no one to go home to, no one to worry about her—why shouldn't she enjoy herself?

Killian paid the barman and turned to face her. The drinks were left on the bar, untouched. Ella tilted her head back, her lips parted.

He took the offer, leaned in, and kissed her.

Ella felt languid in his arms, her weight supported. He held her close as he kissed her, not insistently, but gently.

She broke off the kiss. "I love this tune! Do you know it?"

"No." He smiled.

"Come and dance. Come on!"

Ella dragged him onto the dance floor, and soon he held her in his arms, twirling her. Killian's steps were foreign, but he was sure on his feet. Ella was deft enough to move with him.

Ella's eyes caught some faces from her classes. The girls looked on in envy at the charming man who danced with such grace. The young men frowned.

Ella didn't care. She was lost in the moment.

Ella and Killian stayed at The Prey Turned Hunter until well after midnight, dancing and laughing. They didn't kiss again. Ella was content to merely be close to someone, to be young and happy, just like the others. She frequently ran her fingers over the nape of Killian's neck, feeling his red locks in her fingers. He often kept an arm around her waist, gently feeling the pressure of her body against him, the curve of her hip.

Finally, they tumbled out onto the street, leaving the warm glow of the music hall behind them. Looking around, Ella realized they were among the last people out in the Woltenplats. Many of the public houses had closed, their doors shut and nightlamps deactivated. Only a few hangers-on stayed in The Prey Turned Hunter, eking the last few moments' pleasure out of the night.

Ella was unprepared for the late night chill. It was freezing, and her breath came out in a cloud of vapor. She shivered.

Suddenly she realized how little she knew about this man. He knew so much about her.

"I should be going now," she said.

Apparently sensing the change in mood, Killian made no protest. Ella turned away and took a step before turning back to face him.

"I had . . . I had a wonderful time."

"I am glad. I did too." His smile was broad.

On impulse Ella dashed up to him and brushed her lips against his before walking into the night.

20

While I looked on, the Petryan high lord had his elementalists create a wall of fire. It was like nothing so much as a waterfall, but constructed of bright red flame. He then proceeded to entertain himself by forcing villagers to run through the searing barrier, so hot that I felt it from a great distance away. I can still hear their screams now.

—Toro Marossa, "Explorations," page 106, 423 Y.E.

Miro pulled his green cloak around him. It was unbearably cold, getting worse as they penetrated deeper into Halaran and drew closer to their destination.

It had been a week since the column had crossed the great Bridge of Sutanesta, leaving Altura behind them and entering Halrana lands. Miro had heard descriptions of the bridge but had never seen it. The soldiers said it was as ancient as the Sentinel in the great harbor at Seranthia, that there was no force that could lift such massive stones.

The column moved ponderously along the road, a long unbroken line of officers, nobles, soldiers, administrators, porters, hunters, cooks, tinkers, smiths, carpenters, masons, and assorted camp followers. Stretching as far as the eye could see in either direction, like a rope lined along a curving line to determine its length, it wound its way through villages, over hills, and around forests. But their path was climbing, always climbing, as they headed for the high ground of the Ring Forts.

A group of enchanters mingled with the lords, ready to counter the tricks of the enemy's lore and come up with some tricks of their own. Miro wondered how hard it would be to keep them safe and whether Ella would be sent to the front as their numbers dwindled.

Miro had been grouped with the bladesingers, but at the back, with the other untried and untested recruits. He occasionally noticed the awed glances of the regular soldiers; they didn't realize the distinction between his *raj hada* lined with blue and the blood-red against green of a true bladesinger.

There was little talk around him. Rather than marching like the soldiers, the bladesingers walked casually, gracefully. They murmured to one another in soft tones, long association and familiarity obvious with every contact. Miro was definitely on the outside of that circle.

There were two other recruits with him: a young man named Bartolo Thorn and another named Ronell Kendra. Both were deadly with a sword—they had to be to have made it this far—but in looks and attitude they were completely different. Bartolo had a certain panache, a way of walking and talking that was vigorous and expressive. He was a little darker than Miro, with a tiny moustache in the Halrana style and curly black locks. Ronell was more steady, and he often wore a somber expression as if the bearer of bad news. He had close-cropped brown hair and sad brown eyes, but when he laughed, his whole body shook.

Unlike soldiers, bladesingers—even recruits—were allowed to wear their hair any way they chose. Miro's black hair had grown long, and he now wore it tied back behind his head. He was the tallest of the recruits—even his scabbard was longer than the others', and he wore it strapped to his back.

Miro still couldn't believe they had been given zenblades. Apparently, it was the first time in living memory for zenblades to be given to recruits. Usually only full bladesingers were entrusted with the deadly weapons. The argument between Blademaster Rogan, leader of the bladesingers, and the newly promoted Prince Leopold had been long and bitter, and, it seemed, heard by everyone.

Blademaster Rogan had said there was no purpose in calling half-trained bladesingers to the front without giving them zenblades. Prince Leopold had said there was no way he was going to have recruits carry such powerful weapons into the thick of battle. The men were just too packed together—it would be a disaster waiting to happen. Blademaster Rogan had taken a breath and said simply:

"Either you take them out of armorsilk and put them with the soldiers, or you give them zenblades and treat them like men. Because when they go into battle in the uniform of a bladesinger, they are going to be a target for every weapon the emperor can throw at them. At least give them a fighting chance, for otherwise you'll be sending them to their deaths."

It was settled. It hadn't done much for the relationship between the blademaster and his new lord marshal, though. Prince Leopold cut a dashing figure in his green uniform, with his light hair and regular features, but Miro knew that most of the officers would be looking to others for leadership.

Captain Sloan had also been promoted to marshal. It was hoped that his experience would temper the young prince.

Lord Marshal Devon was sorely missed.

Miro was determined to live up to the bladesinger reputation. He was sure he knew what to do; the complex activation sequences for both his armorsilk and his zenblade had been taught. They had been drilled into him, the song like a chant in his mind, ready to be called on. He just hoped it would still be with him when the time came.

As Miro gazed ahead, something crested the hill in front. Strange birds like dark specks, growing larger.

As Miro watched, they took form. His heart lurched like a stone punching him in the chest. He realized what they must be at the same time as he heard the cry.

"Air attack!"

They had been drilled, but there was a difference between a drill and the real thing. Miro's pulse raced as he looked up and down the column. They were completely defenseless.

"Everyone get down!" one of the officers shouted, running along the line.

Miro couldn't believe this was the best defense they could come up with—to get down. The leading dirigible reached those at the front of the column. It was the first time Miro had seen one with his own eyes.

It was a strange contraption: a boatlike wooden tub attached by wires to some kind of elongated air balloon above. The balloon and cabin both glowed with the complex matrices of the artificers' runes. Miro wondered why they didn't have their own dirigibles. Was this some oversight of the Alturan command?

Something small and spherical dropped down from the air. It missed the column, landing about a hundred paces away.

The ground erupted in explosions of flame and earth as the prismatic orb detonated. Miro blanched. He hurriedly activated the basic protection sequence for his armorsilk. Looking around him, he realized the other bladesingers had already done so.

Miro chose strength over agility—there was little use in flexibility in this kind of situation—feeling his armorsilk tighten around his shoulders. His voice murmured the runes, the words coming out, one after another, so quickly that it blurred into a strange song. The songs of the individual bladesingers merged, rising and falling but maintaining a steady low volume.

The second dirigible reached the front of the column. It swooped low, the pilot choosing his target carefully. The orb fell through the air. Miro could feel the tension around him.

The device exploded thunderously, the booming sound like the loudest thunder, so close it hurt Miro's ears. Men were thrown in all directions, flying through the air, their bodies torn into pieces by the force of the explosion.

It was Miro's first experience of war. It was slaughter.

The orbs began to rain down, heavier now, a deadly hail. Blood sprayed, and limbs were ripped free from their owners' bodies.

The soldiers began to break ranks; the dirigibles were fast, and to stay invited destruction. Miro didn't blame them. It was murder, pure and simple. He was infinitely glad for his armorsilk. The murmuring of the bladesingers continued steadily.

"Hold, Skylord scratch you! Hold, I say!" the officers yelled.

A small group of soldiers buckled and left the column, running like the wind. Miro knew that one moment more and it would be a rout. If the army broke up, they would be easy prey for a ground attack.

"Someone run this over to the mortar team!" an officer yelled nearby. He held a basket of small, rune-covered orbs.

Miro knew he probably stood a much greater chance than an ordinary soldier of making it. He also knew he was probably the fastest runner: the soldiers were all weighed down with their armor.

Without giving it further thought, Miro changed his song. The runes on his armorsilk shifted hue; the way they pulsed became more of a shimmer. He kept some of the protective strength but added a large degree of agility.

He met the officer's gaze and took the basket. "Where?" he said.

"Near the enchanters. Behind us."

Miro didn't look for approval. Bladesingers were allowed to work on their own initiative.

He broke away and began to run alongside the column, the large basket held awkwardly at his side, clutched in one arm, impeding his progress. His heart pumped, and his breath deepened.

Miro saw sights along the way that he knew would stay with him forever. A cook's assistant, her arm torn away. A group of legless soldiers all writhing together, trying in vain to staunch the flow of blood. People from his homeland, dying.

Miro ran like he had never run before.

The enchanters were recognizable by their flowing green silk, standing out among the soldiers like flowers in mud. Miro saw the enchanters well before he reached them. He looked for the mortar teams but couldn't see them.

Miro ducked when a dirigible buzzed low above his head. He saw a prismatic orb drop, scoring a direct hit on the soldiers below. In the same instant, an enterprising soldier with a strong arm threw up his own glowing sphere.

The twin explosions threw Miro to the ground. Both the dirigible and the soldier were destroyed by the blast. There was nothing left but soot and charred earth.

Miro picked himself up and looked around. His basket was upturned, the orbs scattered about.

He began to gather them, ignoring the chaos around him.

A soldier joined him in gathering the orbs; then another, wordlessly handed him the heavy objects. Soon the bucket was full.

"Thank you," Miro said.

"Go with speed, bladesinger," one of the soldiers said, nodding.

Miro touched his fingers to his lips and, balancing the basket on his side, ran on, feeling pain in his side but ignoring it.

Miro finally reached the enchanters and saw them standing in a terrified bunch. Enchantment took time and care; there was nothing they could do here. "Where are the mortar teams?" he panted.

An officer grabbed him from behind. "Lord of the Sky, the orbs, here they are! Where are the rest of them?"

"The rest?"

"We need more! Many more!"

Miro's breathing was labored. He yelled above the din. "I don't know why, but they're closer to the front. An officer there gave these to me."

"Just get more!"

The officer took the basket from his hands. Miro, turning, felt a grip on his arm. "Bladesinger?"

"Yes?"

"Your song."

Miro realized his armorsilk had grown limp, the runes faded. His heart thudded as he thought about how close he'd come to the explosions.

"Thank you."

On the run back, Miro learned something. He learned that if running with a basket was hard, running while chanting a series of complex runes was very, very hard.

"Lord of the Sky, are you all right?" Ronell said.

"More," Miro panted. "We need more. Orbs. For the mortars. Help."

Ronell and Bartolo looked at each other. "Where do we find them?"

Miro's struggle became a nightmare of running through barely missed explosions. He chanted as he ran, the glowing armorsilk saving his life more than once, the other two recruits following his lead.

Then he felt the atmosphere change as the Alturans began to fight back.

Great bursts of flame flared against the sky, again and again. A dirigible went up in flames, still in the air, its occupants screaming.

The Alturans cheered.

As the orbs found their way to the mortar teams, the frequency of the explosions in the sky increased. Soon two more dirigibles were down and another partly destroyed, its occupants fleeing as smoke poured from its cabin. The remaining pilots decided they had taken their best shots—and they too fled.

___

The army struggled to pull together. A great many soldiers and workers as well as invaluable supplies had been lost. The question on everyone's lips was the same: How had this happened?

The officers gathered the column and together they made a hasty camp on the outskirts of a forest, where the commanders hoped the thick treetops and rocky hills nearby would help prevent another attack.

The enchanters didn't have the skills of builders, but were able to construct some rune-covered fortifications and alert systems— tall towers encircling the camp—giving the soldiers a much-needed feeling of protection.

The huge command tent was raised in the center of the camp, a circle of bladesingers providing one level of protection and a series of activated sentry devices providing another.

Miro was posted with the circle of bladesinger guards: some kind of reward for the exertions of the day, he supposed.

The loud voices of the commanders were audible to all. Prince Leopold's cultured accent was a crisp contrast to Marshal Sloan's rasping soldier's voice and Blademaster Rogan's gravelly baritone.

"We have to face the possibility that the Ring Forts have been overrun," said Marshal Sloan.

"That's impossible," said Prince Leopold.

"Then how do you explain what happened today?" said Sloan.

"I don't know!"

"Then guess," said Blademaster Rogan.

There was no response.

"The fact is, we need more information," Sloan said. "I've dispatched runners to Mornhaven and Sark. Hopefully, that will give us some answers, but until then we need a plan of action."

"What do you recommend?"

"This is a good position; we should dig in here. At the very least, it will give us a chance to redefine our tactics and gather information. We can't let another disaster like today happen again. We were completely unprepared."

"That's because we're supposed to be under the protection of the Ring Forts," Leopold said.

"I know that!" said Sloan. "But it shouldn't have happened. If we'd been marching in proper order, we would have saved lives."

Rogan Jarvish spoke, "We all failed here. We know now we can't make assumptions. From now on we must treat the situation as if we're in enemy territory rather than friendly lands. And we must face the fact that the Ring Forts may no longer be under our control."

"I can't believe they've been overrun," Leopold said.

"There's always betrayal," said Rogan. "It's happened before."

"Let's not jump to conclusions," said Marshal Sloan. "At this stage we simply don't know."

———

When the news arrived, it was completely unexpected. The Ring Forts had not been overrun.

It was much, much worse.

"I still don't understand," said Ronell, frowning into the glow of a nightlamp.

They had all heard the same rumors, and finally one of the bladesingers had explained it clearly to the recruits. Miro didn't know whether Ronell was being stubborn or really couldn't understand. He sat down next to Ronell, Bartolo on the other side.

"The Ring Forts line the eastern Halrana border with Torakon," said Bartolo.

"I know that." Ronell scowled.

". . . and the builders of Torakon are old allies of the Imperial House. For example, in the Rebellion, the builders gave the emperor passage through their lands."

"Which is what happened here?"

Bartolo spoke forcefully. "No. This war is different. The Toraks and the Imperial Legion are acting as one. They've effectively become one house, and the Torak high lord has given the emperor their Lexicon."

"Yes, and no one knows why. I know all that."

Bartolo continued, "Everyone expected the Black Army to attack the Ring Forts, the same way the emperor did during the Rebellion. But the Halrana also share a northern border with Loua Louna, the land of the artificers."

Miro thought again of the artificers of House Loua Louna—crafty merchants and masters of lore, eternally neutral, hungry for gilden, and never directly taking part in war. He still couldn't believe it himself.

In a completely unexpected move, the emperor had driven an army of the Imperial Legion deep into Louan territory and straight into the capital of Mara Maya. They'd stayed there only long enough to re-supply before driving farther.

The legion had then taken the towns of Mourie and Norcia. They never stood a chance.

And now the Black Army was encamped outside Ralanast, capital of Halaran.

It came as a complete shock. House Loua Louna, which was neutral in every conflict and existed only for wealth, had been over-run. No one attacked the artificers, for without the tools of war no war could be won.

The commanders of the Alturan army could see only three options: either the emperor was so confident of victory, he was will-ing to marginalize every neutral house, or he was executing some brilliant tactic that could not yet be understood, or he was mad. For the Ring Forts still lay unconquered, the armies of Altura and Halaran undefeated.

Then came the most shocking news of all. It appeared Loua Louna had taken on the white and black standard; the Louans had joined forces with the emperor.

Indecisive, uncertain, the army of Altura lay encamped, waiting for some sign of what to do next.

Should they try to link with the armies at the Ring Forts? Or should they head for Ralanast to try to rescue their ally's capital from certain destruction?

The commanders spent their days arguing, with Prince Leopold trying to take charge but suggesting strategies his subcommanders considered ill advised. The men spent their nights shivering. They felt defeated, and they had yet to face their enemy.

21

Show humility to your neighbors, and make friends of your enemies.
People fight when they feel threatened. Show you are no threat,
and they will open their arms.

—*The Evermen Cycles,* 16:2

In the end, the Alturan army's decision was made for them. A Halrana messenger gave them the news, his face streaked with tears that carved a path through the grime on his skin.

Ralanast, the Halrana capital, had been conquered by the Black Army. The great city that had lasted through the Rebellion, when the spirit of Halaran could never be broken, was taken in a day.

The commanders were now faced with no choice but to try to link with the Ring Forts, to create a unified front in Halaran's south and push forward, trying to retake the territory that had been lost so quickly.

Continuing eastward now, the army began to encounter small groups of Halrana soldiers and even partisan groups, locals who had been forced into hiding by the legion. Refugees brought horrific stories of butchery and pillage. The Alturan army passed them in the thousands, those who had lost everything and now had nothing.

The fleeing soldiers brought useful information on enemy numbers and capabilities. They said the black flag could now be seen across most of northern Halaran. It was now definite—the Louans had joined with the emperor. The Black Army had now swallowed two houses.

Nothing had been heard from the nations of Vezna or Petrya. Perhaps they were still uncommitted. And still nothing had been heard from the primate. None said it aloud, but all wondered why. The primate and his templars in Aynar controlled the essence. Though they had no lore, and weren't even considered a house, the templars were now perhaps the only ones who could bring a swift end to the war.

No word had been received from the Halrana high lord in some time. Prince Leopold's messages to Mornhaven, where High Lord Legasa waited in supposed strength, received no reply.

It was impossible to hide the fundamentals from the soldiers. The men felt terribly alone.

There had been some brief engagements, but nothing that could be called a battle. Some explosions in the night as their defenses were tested. A quick skirmish with some of the legion, quickly decided in the Alturans' favor.

Fortunately they hadn't been surprised by the dirigibles again—they'd learned their lesson well. It was about the best thing that could be said, the only positive so far. Morale was low.

It was now raining, a steady cold drizzle that seemed it would never stop. Miro, Ronell, and Bartolo shared a cold meal under the branches of an alpin. It did little to ward off the rain, and Miro shivered.

"I can't believe it took them so long to tell us," Ronell grunted.

"At least they did eventually," said Bartolo.

"Four days. Four days I've been walking around completely sodden."

"It could have been a week," said Bartolo.

It didn't matter what they were talking about; Ronell and Bartolo always disagreed. Miro often had to act as mediator. Otherwise, he was sure a fight would have broken out by now.

"What are you saying? You'd rather they didn't tell us?" Ronell said.

Miro tried not to think about what he was eating. He just focused on the action of bringing the spoon to his mouth and swallowing.

"No, of course not. I just think they're not used to having people like us in the field, that's all," Bartolo said.

"People like us?"

"You know what I mean," Bartolo said. "Recruits. We're supposed to be in the Dunwood learning these things. Not here."

"If you can't handle it, I'm sure they'll let you go home," said Ronell.

"Hey! You were the one complaining just now."

"Quit it, you two," said Miro. "They just forgot. That's all."

One of the bladesingers, Huron Gower, probably the friendliest of the aloof bunch, had chuckled when he saw the sodden recruits one day.

"Try this," he had laughed, naming a sequence of runes. "Have some dignity and never fear—you'll be bladesingers one day."

Since then, they'd all glowed softly, the rain sliding off their armorsilk rather than wetting it through. It was a great improvement, to say the least. The rain still got under their clothing, still wet their hair and ran down their necks, but their enchanted garments stayed dry.

"Think of those poor guys," said Bartolo, indicating with his head.

They could hear it at all times, the pinging sound of the rain bouncing off the steel of the soldiers' armor.

"What we need is action," said Miro. "We need to take the initiative instead of moving slowly through the forest like a lumbering beast bashing its way through the undergrowth."

"What would you do?" said Ronell.

Bartolo interjected, "I'd get the primate to cut off the emperor's essence, sit the high lords down in a small room, and not let them come out until they've agreed we need a new emperor."

"I know, I know," said Ronell. "Miro?"

The speed of Miro's response made it clear he'd thought about it. "Attack. Take the initiative. I'd split the army and form a second, fast-moving force—"

"Bladesingers gather!" the blademaster's voice called out. "Raiding party!"

"Be careful what you wish for," Ronell said soberly.

Ronell glanced at Bartolo, who glanced at Miro.

They stood in a large circle. It was the way the bladesingers always held their meetings. Miro counted roughly seventy bladesingers, a lethal force, but not a huge one. They stood impassively—weapons that had yet to be unleashed. The rain didn't appear to bother them at all. They all glowed softly; the drops never seemed to touch them.

Blademaster Rogan waited until they were assembled and then spoke without preamble.

"A division of the legion is encamped inside a narrow gorge, Harlan's Canyon, the Halrana call it. The scouts have reported they're unaware of this army so close by.

"We can't leave them at our backs. Prince Leopold has come up with a plan to bottle them up with a force at either end of the canyon. Bear in mind—the canyon is narrow. So narrow that it will be strength, rather than numbers, that will win the day. That's where we come in.

"The plan is to put an elite group at either end of the gorge. At one end will be the veterans, the most experienced of our soldiers, equipped with enchanted armor, shields, swords, and spears. At the other end will be us, the bladesingers." He looked around steadily. "This army's deadliest weapon."

"Altura!" the men growled, their voices deep.

Rogan continued. "After engagement, the more mobile of the two forces, the bladesingers, are to melt back into the valley, where the legion will pursue us and encounter our main force. The remainder of this army will lie in wait."

There was silence for a moment.

Bladesinger Porlen spoke up. A small man with wiry strength, he was one of the more vocal bladesingers. "This is not a good plan. You do not cage a beast."

"Care to be more specific?" Blademaster Rogan said.

"The legion's backs will be against the wall. There is nowhere for them to run. You should always give your enemy an escape route."

"Prince Leopold's plan is for them to have that escape route."

Porlen shook his head. "But not initially. They will see fierce enemies on all sides. They will fight like demons, for they will see it is a fight to the death."

"All the more reason for us to follow the plan to the letter, then."

Porlen just shook his head, murmuring to one of his fellows.

Rogan spoke for some time more, outlining the further details. "We leave at dusk. It's three hours' journey, so get some rest now. When the moon rises, we will light a beacon, attached to a small dirigible. This is the signal to attack. That is all."

Miro could tell by the blademaster's tone that he didn't believe in the plan either. On the face of it, it seemed good—the chance to wipe out an entire division of the legion—but the risk was there for all to see. It was dangerous.

Ronell grumbled when they returned to the remains of their meal. "I don't like the sound of this."

Around them, Miro could hear the common soldiers talking to each other, sharing their fear. The bladesingers radiated confidence, but the general mood of the men was crucial.

Miro projected composure he didn't feel. "Our part will be simple—to draw the Imperials back to the main force. As long as we make that our goal and do nothing brave—and by brave I mean foolish—we'll be fine."

"How close behind us will the main Alturan army be? How long will we have to lead the enemy?"

Miro shrugged. "I don't know. We move a lot quicker than the main force, so perhaps an hour?"

"An hour!"

"Or it could be less."

"Or more," grinned Bartolo. Miro shot him a dirty look.

"Yes, or more."

"Lord of the Sky," Ronell muttered.

Miro knew Ronell was just voicing his nerves, the fear they all felt. They said nothing more as they settled in to get some sleep.

But none of them did.

22

Do not merely give lip service to the Evermen.
Give yourself in your heart. Serve the poor and the needy.
The greatest threat to the future is indifference.
                    —Sermons of Primate Melovar Aspen, 538 Y.E.

"Quiet. Do you hear something?" Bartolo said.

A small hare burst out of the bushes. The runes on Ronell's armorsilk flared brightly as he instantly responded with an activation sequence.

"Change your sequence, now!" a voice hissed. It was Bladesinger Huron, the next ahead of them.

Ronell's chanting changed, and the glow instantly stilled. There was a whole new inflection just for dimming the glow of the runes while they were activated. The chanting stopped completely as Ronell deactivated. Miro didn't blame him. He wasn't chanting himself. It was simply too hard to do it quietly.

They walked in single file through the damp forest, their breath steaming in the frigid air. The sound of water dripping onto leaves was incessant, but for some reason the sounds of the forest were completely absent. No insects buzzed; no animals called. Perhaps they sensed the presence of intruders.

Miro felt a hand restrain him. The trees thinned ahead, and they would soon be losing their cover. Part of him longed to get out of the dripping thickets, but another part didn't want to leave their protection. Miro guessed no one was looking forward to the exposure out on the hills.

It had been a grueling journey, trudging through swamps and thick forests, with fear always at the back of their minds. The most difficult part was the silence. The bladesingers didn't speak—their communications were all made through a complex language of hand signals that Miro and the other two recruits were still learning.

The waiting finally ended, and the bladesingers left the cover of the forest, moving in a single line through the hills.

It was rough, rocky ground, littered with stones of all sizes, ranging from tiny pebbles to massive boulders. Miro stepped carefully to avoid displacing the stones.

The moon rose as the bladesingers sped across the ground, a deadly force, but with Miro feeling exposed. In the silver moonlight Miro could see the ground rise on either side to form a gentle valley. As they moved closer, the walls of the valley grew steeper until it became the mouth of a canyon.

Miro realized the difficulty of their task now, how the reality of the situation was so different from what he had imagined.

It was open ground, well lit, with minimal cover. Miro didn't know what the other end of the canyon was like, but he hoped it was better than this. It would be simplicity itself for scouts to be posted who could easily see the dark shapes moving toward the canyon. They should stop now.

The group halted behind a huge rock, the best cover they would find for some time. The bladesingers huddled together, conferring.

Bladesinger Huron breathed into Miro's ear. "Shadow. Activate. Quietly."

Miro passed the message along to Ronell and Bartolo. He held eye contact with each in turn for a moment. First Bartolo nodded, and then Ronell.

This would be the first true test of their training.

First, Miro began a slow steady chant, the volume of his voice as low as he could make it, naming the runes one after another. He started with the inflection that dimmed the glowing, and then added agility. He thought of adding protection and slowed his rhythm, first making sure he was grasping the current sequence. Then Miro added protection, the runes glowing softly, almost dark. He felt the armorsilk strengthen as the material became imbued with the power to turn the strongest steel.

Miro concentrated, his breath rising and falling evenly. Then he added shadow. His chanting was slow and even, the way he had been taught.

He looked around proudly. He'd done it. As his lips moved, he found he was able to compartmentalize his mind, to continue the chanting as part of his breathing. The sequences took on a singsong quality like a softly sighing ocean, the lightest of men's voices raised in harmony. The need to keep their voices quiet gave the song an eeriness Miro had never experienced before.

Miro saw the bladesingers waiting for the recruits, radiating utter calm and confidence, the song expertly woven around them. Their runes glowed so softly they were almost imperceptible—part of the shadow effect. The rain fell around them strangely as it hit their near-invisible bodies. It was incredibly disconcerting, seeing the rain fall on nothing. All that was visible above their armorsilk now were their heads and hands; the rest was ghostly. Miro wondered if this contributed to the bladesinger legend. He shivered with pride to be here.

Ronell's chanting also came slow and even, and Miro's smile at his fellow recruit was shakily returned.

Everyone turned to Bartolo, who was having trouble. Miro let Bartolo see his lips, trying to guide him through the process. Finally, the recruit nodded, finding his rhythm, and his song joined the others.

Miro saw a bright light rise into the sky, somewhere in the distance. It was the signal.

A hand was raised and then lowered. The bladesingers ran now, creatures of the night, their song rising and falling with their breath.

Like a flock of predatory birds descending, the force entered Harlan's Canyon. It was as dark as pitch, and Miro found it difficult to keep with the group. He followed them by their singing, but the sound of his own voice made it difficult.

The sheer walls of the canyon rose on either side. The night sky was bright above, but the moonlight was unable to stretch down this deep. Miro looked up, his head tilted back to see the high summit of the cliffs.

At the same time as he saw the sentry, looking down from the heights of the cliffs, the man saw him.

"Attack! Bladesingers!" the figure called. A whirling disk flew from one of the bladesinger's hands to strike the figure. The voice was quickly cut off.

But it was too late. The canyon erupted in chaos.

Suddenly Miro saw there were soldiers everywhere, some prone on the ground, blinking with sleep, others in armor, holding swords and spears.

Miro hadn't realized how far they were into the legion's camp.

A bright light flared up, the shine of a prismatic orb. It flew through the air in a graceful curve to land among the bladesingers.

They all dove to the side as the device detonated, sending rock and dirt everywhere. The bladesingers' runes flared up as the blast was deflected by the armorsilk. Miro saw cuts on some of his companions' faces.

Miro realized that the top of the canyon was lined with soldiers, the height giving the Imperials a deadly advantage. Orbs began to rain down on them, exploding with lethal force, the bladesingers still far enough from the main encampment for the enemy to be confident of missing friendly forces. The need for stealth gone, Miro's voice rose as he added more powerful protection sequences to his chant.

Then, as one, the bladesingers drew their zenblades. Miro drew his with them, feeling the power of it in his hands.

He added its song. His zenblade flared, bright as the sun as it was activated.

"Altura!" the bladesingers took up the cry.

In the bright blaze of light, Miro realized the sheer number of black-garbed warriors, already forming into squares as their officers took control. He saw mortar teams readying the lethal weapons. It was insane for seventy men to face up to a force of thousands.

The bladesingers threw themselves at the legion.

Miro ducked the spear of a warrior and thrust out with his sword. The man's body exploded, blood spraying out. Miro carried the force of the blow through the legionnaire and into the next man, cutting off an arm before the movement turned him away.

Miro's voice came strong. He felt it in his blood, in his armor, in his zenblade. He blazed like a wildfire into a score of legionnaires, scattering them before him. He felt a spear slide off his armorsilk and launched himself at the soldier who held it. The soldier backed away but thrust again, trying to find where Miro's body wasn't protected by the enchanted silk.

Miro felt another spear graze him, again deflected by his armor. Looking around, he realized he had perhaps leapt too far into the throng of enemy warriors. He was surrounded by spears. If a spear caught his face, if he faltered, he was dead.

An idea occurred to him, and he added shadow, quieting the brightness of the runes. Miro's body disappeared. But for the glowing runes, he was just a face, hands, and sword.

It gave him the edge he needed. Miro leapt and darted among the legionnaires. He thrust his sword into a man's side. Blood burst from the warrior's body. Miro's zenblade sparked against a shield, cutting it in half.

Miro's vision was a blur of grunting, thrusting men. Then he saw a commotion in the distance. The second Alturan force must have arrived at the other end of the canyon. Miro felt the pressure of the warriors increase. There were just so many of them. They were unstoppable, like a wall of flesh.

Miro looked around and saw the other bladesingers begin to fall back.

The Imperials felt their opponents turn, and pushed by the force behind them, they eagerly surged forward.

Miro saw a bladesinger go down under the throng, the rushing crowd simply too fast, too powerful. With the bladesinger's song disrupted, the runes began to fade. Legionnaires crowded around the fallen figure, hacking at it with their swords. A huge man, his head shaved, suddenly held up a human head. The Imperials cheered.

"Fall back!" a bladesinger cried.

The legion roared in response.

The bladesingers began a strictly controlled withdrawal action. Half the glowing warriors would fight a delaying action against the horde, while the other half fell back and then, taking positions, fought while the others withdrew.

A buzzing sound grew louder before the swift shape of a dirigible flew overhead. Prismatic orbs again rained down from above. An explosion sent clouds of smoke billowing, blinding those below. Miro added as much protection as he was able, but the complexity grew too hard to follow, and he started to falter. He gave up shadow and was just able to keep the sequence going.

Miro saw Ronell ahead, the runes starting to darken as the panicked recruit appeared about to lose his song. Then Miro was forced to fight, turning back to face the horde.

Miro parried a vicious blow from the two-handed sword of a black-armored soldier twice his size. The force of the blow pounded at his head, but his crossed zenblade managed to block it just in time. The legionnaire's weapon had silver runes glowing along its length—explaining how it had survived the clash with the zenblade. Miro pushed against the legionnaire with the full weight of his body. The legionnaire fell back for an instant only, before recovering and smashing his shield against Miro's body. The armorsilk flared as it hit the shield.

Miro realized that in a contest of brute force he was never going to survive. He swung twice in quick succession, forcing his opponent back. Looking over the legionnaire's shoulder, he saw rank after rank of the enemy. Miro started to back away. Seeing his enemy draw back, the legionnaire's confidence grew, and he raised his arms to strike. It was the opportunity Miro had been looking for. He ducked and hacked at the legionnaire's legs. The zenblade carved through his knees as if they weren't there. The legionnaire screamed, a terrible sound.

Miro understood that he needed to pull back; he was among the last of the bladesingers facing the enemy. He removed a prismatic orb from the belt at his waist.

"*Kuhn-rah!*" Miro activated the orb, his song momentarily lost as he did so. A spear flew through the air at him, scoring his shoulder—a messy wound, but fortunately not deep. Miro threw the orb into the crowd of black-clad soldiers, resuming his song as he turned.

He never saw the explosion behind him, but he felt the blood splatter against his back.

Miro ran to catch up with the bladesingers. He found Ronell panting, prone against a wall, an expression of terror on his face. Ronell's runes were completely dark.

"Ronell!" Miro cried. He grabbed hold of the recruit, shaking him. "You need to resume your song!"

"Can't . . . do . . . it . . ." Ronell panted. "No . . . breath . . ."

Looking back, Miro saw the horde running for them, only moments away.

"Slow your breathing. Start with protection only."

The effort of talking while interspersing his sequences was taking its toll on Miro too. He stopped trying to talk and, taking Ronell by the arm, began to run. Miro could just see the other bladesingers in the distance.

Fortunately, their armorsilk was infinitely lighter than the heavy armor worn by the legionnaires. The two recruits quickly drew away but ran for only a few minutes before they both tripped over something.

It was the broken body of a bladesinger, his green armorsilk dark. Fire had taken most of his upper body, leaving the lower half remarkably intact.

Ronell stared at the man in horror, his breath steaming. The recruit's armorsilk was still dark.

Miro stopped his song, losing his own protection.

"You need to resume your song. Quickly, just start with the first sequence for protection."

Ronell panted, his breathing coming ragged. "Just leave me . . . just for a moment . . . When . . . breath comes back . . . no problem . . . song."

Miro looked over Ronell's shoulder. They had gained in height, and in the distance he could now see the green of the Alturan heavy infantry chasing the swarm of legionnaires, pushing them hard from behind. The bladesingers were nowhere to be seen. The Imperials would be upon them in moments.

"I can't let you stay. You have to keep running!"

Miro took the resisting recruit by the hand. Resuming his own song, Miro began to drag Ronell forward.

A silver orb left its mortar and sailed in a huge arc, glowing brighter and brighter as it fell toward the ground.

The explosion was like white fire, blinding Miro's vision. It was directly above their heads, perfectly timed to detonate at lethal proximity.

Miro was the closer of the two. His body shielded Ronell slightly from the blast, throwing them both forward like dolls.

For a moment, all was white with pain before Miro's vision slowly returned. He could hear the cries of the legionnaires behind him, drawing ever closer. Miro's face was pressed against the dirt. He looked in front of him.

Ronell had been scorched to the bone. His left arm was just a stump below the elbow and his entire back was raw flesh. His hair had been burnt away, leaving a pink patch of bloody scalp.

He was still alive. Miro could have cried at the pain Ronell must have been in.

Summoning strength he hadn't known he had, Miro stood up, and though his song came hoarse and from dry lips, it came strong.

His armorsilk flared. He stooped, and picked Ronell up like a child in his arms. Miro started to run.

23

Never defend a city. Instead, move your army to a more
offensive position. Let the angry citizens defend it for you.
—Memoirs of Emperor Xenovere I, page 319, 381 Y.E.

The bladesingers ahead left the canyon behind as they ran in a rough vee pattern—glowing like fire, seemingly invincible. Miro's strength eventually began to give out, but another bladesinger turned back, helping him lift Ronell over the last craggy rise, though Miro still didn't relinquish his burden. The whole skirmish had lasted perhaps ten minutes.

Behind the bladesingers, the legionnaires took the bait. They came storming out of the canyon, those in front lusting for blood, those behind pushed relentlessly by the force of Altura's elite infantry.

The hills ahead were suddenly teeming with men.

They rose over the ridges, poured out of the valleys—too many men to count, the numbers overwhelming. The bladesingers melted away as the great army encircled the legion in its mighty arms.

"Let go! I said, let go of him, man!"

Concentrating only on running, Miro realized he was up on the ridges and two Alturan soldiers were trying to relieve him of Ronell's weight. Miro's arms and legs were so stiff they had to pry the injured youth from him.

Miro fell onto his back as they took Ronell away. He couldn't move a muscle, could only roll over and watch the scene below him, the hills and rocks lit up like daylight in the glow of the runes and the explosions of the orbs.

The Imperial Legion was caught between one overwhelming force and another. The Alturan veterans all glowed silver, their enchanted weapons devastating the weaker units they encountered. A mortar team in their midst launched salvo after salvo into the Imperials, scattering bodies like sand before a wind.

The main allied army surged forward. Soldiers in Alturan green and Halrana brown mingled together, becoming one living entity joined by rage.

There were simply too many soldiers for all to have a chance to combat the Imperials. The hills were soon heaving as everyone tried to get a part of the action, with Miro too far away and too exhausted to do anything but watch.

But there was still a part of the legion, a core that held together through the worst of the fighting. As Miro looked on, he saw a dozen Alturan soldiers who came too close to the core tossed into the air by some massive force—thrown hundreds of paces.

As the fighting surged and ebbed, the core came closer. The mortar rounds of the green and brown soldiers started to find their mark, and a bright explosion lit up the scene so that for the first time Miro had a glimpse of the emperor's deadliest. It was for moments only, and soon the scene went dark again.

There were perhaps half a dozen of them, with the shape of humans but warped by the unique arts of House Tingara's lore.

Miro had heard of meldings, but he'd never heard of creatures like these.

The closest had its face to Miro, a face of horror and flame, the eyes like slits, glowing with malice. It was some kind of monster, a creature of metal and cloth, glowing with purple runes. Its right arm had been warped, twisted into a thing part steel and part flesh—a black sword, eight feet long and glowing vermillion, had been grafted to the arm. In its left hand the creature held a flail, the long twists of braided steel ending in spikes the size of a man's hand.

It twisted and lurched, each movement sending its body through the Alturan army like a scythe through wheat. It impaled a man on its sword and flung his body into a soldier twenty paces away. The flail tore into the men, shredding them into pieces of meat.

A group of soldiers in the brown of Halaran moved to intercept one of the monsters, flaring brightly as they enhanced already activated armor. Working together as a team, the first soldiers distracted the abomination with prismatic orbs, while the others circled round, trying to find an opening.

The flail shot forward and took one of the soldiers in a single sweep, turning his body into a spray of red. Seeing an opportunity, one of the Halrana ran and hacked futilely at the creature's neck. He was thrown to the ground and immediately impaled with the huge black sword. A third soldier thrust his spear at the monster's face. The whip of metal spikes caught him on the back swing, taking off his head. There was now only one Halrana left. He screamed something and leapt on top of the creature. In each hand he held a glowing orb. He clapped each orb to the sides of the creature's head. The resulting explosion boomed across the battlefield, and both the monster and the Halrana were no more.

The army exerted itself to greater efforts. There were so many of them, yet this fighting core of the legion would not back down, could not be defeated by numbers alone.

Then the army cleared way as a glowing dagger of light threaded its way through the ranks—a bright column of warriors that pushed forward, deep into the core of the fighting.

The bladesingers had regrouped.

Men in green and brown stopped and cheered, both those on the outskirts of the battle, as well as those on the edge of the fighting, who had seen their kin destroyed beyond recognition.

"Bladesingers! Altura, Altura!" they cried.

Miro watched it all, transfixed. He could not look away.

The soldiers cleared, drawing slowly back, opening up the terrain. The evil creatures, perhaps sensing their match, formed a ragged line. There were five of them still standing.

The bladesingers, voices raised as if singing an ode to war, lined up against them, some sixty or seventy strong. They glowed so brightly Miro fought to look on. Their zenblades were like ribbons of fire; there was no way to tell where the man ended and the sword began; each was like a being of light.

One of the bladesingers—Miro couldn't tell whom—raised his arm and then lowered it.

They ran in, perhaps a dozen men to each creature.

Two bladesingers were swept away like flies. Their armorsilk protected them, but it didn't stop them from flying hundreds of paces away. A zenblade crashed into a horrible arm; sparks fountained off and a sound like the crack of a whip echoed off the hills. It was like a dance of energy, the moves too quick to follow.

Suddenly, a flail went shooting into the crowd of soldiers, still attached to the arm that held it. A green warrior jumped, high, impossibly high, his sword raised above his head. His face set in determination, the zenblade shot out, taking a creature's head and shoulders off in a single blow.

As two of the creatures were dispatched, so the number of bladesingers attacking each grew. The great flails sent four more men flying, but the rest slowed, awaiting their opportunity.

In an instant two more creatures went down. All Miro could see were stabbing swords and the twitching and writhing of the creatures in their death throes.

The breath knocked out of him, a bladesinger's voice stopped and he went down to his knees. Miro watched in dread. The last creature's great sword arm probed, finding a gap in the bladesinger's defenses, and then thrust forward. Blood gushed from the bladesinger's mouth.

Screaming with rage, the remaining bladesingers leapt forward. In a flash of light and twisting figures, bits of metal flew, flesh parted. The final monster was no more.

As if waiting for the last act in some macabre stage show, the army swamped the legion's remaining pockets of resistance.

The battle was over. They had survived their first real encounter with the enemy. Miro fell back against the hill. The grass felt like the softest linen.

———◆———

Miro paced around the camp, unwilling to sit still.

"Stop that. There's nothing you can do. Lord of the Sky, look at you. You need to rest."

Miro turned to face Bartolo. "Did you see him?"

Bartolo sighed. "No, I didn't. I hear he was in a bad way, though."

Miro nodded. "Really bad. I . . . I tried . . . I couldn't help him."

"You probably saved his life, Miro. Isn't that enough?"

"What if that had been me?" Miro trailed off. Bartolo sighed.

Prince Leopold was calling it a great victory. Blademaster Rogan thought it was a disaster. They'd lost eight irreplaceable bladesingers, and total casualties were eight hundred dead, with four hundred more wounded. They had defeated an army of four thousand.

"I can't believe you were with them, fighting those things," Miro said, shaking his head.

"To be honest? I can't believe I was either. I was sick when I came back, really sick. I still can't hold food down." Bartolo's face was ashen. "I almost died out there."

"What were they? I never knew such things existed."

"Neither did I, not until today. Imperial avengers, the bladesingers called them. Like bladesingers, but rather than chanting runes and wearing armor and weapons, with avengers, it's a part of them. The lore is sculpted into their bodies."

"How can such a thing exist? Lore on living flesh . . . It should kill them. As soon as the essence touches the skin . . ."

"That's the thing. I don't understand it really, but they say the runes never touch their flesh, just the bits of metal and cloth melded to their bodies."

Miro shuddered. "I can't believe anyone would make such a thing, do such a thing to a person."

"Believe it," said Bartolo. "There's worse to come."

Ronell lingered on the cusp of death for days. Miro constantly hovered outside the makeshift infirmary, where the battle surgeon practiced his grisly art, hacking at torn flesh and hoping for the best.

The cold and wet continued, with water getting into everything. The essence cost to use heatplates was considered too high, so they supped on cold rations, anything to fill stomachs and keep their strength up.

Prince Leopold made a speech, saying they'd won a great victory, evidently expecting an improvement to morale, but the horrors of the battle were too fresh. The Alturans screamed in their sleep and spoke of grotesque monsters running through the streets of Sarostar, plunging their blades into women and children. The Halrana were the worst of all, many having already lost their families to the Black Army. And so the army stayed in their forest camp, constantly on edge, waiting for news from outside.

Miro and Bartolo noticed a definite change in the bladesingers' attitude toward them. Perhaps the bladesingers felt the recruits had been tested in fire. Both of the young warriors made firm resolutions to improve on their skills and spent much of their time using each other for practice, sharing their strengths and learning from weaknesses. It brought Miro and Bartolo closer together, but Miro couldn't shake a feeling of guilt when he thought about Ronell.

Then, one cold morning Miro woke to find Bartolo looking down at him, a strange expression on his face.

"I thought you should know," Bartolo said. "Ronell . . . he's awake."

Miro leapt up.

"Miro," said Bartolo. "I don't think you should . . ."

Miro ran through the camp and over to the infirmary. Recognizing Miro, the surgeon tried to restrain him. "You shouldn't . . ."

Miro pushed past the surgeon and opened the canvas with a sweep of his arm. He pulled back in shock.

It was Ronell, but like no Ronell that Miro could remember. The height was the same, and the clothing. But where Ronell's left arm had been, there was nothing but a stump, covered in bandages and weeping red. Only his eyes were recognizable; the rest of his face was a mass of lines, the torn, bloody skin wrinkled and monstrous.

"You," the apparition said.

Miro stopped, unable to speak.

"You. You did this to me! You!"

"Ronell, I . . ."

"I needed to get my breath, to say the runes. But you made me run. You could have left me, but you made me run."

"Ronell, it didn't happen like that at all. I was trying to save you."

"Save me? *Save* me?" a whine came from the man's throat, a hoarse wheezing. "You didn't save me. You've killed me! Everything that I was! Get out! *Get out!*"

Another surgeon arrived, trying to remove Miro from the room. Miro was shocked, unable to speak.

He turned and fled.

24

Every time history repeats itself, the price goes up.
  —Memoirs of Emperor Xenovere I, page 286, 381 Y.E.

The small pleasure skiff made its way ponderously down the Sarsen, requiring only the gentlest of paddling to stay on its course. Ella leaned against the rail and watched the world sliding past like some grand play following the theme of nature's beauty.

Ice had built up along the riverbanks where the water was more sluggish, and Ella wore a heavy shawl against winter's chill. People generally spent their time indoors now—there was certainly enough to do. Ella's hands were growing calloused from holding a scrill; her satchel containing the tools of her trade was now always by her side.

It was the first occasion she'd had to see Killian since the night out in the Woltenplats, but somehow she knew their time was coming to an end. He'd been waiting outside the Crystal Palace. He always seemed so fascinated by it; it had become the one place she knew she might find him, and she always included it on her walks.

Ella didn't ask him where he'd been, and she made no mention of their time together. She'd made the suggestion to take out a boat on the river. Killian had seemed a little hesitant, given the frigid weather, but he'd agreed readily enough.

He'd had one more thoughtful look at the palace before moving away with her, smiling, the way he always did.

Yet the day hadn't passed the way Ella had expected. Killian appeared pensive and distracted. They hadn't been close—in fact they'd barely touched. He'd helped her into the boat, always polite, but that was all.

Killian sat a few paces from her, the paddle in his hand. His vivid blue eyes appeared pale gray in the low winter light, and he wore a thin shirt and trousers, seemingly unaware of the cold.

Ella could see the Long Bridge approaching, with the Runebridge behind it, signaling the end. The Crystal Palace sparkled, glowing softly: the high lord had decided to leave the palace lights permanently activated to improve morale. All it served was to remind Ella of the war, that her brother was out there somewhere. She worried about Miro constantly.

Ella heard the sound of Killian putting down his paddle. She could see him playing with something out of the corner of her eye, but she wasn't sure what it was.

Ella had been avoiding looking at him, but she now turned. He'd been idly looking through her satchel, curious. Ella's breath caught. She was sure she'd sealed her satchel. How had he opened it? Why would he break her seal?

"What's this?" he said.

Killian held a small crystal bottle in one hand. The bottle was intricately designed, like a small jewel.

Ella's heart skipped a beat. The bottle was filled with an oily, black liquid. It was Ella's bottle of essence, the gift she'd received at graduation.

Killian held the stopper in his other hand. He'd removed it, peering down at the liquid in the bottle.

Ella turned white. "Killian. Listen to me. Listen to me very, very carefully."

"What? What is it?"

"Do not move. Don't move one little bit. I'm going to come over to you."

The river had been so placid before, but now Ella was acutely aware of every tiny jolt the skiff made, the smallest rocking. Lord of the Sky, they would have to be in a boat!

Ella started to move in the skiff, and then stopped when her movements caused the boat to rock still more. Killian had a strange expression on his face.

"What are you doing?" he said.

"Killian, I need you to very, very carefully put the stopper back in the bottle."

"Why?"

"Please!" Ella cried, her voice quivering with suppressed emotion. "Just put the stopper back in the bottle."

Ella looked up and saw the shore coming at them. Fast.

It happened all at once. Ella screamed as the boat smashed hard against the riverbank.

The bottle was at an angle; Killian had ignored Ella's request to replace the stopper. Ella watched in horror as the black liquid spilled out, running, dripping down Killian's hand.

He dropped the bottle. Time slowed to a snail's pace. Ella stared in horror at the essence splattered on Killian's arm.

An expression of shock and surprise on his face, Killian staggered with the rocking of the skiff. He stumbled and lurched backward.

Ella watched as he fell into the frigid waters of the Sarsen. Killian's body landed in the water with a splash and began to sink out of sight.

"Killian!" Ella cried.

Ella leapt out of the boat and rolled onto the bank, immediately peering into the dark water, looking for any trace, any flash of skin or clothing.

Gathering herself, Ella threw off her shawl. She took a breath, and dove into the icy water, head first.

The sensation was like being pierced again and again with tiny sharp knives. Pure pain drove through Ella's body and inside her head. Her teeth clacked together, nearly biting her tongue in two. The shock drove the wind from her lungs, and she took a deep involuntary breath, choking and spluttering on the chill water of the Sarsen.

Fortunately, Ella found him almost immediately, her arm brushing against some part of his body. She grabbed at Killian and missed, then rose to the surface. Quickly taking a breath, Ella ducked under again, feeling ahead with her arms.

Ella touched something soft and grabbed Killian by the hair, pulling, and as he rose, she reached forward again and took hold of his arm. Kicking with her legs, and with heavy strokes of her free arm, Ella finally breached the surface, taking a painful, gasping breath.

Some townsfolk were on the bank, attracted by the commotion.

"Take him under the arms!" Ella yelled.

A burly man ran forward and took hold of first one of Killian's arms, then the other, until finally he had a grip under Killian's armpits. He heaved; Killian wasn't a small man. The burly man's face grew red, and with a great effort he pulled, then fell backward. Killian rolled with him to lie motionless on the bank.

Ella coughed in the water and felt another man reach for her arm. He linked arms with her and helped Ella climb out of the river.

Shuddering and wheezing, Ella immediately lurched over to Killian's prone figure. He lay on his back, his lips blue. He was deathly still.

"What happened?" someone said.

"Essence poisoning," Ella gasped.

Immediately the townsfolk all drew back, fearfully checking their skin and clothing.

"What do we do?" the burly man said, sitting up. He had the courage, at least, not to back away.

"I don't know," Ella muttered. "I don't know!"

They were close enough to the Crystal Palace that one of the soldiers approached. "What's happening here?"

"She says he was poisoned by essence." The burly man pointed at Ella.

The soldier frowned. "Shouldn't he be dead then?"

The burly man shrugged. "Maybe the water? The cold? Do you know?"

All attention was on the soldier. He backed away, his hands spread. "How would I know?"

Ella felt time running by swiftly. She shivered, rocking back and forth. Someone offered her a coat, but she ignored the offer.

Then she had an idea. "The high enchantress."

Looking around her, she realized the crowd had grown larger. There was general assent, relief at being able to pass on the burden.

"Of course," said the soldier. "She's at the palace."

"Can we move him?" said the burly man.

"I don't know," said the soldier.

"I'm a qualified enchantress," Ella said briskly. "I'm sure it will be fine."

The soldier and the burly man lifted Killian's prone figure, standing him up, one on either side. They started the walk to the palace, moving with great difficulty, Killian's feet dragging on the ground.

More soldiers came to join them and eventually brought a stretcher. Ella quailed at the sight of Killian's dead white skin as they laid him down prone, his lips blue and body limp.

Ella never took her eyes off him, hovering behind the stretcher, wringing her hands. She didn't even notice when they passed through the main palace gates, and was barely aware when the floor changed to polished marble. Ella only looked up when she felt a strong grip on her arm, pinching her flesh tightly.

"What have you done, girl?"

High Enchantress Evora Guinestor stood in front of her. Evora's lips were thin; she was furious. The woman's eyes blazed, and Ella realized how tall the woman was; the high enchantress loomed over her.

"She said he was poisoned . . ." a soldier began.

The high enchantress raised her hand. The soldier trailed off.

"I asked you what happened," Evora said. She never released the pressure on Ella's arm. Ella felt her hand begin to go numb.

Ella still couldn't take her eyes of Killian's still body. "He . . . I . . . he found . . . oh, Lord of the Sky . . ."

"Tell me!" The high enchantress shook her.

"Essence. He found it. In my satchel. It was guarded, I swear. I don't see how he could have opened it."

Ella felt her world crashing down around her.

"What happened?" Evora said in a frigid voice. "How much went onto his skin? Where did it touch him?"

"His hand. He opened the bottle; he didn't realize what it was. We were in a boat, and it hit the bank. Some went onto his hand. His arm as well. But he fell in the water straight away."

"Which hand? Which arm?"

"His right."

"How long was it on his skin? How soon did he fall in the water?"

"Right away, maybe the time it takes to take a breath."

The high enchantress nodded, turning back to Killian. His still form lay cold and unresponsive on the stretcher in the palace corridor. Evora began to examine the skin of his hand and his arm, bit by bit. She suddenly ripped his shirt open, removing it to expose the muscles of his chest and the curls of his body hair. Aside from a small pendant on a chain, Killian now wore only his trousers. Ella would have thought he was dead but for the rise and fall of his chest. The high enchantress grunted inconclusively.

"High Enchantress?" Ella said. "Will he be all right? Did it wash off his skin? Did the cold do something?"

The high enchantress looked up at Ella, and her expression grew puzzled. "To be honest? I don't know. I need to spend more time with him. I must consult some texts." Evora frowned down at Killian. "Do you see these marks?" She lifted his arm, displaying an ugly blue stain on Killian's skin. "This is where the essence touched him. It always leaves these marks. But I do not know how he comes to still be alive or what will happen next. It could be that the cold or the water did something to impede the poison's progress."

"So he might recover?"

"He could return to full health with no further problems, or he could die as we speak."

"I swear it's not my fault," Ella whispered.

"Wash him thoroughly, and take him to my sanctum," the high enchantress instructed the palace guards. "You may leave now, young lady. I expect we'll be speaking again soon enough."

"Please let me stay with him," Ella pleaded.

"Leave at once. Guards!"

"No, let me stay," Ella cried. "High Enchantress!"

The high enchantress merely cast a dark look over her shoulder as she walked away.

The soldiers forcibly marched Ella out of the palace. She fought them, but her spirit finally left her as she stood at the Crystal Palace's great doors. The guards watched her warily.

"Enchantress," one of the soldiers spoke.

"It's all right. I'm leaving," Ella said.

25

We had been out of port for eleven weeks. We were running out of food and water, and in the end the captain would go no farther. Against my arguments, we turned back for Castlemere. I still maintain that the Great Western Ocean is not endless, merely very large. Perhaps the barren islands we discovered could be used as a staging point for another mission. Perhaps the Buchalanti will answer my questions if I ask them in the right way. I would give anything to see what is on the other side of the world.

—Toro Marossa, "Explorations," page 122, 423 Y.E.

Killian opened his eyes and shivered. It was cold beneath the Crystal Palace, and it didn't help that most of his clothes had been removed.

Was this how the high enchantress thought to help someone who had fallen into a frozen river? No roaring fires, no blankets, nothing of the sort. Instead, he'd been laid out on a marble slab like some strange experiment, his lips blue and skin white.

Well, he couldn't blame her really. She probably thought it was the cold that had stopped the essence from turning him into a disgusting mess like that boy Ella had described. It showed that these people knew nothing about essence. They didn't know a talent such as his existed.

Killian sat up and regarded himself, rubbing his arms to bring back some warmth back to his chill flesh. At least they'd left the pendant hanging in its place about his neck. His task would be much more difficult without it.

He felt a twinge when he thought of Ella, but had to thank the Lord of the Sun for such a fortuitous passage of events. He had to congratulate himself too; one makes one's own luck, after all, and the entire deception had been masterfully planned. The hardest part had been summoning the nerve to get into that scratched water. He shivered again at the thought of the plunge into its icy depths.

Still, it had given him a nicely dead look. Holding his hand in front of his face, even Killian thought the blue-tinged fingernails were nothing that could be faked. It had been a feat of the utmost self-control not to shiver when they'd laid him out on that stretcher while the high enchantress had her tirade at the girl. A job well done.

Killian could feel the tingle of the essence working through his veins; he'd managed to get a good splash out of the bottle—enough to terrify the girl. And just as he'd expected—and hoped—she'd run straight to the high enchantress.

And now here he was, in this, the most difficult of places to get into.

Killian looked around him. So this was the high enchantress's sanctum, her place of power. He was sure she'd have plenty of traps laid about, especially the closer he came to his target. Killian nervously fingered the thin scar on his left bicep. Hopefully, she'd kept her traps to the typical; the hidden golem in Ralanast had proven to be particularly troublesome. Very skillful of their high animator, automating a construct like that.

Scanning the area, Killian could see a series of rooms connected by wide corridors. Chamber after chamber ran before, beside, and behind him. Where to begin?

Killian stood, and picking a direction at random, he began to explore.

⸻

Down in the huge spaces set aside for the high enchantress's use beneath the Crystal Palace, there was no sense of time, no sense of the moon's rise and passage across the night sky.

It was cold. Cold and empty. Although the rooms were filled with all manner of tools, weapons, armor, books, bubbling pots, strange odors, and works in progress, they were still empty, lacking in life. It was clear to Killian that Evora Guinestor hoarded her work, sharing the load with no one. For her the joys of knowledge and discovery were a private thing.

The chambers were covered with thick silk carpets, and Killian tossed a vial of essence in his hand as he walked, enjoying the soft feel of the silk on his bare feet and the weight of the bottle in his hand. It hadn't taken him long to find the bottle, even if it was small; the high lord must keep the main stockpiles somewhere else. It was good to have a supply again. He now had options.

Killian heard a voice and paused. There was someone in the next chamber, walking about. Killian drew behind a cupboard door that was hanging ajar, peering around its edge.

It was the high enchantress, a frown on her face. She was alone, muttering under her breath—probably a habit she'd picked up from spending so much time by herself.

Killian hadn't managed to look at High Enchantress Evora Guinestor, playing dead as he'd been at the time. She was actually quite beautiful in an imposing, regal way. She was tall, even taller than him, and slim. Her hooded silk dress hung about her, decorated and etched with silver runes in intricate patterns. Killian had no intention of finding out what they meant.

He guessed she was looking for a book of some kind; he'd heard her mention to Ella something about books. Was she going to go to the cold slab where he'd been laid out? Perhaps to look at the half-dead, half-frozen stranger? Killian certainly hoped not.

Evora turned toward the room containing the slab, and Killian's breath caught but then was released as she turned away. Evora instead walked into a chamber that was the first in a series of libraries. Books lined the walls from floor to ceiling, an orderly collection of lifetimes of knowledge. From heavy volumes half the size of a man to tiny notebooks the size of a palm, there were books of every type and description.

Killian thought hard. There was an opportunity here he couldn't miss. He had to follow her, and he couldn't afford to be seen. When he felt she'd settled in, Killian quickly slipped into a well-lit chamber in the opposite direction. He searched and then found what he was looking for: a workbench and a scrill.

He didn't have much time. It was complicated, this process, and if he didn't do it right, he'd have to start all over again. The high enchantress made liberal use of bright nightlamps—a second-rate effort wouldn't be good enough.

Killian unclasped the silver chain from his neck, placing the pendant bottom-side up on the workbench so he could see the matrix of runes inscribed on the back. He sat the essence vial on the bench and removed the stopper. He then took the scrill and dipped the sharp end into the bottle. When he took the scrill out, its end dripped black, oily liquid.

Killian began to copy the runes onto the bare skin of his chest.

He tried to keep his hand steady, but his breathing made it difficult. Smoke hissed up from the end of the scrill, but he felt no pain, just a slight tingling sensation.

Killian finished the first rune. Comparing it to the rune on the pendant, he decided he'd made a reasonable job of it. He began on the second rune. It was more complex than the first, with some difficult bridges and whorls. Finishing it, he began on the third rune. The sound of muttering bounced off the walls.

The high enchantress was coming.

Killian started to move the scrill more quickly, but he knew he couldn't make the slightest mistake or it would all be for nothing. The muttering grew louder. The smoke drifted into his nose, irritating him, and the hissing as his hand moved seemed so loud that surely she must be able to hear. Killian began tracing the final rune. The high enchantress walked into the chamber.

"Sur-an-ahman," Killian whispered under his breath.

And then he vanished.

Evora seemed to sense a change in the chamber. She frowned as she scanned the room, and then her eyes lit up. Taking a small stone tablet from a shelf, she left the chamber, clutching the tablet to her chest.

Killian breathed: a slow, steady sigh of relief. His trousers were in a pile on the floor; he'd removed them and kicked them under a table just before the high enchantress looked his way. He stood naked now and completely invisible. The pendant was clasped in one hand, hidden by his skin, the vial of essence in the other. It had been close—too close.

Regaining his composure, Killian followed Evora from the room. The high enchantress walked back into one of the libraries and sat down next to a shelf. She proceeded to compare what was inscribed on the tablet to the contents of one of the large books, keeping her back to him.

Killian sat near her as she worked. His confidence returned, but alongside it was frustration. How would he find what he was looking for? He decided to leave her for a moment and continue his search elsewhere.

Killian had been wandering for what seemed like hours. He'd come across no fewer than five traps—wards that would most likely boil an ordinary intruder's blood. His special ability allowed him to pass through them like they weren't there.

But Killian's time was running short, and he could now make out the faint outline of the runes on his skin as they glowed softly silver. Soon the effect would end. Killian had to find the Alturan Lexicon, and he had to do it quickly.

He suddenly heard voices.

"He can't have made it far," a soldier's curt speech. "He probably just woke up in a strange place and tried to find his way out."

Killian heard the high enchantress. He didn't quite catch what she said, but she sounded troubled.

He edged forward until he could see them, standing in a group.

The high enchantress and a dozen armored palace soldiers were searching the chambers.

"Be careful not to touch anything," one of the soldiers said.

There were even two bladesingers present. Killian wasn't happy at all to see them; he'd heard rumors about their abilities.

"He must still be here," the high enchantress muttered.

Killian knew he had moments only. Thoughts of the Alturan Lexicon left him—there was nothing for it; he would have to think of a different tactic and come back another time. Yet what chance would he have then?

Sighing, he remembered from his previous explorations where the stairs upward were and turned in that direction. Killian passed through the libraries on the way. *Plenty of books here,* he thought wryly.

Then he stopped in his tracks. A path had been worn into the carpets, the passage of feet so regular it was discernible.

His heart racing, Killian followed the slightly worn trail into one of the libraries. It was the room the high enchantress had been occupied in, comparing the stone tablet to something in one of the great books.

Of course! She'd never be able to hide the Lexicon away—she would need to work with it constantly. Not only would she need to refer to it in her work, but also if she didn't renew it regularly, the enchanters' runes would fade. Killian had stood right next to the prize and left Evora with the Lexicon while he'd run off on his fool's errand.

She'd hidden the Lexicon in the best possible place—among thousands of other books.

"Lord of the Sun scratch you, woman," Killian cursed the high enchantress.

He sat down where she had knelt, facing a row of large books. Killian opened the first book. Strange creatures leapt from its pages, vivid drawings of monsters the like of which he'd never seen. He put it back and withdrew the second book. It was some kind of text, a story, illustrated and captioned: the travels of an Alturan from long ago. Killian returned it to the shelf. The next book was full of numbers, column upon column of numbers. Some kind of reference? Replacing it, Killian turned to the next book.

It was of a different kind than the other books. This book's pages were made of a silver, almost metallic material, the sheets so thin that the book had a great many more pages than it had at first seemed. It was surprisingly light, untouched by age, and felt foreign, almost alien. It didn't feel like the creation of man.

The cover of the book was green, and on the cover of the book was a rune: the number one. Killian opened the book as curiosity overwhelmed him. Runes stared back at him, undeniably perfect. This was the work of the Evermen, a relic of unimaginable power.

A voice broke the spell—a woman's voice screaming, crying with all of its power. "Guards!"

Killian tucked the book under his arm, trying to obscure it as much as possible with his body. A body that was weak, naked, and starting to betray him.

He ran.

———————⚬———————

The Crystal Palace reverberated with a commotion: the sound of soldiers' boots, calls, and shouts. It was perhaps three hours before dawn, the time when spirits were at their lowest and men fought to blink away sleep.

A passerby looking directly at the Crystal Palace would have blinked and rubbed at his eyes as an ethereal shape stole out, hiding behind a column before soundlessly creeping down the marble steps, slipping from shadow to shadow.

Killian's heart pounded, and he fought to keep his breath silent. There were two guards at the bottom of the steps, made alert by the commotion. Killian stilled his breath further, attempting to slow his heaving chest. He would have to walk directly between the guards, a space barely wide enough for his body to fit through.

"Have you seen anything?" a voice called from behind him.

"No, nothing," one of the guards responded.

"He must come this way. He must," the voice said. "I think I'll wait with you."

"Of course, bladesinger," the guard replied.

Killian felt like he had been punched in the chest—a bladesinger, directly behind him. He prayed for the light to stay dim; he prayed to the Sunlord that the bladesinger wouldn't see him.

Killian moved to the shadow of another column, creeping toward the guards. The gap was ahead of him; he just needed to slip through.

He heard it then, just at the edge of his hearing; he never would have heard it if he hadn't been so close.

"*Tun-ahreen-lahsa,*" the bladesinger whispered.

Killian ducked, and in the same instant, so fast it was blinding, a piece of light thrust where Killian's head had been less than a heartbeat before. The bladesinger moved like a coiled spring. If it hadn't been for the two guards in the way, Killian knew he would have been sliced in two.

He was now behind the column closest to freedom, and tucked under his arm, the book felt like it was writhing, trying to save itself from the trespasser.

Killian noticed the runes dimming on his chest. He could see his fingers now, make out their definition. It was now or never.

Killian ducked and threw himself between the two guards.

"Get out of the way!" the bladesinger snarled.

Completely lost in this strange battle of whirling forces, the two guards tried to back up the steps. The bladesinger moved like the wind, his song rising from his lips. He jumped over their heads, his sword held before him in a striking position, before he landed softly on two feet, scanning from side to side. Making a swift judgment, the bladesinger cut across the air in front of him viciously: once, twice, the vibrant zenblade making a sizzling sound like meat on a fire.

Killian knew he had to get away. As he rolled to a standing position at the bottom of the stairs, he felt something slice across his back, the lightest touch, but followed by a searing pain like nothing he'd ever felt. Gritting his teeth, he lurched to his feet and began to run.

Blood ran down his back; he could feel it dripping to the ground.

"Now I have you," he heard the voice behind him.

Killian knew it was over. Wounded, no longer invisible, with an angry bladesinger, he didn't stand a chance.

In one hand was the book, clutched under his arm as he ran. What was in the other? His pendant and . . . something else.

Killian stopped and turned, facing the bladesinger. Surprised, the glowing warrior slowed.

Killian stood painfully, completely naked with the Alturan Lexicon clutched under his arm. Blood dripped down his back and onto the ground. Soldiers called in the distance.

"Back away," Killian said.

"You won't be seeing the dawn, thief," the bladesinger said with venom.

Killian dropped the Lexicon to the ground.

"Good," said the bladesinger.

Killian removed the stopper from the vial of essence, and as fast as he could, he flung his arm out, spraying the black liquid in all directions, careless of whether he hit himself.

The bladesinger moved to attack, too quickly for Killian to see if he'd hit him with the essence. Then the warrior slowed, and Killian saw the bladesinger on his knees, an expression of pain and horror on his face.

Picking up the book, Killian ran until the forest hid him.

And then he ran some more.

26

Peace may cost as much as war, but it is a better trade.
—Memoirs of Emperor Xenovere I, page 87, 381 Y.E.

"Please, you're not going to leave, are you?" Varana said.

Miro turned away from the window. He'd been watching the town hall, recently appropriated by the army's command. Varana lay on her side on the soft bed, her head raised on her elbow. Her dark Halrana curls spilled in a cloud around her; her eyes were smoky brown. She had the cover pulled up over the lower half of her body, but the rest was open to his gaze, her breasts heavy, stomach flat.

Varana caught his gaze, "Come here—come and lie with me. Please, my bladesinger."

"Don't call me that," Miro said.

She pouted. "Don't you want me?"

Miro walked over to the bed and sat next to her. He began to stroke her thick, lustrous hair, watching how it glistened in the flickering light of the candle. Candles were becoming popular now, with essence strictly rationed by the military. It was still fairly light outside but the thick, stone walls the Halrana favored let in little sunshine.

Miro wondered if there would come a time when even candles were seen as a luxury. He shuddered.

"Oh, my baby. You're cold. Come." Varana raised the cover, offering Miro a tantalizing glimpse of her body. "Come in, join me."

Miro didn't move, just continued to stroke Varana's hair away from her face, playing with the wispy tufts at the back of her neck. He wondered if life would ever return to normal. Had it ever been normal?

After the battle the army had licked its wounds on the edge of the Wrenwood. The bladesingers were furious. There had been loud arguments between Prince Leopold and Blademaster Rogan, who had seen some of his best men lost due to poorly scouted terrain and a dangerous battle plan. The prince kept pointing to the victory as justification. The blademaster said that if that was the price of victory, there would be no soldiers left by the end of the war and no bladesingers left by the end of the season.

The rain finally stopped. The injured were sent home, the dead burnt on the pyres. The army had decamped, and with a much better idea about how to organize a column, they had moved deeper into Halaran. The billowing smoke of the funeral pyres was a reminder of their first taste of a major battle.

Word finally arrived from High Lord Legasa in Mornhaven. His armies were mostly intact, the men restless. They were shut away from the west, blockaded by the forces of Torakon and a horde of the legion. High Lord Legasa proposed that Prince Leopold and the bulk of the Alturan forces, together with the elements of the Halrana who had joined them, should attempt to break through and link with Mornhaven and the Ring Forts. With lines of communication and supply opened from Mornhaven to Sarostar, they would be able to regroup and begin the re-conquest of Halrana territory.

Prince Leopold dithered, eventually sending a messenger to High Lord Tessolar back in Sarostar, requesting advice. He had decided to billet the men in the Halrana town of Sallat while they waited for a reply. Some of the men still slept in tents, but Miro wasn't the only Alturan who'd found a home with a Halrana woman. Miro didn't know if Varana had lost her man or if she was simply lonely, and he hadn't asked.

"What is it? What are you thinking? Are you leaving?" Varana said.

"No, I'm not leaving you."

Miro's hand continued stroking her hair, and then as if of its own accord, began to stroke the pale skin of Varana's shoulder. He caressed Varana's shoulder blade, and his fingers moved to the small of her back.

"Mmm," she said, arching her back like a cat. "That's nice."

Miro leaned down and softly kissed her parted lips. "You're nice."

Varana smiled in happiness. It was what he liked about her, her completely unguarded nature, the way she spoke what she felt and showed her emotions openly. She was perhaps five years his senior, but she acted like a little girl, responding to a harsh tone with tears, to a smile with laughter. She reminded Miro of Amber.

"What are you thinking about?" she said.

"Hmm? Nothing."

"Tell me."

"No, it's nothing. I was just thinking about . . . about the prince."

"You were kissing me and thinking of another man?"

He laughed. "No, nothing like that."

Miro continued to stroke her, his hand traveling from her back over her hip, feeling its curve. She had the most curvaceous body— her breasts full, her nipples large, thighs soft and white.

"Mmm," Varana said. She rolled onto her back and grinned impishly at the obvious suggestion. Miro smiled along, his hand tickling her flat stomach.

Miro bent down and kissed her left breast before taking the nipple into his mouth, pulling on it gently. Becoming aroused, he stood up and threw off his clothes before moving onto the space Varana made for him on the cushioned bed.

Miro resumed where he'd left off, kissing her breast, the smell of her bringing forth his passion.

She whimpered, "And the other one."

He chuckled and moved to Varana's right breast, his lips teasing. Miro's hand came up and squeezed the breasts gently as he kissed the nipples in turn, devoting his attention first to one, then the other.

Varana shifted her body, and her legs were on either side of Miro's waist as he moved down her body, kissing her stomach, then the soft hair below her navel.

A clarion sounded. The noise was unmistakable.

"No!" cried Varana as, cursing, Miro rose. "Just ignore it."

Miro dressed quickly, first pulling on his woolen undergarments, then the armorsilk above. He slipped on the soft shoes and then slung the zenblade in its scabbard onto his back, feeling it hard against his shoulder blades.

Miro looked out of the window as he dressed. He could see a commotion in the town square. Half-dressed soldiers were running to get the news, then running back into their billets to grab their gear.

"What is it? Tell me what it is."

"I don't know," Miro said as he turned to the door.

"You're leaving—I know you are!" Varana cried.

Miro looked over his shoulder and moved to face her. She sat up naked on the bed, her beautiful body abandoned before it could be given the homage it deserved. She was quivering, tears pouring down her cheeks.

"I don't know what it is. I'm going to find out," Miro said.

He opened the door and left her there.

———————◆———————

There was a crowd gathering outside the town hall, soldiers and locals, all sharing anxious expressions, desperate for news.

A messenger had arrived from Altura, the *raj hada* on his cloak proclaiming him an official courier. He must have come from the high lord.

Miro stood aside to let Marshal Sloan past, flanked by two aides. Blademaster Rogan strode past a moment later, the soldiers making ample room for him to pass.

The crowd grew; rumors abounded. Miro saw Bartolo some distance away and nodded a greeting. Ronell was near the other bladesingers, standing somewhat apart, unmistakable by the scarring on his face, the empty sleeve of his armorsilk. There was no friendship there, only enmity.

It seemed like an age that they stood, waiting for news. Any news.

Finally Prince Leopold came to stand on a podium facing the soldiers and townsfolk. Rogan and Sloan murmured behind him, deep in conversation.

"I have now received word from High Lord Tessolar. He sends his deepest respect and honor for the soldiers of Halaran and Altura who now stand together in this great army." There was a ragged cheer from the soldiers. "People of Halaran, soldiers and citizens alike, your high lord needs you. He is beset by enemies on all sides. He has with him the greatest part of your armies as well as many of Altura's best men. He is cut off from all supply and communication. He needs our help."

Prince Leopold paused, gazing around him, sensing the mood. They had been good to the men, these Halrana of Sallat. They had housed and fed them. Many of the soldiers had met women among the townsfolk, women whose men had been gone for month upon month, with not a word or message to keep hope alive.

Miro realized what was going through the prince's mind. He thought he knew what was coming next.

"And so it is our duty that calls us forth, to do battle against a remorseless and unyielding foe. People of Sallat, we thank you from the bottom of our hearts. Your kindness and your generosity will not be forgotten. As we leave on the morrow, we leave with the memory of your spirit in our hearts, for you are what we are fighting for." His head bowed for a moment. Miro had to admit, he was quite an orator. "May the Lord of the Sky raise you up." He touched his lips and forehead in the Alturan manner. "And may the Lord of the Earth bless you always." He pressed his palms together.

Without another word, Prince Leopold left the stage.

Miro met Bartolo's eyes. Bartolo shook his head, a sad gesture. The soldiers around them tried to avoid the eyes of the townsfolk, but it was impossible. There wasn't a soldier that didn't feel a terrible guilt. They had brought their strength and protection to this town. In return Sallat had given everything. Without them the town would be a tempting target for the enemy.

That night Miro made love to Varana remorselessly, as if to blot out the guilt and pain. She didn't say a word, only clung on to him tightly. They spent their last night together in each other's arms. Miro tried to sleep, but the tears falling soundlessly down Varana's face stabbed at his heart like the sharpest knife.

"I'm sorry," he whispered into the night, too softly for her to hear.

The bladesingers were posted along the flanks of the army, the first line of defense in case of trouble. Scouts were sent in all directions. Mortar teams were evenly spaced along the line of the column, ammunition near at hand. The enchanters had been placed with the most important of the workers at the rear of the column, surrounded by elements of the Alturan veterans. They were ready to move out.

Some of the townsfolk waited in a small crowd to see them off, but most had either stayed indoors or were already at work, trying to get whatever crop they could out of the dry winter soil to help replace the stocks that had been devastated by the army.

Still it was with red eyes and occasional sobs that the crowd—mostly women—watched the soldiers depart. Miro looked for Varana but didn't see her. It was better this way; they'd said their good-byes the night before. Gazing stone-faced ahead of him, he looked about for any sign of trouble, willing some of the enemy to take him on now.

Miro was near the front of the bladesingers this time. He watched Prince Leopold conferring with one of the officers, waving his arms vigorously as he talked.

A few hours into the march, a scout ran up, red-faced and exhausted. He touched his lips and forehead in a token of politeness before gushing out his report.

"Imperials, sir. A whole host of them," the scout pointed in the distance. A great dust cloud had risen on the horizon.

"How many?"

"Thousands, perhaps half our number."

"They know we're here?"

"I don't think so."

Then Miro realized where the scout was pointing. Back, in the direction of Sallat. "No," he said. He hadn't even realized he was saying it.

One of the officers spoke up. "Prince Leopold . . ."

"There's nothing we can do," Prince Leopold said, his face like stone.

"Lord Marshal . . ."

"I said, there's nothing we can do!" Prince Leopold met the man's eyes. The officer dropped his gaze.

Already grim faces turned ashen. Miro tried desperately to think of something, anything, to take his mind off Varana. It was hopeless.

———◆———

Varana busied herself about the house, the familiar chores soothing frayed nerves. Her eyes were red. She had watched the men leave, trying not to attempt to pick out Miro's form, but her eyes were already roving. It wasn't too hard, there were so few of the self-possessed men in green silk. She'd watched his tall figure with his long dark hair while pretending not to, finding reasons to stop by the window. Many of the townsfolk waited until the very end, waving pathetically until the last man was out of sight, waving until there was nothing but the trodden earth to show they had ever been there.

He won't come back, she kept telling herself. *He won't come back.*

Varana now glanced at the timepiece on the wall, a valuable artifact that had been in her family for generations. Its runes still glowed with life, nearly as bright as they had been a hundred years ago.

Only a few hours had passed since he had left. It felt like a lifetime.

Varana sighed and suddenly fell down on the bed, sobbing into the pillow. She could still see where his weight had pressed down on the blankets. She could still smell him in the fabric.

At first, the screams didn't register, so lost was she in her misery. Then they joined into a chorus, and leaping out of the bed, Varana ran to the window.

People were running down the main street, some carrying bags of possessions, others carrying children. They ran with expressions of terror on their faces—the kind of terror that could be felt and communicated with a single glance at a stricken face.

Some of the town's men were running in the opposite direction, carrying ancient swords and wearing steel caps. A score of young lads shouted to those around them, urging them to join the fight.

"House Halaran!" Varana heard the cry. It was taken up by few.

The tide of fleeing townsfolk grew stronger. Varana stood transfixed, watching through the window, unable to move. It was dreamlike, unreal.

Varana saw a man drop all of his family's possessions, leaving them by the side of the road as he scooped up a child who was lagging behind. His other two children ran close by his legs. His wife carried a small howling dog.

A few more of the townsfolk emerged with weapons. Stop! Varana wanted to tell them. Give up! You'll only make it worse!

There was a sickening, crashing noise in the distance, in the direction the militia were running toward. Then all Varana could hear was the sound of marching boots. A young Halrana boy ran by, away from the fighting. His sword was gone, and blood covered his chest. Then another came—this time an older man, his head balding. Where his right arm had been was now just a bloody stump. He didn't make it far. The old man collapsed, his lifeblood pouring onto the dust.

In the distance buildings went up in flames. Soon Varana's vista was one long line of smoke as the town was systematically burned.

A crashing sound behind her forced Varana to tear her gaze from the window. The bedroom door burst inward, and a huge bare-chested man entered, carrying a curved sword in his hands. His shaved head bore a sun tattoo, spread across his scalp, and his face was scarred. He was old, as old as Varana's father, and he grinned when he saw Varana.

"Ah, that's more like it. Hey, Renitt, this one's much better than that one in Ralanast."

There was a sound behind him, and another warrior peered from behind the huge man's shoulder. "Much better. C'mon, Skarl, me first this time. You got . . ."

Rennitt was cut off by Skarl's elbow in his gut. He coughed.

"Shut yer mouth and wait by the door. Watch out for officers."

Skarl moved forward, a wide grin on his face. Varana noticed half of his teeth were broken. She felt detached from her body and just stood by the bed, a basket of laundry in her hands.

With a grumble, Rennitt leaned against the door, his arms folded across his chest.

"There, there, love. You won't be needin' that." Skarl pretended to reach for the basket but then smashed his fists down onto it, knocking the basket from her hands. Varana shrieked. She couldn't move.

He chuckled. "There, there. No need for noise. Some folks, they like a bit of noise while they're at it. Not me, not Skarl. You just be nice 'n quiet. That's the way, nothing to make a fuss over."

Skarl reached over and slipped Varana's dress first off one shoulder, then the other. He drew it slowly down and Varana's breasts burst free. From the doorway, Rennitt made a sound of appreciation. Skarl reached over and roughly grabbed Varana's breast, squeezing the nipple painfully between his thumb and forefinger. Varana cowered, shivering at his touch. It wasn't happening. This would end soon.

"Nice. Very nice," Skarl said to himself.

"Hurry up then. Don't want the officers to get here, do we?" Rennitt called.

With a grunt, Skarl nodded. In one motion he grabbed hold of Varana's dress and ripped it away from her body, tearing until the material was in a mess on the ground.

Varana stood in front of them, eyes closed, her hands crossed in front of her breasts, her legs together. Both men chuckled.

"Look at 'er," said Skarl. "Today's our lucky day."

"Just hurry up," said Rennitt.

Skarl stood menacingly close to Varana. He raised his arm. She could barely open her eyes, terrified he was going to hit her. Terrified of what else he would do.

He pushed her, hard. Varana fell back onto the bed, and suddenly Skarl was on top of her, his weight crushing her, taking her breath. His mouth tried to latch onto any part of her skin it could find—her neck, her lips, and her breasts. He tried to push Varana's legs apart with his knees, while she tried to keep them shut with every bit of strength she possessed.

"That's the way it's gonna be then?" Skarl said.

His fist lashed out, smashing into her cheek. Varana blacked out for an instant, and in that moment he drew her legs apart. Skarl fumbled with his trousers.

"Hurry u—" said Rennitt, his voice suddenly cut off mid-sentence.

Skarl ignored Rennitt and continued to pull his trousers open. Then all of his weight came down on top of Varana, and he stopped moving.

Varana felt something warm and wet spreading over her. She looked wildly about. Skarl's dead eyes stared back at her. The weight suddenly lifted from her body.

A man stood above her. His head was also shaved, but he wore delicate plated armor, black as night. Strange symbols were etched across the steel.

Varana slowly sat up. Skarl's head lolled back beside her. His throat had been neatly cut from behind. Rennitt's limp body was by the door.

"Can't have this sort of thing going on, you understand. It's bad for discipline," the newcomer said. He turned to another soldier behind him. "Burn the house. Any looting will be punished. Severely."

The soldier nodded. "Yes, sir."

"Please . . ." said Varana.

"Oh, I almost forgot."

The man's hand whipped out, fast as a snake. Something sliced across Varana's throat, and she fell back on the bed.

As her heart pumped the blood from her body, Varana looked at the timepiece on the wall. It had been in her family for generations.

Everything went dark.

27

Perhaps having the skin boiled off your bones will help you remember.
People, take note: Even the high elementalist can forget his duty.
You think renewing a Lexicon is difficult? Try keeping House Petrya
secure from our enemies.
—High Lord Apit Neffer at the trial of High Elementalist
Popan Mimphet, 440 Y.E.

Ella woke out of a nightmare, some terrible monster plaguing her even in the refuge of sleep.

"Ho, the house!" a male voice called. "Enchantress, are you here?"

Ella lifted her body out of bed. It was time to face the news.

"Enchantress Ella?"

Ella's heart thudded when she thought of Killian. Was he alive? Had he died during the night? She tipped some water from the ewer into the basin and washed her face.

She was terrified to hear what the man had to say.

"Ella!"

Ella slipped on her soft yellow dress, a simple garment that reminded her of summer. It set off her pale blonde hair, contrasted with her brilliant green eyes.

A pounding sounded at the door, growing steadily louder. Ella turned and walked to the door. A palace guard stood on the porch, his face grim.

"Enchantress, there you are. Please, you must come with me at once!"

Ella drew in a shaky breath. "It's bad news then. Killian . . . Is he . . . ?"

"You know?" He seemed shocked. "How could you know?"

Ella looked at him, perplexed.

"He's gone," the soldier said. "Gone." Ella drew back, stunned. "And we need you to tell us where he went."

Ella had never seen the palace guards so tense, so many of them with faces like cornered animals. They surrounded the Crystal Palace, out in force.

The cold winter sun had only just risen, sending scant warmth through the clouds overhead. Palace officials stood huddled in heavy woolen coats, talking together in hushed tones. There was something odd about the scene, something indefinable. It was as if a terrible tragedy had occurred, and the people were now looking for someone to blame.

Ella couldn't make sense of what the soldier said. He'd kept his lips firmly sealed, responding to none of her questions, just shaking his head and herding her in a direct line for the palace.

On the palace steps Ella could make out the forms of the high enchantress and two lords, flanking an old man. At first Ella just saw the wisps of gray hair, a flowing green cloak and an immense stiff collar. Then she realized who it was.

"Is that the high lord?"

"It certainly is," said the soldier. "And you are about to meet him."

The soldier led Ella to the palace steps, until the two of them came to stand before the high lord. If he hadn't been a couple of steps above her, Tessolar would have been much shorter than Ella. The soldier departed without a word.

Remembering her manners, Ella dipped her body and put her right hand over her heart while the fingertips of her left hand touched first her lips and then her forehead. She thought again about Lady Katherine, mysteriously drowned. How could she have married such a grim man, even if he was the high lord?

"High Lord, this is the girl," said High Enchantress Evora Guinestor.

"High Lord, it is an honor," said Ella, not knowing what else to say.

He grunted—a surprisingly human sound to come out of his ancient face. From a short distance away the two lords looked on. "Ella?" High Lord Tessolar said in a hoarse voice. For some reason he wouldn't meet her eyes. "Tell us of this man this thief who steals in the night."

Ella's brow furrowed. "High Lord, I don't understand. What happened? I take it he lived?"

Evora spoke. "Lived? I doubt he was ever unwell."

"I . . . I don't understand."

"Child, he was a thief. Last night, when most everyone in the palace was fast asleep, he searched my chambers, passed unhurt through my protective enchantments, found our Lexicon, and took it from under our very eyes."

"He did *what*?" Ella spluttered. She knew she wasn't supposed to speak in this way in front of the high lord.

"He stole our Lexicon," said High Lord Tessolar. "I assume he was the same thief who stole the Halrana Lexicon. Much becomes clear now."

"Clear and yet full of unknowing." The high enchantress frowned at the high lord. "It should never have been possible."

"The animators' Lexicon has also been stolen?" Ella said.

"Forget you ever heard that," said the high enchantress.

"Bah, our enemies know," said Tessolar. "The emperor knows. This is all his doing."

"We don't know that," said Evora. "There is much we are dealing with that we do not understand."

"Skylord scratch his name!" the high lord cursed.

Ella was shocked to hear the high lord swear. She spoke up. "But I saw the essence. It was real essence, I should know. It touched his skin."

"I believe you," said the high enchantress.

"You believe me? So . . . ?"

"Somehow, the essence did not kill him. Somehow, he was able to move about in my chambers undetected. He passed through our wards like they didn't exist. He walked past hundreds of people without being seen. Ella, I need to know what you know. Who is this young man?"

Realization came over Ella slowly, the shock of recent events fogging her mind. She'd been tricked. It had been a ploy, all of it. She'd thought she'd killed him, that Killian would die in the same manner as Talwin. She felt sick.

"He said his name was Killian." She swallowed. "I . . . I don't really know much about him. He had an accent. He told me he was from a distant land, here to trade goods."

The high lord snorted. The high enchantress shot him a warning glare.

"Continue, Ella."

"I showed him around Sarostar. He seemed interested in the palace. I told him everything I knew. I didn't know there could be any harm in it. Lord of the Sky, how could I have known?"

"Is there more? Were you . . . intimate?"

Ella blushed. "No, nothing like that. Well, we kissed. Just once." She found it made her angry the way the high enchantress was nodding. "We spent some time together, that's all."

A palace guard came over and made a formal greeting to the high lord and the high enchantress. "You asked for me, High Enchantress?"

"Ah, yes. High Lord, this is Sorrell Ronin, one of the guards."

"Soldier," said the high lord with a nod.

"Enchantress Ella, Sorrell here had an encounter with your young man. Sorrell, could you describe what you saw?"

Ella turned to the guard.

"He was quick—obviously he had some skill. Not as fast as our bladesingers, though—nothing like that. The invisibility though, that was the hard part. Other than that he was naked, didn't stand a chance if he hadn't had that essence."

"Invisibility?" Ella said, incredulous.

"Like our bladesingers' shadow. But where they make light pass through their armorsilk, he'd somehow made the light pass through his skin. He could hardly be seen."

"Do you know anything about this?" the high enchantress asked.

"No, of course not. How could such a thing be possible? Was he wearing something over his skin?"

The soldier shook his head definitively. "Not a thing. He was completely naked. The bladesinger—he nearly had him, though. Almost cut him in half with his zenblade."

"Almost?" Ella said. "What happened?"

The soldier's face grew grim. "The thief threw essence at the bladesinger. Sprayed it out of a bottle he'd stolen. Lord of the Sky, I hope I die in my sleep, I never want to go like that."

"That is all, thank you, soldier," said the high enchantress. She looked hard into Ella's eyes. "Is there anything, anything else, anything at all?"

Ella slowly shook her head, trying to think of something that could help. The realization steadily dawned—Ella's brother was out there fighting, and she'd helped give the enemy a great weapon against them, at the same time crippling her house.

Ella swallowed. "Only that he had red hair and an unusual name. He just asked me a lot of questions. I don't know what else to say."

The high enchantress sighed and nodded.

"What do you plan to do next? How can we recover our Lexicon?" said High Lord Tessolar.

"I'll make plans to track him down. It's our only option," said the high enchantress. "I renewed the Lexicon recently. It will take time for the runes to fade." She scowled. "Where are those trackers?"

"It will take a few hours to round them up. Nevertheless, he should stand out with that red hair," the high lord said. "Just remember what happened to the high animator. We can't afford to lose you too, Evora."

Evora nodded. She looked at Ella standing by, twisting her fingers in her dress. "That will be all, Ella. Please forgive my harsh words. Next time a young man shows an interest in you, though, make sure you find out a little about him."

Ella bowed her head and turned away but heard a voice behind her.

"Oh, I almost forgot. It was in the boat. There's only about half left, but fortunately it fell on its side."

The high enchantress handed Ella the intricately worked crystal bottle, the stopper now where it should be, firmly sealing the bottle. "Here you go," Evora said.

Ella thanked Evora and once more turned to leave, when another soldier came running forward. "High Lord! One of the city watchmen saw a man in rags heading north out of the city in the early hours of the morning."

Evora and Tessolar exchanged glances. "It could only be him," High Lord Tessolar said.

"But north?" Evora questioned. "I would have thought east, to Halaran, or more likely south, to Petrya. The Petryans were never our friends."

"North implies he's heading for Vezna. The cultivators still have not taken a stance and may have gone to the side of our enemy. Go, Evora," Tessolar ordered. "I'll send the trackers to catch up to you. Every moment that passes takes our Lexicon farther away."

"Can I help?" Ella said.

"No, Ella. There's nothing you can do."

Ella walked away as Evora rushed off, the soldiers scurrying to keep up with her long strides.

Ella thought about Killian as she saw bladesingers and soldiers prowling the outskirts of a small copse of trees. A few stood looking at something on the ground. Getting closer, Ella felt an initial sense of revulsion, and then pity when she realized it was blood. There was so much of it. Surely it couldn't all be the bladesinger's? She tried to avoid picturing Talwin, his insides turned to liquid. There had been plenty of blood then.

Smaller splashes of blood led to a copse of trees, a pleasure park more than a real forest. This was where they'd tracked him to. Sarostar was surrounded by forest, and Killian would undoubtedly use the forest as cover. Some of the high lord's best trackers were being summoned to join the high enchantress in the hunt.

Ella stood looking at the blood, feeling a strange mix of pity and hate. The rage began to build in her. It had all been an act. Killian had probably laughed to himself as she'd offered him her kiss. She was just a steppingstone to take him a little closer to his goal, a stupid, naive girl, lonely and looking for love.

Tears welled behind Ella's eyes. She didn't blink, refused to acknowledge them. She hadn't cried since Miro had left, sent to the front, and she wouldn't cry now, not over *him*.

All that talking, the subtle meeting of eyes and the gentle touches, they were a lie. A trick.

Ella couldn't believe she'd shared with him her innermost emotions: the guilt she felt at Talwin's death, the resultant sickness, Amber's wedding, and her solitude.

Ella caught some sidelong glances from the soldiers. She knew she must look a sight, dressed as if for a summer garden party, forlorn, staring at a pool of blood as if at her worst enemy.

Killian had stolen the most important relic of her house, and because of him Ella's brother could die.

Ella pictured Killian: wounded, naked, fleeing through the forest with no clothing and no possessions. Good. She hoped Evora gave him the fate he deserved.

She frowned. There must be something she could do to help. Yet the high lord's trackers were woodsmen born and bred, and Ella knew nothing about tracking. The forest was vast, and only the Dunfolk knew it better than the high lord's men.

Ella stopped.

The Dunfolk!

———◆———

Ella pushed through the undergrowth, doing nothing to hide her presence, remembering Amber's story and heading north from Mallorin. The shrubs grabbed at her legs and tore at her dress—she'd come straight from the palace and neglected to change—but she set her mouth with determination as she forged a path deeper and deeper into the forest.

Without a seeker she could only guess at her direction, but she eventually found a narrow path through the forest that appeared to have been made by tiny feet. From what she'd heard, the Dunfolk would find her.

The air became thick and heavy as Ella traveled for hour after hour. The canopy overhead covered the sky so that it was hard for Ella to tell what time it was; she'd set off in the morning, and she assumed it must now be early afternoon. Birds called to one another, and the hum of insects filled her senses. Ella could smell moisture and growth, and her vision was filled with a thousand shades of green.

The path led her to a part of the Dunwood where huge trees took place of the shrubs and bushes. Ella cocked her head to the side and suddenly stopped.

The sounds of the forest were gone.

She wondered how long she'd been walking through the strange silence. Had something disturbed the creatures of the woods?

Listening intently, Ella heard whispers.

"Who's there?" Ella called out. She looked to the left and the right, but could see only trees.

Ella felt a strong sensation of being watched, but she frowned and fought down her rising trepidation. The silence persisted as she traveled still farther into the forest, and then a figure stepped out from behind the wide trunk of an evergreen.

She was a small woman with ruddy skin, dressed in clothing of stitched leather and fur. She wore a silver fox pelt on her shoulders and had her arms crossed in front of her chest as she regarded Ella inscrutably.

"Ella," the woman said. "I am pleased to see you well, but what are you doing here, close to Dunholme?"

Ella breathed a sigh of relief. "I . . . I'm here for two reasons. One is that I want to thank you, Layla. You are Layla, aren't you?"

The Dunfolk healer nodded.

"I want to thank you for healing me. I'll always be grateful to you and to your people."

"Yes, yes," Layla said. "What is this other matter that brings you to my home?"

"Layla, I need your help. A man, a thief, stole something extremely important from my people. This thing he stole, our Lexicon, means that the lore of my people cannot be renewed and will fade. You may know that there is a war being fought to keep these lands safe. If we can't retrieve our Lexicon, we will lose this war, and many of my people will die. My brother, Miro, will die. Altura will fall." Ella took a deep breath. "The thief fled into the forest, and I need your help finding him."

"Can your own people not find this thief?"

"They're searching, but the forest is vast."

"Then how do you plan to get your Lexicon back?" Layla inquired.

"Can you track?"

"Track? You mean magarana?"

"I . . . I think so. Can you follow a man by reading signs in the earth?"

"Of course," Layla said. "All of my people can. But why would we help you?"

"Our enemies bear no love for your people. By helping me, you'll be helping yourselves."

Layla shrugged. "It is no concern of ours. Go home, Ella."

Ella opened her mouth to speak, but Layla held up her hand.

"Go home," Layla repeated again, her voice firm. "It is good to see you well. If you turn back now, you will reach your home before dark."

Ella hung her head.

"Please . . ." Ella started, raising her head.

But Layla was gone, and the sounds of the forest had returned.

28

A thief believes everybody steals.

—Torak proverb

Killian's flight through Altura's south had been planned long in advance, his situation changing as swiftly as his loping run through the forest. When he left Sarostar, he was naked and bleeding, but he'd found the first of his caches. He'd treated his wound as well as he could, and with clothing and supplies his confidence improved.

Killian now wore his disguise, a white smock with a double black stripe—the garb of an acolyte priest. His clothing would stand out in the forest, but he didn't plan on spending time in these parts. He would find the next of his buried caches and leave some surprises to slow down any pursuit, and then he would leave the woods, find the road, and travel farther south to Petrya, a land of devout people hostile to Altura, a place where any pursuers would have a difficult time following.

Killian knew High Enchantress Evora Guinestor would be in pursuit, and Evora was a woman he had no desire to encounter again in his lifetime.

A branch slapped at his face, stinging his cheek, and he grimaced. The undergrowth was thicker than he remembered, but then again, he hadn't planned on being wounded.

His foresight meant he could travel swiftly and light, rather than carry his supplies with him, and aside from the emerald-covered Alturan Lexicon, Killian's satchel contained no more food.

Killian's belly rumbled. He would soon be on the next of his buried caches. The trail rations he found would be cold, but they would provide sustenance.

He'd buried the next cache near the stream he was currently following, at the base of a huge tree with red bark, and he recognized this bend in the stream. Killian was close, and he was hungry.

The burbling of the stream nearly covered the sound, but Killian was still on high alert, and when he heard it, he froze.

It was the sound of chirping voices.

Killian immediately dropped to the ground and waited, but the sound of two male voices chatting continued; he hadn't been seen or heard. He crept forward, cursing the color of his clothing, and parted two branches with slow movements to see what lay ahead.

Two small men crouched in a clearing not a dozen paces from the huge red tree where Killian's cache was buried. They were evidently hunters: both were using wicked knives to remove the entrails from a fallen doe.

He watched the two hunters as they worked. He'd heard of Dunfolk, but he'd never seen one in the flesh before and was curious despite himself. The hunters wore skins, but the fabric was well stitched and didn't make them appear as barbaric as he'd heard they were. The two small men evidently took pleasure in their work, grinning as they spoke and helping each other clean the carcass. Yet Killian had heard they didn't take well to outsiders and were more violent than they appeared. Those knives looked sharp.

Killian inwardly cursed. After his trouble leaving the Crystal Palace, he wasn't looking for another fight.

Killian wondered if he should leave the cache where it was.

But he needed his strength, and it would be a day before he reached the next supplies. The urgency of his quest spurred him on. He needed to get the Alturan Lexicon out of these lands.

What if he simply talked to them? Killian shook his head. There were two of them and only one of him. They had weapons and he was unarmed.

Killian looked around and spotted a stick the thickness of his arm that would make a handy cudgel. He had no argument with these men and didn't want to hurt them, but one way or another, he was going to get to his buried supplies.

Killian watched the two hunters as he waited. He knew an opportunity would come. He would dash for his supplies, and if they gave him trouble, he would defend himself.

His chance came when one of the hunters put aside his knife and went to the stream to wash the blood from his hands. The other hunter set down his own knife and rose from a crouch, stretching.

Killian stood and took a deep breath. If he entered now, he would only face one hunter and could get his food and flee.

He dashed into the clearing. The remaining hunter lunged with surprising speed for his hunting knife.

Killian hesitated, but he had no other choice. He smashed his cudgel down on the hunter's hand. The hunter dropped the knife, howling in pain as the stick hit his wrist with a crack. Killian then ran past and, reaching the base of the red tree, he began scrabbling at the ground.

Something jumped onto his back.

The second hunter had run to the aid of his companion and began to pummel Killian with clenched fists. Killian could only thank the Lord of the Sun that the small man had neglected to run for his knife.

"It's our meat!" the hunter cried as he tried to grab Killian's throat in a stranglehold.

"I don't want your meat," Killian grunted.

He finally reached over his shoulder and grabbed the flailing hunter by his clothing. In Killian's life he'd had two occupations: a thief and, in nobler days, an acrobat.

With great agility, he threw the Dunfolk hunter over his head, sending him crashing into the hard bark of a tree. The hunter crumpled to the ground, groaning.

Killian dug at the ground until his fingers touched cloth, and a moment later he recovered the small sack. He stood and turned back to regard the two wounded hunters, one rocking back and forth and clutching his wrist, the other moaning at the base of a tree.

"I didn't mean you any harm," he said.

With a final glance, Killian left them behind.

He was in a hurry.

Ella closed the book, looking out from the porch with a sigh. She shuffled uncomfortably; she'd been seated for hours.

In addition to her scheduled work at the Academy of Enchanters, making weapons and armor for Altura's soldiers, Ella had brought home stacks of books from the libraries and scanned them ceaselessly. Yet try as she might, she was no closer to discovering Killian's secret. How could he survive the touch of essence? How could he enhance his very skin?

Ella had spoken with Amber at the Academy, and when Amber's shift ended, she was coming to Mallorin to help. Perhaps Amber would be able to succeed where Ella had failed, and together they would solve the mystery of this man.

As if echoing her thoughts, Ella heard a soft voice. "We didn't find your thief, but he found us."

Layla stood at the base of the steps leading up to the porch. After closing her book, Ella had been gazing at the forest, but she hadn't even seen the Dunfolk healer approach.

"What did you just say?" Ella gripped the arms of her chair.

"A man dressed as a priest attacked two of our hunters. I just returned from tending their wounds."

Ella stood. "Where? Where did this happen?"

"In the forest. South of Sarostar."

"What did he look like? The man we're looking for isn't a priest."

"The hunters said he was dressed in white. They said he had wild hair, the color of fire."

Ella's felt the blood drain from her face. Evora's party had left for the north.

"You said it was important, so I came to tell you. I have done so now. Good-bye, Ella."

Layla turned to depart.

"Wait," Ella called. "Wait!"

"What is it? I came to tell you. I'm leaving now."

Ella thought furiously. Evora was heading north, whereas Killian was on his way south. Every moment that passed he was getting farther and farther away.

"Wait! Layla, will you help me? Please. It's very, very important. If we don't recover our Lexicon, evil men will occupy these lands."

Layla's face was blank. "Your people are not my people. See my skin? It's different from yours."

"Yes, we are different. But if these lands are conquered, your people will die too."

Layla spread her palms. It meant nothing to her. She stepped down from the steps, and Ella knew that in seconds she would disappear into the trees.

Ella thought of all she knew about the Dunfolk. "I know! I'll give you a gift."

Layla stopped. She turned, regarding Ella with suspicion. "What gift?"

"How about armor made of cloth, soft and supple but able to stop the strongest sword blow?"

Layla shrugged.

"I know: a set of stones. Placed around the inside of a building, they create warmth, enough warmth to survive a hundred winters in comfort."

Layla walked up to Ella. She was a full head shorter, yet possessed a confidence that Ella felt she herself lacked.

Suddenly, Layla stepped around Ella and entered Ella's home. She started to rummage inside while Ella stood too stunned to react. Finally, Layla emerged once more, and this time she held something up.

It was a silk dress, simply designed, functional yet graceful. It was a deep brown, the color of the earth, its hem gold.

"I want a dress like this," Layla said simply.

Ella smiled. "It's yours. That very one. I'll alter it to fit you on the journey."

For the first time, Ella saw Layla smile too.

Ella dashed into the house and began to throw random items of clothing into a bag. She followed with some gilden. What else would she need? She packed bread, cheese, and a few packets of dried beans. A small pot. The heatplate was too big, and it hardly worked anyway. Some candles. An igniter. She'd made that herself; it worked, at least.

Then she remembered—the essence. The high enchantress had given her essence back to her.

Ella added two scrills: one for fine work, the other suitable for most purposes. And of course, her green silk dress. She was an enchantress, after all.

She felt much better. Anything she didn't have she could either make herself, or she could trade enchanted items for what she needed.

Ella added a few more items and then stopped. The satchel was looking heavy enough.

She finally left a note for Amber, asking her to send word to the palace. Evora was looking in the wrong place: Killian was heading south, toward Petrya, just as Evora had thought he would.

Ella finally decided she was ready. She didn't know how she would do it, but she would stop Killian and get back her house's Lexicon. Help would be right behind her.

Ella took a deep breath and then followed Layla into the forest.

29

*The fortresses of Manrith, Penton, Ramrar, Charing,
and Sark, known as the Ring Forts, are to remain in
Tingaran possession for a period of no less than thirteen years.
At the end of this time the aforementioned shall revert to
the control of House Halaran.*

—Treaty of Mornhaven, Clause 53

"Run! Back to the men," Miro hissed. He sprinted away from the wall as fast as his legs could carry him. The darkness of the night quickly enveloped him.

He was wearing black, and a hood covered his head. The dark clothing had been quickly put together by the enchanters at Miro's request. The garments had many of the abilities of armor-silk, but some protective strength had been sacrificed for greater stealth.

Miro could sense the other men behind him—regular soldiers also dressed in black—and could hear the thudding of their boots combined with the heaving of their breath as he led them away from the enemy encampment. Miro could make out Tuok's stocky form just ahead.

The bladesingers had been split up and distributed among the ranks of the soldiers. It was thought their confidence would rub off on the men and help prepare them for the battles to come.

For Miro, it was a chance to fight the war the way he thought it should be fought. After the battle of Harlan's Canyon, the bladesingers had developed an almost mythical reputation, and the soldiers automatically deferred to him, in awe of a bladesinger, even one so young.

They'd been fighting to reconnect with the main Halrana force holed up in the Ring Forts for weeks now. The soldiers of the Black Army were well dug in, effectively blocking Prince Leopold's army from the Ring Forts and the town of Mornhaven, where High Lord Legasa waited in strength.

Even if they managed to link with the Halrana high lord, they still had yet to face the huge army encamped on the Azure Plains below the forts. It was as if the emperor were simply trying to buy time, to tie up the Alturan and Halrana forces in a protracted and bloody war while he pursued a private agenda.

Miro glanced behind him as he ran, looking back at the enemy encampment and praying for success. The builders of Torakon had been hard at work, and this gamble had to pay off. A low wall, reinforced with glowing runes, had been built around the main enemy encampment. Great towers were evenly spaced along its length. A mortar fired from one of the towers could reach a phenomenal distance.

There were over fifty towers.

Leading up to the wall were deep trenches and holes riddled with wicked spikes. Miro and the other soldiers had fought over each trench, bloody hand-to-hand combat, with explosions raining down from above. One by one the Alturans and Halrana took them, incurring heavy losses and then dispiritedly watching the enemy withdraw to the next trench, with the walls yet to be breached.

And yet despite it all, the men in green and brown were actually gaining the upper hand.

The allied soldiers in the Ring Forts constantly swooped down to harass the enemy. Unlike the Azure Plains, so far below, the Halrana lands held in enemy hands were easily accessible from Sark and the four other strongholds.

Pressed by the Ring Forts on one side and the Alturan army on the other, the combined forces of House Tingara, House Torakon, and House Loua Louna were gradually being pushed back.

Nevertheless, Miro thought, with Petrya in the south and Vezna in the north undeclared, the war could still go in any direction. He hoped that High Lord Tessolar, back in Sarostar, was hard at work securing the support they needed.

The boom of the explosion almost knocked Miro off his feet. It was so loud that he clapped both of his hands to his ears while he ran. The runebomb he and his men had laid had been crude—the enchanters didn't have anything like the skills of the artificers—but it had been big.

The scene behind him was lit briefly, but the shooting gout of smoke and flame obscured the great enemy encampment. The huge fortress Sark stood mighty above all, glaring down as if angry at the trespassers in Halrana territory. Miro could see the four other peaks of Manrith, Penton, Ramrar, and Charing. Under their protection was the border town of Mornhaven.

"Bladesinger, it worked!" a messenger running alongside him panted. "Should I tell Lord Marshal Leopold?"

Miro nodded and then realized the messenger couldn't see him in the darkness. "Yes, tell him there is a breach in the northwestern quarter of the wall. Hopefully, he'll send in the ironmen."

◆

It was only recently that a division of Halrana animators had joined them. They made slow progress, weighed down by their equipment and constructs. The train of carts took an age to make the small distance from their fortified camp to the front line. Miro had thought it a terrible disadvantage—their constructs required so much essence that the animators feared activating them until truly necessary.

Then Miro saw them in battle.

It had been a battle of their own choosing, a hard probe at the enemy's defenses, an attack at all sides of the fortified encampment. The army had formed up: a massive force of common Alturan soldiers wielding swords, Alturan veterans with heavy enchanted armor, Halrana pikemen, bladesingers, dirigibles, mortar teams, and a motley collection of Halrana partisans armed with whatever weapons they could lay their hands on.

The Halrana animators erected tall steel towers, and then each ascended a tower and took a seat atop its summit. A metal table rested on each animator's knees, and strange spectacles framed their eyes.

Most of the men had never seen the animators in action before, and they stood mesmerized.

Miro moved to watch the animator closest to him—as a bladesinger he was free to move through the lined-up men. From square to square he traveled, weaving through the columns, passing men lined up in perfect symmetry. Finally, he stood close, overcome with curiosity.

Behind each tower was one of the great boxed carts. As Miro watched, his head tilted back, the animator spoke an activation sequence. A rune on the animator's bench flared.

284

There was a thunderous crash. Many of the men around Miro jumped, exchanging sheepish glances. The doors of the carts had fallen down, exposing the cavernous interiors. Miro looked into the closest cart.

It was filled with row upon row of metal men, shorter than golems, perhaps a foot shorter than Miro. The animator spoke again. The ironmen's eyes lit up—yellow like the sun. The runes drawn on their bodies glowed. They walked forward, maintaining perfect order.

Miro moved closer, and the closest group passed him only paces away. They were as black as night, somehow grotesque, a parody of the human form made of burnished metal. They looked unstoppable. And they nearly were.

Miro still couldn't believe that day. The animators sat high on their towers, guiding their creations. At a command, the soldiers drew apart, allowing the animators to push hundreds of ironmen forward, leading the army like the crest of a breaking wave.

On that day, hope came back.

———

The messenger left to pass Miro's message along. Miro realized he'd lost track of Tuok and the men he'd chosen to fight with.

Tall standards sprouted like trees from the army, identifying units grouped into squares. Between the squares were empty passages to allow the flow of supplies, messengers, reinforcements, and the wounded.

Each standard glowed with runes like a nightlamp; Miro soon identified the unit he was after.

"Tuok!" Miro called when he finally saw the grizzled warrior. Tuok had been promoted to sergeant, something he seemed to hate.

"There you are, young lord." Tuok took a sip from a small flask at his belt and grimaced. "Looks like we broke through the wall. My ears'll be ringing for months."

"Looks like it." Miro grinned.

An officer ran along the line. "On my command!"

Miro pointed in the distance. "We'll be following soon. Get ready."

The stilted walk and glowing eyes were unmistakable. The ironmen marched through the fire of the recent explosion, impervious to the terrible heat. The enemy's orbs dropped down like hail, some of the mortars scoring direct hits, the detonations deafening. The blasts heated the air until it wavered like a mirage. Metal melted and twisted. Occasionally the runes darkened, and a construct was stilled.

Their numbers were thinned. Still, the ironmen marched on.

"Attack!" the cry came from somewhere in the distance. It was immediately taken up by every animator, bladesinger, officer, and soldier.

"Attack!"

Holding back nothing, the Alturans and Halrana poured into the breach. A group of twenty bladesingers led the way, their armorsilk flaring as it warded off the terrible heat, hoods pulled low over faces. The blasts continued around them. The Alturan veterans followed.

Bridges had been placed all along the trenches, reinforced with enchantment. Miro leapt over a bridge, hardly seeming to touch it. His song was searing through his veins, heating his blood as he felt it more than he ever had before. Faster than the encumbered soldiers, Miro outdistanced Tuok and his men. His voice grew louder, the runes melding to form one song.

Reaching over his shoulder, Miro felt the comforting presence of his zenblade and drew it as he ran.

The breach was in front of him. Miro could now see the devastating force of the explosion; the stone was twisted, the steel girders melted beyond recognition, and a huge crater had been gouged from the earth.

The heat took the breath out of Miro's lungs, searing his throat. His song rose in tandem, the black armorsilk a comforting presence. Then he was through.

They were inside.

Miro could see enemy soldiers leaping down to close the breach—Tingaran legionnaires, Torak spearmen, and Louan grenadiers.

He held his zenblade in front of him, adding more and more to his song. He didn't know how much of the potential of a zenblade he had drawn on in the past, or how much he was drawing on now. All he knew was that the runes had formed a melody of such complexity that he knew if he stopped to examine it, he would lose it.

The searing light of his zenblade drew the enemy like moths to a flame. Prismatic orbs exploded everywhere around him, killing many of the enemy's own soldiers. If they could take Miro out, they stood a far greater chance of closing the breach. It was worth a few of their own lives.

A spear thrust at Miro's side. He deflected it with his zenblade, shearing the long jagged point off halfway. Sparks flew out in a spray, and the spearman quailed, looking down at his broken weapon. Miro's sword took him through the chest. Before Miro's position could be fixed, he whirled and thrust into the side of an axe-wielding legionnaire—a huge man, his face scarred. Blood burst out of the man's body, though his cry was lost in the chaos.

Miro added shadow, and then for good measure he interspersed his song with the inflections that quieted the glare of the runes.

His enemies drew back, frantic at the ghostly apparition he had now become as he tore into a group of grenadiers. Through the all-over covering of the black armorsilk, Miro knew they could see the surge of the battle behind him, the light coming straight through his near-indiscernible form.

The zenblade thrust and slashed. Gore splashed around Miro as his sword rose and fell like a branch tossed in crimson rapids. He realized now the importance of the once novel sequence to keep off the rain. Without the matrices that allowed the blood to slide right off, he would have long ago been soaked, rendering the shadow ability useless.

Through it all, Miro maintained a steady image in his mind's eye: the sweet, tender smile of Varana, the woman he'd left behind in the Halrana town of Sallat.

Miro dispatched his enemies with cold rage. They roared and threw everything they had at him. Out of the corner of his eye, Miro saw the body of a bladesinger, torn to pieces, only recognizable by the green silk.

Miro's song sounded strong. The enemy knew he was there, but he did everything he could to ensure they could not know where he would be next.

The vision of Varana faltered, replaced by the sight he was trying to forget, a sight that they were all trying to forget.

The huge plume of smoke rising from the town of Sallat had spread to cover the sky in soot and ash. The sunset that night was a terrible red, as red as the blood they all knew had been spilled that day.

In Miro's mind, Varana's eyes grew sad, and she stared at him accusingly. Tears were running from her eyes, tears that turned into blood.

Then her face changed, and it was Amber's face that Miro saw.

Miro's blade swept through the enemy, furious and unforgiving.

The Alturan army poured into the enemy encampment. Support came down from the Ring Forts, massive creatures of wood and iron, crashing through the ditches, bursting through the walls. Soon the enemy was in rout, fleeing for the security of their strength in the north.

Miro tried to focus on nothing. Nothing at all.

It didn't work.

30

Before we can develop an improved future for the
Tingaran Empire, we must first develop the ability to envision it.
—Sermons of Primate Melovar Aspen, 541 Y.E.

Layla stopped, looking at the earth. She crouched down, staring intently at a patch of grass. She picked a blade and put it between her teeth, chewing on it thoughtfully.

"What? What is it?" Ella said.

Layla frowned at her. Ella sighed.

The small woman—Ella had decided "woman" was more appropriate than "girl"—pointed at a patch of ground.

Ella couldn't see anything at all.

"He came this way. He is feeling better now, moving faster, his wound pains him less. He found some herbs to help him." Layla looked at Ella in reproach. "It seems your people are alone in their ignorance about healing."

"Yes, yes. Which direction?"

Layla pointed. "Also, he still wears the white clothing."

"Good." Ella nodded.

Picking up her satchel and throwing it over her shoulder, Ella followed Layla deeper into the trees.

Ella knew she never would have made it this far without the healer. Rather than follow the road, Killian had taken a shortcut through the forest. This new route would make the going more difficult, but the same problem would apply to any pursuers.

As dry twigs and leaves cracked beneath her feet, she wondered how far behind her the high enchantress was. Layla somehow stepped so lightly she didn't make a sound. Ella felt like a lumbering beast in comparison.

Ella removed her shawl, growing warm from the exertions of the walk. Her dreams of altering Layla's dress on the journey had so far come to nothing. Each night she collapsed exhausted, too tired to eat, let alone sew.

She'd eventually had to give up on protecting her own beautiful yellow dress from the ravages of the forest, and wished she had more practical clothing. She looked down at it sadly, the bits of plant entangled in the hem, the threads torn by sharp branches or thorns. Her arms bore the same scratches, but she was somehow sorrier for the dress.

She'd rotated her clothing in the time that they'd been on the trail, so that it was all in the same sorry state. It was fortunate that she'd brought so much, though—the cold at night was formidable. The only dress she kept unworn was her green enchantress's dress. She knew she might need it later.

Frost covered the evergreens every morning. Mist sometimes flowed through the trees so that it was hard to see a few paces ahead.

Growing up on the edge of the Dunwood, Ella was used to the sounds of the forest. But here, in the south, in a different forest with a different name, the sounds were much more ominous. Strange shrieks and terribly humanlike voices cried out in the night. The disdain Layla showed for her fear was comforting; the little woman seemed to fear nothing.

"Tell me something of the Dunfolk," Ella said.

Layla grunted. "For one thing, we are not 'Dunfolk.' That's a word created by you of the houses, and it means 'moss people.' A stupid name. *Loralayalanasa* we are, and we have been in these parts far longer than you. Long enough to see the great trees grow from a tiny seed. Long enough to become a part of this land."

"Oh," said Ella, taken aback, "I didn't mean to offend."

"It is not you we are angry with. Some of your people are good; some of them are evil. For us, though, it is your power that is the problem. You have so much power, the power to burn, to destroy, to kill."

Now it was Ella who took offense. "But also the power to create, to warm, to protect."

"Our people create nothing; we grow. We plant a seed and give it our attention, and it grows. We don't need heat—we have each other for warmth. We give our brothers and sisters love, and they give us their warmth in return. And what do you protect from? From each other. You protect yourselves from the evil ones. And something dies inside of you every time you fight, every time you take on their methods in the name of security."

Ella was surprised at the depth of Layla's understanding. She realized she might have underestimated the small healer—they might have underestimated all the Dunfolk.

"And your leaders. You raise them up, you give them power over you. Then when that thing inside of them dies, when it burns out completely—what then? You tell me this emperor threatens my people. I blame you! Who made him emperor? Who gave him this power to threaten the Loralayalanasa? You did!"

Ella didn't respond, lost in thought. She could see how Layla's reasoning made sense to her. The arguments seemed logical, but she felt Layla was missing something. Something about the will to challenge an oppressor, the nobility of freedom, and how people needed a voice to speak up in freedom's name.

They trudged on in silence. Ella followed Layla into a deep valley. Mist welled out of its depths to spread slowly up the opposite side of the long dale, like the rising of a white tide.

Layla said they were cutting a big loop in the road. She said Killian had obviously come this way before, and when they discovered the caches he was unearthing, it was confirmed.

The two pursuers reached the floor of the valley after an easy downhill stretch. Discovering an ancient riverbed, they followed it as it twisted and turned.

Ella couldn't see how Layla kept to the trail—how she knew they were still tracking Killian. Occasionally, Layla touched her fingers to a patch of dirt or examined some moss on a tree. It made no sense to Ella.

The riverbed led them to a cleft under a huge rock that once must have been the spring's source. From the boulder they were forced to climb.

The ground grew steep, graveled and littered with rubble. Trees were sparser here. Ella's breath grew ragged, and she tried to use the trees for support. Sweat began to pour down her forehead, even in the freezing air. The mist thickened.

"Are you sure he came this way?" Ella panted.

"Yes, I am sure. Would you like to lead instead?" Layla said. She seemed to be finding the going much easier than Ella.

Ella only grunted in reply.

The climb grew even more difficult. They had no chance to talk but could only take one step after another. Even Layla began to pant. The air became thick, the moisture in it a tangible thing. Soon Ella could barely see Layla ahead of her, the small woman's figure almost lost in white.

Then she lost her altogether.

Ella stopped in her tracks. Scrambling, she started climbing the steep slope as fast as her legs could take her. Her feet kicked up bits of stone and dirt, and she clawed at the earth with her hands.

"What are you doing?" Layla asked.

Ella looked up. The slope had ended. Layla was on the top of the crest, resting with one arm against a tree.

"Climbing," Ella panted.

The fog was like a white version of darkness, so thick it appeared impenetrable. Ella stretched as she panted, her muscles aching.

She walked around the flat area. Only now could she appreciate how high they'd come, how steep the slope they had been climbing had been.

"Stop!" Layla suddenly shrieked. She ran at Ella, and grabbed hold of Ella's arm, dragging her to a halt. "Stop!"

"What . . . ?" Ella began.

Then she realized where her feet were taking her. Where they were.

She was standing on the edge of a sharp precipice, an abrupt cliff that fell down until it was lost in the mist.

The edge of Ella's foot was just over the cliff. Another step, and . . .

"Lord of the Sky . . ." Ella breathed.

Layla tugged on her hand as Ella let herself be led away. She couldn't believe how close she'd come. If Layla hadn't been there . . .

"Thank you," Ella said. "Thank you, Layla."

She received only a grunt in reply.

Layla insisted they wait until the mist cleared. They settled down to a cold camp of stale bread with some moldy cheese. Layla supplemented the fare, finding some wild mushrooms with pink stalks she insisted were edible. Ella found to her surprise that they were actually tasty.

"If only we had a bow," Layla grumbled. "I need meat."

It was the first time they'd had a chance for a proper rest without being exhausted from a full day's march. Even so, Ella cursed the mist that was forcing them to wait.

With a sigh, she activated a nightlamp, its light stretching just far enough to create a haven within the fog. Eventually, Ella felt refreshed, and she began to get restless; the fog was going nowhere. Having an idea, she rummaged around in her satchel.

"Stand up," Ella said.

"What do you mean?"

"It's a simple request, stand up."

Layla stood.

Ella slipped the brown silk dress over Layla's head. "Stop struggling," she said.

"I can't breathe!"

"Yes, you can. Don't be a baby."

The dress slid down Layla's small body. Her head popped out, and she looked around in confusion.

"Here, hold the hem or it's going to get dirty," Ella said. "Now stay still."

"Ouch!"

"Sorry." Ella laughed. "I'm just tailoring the dress to fit you. You're very pretty, did you know that?"

"No, I'm not," Layla said in flat voice.

"You are. And you're going to look beautiful in this dress."

Ella could see Layla fingering the supple material as she held the hem, casting her eye over the gold trim. Ella quickly pinned the sides of the dress, tucking it in a little at the waist, letting it out a bit at the hips. She then pinned the hem.

"There we go—done. Hold up your arms. There."

Layla turned to Ella and grinned. It was so rare that she smiled that Ella found herself smiling along.

As Ella worked on the dress, a gentle breeze began to blow against the hill, and the mist began to clear. Ella added some finishing touches and smiled to herself, putting the scrill and essence away. She wondered how long it would take Layla to discover the runes she'd enchanted into the fabric of the dress—whether she'd recognize them for what they were or think they were merely decorative.

"What are you smiling about?" Layla said.

"Nothing," Ella said. "I'm just happy the dress has turned out well. Here," she said, handing it to Layla, "you can try it on another time."

Layla took the dress, handling it with suspicion. But her sparkling eyes showed her interest.

Ella gathered herself and stood. "Look," she said.

The haze below the cliff cleared to reveal a breathtaking panorama. A turbulent river twisted and turned its way through a green valley. Tracing it with her eyes, Ella could see at its source was a majestic waterfall, spouting from the cliff face directly below them. In the far distance she could make out the dusty road, turning ever south and east to the glass-bottle mountains of the Elmas at the extreme limits of her vision.

"If we cross that river, it will be the farthest I've ever been from Loralayalana," Layla said.

Ella followed the healer to the cliff edge. It was sheer, dropping down for hundreds of feet before it began to level off with the ground.

"Surely he didn't come this way?" Ella said.

She drew away at the glare Layla gave her.

"He made his way down unaided," Layla said. "He is very agile."

Ella cursed. Killian may have been able to do it, but for her and Layla the climb would be impossible. She scanned the cliff and then spotted something in the distance. "There," Ella said, pointing.

It was a braided rope, tied to the base of a sturdy tree. Ella and Layla pushed through heavy undergrowth to reach it, but Ella cursed again when she saw that it looked like the rope had been there for a very long time. It was yellowed with age, thinning out in places.

Ella knelt down and began to pull up the rope. A small pile built up on the ground in front of her. Then she pulled up the frayed end.

The old rope was broken. It would never reach down to the bottom of the cliff. It wouldn't even reach halfway.

Layla looked at Ella. "I think we will not be going this way. He planned this. By the time we find another route down from here, he will be long gone, your book with him." She shrugged. "We tried. I am sorry."

Ella sat down hard. She looked at the rope in frustration. Suddenly she picked up the pile of rope. Her fingers worked quickly as she began to unbraid it into its three separate strands.

"What are you doing?" Layla said. "That rope will never be strong enough. Even I would not trust it. You are much bigger than me, much heavier than me. Your body is large."

"Thanks," Ella said wryly. Her fingers continued working.

"We should be going now. I should be going now," Layla said.

"Just wait."

Ella finally completed breaking the rope into three thin lengths. The rope was so old that in some places it had almost broken through.

She rummaged inside her satchel, pulling out the fine scrill and the vial of essence.

"What are you doing?" Layla said.

"Shh," said Ella.

The separate strands of rope were perhaps half the width of Ella's small finger. First she tied the strands together, to make one long piece. Then, sitting down in a place where the light of the sun was the best, Ella began the delicate process of enchantment.

Rope was difficult, but not impossible—the trick was to tie knots into simple rune structures and then trace the essence along those knots. When Ella was done, she looked up triumphantly. Layla was sitting on a tree stump nearby, munching on some forest food she had foraged. Ella picked up the rope in her hands. It was just as light, but she could feel the new strength she had imbued it with. She'd had to keep the runes very, very simple, but she was proud of what she had done.

"Here," Ella said. She threw the rope at Layla, who deftly caught it. "Try to break it. Test its strength."

Layla was red in the face before she would acknowledge that the rope was strong enough.

Ella tied the rope back onto the tree and cast it out over the cliff. She looked at Layla. Layla looked away. Sighing, Ella began to lower herself down the rope.

She soon developed a rhythm, finding holds for her feet first, before gently lowering herself, holding onto the rope with her arms, her feet searching the cliff for new footholds.

Halfway down, Ella began to hear a huge roaring sound. It grew louder the more distance she made down the cliff face. Then she passed a knob of rock, and the source of the sound revealed itself.

A second mighty waterfall, sparkling in the sun, shot out of the cliff. Water sprayed out in a cloud around it, rainbows spraying their color across the air. Butterflies buzzed about, flying up and then down to where the waterfall was lost in the foam churned up by its power. It was an amazing sight, yet the spray made the stone slippery, and Ella had to take special care as she descended down the rocky face.

Ella found the footholds more by touch than by sight, worried that if she looked down, she'd be unable to keep going. Then her right foot felt out into emptiness.

Her scream brought Layla to the top of the cliff, peering down at her. "What is it? I can't help you from up here."

Ella would have laughed if she hadn't been terrified. "I need your help. I need you to look down and tell me where I can put my feet."

Layla frowned down at Ella. "Why don't you just look down yourself?"

The muscles in Ella's arms were growing weak. She tried to regain a foothold with her right foot, to take some of the strain off her arms, but couldn't get a purchase. She slipped.

"Layla! Just help me. I can't look down. I don't want to know how far I have to go."

"I don't understand why you don't just look down."

Ella took a deep breath as she looked down, but her vision was obscured by the jagged features of the cliff. "Because I can't see! Does that answer your question?"

"No need to be angry. The cliff falls away below you, for about ten paces. You need to either slide down or swing to the side to get hold of the cliff with your feet."

"I can't slide. I'll burn my hands and fall!"

"Then swing to the side."

Taking a deep breath, Ella kicked out to the side. She just managed to touch the side of the fissure. She began to swing. Her arms on fire, she kicked out again. She began to swing more. The pressure it was putting on her arms was too much.

She fell. Her hands slid down the rope, scorching her palms, but she couldn't let go, she had to hold on, had to . . .

Her feet touched the ground. The fissure panned out, slowly sloping to become the valley floor.

Something scampered down the rope. Layla landed next to Ella only a moment later.

Ella just stared at her, too angry to speak. Her eyes were wide, her fists clenched at her sides.

"What?" said Layla. "You told me you didn't want to know how far you had to go."

Ella didn't say a word as they continued along the lush ground of the valley. After a while, though, she calmed; the beauty was just too great to maintain a foul mood, and Layla didn't seem affected anyway.

The valley had a microclimate—its own cycle of seasons and warmth, its own species of birds and insects. The warmth rising from the valley finally took the chill from Ella's bones, chill she hadn't known had been there. Butterflies the size of a man's hand and colored like brilliant jewels fluttered about lush green trees. Ella could now see three other waterfalls. The water spilled far out into empty space before disappearing into mist.

"Have you ever seen anything so beautiful?" Ella said softly, almost whispering. "Look at that bird—there on that branch. It's just sitting there, looking at us. Why doesn't it fly away?"

They followed some kind of game trail, either a path made by animals or a track long-neglected by humans. The roaring of the waterfalls grew more distant. Ella didn't ask if they were still on Killian's trail. She was learning to pick up the subtle signs as Layla checked small changes in the plants or the earth.

Ella followed Layla into a wooded glen. A soft gurgling sound came from somewhere ahead, a pleasant tinkling—the sound of running water. Birds fluttered from tree to tree, singing to each other in their high voices.

"Few people come here," said Layla. "The animals have not learned fear."

They emerged from the trees. In front of them was a wide, turbulent river, its water a deep green, splashing against the banks.

"Someone must have come here," said Ella, pointing at something on the bank.

It was a rope bridge, evidently the only way to cross the river.

It was in tatters, deliberately cut after being crossed.

"He covers his tracks well," said Layla.

Ella sighed.

31

*I had finally reached the summit of the mightiest mountain
in the Emdas. The victory was short lived. Some regular
arrangements of stones told me an ancient people
had been there long before me.*
—Toro Marossa, "Explorations," page 189, 423 Y.E.

"Sark. The guest house with the best view in the whole of Halaran,"
a voice came from Miro's shoulder.

Miro started.

"Sorry—I didn't mean to startle you."

It was Bartolo. Miro had been so lost in thought that he hadn't
heard him approach.

Miro turned and smiled. "No, it's good to see you. It's been so
frantic lately. This is the first opportunity I've had to just stop and
think."

"I know what you mean," Bartolo said, looking out over the
disquieting vista below.

They said the army encamped on the Azure Plains was the
biggest that had ever been assembled. It stretched across the land
below, the individual figures as small and numerous as ants. The

might of three houses had combined to an extent never seen before.

The builders never stopped construction, and the catapults and trebuchets never ceased their bombardment of the walls; it had become commonplace now, put to the back of the mind. Ballistae were lined up one after the other, behind the defensive wall below, in a row that just kept going and going.

Signs of the artificers of Loua Louna were everywhere. It was clear to all now that they had thrown their full support behind the emperor. The dirigibles covered the Black Army like a cloud of death. Already the number of wounded who had been sent home with missing limbs had tripled in the week since they'd linked up with High Lord Legasa's force in the Ring Forts. Soldiers complained of hearing the blasts of mortars and prismatic orbs in their sleep. Many who'd survived close encounters had gone deaf, no longer able to communicate, their ears ringing in constant agony.

Binding it all together was the black flag bearing the white sun. Still no one knew why the emperor's colors had been struck for this symbol, or what it really meant. No longer could imperial purple be seen on the tabards of the Tingaran soldiers; no longer the sun and star *raj hada* of the Imperial House. All was black.

After the great encounter—they were calling it the Battle for Mornhaven—the bladesingers had been headquartered in Sark. It was some kind of honor, Miro supposed.

Miro hadn't seen much of Tuok or the other soldiers. The bladesingers had been acting strangely aloof, as if intentionally distancing themselves from the recruits.

Miro had seen Ronell only once, and the look he'd received was pure venom. He'd heard that even fighting with only one arm, Ronell had distinguished himself well in the battle, but there were troubled opinions also. Rumor had it Ronell had the look of someone who didn't care if he lived or died.

"I can leave you, if you'd prefer privacy," said Bartolo.

"No, no. I was just thinking."

"Always a thinker," said Bartolo. "What do you think will happen next?"

"What *will* happen next, or what do I *think* should happen next?"

Bartolo grinned. "That's the Miro I know. What would you do?"

"I would assemble a strike force, the very best."

"And where would you send them?"

"I'd strike through the Elmas, hit the elementalists. Drive straight through to Petrya."

Bartolo's wide eyes said he hadn't been expecting it. "House Petrya hasn't declared yet."

"It's a matter of time. They fought with the emperor in the last war, in the Rebellion."

"Yes, but . . ."

"You think this one will be any different? First Torakon and then Loua Louna. They've both joined with the emperor, given him everything, held back nothing. Why should Petrya be any different?"

"But surely we should give them the benefit of the doubt. To attack, while they're still undeclared . . ."

"The way the emperor attacked Loua Louna? Look where we are now. We're barely holding them off. We've got everything Altura has here—everything. Half of Halaran is lost. Ralanast is lost. We don't have much room for error. No, we need to take the initiative—seize it. Otherwise, we're lost too."

They stood in silence for a moment. The Black Army below lent its grim weight to Miro's words.

"So what do you think our commanders will do?"

"They'll regroup here, join the two armies. Practice some maneuvers. Look down on the enemy below and ignore them. Then, very slowly, they'll send us north and west."

"Ralanast?"

"Ralanast," Miro echoed.

The sound of a man clearing his throat came from behind them. The two recruits turned.

Ten bladesingers stood behind them, expressions grim. One of them ran his eyes over Miro's casual clothing. "Get your armorsilk and your zenblades. You've been summoned. You're coming with us."

They were led into the bowels of the fortress, deep underground. It was damp—damp and dark. The passages were roughly hewn, the stairs uneven. Miro itched in his armorsilk. Something didn't feel right, but he put it down to nerves. His zenblade was strapped to his back. Bartolo walked beside him, his face pale. Neither spoke.

The most senior bladesinger opened a heavy iron door. It creaked and clanged as the man heaved it open, frowning at the two recruits. There was the sound of movement behind Miro, and he turned and saw Ronell, flanked by five more bladesingers. Ronell didn't meet his eyes.

Blademaster Rogan waited as the three recruits entered; beside him were Bladesinger Huron and Bladesinger Porlen. Their expressions were stern, and if Miro hadn't known better, he would have said they were about to be punished.

"Normally, we would be at the Sanctuary, deep in the Dunwood," Blademaster Rogan said. "However, we are not there.

High Lord Legasa of Halaran has graciously lent us these chambers and the assistance of the men we need." He met the eyes of first Ronell, then Bartolo, and finally Miro.

"Recruits, you are about to be tested. You have been hardened in battle. You have developed your skills. What you lack in training, you perhaps make up for in experience fighting legionnaires and common soldiers. But bladesingers are more than soldiers and must be able to combat the strongest opponents with confidence, fighting alone. You must prove your command of the runes without following the lead of your more experienced brethren. This is a rite of passage all of us have taken. Are you ready? We will soon know.

"If you pass this test, you can call yourselves bladesingers, and we will welcome you into our number. If you fail, there is a makeshift infirmary in the next chamber. If you fail, you might not even need it." His look was significant. Miro thought of the rusted knives and bloody aprons of the field surgeons.

"Do not doubt me in this," Rogan Jarvish continued, his voice hard. He bit off his next words: "I will see you dead before I accept a liability. We have all passed this test. I have seen recruits with great potential fail. I am glad they were tested, because in battle their failure might have led to more deaths. You've fought with us in battle against my better judgment. At least here, there can be only one death. Yours."

Miro shifted in his armorsilk. It felt uncomfortable, ill fitting. It was all that stood between him and whatever it was that was about to unfold.

"Now, about the test. The animators have been helping us with it for years. It's something of a contest between us, a chance for us to test the skills of our best against the skills of theirs. It forces our enchanters to constantly innovate, to create better weapons, to enchant better armor. It forces our bladesingers to fight better, learn faster, and adapt their song to new conditions and a new foe.

"I can tell you now, not one of us here has ever fought the foe you are about to fight. We have fought our own enemies, passed our own tests. As we hope our methods of training have improved, so have those of your opponents."

Rogan Jarvish nodded to someone behind the recruits. Miro felt a pressure on both sides. A bladesinger stood by each shoulder, their faces impassive. Miro realized with a pounding heart that there wasn't a choice here. This test wasn't optional. He would face his foe or he would die.

A sheen of sweat began to cover his brow, though it was cold and dry here under the mighty fortress of Sark. He shared a glance with Bartolo. Ronell looked at nothing but the walls, his face impassive but betrayed by the ashen color of his disfigured skin.

The recruits were led down a long corridor, each flanked by their handlers. Miro lost sight of Bartolo and Ronell. He was brought to a halt outside a door.

"Enter here," said one of the bladesingers, his face cold.

Miro opened the door. He was pushed roughly from behind. The door was closed behind him.

Two figures strode up to Miro, meeting him eye to eye, their faces hard as stone. They were dressed in brown robes, the Halrana *raj hada*—a hand with an eye in the center—a bold emblem on their breasts. They were large, burly men, used to physical work. Without a word each took Miro by the arm and led him down another corridor.

At the end of the passage was an open door, inches thick, made of heavy iron, studded and bolted. Somehow Miro knew that whatever was waiting for him would be waiting behind this door. A series of runes had been drawn on the door. Once sealed, even a zenblade wouldn't easily get through it.

One of the Halrana spoke. "This door will be locked behind you. It will be opened only when the battle is over."

Miro was thrust into the room, the slamming of the heavy door echoing in his ears as the bolt was thrown behind him.

It took some time for Miro's eyes to adjust to the dim light provided by some weak nightlamps. The room was massive, the ceiling high, the floor sanded. Littered about the room were stone blocks of uneven sizes, some small enough to throw, others twice a man's breadth and height.

Miro stood at his end of the chamber, ill at ease and conscious of the sealed door behind him. No matter what happened, he wouldn't be able to leave that way. He shifted in the uncomfortable armorsilk. Beads of sweat dripped from his brow.

As his eyes adjusted to the dim light, Miro had a direct line of sight to the other end of the chamber. There was a man seated on a chair, the only piece of furniture in the chamber, wearing a brown robe and a torc around his neck. The torc glowed with strange colors, and Miro saw that at his wrist was another glittering circlet. The man regarded Miro for a moment and then looked down at a rectangular tablet on his knees.

Miro drew in a sharp breath. An animator.

The animator spoke, too softly for Miro to hear. The tablet flared to life, the runes glowing silver. The brown-robed man touched the tablet at a particular place. A matrix of runes there changed color. The animator's lips moved again.

Miro heard a sound from the shadows. Heavy steps, crunched into the sandy floor. A metallic creaking followed.

A construct, black as night, stepped out of the darkness to stand in front of its animator, only paces away, and then turned to face Miro. Its eyes were red, its mouth a narrow gash. Symbols covered every part of it. Some were activated, giving it a soft silver glow. It carried a long black sword.

The construct stood with its chest pulsing, limbs glistening, heaving in a grotesque parody of breathing. A strange sighing sound came from its body as it pulsed. It had been awakened. It was alive.

It was an iron golem.

Miro had only seen an iron golem once before, in the Halrana market house in Seranthia. They were House Halaran's deadliest fighters, but the Halrana didn't have many, and they were rarely seen. Requiring a fearful amount of essence to construct, they were also complex to animate. And Miro was about to fight one.

Miro looked at the robed man. The animator smiled.

He made several more gestures at the tablet and activated more runes, the animator calling them in quick succession.

The iron golem flared and twitched, different colors—greens, blues, and reds—glaring from its body. Its eyes grew bright, still a menacing red. It raised its sword—in salute, Miro realized.

Miro took a deep breath. This was going to require every bit of skill he had. He knew there would be no help from the outside, and a single blow of that sword with the unbelievable strength of those metal limbs behind it would sorely test his armorsilk.

Miro reached over his shoulder, feeling the hilt of his zenblade, comforting in his hands. He drew the sword.

Steadily, with no room for error, he began his song.

His sword grew bright, brighter with each sequence, white as lightning. The armorsilk stayed dark.

The golem started walking toward Miro, its steps ponderous, inevitable.

Miro controlled his panic. He began his song again, this time with the most basic sequence for armorsilk protection, letting the sword fade altogether.

The armorsilk did nothing. Miro's words were having no effect.

The golem drew closer, moving faster now, starting to run. It would soon pin Miro against the wall. Miro leapt to the side.

The sword whistled through the air, where Miro had stood less than a heartbeat ago.

Miro thought furiously. What was happening? He knew his song. The inflections were correct. The sword was behaving as it should.

Then with a heart-stopping lurch, he realized.

A bladesinger's tools were attuned to that particular warrior. His zenblade and armorsilk were coded for a specific activation sequence, slightly different from that of the man next to him. Otherwise, their songs would interfere with each other—their words would clash. Each item had a certain sequence that had to be uttered in the correct part of the song. A bladesinger could easily use another's sword or armor, provided he knew the code.

Miro wasn't wearing his own armorsilk. He'd fetched it from the peg where he'd left it, but it had been substituted with someone else's. He didn't know the sequence for this armorsilk.

He ducked a vicious blow from the golem and lunged to the side as the construct followed it with another, then two more slashes in quick succession. The second slash missed him by a finger's width. Miro dove behind a stone block.

Who had done it? The answer came to him with a cold feeling of dread: Ronell. It would have been simple, no problem at all. Ronell could always plead innocence, and no one would be able to prove otherwise.

With no other choice ahead of him, Miro concentrated on the zenblade. He ignored the sequences for the armorsilk and chanted the runes for the zenblade, one after the other. The sword again turned white as his song came clear from his lips, rising up and echoing from the walls of the cavernous stone chamber.

Miro walked sideways, keeping the golem within his sight at all times. He put a tall column between them. The golem swung its shining metal arms, the sword arcing out faster than the eye could follow, passing through the column like a fish through the water, as if it weren't even there.

The construct hissed—a terrible sound—and leapt forward, pushing itself at Miro, maintaining the initiative. Miro fell back. Suddenly, he tripped over a low block of stone behind him. The golem leapt forward, and Miro swung with his sword as he fell. The zenblade crashed against the black sword with an explosion of sparks. Then the construct thrust its sword in turn, and Miro's back struck the ground as he tried to block it with his own.

The black sword surged forward with enough momentum to easily push past the zenblade. Miro was against the ground, with nowhere to go. The black sword hit Miro low in the abdomen, piercing his side.

The gush of blood told Miro the cut was deep. He rolled to the side as the black sword came down again. With a firm grip on his zenblade, he blocked the next attack and leapt to his feet.

Chest heaving, Miro sought refuge behind a thicker column, this one as wide as three men. Gasping for breath, he put his hand to his chest and pulled it away, dripping with blood. His song faltered, and the sword lost some of its color, the runes fading to silver.

The golem strode toward him. Its runes flared bright—red, blue, green. Miro had been taught to track an enemy's actions by his eyes. The emotionless red glare told him nothing.

The black arms rose.

Miro prepared for an overhead cut. The golem feinted, instead sending a sweeping cut toward Miro's chest. Miro blocked it with the zenblade, but he felt the weakness in his sword; he had to do better. Miro thrust into the golem's backswing, but the attempt was blocked, almost casually, before the construct sent a steel fist crashing into Miro's face.

Miro's skin split, and red filled his vision as blood filled his right eye. The golem followed up with the hilt of its sword, smashing it against Miro's chin.

Miro's lip broke open, and he tasted his own blood. The force of the two successive blows sent him reeling; he almost dropped his sword, barely staying standing as he put space between himself and the construct.

The golem came on, and Miro knew he was going to die.

His voice came hoarse, the runes spoken in staggered syllables through thick lips. The zenblade was faintly silver now. Miro closed his eyes for a moment and wiped the blood from his right eye. He then straightened his back and took a fighting stance.

Miro began his song anew. It was all about the zenblade. With a start, he realized that without having to maintain the armorsilk, he had the ability to truly use the zenblade, to add as much as possible to its song.

He first added strength and lightness. The sword grew bright, the runes shining white. As the sword grew lighter, Miro's arms felt stronger, and he grew more confident. He added sharpness and a searing heat, hot enough to melt iron. The blade's color moved from white to yellow.

The song came strong from Miro's lips now, his breathing continuous.

Miro could almost feel the runes, the chanting pouring forth as if it were a natural thing. He reached the state he had achieved in the Battle for Mornhaven, then passed it, the song coming easier. More inflections. More runes. More power. He didn't know what he was singing now—it was visceral, something from within him.

The zenblade turned from yellow to red. A bright and fiery red, as red as fresh arterial blood.

Miro threw himself at the golem, his blows coming one after the other, again and again. The golem blocked each in turn, but its movements weren't fast enough; there was a small delay, growing with each blow. Miro kept up the continuous barrage until he saw his opening. He would need to be fast, faster than he had ever been before.

Miro feinted and then slashed, in the direction of the golem's neck.

The zenblade hit the metal of the construct squarely in the shoulder, almost shearing off its arm. The clashing of the runes crashed like an explosion of lightning, and for a moment the cavernous room lit up brighter than day. Several of the runes around the golem's upper chest went dim.

The iron construct faltered. Miro saw an opportunity and lunged in again.

Miro realized it was a trick as the construct straightened and the black sword slashed straight at his head. He tried to turn but he felt pain as it sliced down his face.

In rage and frustration, Miro's song entered a new depth. He simply knew where to add the inflections. He didn't think about them; he only felt them. The song was part of him; he was the song.

The zenblade shifted from red through violet. It turned blue.

Miro then added the sequence to dim the runes. The blue grew softer, ghostly and ethereal.

Finally, Miro added shadow.

The zenblade all but disappeared, becoming a thin beam of light. Miro launched a flurry of blows, seeing the golem's head turn from side to side as it ducked and weaved, as fast as anything Miro had ever seen.

In one great swing, the zenblade came through the air at the golem's head. Faster than Miro would have thought possible, the black sword came up. The ethereal blade hit the black sword.

The black sword sheared into two pieces.

The zenblade kept going, hitting the golem squarely on the neck. Sparks sprayed out, the din deafening. The head lifted from the shoulders and fell with a clang to the ground. A moment later the heavy body followed.

There was silence but for the sound of Miro's heaving breath.

Then Miro heard a clapping sound from the end of the chamber. The animator stood.

"Well done, Bladesinger," the animator said.

32

*I asked the High Animator if I could see the Halrana Lexicon.
Of course, he refused. What chance have we to discover more
about lore if even close allies cannot share?*
—Diary of High Enchantress Maya Pallandor,
page 488, 411 Y.E.

Ella woke to the depressing sound of the river. The impassable barrier between her and her goal. With each passing day the Lexicon grew farther away. It would soon need to be renewed, something only the high enchantress could do. And when it wasn't, all enchantments would fade.

Ella sat up and rubbed at her eyes, frowning at the river in consternation.

They'd made camp on its banks while they decided what to do, the warmth of the valley after the cold of their other camps an unexpected treat. Ella had found a flat rock and enchanted it into a heatplate. Layla trapped a small rabbit, and the smell of grilling meat wafted through the trees.

Ella felt vaguely guilty for using essence for such a mundane task. The black liquid was so costly that when a heatplate was made, the stone carvers chose a beautiful piece of marble and enhanced it with intricate designs. And here she was, picking any flat rock that served the purpose.

Still, she reminded herself, it was her essence; she'd been given it, and she was free to do what she wanted with it.

With a hot meal, and the best night's sleep she'd had in weeks behind her, Ella was free to examine their problem.

The river.

She looked over at Layla. The small woman slept with her head piled on her satchel—a tiny bag that carried little else besides a hunting knife, some twine, and the dark brown dress Ella had given her.

Ella smiled. So grumbling and defensive when she was awake, here and now she looked like nothing but a sweet and innocent child.

"What are you looking at?" Layla opened her eyes.

"Nothing," Ella grinned.

"Hmpf," said Layla, closing her eyes again.

Ella decided first to have a look at the broken rope and wood bridge. If it had been cut at the end, maybe someone could swim a line across and they could tie it back up. Not that swimming was an easy option, Ella thought, looking at the turbulent water.

She had no such luck. The bridge had been deliberately broken, rendered unusable, the rope frayed into thin strands. Reaching the bridge would be as difficult as reaching the far bank.

Sighing, she decided to walk along the riverbank.

It was pleasant to be alone in this beautiful valley, yet Ella's quest was constantly at the back of her mind. A thought came to her of Miro, fighting in some great battle, hurt and afraid. Ella had heard about the battlefield surgeons, and her greatest fear was Miro being tended by one. At least in Sarostar they used fresh water and sharp knives.

Ella felt determination return to her. The Lexicon was the backbone of her house; without it they would be crippled. With the Lexicon of Halaran also missing, the allies had little chance of winning this war. Ella was certain Killian had been involved with that theft as well, and finding him was her chance to make right this terrible wrong.

"If you don't want this, I'm going to have it," the voice came from beside Ella. She looked down to see Layla carrying Ella's satchel as well as her own.

Ella laughed. "Thanks."

They followed the riverbank together in silence. Clouds of butterflies rose in the air, drifting on the currents of a gentle breeze. Birdsong lilted and chimed, emanating from a small copse of swaying green trees.

"Maybe I should just try swimming," Ella murmured to herself.

"What did you say?"

"I said I'm going to try swimming," Ella said with determination.

"Swimming? You can swim through this?"

"I don't know. That's what I'm going to try. If I get across, I'll rest and then come back. If I can do it once, I can do it again. It looks difficult, though, so I should try this the first time without a line."

"I don't know if this is a good idea."

"We won't know if we don't try, will we?"

"I suppose so. Are you going to swim in your dress?"

Ella looked down at herself. "I'd rather not," she said.

She put her satchel down on the soft grass and without ceremony lifted her dress above her head. She carefully folded the garment and placed it on the grass. She then removed her underclothes; she would dry faster without them. Layla was looking studiously in the opposite direction.

It felt strange to be naked in the open like this. Ella knew there was no one there to see her—no one except Layla that was—but she still felt a blush rise to her cheeks.

It was almost spring weather, but there was still enough chill in the air to raise goose bumps on her white skin. Her pale blonde hair fell over her small breasts, reaching almost to her midriff.

"Do your people always inspect themselves like this?" Layla said.

Ella turned a deeper shade of red.

"Just watch out for me. See that fallen branch there, the long one? Keep that ready in case I need help."

"Yes, yes."

Ella looked meaningfully at Layla, hoping she'd made her point. Then, before she could think too much about it, she crouched, took a deep breath, and dived head first into the water.

It was icy cold, the water coming directly from its source below the hills. Ella popped to the surface of the river, gasping with the sharpness of the cold. The current was already pushing her downstream, away from the waterfalls above. She'd neglected to mention to Layla to keep up with her as she was pushed down the river. She hoped the healer was quick.

With heavy laboring strokes Ella pushed herself through the river, thankful for all of the time spent swimming in the Sarsen. This was nothing like the Sarsen, though; this was like a wild young buck compared to the sedate old man that was the great river of her homeland. As Ella was pushed one way and then the other, tossed around like a piece of wood, she tried to keep an eye on the bank ahead of her. She couldn't help but glance back to see how far she'd come.

Ella realized she would never make it.

She heard a voice yelling—it must have been Layla. Her hair floating in a cloud around her head, Ella tried to turn in the river. It was like trying to push against a stone wall. The current was speeding up, taking her with it, and she gave up on her overhead stroke, instead trying for a simple paddle. Her body slowly swung around, so she could now come to terms with her position.

The water was beginning to get rough, peaks and troughs forming in permanent waves. Ella suddenly realized there must be rocks under the surface. In panic, she looked further downstream, cursing herself for not scouting downriver before diving in.

The tips of jagged rocks protruded above the surface of the water, sharp enough to slice her open from head to toe.

Layla was running down the bank, shouting and pointing at the rocks. The healer held grimly onto the stick, desperately looking for an opportunity to hand it out. Ella realized she needed to slow down to give Layla an opportunity to get ahead of her, farther down the bank, and hold out the piece of wood.

Summoning the last of her strength, Ella fought against the current in an attempt to bring herself closer to the bank and give Layla the chance she needed.

Then she saw it.

The bank ended in a wall of stone, the river flowing past it into a canyon, sheer cliffs above and rapids below. Layla stood at the very limit, pressed against the rock wall, holding the branch out as far as she could.

Ella felt a rock under her foot, sharp and painful as she kicked it. Her body was thrown down into a trough and then up again, water splashing into her mouth. She spluttered and coughed as the water entered her lungs. She could hear Layla shouting.

With a final effort, she kicked out at the ground, her feet finding the riverbed for a heartbeat. She threw her arm out.

Ella caught hold of the branch, holding it in a grip of death. Layla struggled on the bank, her face red with exertion as she tried to hold Ella's weight against the current. Ella kicked out again, lunging toward the shore. With one hand clutching the branch and the other reaching out, she finally caught hold of the bank, dragging her naked body out of the raging river.

She fell onto her back, catching her breath, realizing how close she'd come to drowning. All because she hadn't taken the time to run down the riverbank and see what lay ahead.

"So stupid," Ella whispered to herself. "So stupid."

Ella woke to a warm liquid being poured down her throat, redolent with the taste of herbs and fungus. She coughed and sat up. She had a terrible headache.

"What . . . ?"

"It's an elixir. You took water from the river into your lungs. You're probably fine, but you need to take some herbs just in case."

"In case of what? What are you talking about?"

"In case bad spirits in the water affect your lungs and you grow sick, especially in your weakened state."

Ella was utterly exhausted. She was still naked, though two blankets now covered her. It had grown dark.

"Bad spirits in water?" she muttered, but her headache was starting to clear. "Thanks."

The healer just grunted.

"Can I have my dress?"

"Here you go. I brought everything down here. I thought you said you could swim the river."

Ella was growing to know Layla enough now to understand her strange sense of humor. She still didn't find it funny, though.

"I said I would try. I tried, and I failed."

"Don't be angry with yourself. It was brave of you to try."

"I'm not angry," Ella took a deep breath. "I'm just frustrated. I'm not sure what to do next."

"When we don't know what to do, we pray to the Eternal."

"The Eternal?"

"It is the spirit of the land, the thing that binds us all together. We are all connected by a strong force of attraction. When we give someone love, or hate, it affects it physically. This is the work of the Eternal."

"Physically?"

"Name when something good has come of hate in your life."

Ella sat up. "What do you mean?"

"Well, first think of something you have hated."

Ella thought of the broken heatplate, back at home in Mallorin. The times she'd cursed it. "How about the heatplate in my home in Sarostar?"

"That will do—it could be anything. How did your hate affect it? Did it respond well? Did it give you what you needed?"

Ella thought about it.

"Well, no. It was always broken. That's why I hated it."

"Now think of how you could have given it love."

Ella looked in the distance, pensive. She was an enchantress, yet she'd never renewed the heatplate, never even taken it in to be renewed. Why not?

"I could have done a lot of things, I guess. But that's just a heatplate. It's not a person."

"Trust me," said Layla. "With a person the effect is much greater. That is the Eternal at work."

Ella remained doubtful. "Is that all?"

"No, there is much more," Layla said. "Think of us. Look around at this valley. Look at the animals, the trees. Then look deeper, at the way the trees reach for the light, how their roots drink the water and eat from the soil. The land feeds the trees, and the sun helps them grow. The trees provide the shelter and food source for the insects, and the birds eat the insects. Do you see it?"

Ella nodded.

"Then answer me this. What if water—the water that falls from the sky—were poisonous? What would happen?"

Ella sat for a moment. "There would be no trees."

"No trees, no grass. No insects, no animals. No people."

"But I don't understand. Water isn't a poison."

"No, it is not. What I am trying to show you is that the land is in a delicate balance. One step in the wrong direction, and we would not be here in this beautiful valley. Who keeps this balance? What force is it that tells a motherless bird, after hatching from its egg, to leap into the air and fly? What force tells a bee to move from flower to flower, sharing the flowers' seed so they can breed? It is a fragile thing, this balance. It was put here by the Eternal, and it is our duty to maintain it."

Ella recalled the lessons of the priests, the stories of the Evermen Cycles. It was a very different sermon she had grown up with, stories of battles and betrayal and the origin of lore.

"So will you pray?" Layla said.

"I'm not sure."

"Then I will pray for both of us."

The next day Ella woke to the calls of the birds, Layla's words still in her ears. Layla's beliefs were so different. It didn't sound like the worship of a deity—a man or woman being with incredible powers. It was instead a worship of the land, of nature itself. The message was simple: give love and you will receive love; keep the balance of nature that was so perfectly created for people to live in.

Layla was already awake, staring into the river.

"Did you pray?" Ella said. Somehow, the image of one of the Dunfolk on their knees making obeisance didn't seem right.

"Of course. I closed my eyes and slept. Did you?"

"Well, if that's what it takes, then I suppose I did."

"And what did you decide?"

Ella realized she had made a decision after all. "We need to build a raft."

———————◆———————

Ella spoke as she worked, tearing one of her favorite dresses into strips. "It will take time to build the raft, most likely the entire day. We've already lost a lot of time and I'm concerned that Killian—I mean, the thief—will be getting away from us."

Layla nodded. "He knows where he is going. It will be difficult to catch up to him."

"We have one advantage, though. The river flows in the direction we need to go in. South." She gestured to the turbulent water. "And as we already know, it's fast."

Layla looked at Ella skeptically. "What do you need me to do?"

"I need you to find me young trees. Preferably dead, but alive will do as well. They need to be of wood that is light, but hard—wood that will be resistant to water." She measured a diameter with her hands, about six inches. "I need about twenty of them."

Layla set off. Ella continued tearing strips until she thought she had enough. She carefully enchanted each strip to be strong yet flexible and to resist the water, a simple enough matrix.

Ella then took Layla's hunting knife and placed it on the tree stump in front of her. She took more care with her enchantment this time—the knife would need to be both sharp and tough enough to cut through wood. She added some extra runes and then decided she was finished.

323

Layla returned. "I have found the trees."

"Show me," said Ella.

Ella put some things in the pocket of her dress and the rest of her tools away in her satchel, and followed Layla to a sparse forest.

"I could not find dead trees, so I found live ones," said Layla.

It wasn't as good, but it would have to do, and the trees were the right size.

"What are you going to do?" Layla said.

"The cultivators of House Vezna use their lore on trees and plants," said Ella. She took the vial of essence from a pocket in her dress. "The problem is, because lore cannot be used on living things, the essence inevitably kills the trees."

She carefully dipped the scrill in essence and touched it to the skin of the first tree. She then moved along the trees, touching a tiny amount of black liquid to each tree in turn.

"Is something supposed to happen?" Layla said.

Ella took Layla's hand and led her to the first tree she had touched. "Watch," she said.

It took some time for there to be a noticeable effect. Then Ella pointed at the leaves of the tree. They'd turned a darker shade of green, sickly veins sprouting along from the place Ella had marked. Some of the leaves began to curl slightly.

"It will take a while longer. We'll return after a meal and see how they're going."

They periodically checked on the saplings as they prepared themselves for the river. By the evening the trees had lost their leaves completely, and the branches were now like skeletons, as dry as bone. Ella still wasn't happy that the trees weren't ready, and she cursed every moment they were delayed.

In the early hours of the morning, Ella was woken by a series of mighty thumps. At first she shot up, fearful and eyes open wide. The sun was just beginning to rise. The morning air was still and cool.

"Good, you are awake," Layla said, standing at the edge of the camp. "The trees—I think they are ready for us to make them into a raft."

The saplings had fallen down under their own weight. Their bark was dry and hard. They were completely dead.

Ella set to work with the hunting knife, which she had enchanted to cut through wood like butter.

"Tu-mah," Ella spoke the activation rune. The knife lit with a satisfying glow.

She first trimmed the branches and roots, then took off the remaining knobs and points, until she was left with twenty fairly straight lengths of wood.

One by one they took the logs to the riverbank. Layla knew some strong knots, and they tied the logs in a row, one to the other. Ella then made some quick rune sequences on the joints to give them added strength.

Ella looked at Layla, taking a slow breath. They regarded the raft.

It was simple—just a platform of logs, really—but it looked strong, and with Ella's added enchantments she thought it would serve their purpose. There was enough space for the two women, their possessions, and little else.

"I think we're ready," said Ella.

"I think you may have missed something," said Layla.

Ella looked over the raft. She checked each joint, each connection. "What?"

Layla reached over to where she had something tucked away, something made of wood.

"I made these," she said. She withdrew two carved paddles.

"Oh," said Ella. How could she have forgotten paddles? "Well done."

Layla smiled.

They were ready.

───◆───

One of their first problems was that the current wanted to carry the raft away before they were ready. They pulled the raft to the shore, with half of it in the water and the other half on the bank. The river pushed at the wooden logs, running up through the spaces in between. Ella quickly put her satchel over her shoulder, Layla already holding hers.

"You go first," Ella said.

Layla jumped onto the raft. Her weight made the raft sink onto the bank.

Ella pushed. The raft moved only slightly. She pushed harder and it began to move, faster as the river caught it. She quickly gave a big push and then jumped on. For a moment her extra weight slowed the motion of the raft, but then suddenly they were in the river. They were away.

The first hazard to negotiate was the series of jagged rocks that had almost caught Ella previously. The two women paddled furiously. The raft tended to plunge into the water at the front, so they tried to keep their weight on the back, Ella paddling on the right side and Layla on the left.

Ella heard a scratching sound as they went over a rock and held her breath. Fortunately, the raft stayed strong.

Then they were heading directly for a sharp stone the size of a man, jutting out of the water. Ella paddled furiously to turn them to the left. Then she realized Layla was doing the same, canceling out her own strokes.

"Paddle backward!" she yelled.

Layla just looked at her blankly. Ella had no choice; she began to paddle backward. They turned to the right, but they were too late, and the raft smashed against the side of the rock, scraping against it. Layla was nearly knocked off the raft, but Ella reached for her, the raft tilting dangerously until Layla regained her position.

Then they entered calmer, deeper water. They were past danger for the time being.

Ella let out a breath of relief. The river still flowed with speed, and she judged them to be traveling faster than a running man. Ella and Layla continued to paddle, increasing their speed still further. They were regaining the time they had lost.

They would occasionally see strange birds and animals on the banks. A tall bird with thick legs ducked its entire head under the water and kept it there for a surprising amount of time before reappearing with a fish in its beak. A capering, cat-sized animal with brown fur and small horns danced in the treetops.

Butterflies twisted and turned in a growing breeze, the rushing sound of the river combining with the buzz of insects to create a general background hum, the song of nature.

As the morning moved into midday, the sun came out in force, dispelling the chill of the night. Ella even started to feel hot, working up a sweat with the constant paddling.

The river grew still wider, slowing its frantic pace. It looked like a good time to break their fast with some cold rabbit and wild mushrooms.

"I miss my people," said Layla suddenly.

Ella nodded as she sighed. She had wondered when this would be coming. Layla had proved to be an invaluable tracker and traveling companion. Ella might even call her a friend.

"When we come to the road and we've confirmed that he's still going in the same direction, you can go home then," Ella said.

Layla nodded. "I will go home then."

"I . . . I want to thank you for helping me," Ella said.

"You have given me a gift."

"Is that the only reason you're helping me? Because I gave you something in return?"

Layla was pensive for a moment. "It has been good to come to understand you a little, your people, your ways. You are different. I think you still have a lot to learn about the world."

"I guess we all do." Ella paused, watching the bank roll by. "Layla, do you think I could call you my friend?"

Ella wasn't sure what answer she expected. She realized then, that after Miro and Amber, she didn't really have any other friends. Even though Layla was so different, with Miro gone and Amber married, it was good to have someone to talk to.

She turned and met Layla's eyes. Dunfolk eyes. "We are friends, Ella. Of course we are. Did you think we weren't?"

* * *

Ella was pleased with the progress they made. The river had narrowed again, and with it came a corresponding increase in speed. At one stage they passed through a great canyon, its sides made of shiny black volcanic glass. At other places the bank was wide and marshy, with tall tufted grass that played host to a myriad of wildlife. The sun sank in the sky, and as the last vestiges of a vermillion sunset disappeared into darkness, Ella took out the rock she had made into a nightlamp.

"Tish-tassine," she intoned, the warm glow of the runes lighting up the raft.

Shortly after, a crescent moon outlined a broad shape against the night sky. A bridge.

"The road." Ella grinned.

"Yes, the road," Layla echoed.

"Quick—we need to stop."

Ella began to paddle toward the narrow strip of riverbank. The raft moved ponderously; they were in the middle of a wide part in the river here, but the flow was still fast. Surprisingly fast. Ella could hear a sound carried on the night air.

"What's that sound?" Ella said.

It grew louder until it became a gentle roar. It sounded like heavy rain or a furious wind. Ella began to grown concerned as she saw they were still far from the bank. The current grew rapid, swifter than ever before. The raft bobbed along, caught in the inevitable surge.

Ella realized what the sound was.

"Paddle!" she cried. "It's a waterfall!"

Ella pulled at the paddle as hard as she could, and the raft slowly moved across the river as the bank sped by.

Ella heard a shriek and turned. Layla was staring, transfixed, her hand across her mouth. Then Ella saw it too.

Just ahead, the river fell away into nothingness. They would never make it.

Ella's mind went blank. She thought of nothing, just gazed at her impending doom.

The raft flew on the swift water.

They went over.

Ella screamed as she fell. She lost contact with the raft immediately. The nightlamp was lost, and suddenly everything was in darkness. She could only hear the roar of the cascading water. Her body twisted one way, then another, as she plummeted through the air.

Then she hit where the water churned itself into froth. For a heartbeat Ella floated on the foam before she was slammed deep underwater, pummeled mercilessly with the strength of a thousand hammers into the cavity created by the action of eons.

Ella's vision turned black, then white. Her ears hummed and shrieked, while her head felt like it would explode. Her lungs screamed from the lack of air, desperately trying to convince her to open her mouth and suck in whatever she might find. Some sensible part of Ella held fast.

The water rolled her over again and again, and Ella lost all sense of up and down. Suddenly the pressure eased, and she knew she was away from the base of the waterfall.

Still underwater, Ella opened her eyes but could see only shadows. Her lungs screaming, she picked a direction and swam. Her head smashed into a rock and she almost blacked out, taking in a mouthful of water. With her arms in front of her head, she tried again. Finally, Ella's head broke free of the surface and she gasped in sweet air.

Coughing and choking, she gathered herself and looked around. Where was Layla? Where was the raft?

There were shapes poking their heads out of the water, many of them. Ella peered into the dark, then realized what they were. More rocks. She had to get out of the water.

She tried to swim but her arm was tangled in something. Ella realized it was her satchel; she'd somehow kept it. She untangled herself, her dress dragging her down, her satchel making it difficult to move her arms for fear of losing it. With a great effort she swam the distance to the rocky bank without cutting herself on the sharp stones.

Heaving herself out of the water, Ella finally found dry ground. She collapsed and fell into darkness.

33

*What lies behind us and what lies before us are as nothing when
compared to what lies within us.*
> —Sermons of Primate Melovar Aspen, 536 Y.E.

Miro gingerly touched the scar on his cheek. It was about a finger's
width, running from below his left eye to his jaw line.

He stood, stone faced, in the circle of the bladesingers' conference as Blademaster Rogan prepared to speak.

The bladesingers looked on, their matching green silk and *raj hada*
bold and challenging. Something of import was about to be said.

Much had changed after the test. Miro had barely come away from
it with his life; the wound in his side had been deep. Fortunately,
the surgeon had a steady hand, and some honey and wine had prevented the spread of infection. The slice across Miro's face was less
serious, but it also needed stitching.

Bartolo had almost bled to death. His grueling fight had lasted
for so long that Bartolo only won through sheer tenacity when the

lore in the golem's limbs became depleted, but not before he took a wound on his upper thigh that caused his life's blood to spill out onto the sandy floor.

Ronell had taken a different tactic. He had toyed with the golem, merely defending, trying to get it far enough away that it couldn't protect its controller.

Then he'd killed the animator.

The bladesingers now had three new men to their number. Miro's armorsilk—his own this time, not the set Ronell had substituted—now bore the red-trimmed *raj hada* of a full bladesinger. Nevertheless, the three new recruits were nowhere near enough to replace the bladesingers' losses.

When their new members had healed sufficiently, they were welcomed into the fraternity with a feast. Conversation had naturally revolved around the war. The Halrana were completely focused around taking back their capital, Ralanast, and sealing their border with Loua Louna in the north. Miro didn't hear the undeclared houses discussed once. Prince Leopold was proving to be an indecisive commander, more willing to follow the lead of others than lead himself. The result was that their entire combined force was focused on the re-conquest of Ralanast.

Miro could understand their motivation. Ralanast was a wealthy city of large population. Her people would be crying for freedom from the tyranny of the Black Army.

But the Halrana capital had little strategic importance. They were taking men out of the Ring Forts, weakening their strongest position, and sending them into what would inevitably be a deadly conflict. A conflict that could very likely see much of Ralanast destroyed.

That had been two weeks ago. Sark was now a memory.

Their great army had pushed forward. The Alturans with their bladesingers, enchanters, and well-equipped heavy infantry; the Halrana with their smaller numbers of regular infantry, but cart upon cart of constructs. The huge carts were pulled along by drudges—menial constructs made of wood, strong and simple. Interspersed down the long train and guiding the drudges were the animators themselves.

Dirigibles floated overhead, providing warning about lurking enemy forces. Scouts ran in all directions, seeking news of enemy movements and testing the lay of the land. At night the enchanters set up wards and alarms; the animators put out iron golem sentries.

The enemy had backed away, leaving barren ground and little else. They'd pulled back north, past the upper reaches of the Ring Forts. Leaving the fortresses' protection completely, the army had followed them into northern Halaran.

Blademaster Rogan now openly derided their strategy. He knew what was about to happen, with a dangerous foe withdrawing to the north and the occupied city of Ralanast now to the west.

Prince Leopold gave the order to split the army. Some would stay to guard against the enemy to the north, but the bulk would try to take back Ralanast.

No one said it, but everyone knew. Neither of the new armies would be sufficiently close for the Ring Forts to provide reinforcement in the event of a defeat.

With the split expected any day, the blademaster addressed his men.

"Bladesingers, this is the farthest north we have come in our travels," Rogan said. "As you know, we lie between the borders of two nations—Halaran and Loua Louna." He paused for effect. "But to our north lies the border of another house." He gazed around, meeting the eyes of each man in turn. "Vezna, the land of the cultivators. They stay silent while around us men die. We cannot miss this opportunity. I have no permission from high command; I have sought none. But I propose we find out where the cultivators stand rather than **idly sit by** and **wait for them** to throw their lot in with the Black Army. We need to find out what's causing the other high lords to join with the emperor. Perhaps our answers lie with the Veznans. Can I hear support for my proposal?"

"Altura!" the bladesingers shouted.

Rogan smiled. "Good. I will hear plans for an information-gathering mission. Remember, stealth and secrecy are the priorities here."

He withdrew into the perimeter of the circle. Bladesinger Huron Gower walked into the middle.

"Once in Veznan lands, the trees will provide plenty of cover. It's getting through enemy lines that will be the problem. Our best bet is to use the cover of Tovitch Forest, then the Sarsen itself—it's shallow and wide in these parts."

He received a rumble of assent from the circle.

Huron continued. "One man. One man only, in the black armorsilk. He can be shadowed by the rest of us for part of the way, protected for a time. We can provide a distraction, but it is my opinion that one man stands the best chance of slipping through enemy lines alone."

"But who?" called one of the bladesingers from the circle.

Some names were bandied about. Then, to Miro's complete surprise, he heard his own name.

Perhaps he shouldn't have been surprised. Something of a legend had grown up around him since the test. He probably had the animator to thank for that. The Halrana simply couldn't believe that an unarmored man had defeated an iron golem, even with a zenblade. Miro had been quizzed at length, but with nothing to prove about Ronell's involvement, he just said he'd picked up the wrong set of armorsilk. The bladesingers thought it was hilarious. But they'd also looked at him with a new respect.

"Miro," someone else said his name again.

Huron nodded. "It was Miro who asked the enchanters for the black armorsilk. He can obviously fight without the full armor—something some of us may depend too much on—and he is not one I would wish to face in battle." He grinned. "Plus, he had a problem with his last testing, so this would be a good final test."

Blademaster Rogan called out, "Can I hear an assent?"

"Aye!"

"Miro, do you accept the request?"

Miro felt he was being swept up in the tide of events. "I do."

"Good. Let's work out the details. We'll leave tonight."

***

They swept through their own army, a single man in black followed by a phalanx in green silk. Not one soldier queried them on the way. None were prepared to challenge the bladesingers.

The moon cast a silver glow on the hills that separated the two armies. The enemy were encamped in a wide crescent, the western edge of which touched on Tovitch Forest to the north. There was no chance of going unseen—the Black Army had erected huge towers on all fronts, dirigibles floated above, and sentries patrolled ceaselessly.

At some unspoken command, first one and then another of the bladesingers began his song. The runes flared as they were activated, and the armorsilk took on the strength of mountains, the lightness of air.

They ran like the wind over and down the hills, a speeding triangle of elemental figures. As they ran, they drew their swords and added the zenblades' song.

335

The enemy responded with deadly speed. Soldiers poured down to support the western point of the encampment. Mortars sparked, and orbs began to rain down in the midst of the bladesingers. Six dirigibles covered the approach before the bladesingers had even reached the defenses, ready to pour fire on those below.

Slightly to the side, unseen and unnoticed in the commotion, Miro ran with them. He sang only for lightness, speed, and shadow. He was a black void among bright stars. Their song stirred his blood, and he wanted nothing more than to draw his zenblade and join them in the attack.

Miro suddenly saw a wide ditch yawning ahead of him, the bottom lined with steel spikes. It was thirty paces wide, as long as five men were tall. He saw his comrades about him leaping like birds as he took a breath, timing it to his chant, and jumped. The air whistled past his ears; he landed with a thud and kept running.

Dirigibles dropped prismatic orbs onto the bladesingers, who made for easy targets. Plumes of flame and smoke rose as detonations tore up the ground. Explosions sounded again and again. Not far from Miro, dirt spewed out of the ground, tossing a bladesinger into the air. He kept singing, though, and landed deftly on his feet.

Miro heard the clash of arms as battle was joined, and veered off. He entered Tovitch Forest.

The trees here were different from the trees of the Dunwood. The Dunwood was wild and untamed; this forest was more sculpted. The evergreens were evenly spaced a few paces apart, and he had no trouble weaving through them.

Miro slowed to a ground-eating lope, but thoughts rushed through his mind. He knew how important his mission was. Prince Leopold only saw the immediate, only thought about the next coming battle. But there were many who knew there was some strange force at play, that there were greater questions that needed answering.

The moon passed across the sky as Miro ran through the night. The trees of Tovitch Forest thinned, and he saw the glint of water ahead and gave up his chanting. Plunging into the icy water of the Sarsen, Miro waded to the other side, then stood on the bank for a moment, panting, his breath coming out as steam. The water ran down his black silk; at least he had that comfort.

Miro regarded Veznan lands for a moment, then entered.

This was a new forest—that much was clear. The trees were even more planned than those before, grove upon grove of every species carefully given its own space and separated from the others.

As Miro penetrated deeper into the forest, the species grew ever stranger. Soon he saw trees with two trunks, each at an angle to the other like legs. The big gnarled branches looked like arms, each the size of a man. They were still trees, though, sleeping, unmoving.

The questions became clearer now.

Who was leading the Black Army? What motive brought their enemy together in war, a war that meant only death and disaster? What strange force was taking away the houses' independence?

If the high lord of House Vezna was going to throw his lot in with the emperor, now would be the time. Perhaps Miro would find the answers they were all looking for.

Perhaps Miro was about to find out the truth.

34

*We need to always ensure there are safeguards against the
Tingaran emperor seizing control of Stonewater. Reader,
you may think this a strange note of caution, coming from me,
but this new balance is an effective one. We are like a three-legged
table. Each leg is balanced by the other two—the Houses
balance the Assembly of Templars, the Assembly balances the
Imperial House, and the Imperial House balances the other houses.
If the Imperial House were to control the source of essence,
the houses would become powerless. The emperor would be
a leader no more. He would be a tyrant.*
—Memoirs of Emperor Xenovere I, page 195, 381 Y.E.

Vezna's capital of Rosarva could not really be termed a city. It was
more like an organism, but an organism that, like many things
Veznan, was planned in detail.

Inhabitants were allowed to apply for a permit to move their
dwelling, perhaps to be closer to work or family. If the permit was
granted, the four trees that made up the dwelling's supports, walls, and
ceiling walked to a different part of Rosarva and replanted their roots.

Rosarva's avenues were broad and lined with carefully pruned hedges to separate one flow of traffic from another. Walking on the wrong side was a punishable crime. Still, the many rules that governed a Veznan's life were necessary—in a place that changed with the seasons, where services changed location from month to month, the regulations provided a much-needed sense of order.

There was an area, though, that hadn't changed in centuries.

The Borlag.

It was an island, separated from the rest of Rosarva by a wide moat. People didn't loiter near the Borlag. They entered, conducted their business, and quickly left with their eyes downcast. Intruders weren't tolerated—the seemingly innocuous lily pads floating in the water needed regular feeding.

The Borlag was only accessible via the Juno Bridge—a narrow, living bridge that needed to be replanted at regular intervals after the essence worked its way through the bridge's system and killed it. An activation sequence, known only to a select few, had to be spoken in order for a man to be allowed on the Juno Bridge. If any other tried to cross the bridge, giant thorns came out of the wood, impaling the man instantly.

Uninvited guests were not tolerated in the Borlag.

On the island itself, soldiers patrolled a wide park surrounding a great palace made of stone and wood. This was the residence of the Veznan high lord.

High Lord Vladimir Corizon and his son, Prince Dimitri, sat in an audience chamber, high in the upper levels of the immense palace. They were dressed in Veznan formal wear, plaited orange garments with bows and stripes. A thin man in white—so thin as to be emaciated—conversed with them. Next to him sat a tall man with a shaved head. Where the tall man's right arm should have been was an arm of metal.

"I noticed your gaze, young Prince Dimitri. Please do not mind Moragon here," the thin man said, his tone friendly. "He lost his arm in an accident. It was a miracle of the emperor's arts that they were able to graft an arm of lore onto his living flesh."

"My son may be curious, Primate, but he is not fearful. Just tell us what we need to know," said High Lord Vladimir.

The thin man continued. "Of course, High Lord," he gave a small bow. "Please indulge me for a moment, though. You see, it's important that we are on an equal footing, that we know all of the facts before negotiations can begin. My role as primate has changed slightly. My Assembly of Templars itself has . . . changed. Knowledge is a powerful thing."

"Changed? In what way?"

The primate didn't answer immediately. He swirled a glass in his hand, gazing into its depths as light glistened off the surface of the oily black liquid inside. He took a small sip, grimacing at the taste, and then looked up. The primate's eyes had a strange yellow sheen, yet he seemed perfectly healthy.

"There are many things one learns, being the custodian of a substance as powerful as *raj ichor*. Essence, you may prefer to call it. I came upon this secret many years ago, quite by accident. It was in an ancient book, a relic of the Evermen. I could scarcely believe it at first—after all, what do I know about lore? I do know something about essence, however. And what I discovered promised to change the world forever."

"I thought we were here to discuss treaties," said High Lord Vladimir. "You've changed, Melovar Aspen, I can see that. Yet I don't really care for what you have to say. All I care about is the safety of my people."

"Hush, High Lord," said Primate Melovar Aspen. "My meaning will become clear soon enough."

"Be careful of how you speak to my father," said Dimitri Corizon. "He deserves respect."

"Yes, Prince. Of course. Now, if I may continue?" The primate took another sip of the drink. "Where was I? Ah, that's right. My discovery. I found it in a book, yes; however, the book was not in my possession, and I was not able to take the book by force. I really wanted this information, you see.

"I knew someone who was close to this book, so I had sections of it copied by one I converted to my cause, however reluctant she was at the start. It was difficult, but it was important, perhaps the most important discovery of all time."

"What are you talking about?" the Veznan high lord said.

"You see, in this book I discovered that essence has an opposite. I was upset to discover this, because it is my duty to know all there is to know about *raj ichor*. But, yes, essence has an opposite. It's called *raj nilas*." The thin man paused. "What does that mean? Well, where essence creates the rune structures, *raj nilas* destroys them. Permanently. Do you understand, High Lord, Prince? I had found a way to destroy the runes. But there was also a second discovery, perhaps just as important. For where *raj ichor* is a poison—perhaps the deadliest poison in existence—*raj nilas* is an elixir. In fact, that's the name I have given my new liquid. Elixir."

The primate took another sip from his glass.

"It took me many years. I can't tell you how many men died until I had the formula right—they must number in the thousands." He frowned. "I suspect my contact was withholding information. There were some early . . . mistakes. My will endured, however, and I eventually had something I could work with."

The thin man in white continued to swirl the liquid, as if finding some secret in the crystal glass. "It has unbelievable properties, this liquid. It stops the aging process completely." He chuckled, a dry rasping sound. "It's a shame I was already so old." He took another tiny sip, his face contorting in distaste as he swallowed. "It also increases the regenerative powers of the body, to a fantastic extent. Behold."

The primate drew a rune-covered knife from his belt, and without warning slashed it across Moragon's living hand. The man with the shaved head and grafted arm simply smiled, not even flinching. As the Veznans gaped, the wound resealed itself, leaving only the faintest hint of a scar.

"Such a tedious task, managing the essence quotas, keeping the houses balanced. Even the emperor needed his share. It was easy, though—if the emperor wants too much, tell the houses and he'll back down. If the houses want too much, tell the emperor, and they'll back down. The houses watch each other. A delicate balance, but one that has worked for many years, to a greater or lesser extent." The primate licked his lips. "However, there is one group for whom the balance has not worked out so well. The wives without husbands and children without parents. The dispossessed: victims of the past wars among the houses. We get thousands of them coming to us templars every year. But what can we do to help? We have no lore, and so we have no gilden. In fact, what does lore really do for the world? All it seems to do is provide us with more efficient ways of killing each other. There is much technical progress that was lost in our pursuit of lore. Perhaps we might all be better off without it."

Primate Melovar Aspen tilted the glass back again, finishing the contents. He sighed and looked up, noting the Veznans' glances at each other. At Moragon.

"Trust me. You will be interested in my offer. Where was I? Ah, that's right. The secret. High Lord Vladimir, may I ask you, would you like to live forever? To stop aging?"

"At what cost? What is it you aren't telling me?" the high lord said. "I thought we were here to discuss a treaty, not to talk about eternal life. What is this madness?"

"But we are, High Lord. We are discussing a treaty. I'm here to give you a choice. You can have the terms you are seeking. You will contribute your forces to my Black Army, as have the high lords of House Torakon and House Loua Louna before you, and we will keep you safe. All I ask is that you have a small taste of what I offer. You will have the peace you seek, your borders will be protected, and you will have all your many, many years to see your people prosper."

"No," said the high lord.

"Why not?" said the thin man in white. He glanced at the son, Dimitri.

"Father, he is drinking it as we speak. What harm can it do? Even if it doesn't do everything he claims, we can help our people."

"Dimitri, do as I say. Do not accept this man's gifts."

Prince Dimitri Corizon eyed the flask of black liquid resting on a low table next to the primate. The thoughts were visibly crossing his face: eternal youth, powers of regeneration.

"Oh, and your other option? Your other option is that I can destroy your Lexicon. I am not speaking about lack of renewal, about allowing your magic to fade. I am speaking of permanent destruction, made possible by *raj nilas*. House Vezna will be no more. Your civilization will sink into the swamp. Your famous living city will rot and die."

"You don't have our Lexicon, and nor will you."

"Do you really think you can last? I've already given the same offer to the emperor. To High Lord Koraku of Torakon. To High Lord Raoul of the artificers. You know where they stand. You can join them by standing with me. Think of what I offer—the death of your house or eternal life. Here, taste it."

The thin man smiled and refilled his glass from the flask. He held it out to Prince Dimitri.

In an instant Dimitri took the glass and touched it to his lips.

"Dimitri, no," said the high lord.

Prince Dimitri took the smallest of sips, grimacing at the taste and set the glass down. The thin man took the glass back, while Moragon leaned forward in his seat, his smile broadening.

High Lord Vladimir shook his head. "You should not have done that, my son."

"It was just a taste," said Dimitri.

"Well done, Prince Dimitri," said the primate. "The borders of your land are now secure. Once your people join with us, you will be part of something bigger, something great, a new order for the world." His gaze became unfocused. "The high lords will live forever. There will be no more displacement of power, no voids left by departing rulers. People will live and work together in harmony. No more disparate houses. And eventually, elixir will be available to all. Tell me, Dimitri, how do you feel?"

"It feels . . . amazing. I feel strong." The young prince's expression was rapturous.

"Join with you?" High Lord Vladimir said with contempt. "You are nothing but a servant, a priest, a templar. Why would anyone follow you? This meeting is over."

The primate smiled. "I was discussing the properties of this amazing liquid," he said. "It comes from the further processing of essence. Did I mention that? There is only one small drawback for so many benefits." His smile widened. "It is addictive. Like nothing you have ever experienced. And," he nodded at Dimitri, "because this is your first time, you are going to feel it with full force."

Dimitri shook his head.

"I've heard the pain of withdrawal from this liquid is similar to the pain of essence poisoning. You'll be starting to feel it now. Ah, yes, there it goes. Remember, my son, all you need to make the pain go away is a little more."

Dimitri's eyes began to look feverish, and sweat rose on his brow. "Make it stop."

"A little more?" the primate handed the glass out again.

"No!" the high lord said.

Dimitri reached for the glass, but High Lord Vladimir knocked it out of the primate's hands.

"Guards!" the high lord called.

Moragon moved, faster than the eye could follow—a blur of motion. He latched the heavy door, and then, before either Veznan could react, he pinned the high lord's arms back behind him.

"Now, I'll be happy to give you a little more, Prince Dimitri, but first there is something I need you to do. Just a simple task, and then you can have all you want. Are you ready?" Dimitri whimpered. "I want you to kill your father," the primate said, smiling.

Guards began to pound on the door.

"Never," Dimitri said. His eyes were turning red; he started to twitch. "It hurts so much."

"A little more?" the primate asked again, looking at the flask and raising an inquiring eyebrow.

The guards called out. They began to attempt to knock down the sturdy door.

Moragon grinned.

Dimitri started to groan. A keening sound came from his mouth. "It hurts, oh, it hurts so much! Give it to me!"

Prince Dimitri suddenly lunged at the primate, who danced out of reach, his agility defying his apparent frailty. Panting, Dimitri fell to the floor.

"Kill your father," the primate said. He held out a knife, while Moragon kept the high lord pinned to his chair.

"Have strength," High Lord Vladimir Corizon whispered.

Dimitri began to writhe. His eyes developed a yellow hue, and foam started to appear at his lips.

"You know what you need to do," Moragon said.

With a great effort, Dimitri stood, lurching like a drunken man. For a moment, it seemed he would attack the primate. Then he snatched the knife from the primate's hand and ran the cutting edge across his own throat.

The wound lay open for a heartbeat before resealing itself.

Dimitri screamed with anguish; there was no refuge, no escape from the pain. His eyes darted about before he made his decision.

The blade in Dimitri's trembling hand lashed out, slicing across High Lord Vladimir Corizon's throat.

"Now, give me more," Dimitri said.

The primate handed over the black liquid. Dimitri tipped it back. He fell into his chair, the strength gone out of him.

Moragon heaved the corpse of the Veznan high lord onto his shoulder and walked to the open window. Without ceremony Moragon dropped the body, and a moment later a great splash sounded as the high lord's corpse entered the moat that surrounded the Borlag.

"Congratulations, High Lord Dimitri Corizon. Now, inform the guards of your new position. And if you have any doubts, remember: I am your only source for the elixir."

"What . . . what do I say?"

The primate shrugged. "Assassin? I'm sure you'll think of something."

Moragon unlatched the door. Several soldiers in the orange of House Vezna stood in the doorway with weapons bared. Dimitri Corizon rushed forward to confront the guards before they saw the pool of blood.

"Quickly, I think there's an assassin! My father was at the window, looking out. He saw something and cried out. I think he fell into the moat!"

The guard paled as he looked past the prince's shoulder at the open window and gestured to the other soldiers. "The grounds. Come on!"

The guards rushed away as Dimitri put his head in his hands.

"Well done, my son. We will make a proud ruler of you yet." The primate leaned forward, offering the flask. "Another drink?"

There was a noise from immediately outside: a human sound of pain that seemed to come from the window ledge.

Guards called to each other from below, coordinating their efforts.

"I think there really is someone out there," said Moragon.

A black figure moved past the window.

35

The Buchalanti are my most beloved of the many houses.
There are no people more free. Perhaps I was raised by
House Buchalantas in another life.
—Toro Marossa, "Explorations," page 162, 423 Y.E.

High Enchantress Evora Guinestor hid her impatience as she waited for the men to deploy. The four bladesingers with her chatted quietly among themselves, calm and unperturbed as always. Joram, the captain of her guard, sent scouts in all directions. He checked over each man in turn, frowning at one, before he turned to the high enchantress.

"Ready to move out, High Enchantress."

"Thank you, Captain." Evora's voice was dry; she didn't care any more whether he would detect it.

They had made camp on the floor of the valley while the men attempted to turn the remnants of the rope bridge into a working version. Forced to wait, Evora had to admit, it was a beautiful valley.

If only she weren't seething inside.

Soon, the power of the Lexicon would fade, and every object that had been enchanted with its runes would fail. Unless she could renew the Lexicon in time, Altura's lore would fail, most likely when those fighting needed it the most.

The enemy's Alturan-made weapons would also fail, but the builders would still build, the artificers' dirigibles would still fly, and the emperor's avengers would still fight on.

It would be a massacre.

Every moment lost was a moment further that the thief had to escape. Evora understood her men felt the need to protect her, especially given what had happened to the Halrana high animator, but it was taking too much time.

Evora had received Ella's message that the thief had gone south rather than north just as she caught up with the ragged beggar they'd been chasing all this time. Evora had almost gone from being furious with the girl to investing in her, hoping that at least someone would catch up with the thief. Ella was an enchantress after all—she stood some chance, didn't she?

Evora's lips thinned. What chance did Ella have against the thief who stole Altura's Lexicon from the heart of the Crystal Palace, killing a bladesinger on the way out? Not much of one.

Still, the young enchantress had proven to be remarkably resourceful. Her trackers had confirmed that Ella was on the correct path, that a few days behind the path of the thief were the tracks of a young woman and the less discernible tracks of a smaller woman. One of the Dunfolk, she must be.

Evora had no idea how Ella had managed to get one of the Dunfolk to help her. But the girl had done it, and here she was, making a mockery of Evora's own efforts to track down the thief.

"The Dunfolk woman is very good, High Enchantress," Joram said. "We almost lost him on the cliff. If it hadn't been for the rope hanging down . . ."

Evora bridled. Was she that obvious? Had this become some kind of pathetic contest? Then she relaxed her shoulders. The result was the only thing that mattered. The rope had shown just how resourceful Ella could be. If only they'd figured out how she'd crossed the river. The trackers had said it looked like Ella had entered the water, and looking for a hundred paces down the river, they hadn't found an exit point. The Dunfolk woman's tracks were nearly invisible at the best of times.

Enough thinking about them. "The rope bridge—is it done?"

"Yes, High Enchantress."

"Then let us cross in haste."

"At once, High Enchantress."

Evora sighed. She hoped that whatever happened, Ella would slow the thief down. Even if it meant the girl came to harm at his hands. The return of the Lexicon was worth it.

Evora felt guilty at the thought.

The bladesingers moved out, radiating calm as always. The high enchantress strode forward, her head high. Her green silk dress drew glances from the men. She knew they wondered what she was capable of; the soldiers stayed carefully out of her way.

Suddenly, before crossing the precarious-looking rope bridge, Evora stopped, looking at the soldiers around her—nearly forty fighting men. "From the other side of this bridge we increase our speed," she said. "We march from two hours before dawn to two hours after sunset. Nightlamps will guide our way. Soldiers, you are on the most important mission of your lives. I want speed." She locked eyes with Captain Joram. "Give me speed."

"You heard the high enchantress: Move out. Double time."

Her mouth set in a grim line, Evora set the pace.

36

If you don't climb the mountain, you cannot view the plain.
—Sermons of Primate Melovar Aspen, 536 Y.E.

Ella woke some time before dawn to bruised ribs and freezing cold. As she shivered, her mind numb, she fumbled around for her satchel. Inside it was the simple heatplate. She took it out and placed it on the ground.

"*Sahl-an-tour.*" The runes came to life, instantly emitting a soft glow and gentle heat.

For a long moment Ella just held her hands over the heat until the shivering subsided and she could think clearly enough to take stock of her situation.

She was still in her wet dress. She wasn't sure if it was better to stay in wet clothing or to take it off, but decided it would dry more quickly if she removed it. Gasping and wheezing with the cold, Ella found a long branch and erected it over the heatplate. Then she removed her clothing and draped it over the branch. Naked now, she brought her body as close as she could to the life-giving warmth.

She had her satchel, but she knew she'd lost the nightlamp. Suddenly frantic, she searched the bag, breathing a sigh of relief when she found the essence and two scrills. The precious liquid was starting to run low, but at least the bottle had stayed intact. The rest of Ella's clothing was completely soaked through. She moved the bag closer to the heatplate. Hopefully, some of the warmth would reach through to it.

Thinking dark thoughts, Ella curled up next to her satchel and fell asleep.

When Ella woke again, she squinted against bright sunlight. It felt like midmorning, but she was cold again. Sitting up, she saw that the heatplate's runes had faded. It needed to be re-enchanted if it were to ever again provide warmth. Rather than giving the heatplate anger for running out, she thought of Layla and sent it love for saving her life.

Layla!

Ella hurriedly put on her now dry clothing. Scooping her belongings into her bag, she started to search the area.

"Layla!" she called again and again.

She looked all along the bank up toward the waterfall, then back down, past the place where she had washed up. She looked everywhere, scanning the opposite bank, searching the reeds for sign of the raft or Layla's possessions.

Then, walking up a hill to get a better view, Ella saw the road, only a few dozen paces away.

The road.

Ella looked south, conflicted. Killian had undoubtedly taken this road toward Petrya. She'd probably made up a lot of time on the river, and he might only be just ahead of her. Ella needed to catch him, find out whom he was working for, and get back her house's Lexicon.

Then she looked north. In this direction was Layla's homeland and her own. If Layla had perished in the waterfall, there was no use in going this way. If she'd survived and gone back to the Dunwood, there was also little use.

Ella had checked the river. She felt certain Layla wasn't there. As certain as she could be.

Ella stood there for a long time. Layla was her friend. But her people needed her. Miro needed her.

With a heavy heart, she turned south.

———————◆———————

After traveling the road for days, the forest thinned and Ella began to see signs of civilization again. She passed cottages and farmland, much of the earth lying fallow in winter's heart. She slept under hedges, ate apples, and drank from streams, but Ella knew she needed real food.

As if in answer to her prayers, Ella spied a small farmer's market ahead. With a heart-stopping lurch of hope, Ella clutched at the inner pocket of her dress.

They were still there, two deen coins and twelve cendeens.

As her stomach groaned, Ella bought eight crusty white bread rolls and a block of hard, ripe cheese. Unable to stop herself she followed the purchases with some cured sausage, a pot of jam, a bottle of fresh milk, two large sourmelons, and three bottles of dark beer.

She received a few strange looks as she heaved her satchel to her shoulder and, without stopping, began to assemble her lunch.

Ella ate while she walked, the bag getting lighter with every mouthful.

It was easy going for the most part. The road was dry and dusty, and the temperature during the daytime was cool enough that the walk wasn't uncomfortable, though nights were cold. Ella often marveled at the towering trees that lined either side of her path, beautiful evergreens with their leaves rustling in the gentle breeze. This was the great farmland of Altura's south.

Always at the back of Ella's mind was the importance of her task. Her long legs found their traveler's pace, and she focused on landmarks in front of her, determined to reach them in the shortest time possible.

Two more days found Ella still walking as the sun started to sink into the horizon, the rays casting a glow on endless fields of sugarwort, covering the land with red and orange colors. As the road turned slowly east, Ella could now see the forbidding peaks of the Elmas in the distance, the natural barrier that separated the lands of Altura from the lands of Petrya.

Ella knew where Killian was headed.

There was only one route through the Elmas, one way to leave Altura behind and head for Petrya in the south before traveling to Tingara in the east: Wondhip Pass.

All Ella knew about the pass was that it was a route rarely taken, a place of treacherous terrain and dangerous outlaws.

Ella walked while it was still light enough to see and then, as exhaustion tugged at her eyelids, she stopped at the next hamlet she came upon, a tidy little place with a sign proclaiming it the village of Rowen.

Facing the road was a small inn: The Steady Hand. Before she entered, Ella looked down at herself. Her blue dress was scratched and torn. The cloth around her knees was dirty, and the hem had obviously been dragged in the mud. Her hair was a tangled mess. Making a decision, Ella held a few coins ready in her palm and walked around the back of the inn, rather than entering through the front.

Ella found a huge woman behind the building, sweat pouring down her forehead as she pounded at some stubborn laundry stains. Water and soap sloshed down her jiggling arms. A barking dog challenged Ella, and the woman looked up.

"Lord of the Sky, dear! What are you doing back here?"

"I'm seeking lodging for the night," Ella began.

"Then you'll be wanting to talk to my husband, Oerl." The woman looked Ella up and down. She smiled over her wobbly chins, a kind smile. "On second thought, perhaps you'll be more comfortable if I let you in back here and get you settled, yes?"

Ella nodded.

"You have . . . ahem . . . you have got . . ."

"I've got money," Ella said, opening her palm.

"Ah, no problem, no problems at all. Come with me, lass, and we'll get you settled. It looks like you've a story to tell, but you'll be wanting to tell it clean, I'm thinking." She caught Ella's expression. "Or not at all, as the case may be. Ahem. Yes, now come with me. That's the way. Wait here and I'll see if I can get you a nice warm room."

Ella followed her to a set of stairs. It felt strange to have someone fuss over her. Even in Sarostar she'd always had to look after herself. The woman gestured.

"Here you go, top of the stairs and second on the left. Number four. You won't be needing help with your things? Good, good. You have a nice wash, and come down for some supper when you're ready. Any clothes you want washing, just put them outside your door and I'll see to it. Any mending also. I'll send some hot water up in just a moment."

The woman trailed off as Ella closed the door behind her.

Ella couldn't believe the sight that greeted her. A bed, with a real mattress and warm woolen covers. Even through her fatigue, she suddenly felt completely, utterly filthy. Turning and encountering a mirror only confirmed it for her.

There was a soft knock on the door. Ella opened it to see a young, round-faced girl holding two large buckets of steaming water.

"Water for the bath," the girl said.

"Come right in," Ella said with a smile.

Even though she was wearing one of her dirty dresses—the least damaged of the bunch—Ella felt wonderfully clean as she descended the stairs and smelled the first aromas of a hot dinner wafting from the public room.

There were far more tables than people. Ella chose one near the open fire, the warmth finally driving the last of the cold out of her bones.

The innkeeper's wife approached. She'd changed into a matronly white costume with a black apron. It seemed amazing that she'd found one to fit her immense girth. She was all smiles as she approached Ella.

"Look at you, dear. Now who would have known there was a beautiful woman under all that dirt? I've just now realized I never gave you my name. Never forgive me, my old mum would. I'm Tessa Lowellen, and my husband's name is Oerl. What's your name now?"

"I'm Ella."

"Ella. That's a nice name now. And where might you be from, Ella?"

"I'm from . . . Schalberg, near Castlemere, on the Basch Coast."

"My, my. Such a long way away. I would have picked you to be from Sarostar, myself. Your voice, and you've got the look. I spent some time round there when I visited the Dunfolk."

"You know the Dunfolk?" Ella blurted.

"Oh yes, I spent some time there learning about medicine when I was younger. I'm Rowen's local healer, you see. Learned a lot about herbs. Hopefully it shows in my cooking, speaking of which, what will you have?" She dropped her voice to a confidential whisper. "I recommend the hunter's pie with black bread."

Ella laughed. "I think I'll have hunter's pie then."

"Good choice," the woman said, and laughing, she departed.

The food was delicious and Ella found herself warming to Tessa Lowellen, but she retired early, desperate for rest. As she went to sleep, Ella thought about Layla and Miro and Amber. Killian's face danced in front of her.

For some reason she found herself thinking about his smile. His warm touch. Gentle eyes.

———————

"You sure you won't be staying longer? The sun's barely up. Ah, all right then," Tessa said as she took Ella's breakfast plate away. Spontaneously, Tessa dropped down onto the bench opposite Ella and looked at her with serious eyes.

"Just remember, dear, no matter what you are running from, family is what counts. I just hope that's who you're running to."

"My parents are dead." Ella didn't know why she said it.

The woman's eyes grew sad, and for some reason tears came unbidden to Ella's eyes.

"It's this cursed war," Tessa said. "Just be careful, do you hear? A young girl like you, alone, with rampaging soldiers about. Don't trust anyone, hear me? Not even the soldiers on our side—not unless you see a lord or an officer about and are pretty sure you know what you're doing."

"I'll do my best."

"Take care, dear." Tessa's expression grew uncomfortable. "My Oerl, he wants to see you now. The room, you see."

Ella smiled. "Of course. Thank you."

Ella went up to her room and gathered her things. Seeing that Tessa had mended and washed her clothes, Ella felt eternally grateful.

Oerl was at the front of the inn, polishing the nightlamp that lit up The Steady Hand's sign.

"Mr. Lowellen? Your wife said I could pay you for the room."

"Ah yes." Oerl was a worried-looking man with thin hair. "Lass, my wife, when she gets something in her mind, she's hard to stop. We've got to cover costs, though, what with fewer and fewer people traveling 'cause of the war."

Ella tried to hush him, but Tessa's husband seemed desperate to tell her why he had to charge her.

"Plus there are plenty of thieves about, let me assure you of that," Oerl sighed, a long deep tribute to trial. "Half a deen should do, lass."

Ella handed him the money. "Thank you," she said, smiling.

"Thank you, lass," Oerl said, the worried expression never leaving his face. He examined the coin before putting it into a pocket.

Ella turned to leave, but then had a thought. "Did you mention thieves? Anything recent?"

"Why, you wouldn't believe it, but a man passed me my own stolen money, he did. First he steals it from me, and then he uses it to pay his bill. The nerve!" Oerl's voice trailed off as he returned to the sign.

"What did you say?"

Oerl sighed, "Perhaps you can shed some light on it. It was two days ago. A man stayed here—a priest by the way he was clothed, though he had the look of one well traveled, I'll say that. I don't know how it happened, but you see I remember coins, I do. Some people remember faces; I remember coins. Anyways, when he came to leave, he paid me with one of my coins. I wasn't sure of it, so I let him go. It's a strange thing to accuse someone of. But after he left, I checked my strongbox, and sure enough it was down by three coins. That was all he took—just three coins—and one of them he used to pay me. A strange episode, if you ask me." He stopped, as if exhausted by such a long speech.

"This man, did he have red hair? Long, nearly to his shoulders? And blue eyes?"

Oerl stared. "You know him?"

"He's a thief. He stole something from me. How long ago did you say he passed through here?"

Oerl just stared at her.

"How long?"

Oerl started, "It was two days ago that he left. Not yesterday morning, the one before. Left early."

Ella started to run, leaving with a wave of her hand. Glancing back, she saw Oerl following her with his eyes and shaking his head.

Two days. Ella was only two days behind him. The knowledge lent a spring to her step, and the shoulder bag felt lighter.

It was good to be running, and Ella determined to make as much progress as she could. She soon left the small village behind her, and when the road curved around a field, Ella cut across it,

37

The life of worship is a life of paradox. We must give to receive,
realize we are blind to see, become simple to be wise,
suffer for gain, and die to live.
　　　　　—Sermons of Primate Melovar Aspen, 539 y.e.

"Ah, good to see you've returned to us, young lady." The voice spoke in a rich deep timbre.

Ella lifted her head. The large wooden wagon she found herself in was being pulled by two small drudges, the simple constructs making speedy headway on the level road, faster than walking pace, but not quite as fast as a running man. The driver, evidently a Halrana, kept one eye on the drudges and the other on Ella.

She was lying on top of a woolen rug in the back of the wagon. Ella sat up and clambered forward to join the driver, perched on a sill at the front of the cart.

"How long?"

"How long? Six days, you've been unconscious."

"Six days?"

Ella looked at the old man. He wore a dirty brown robe on which the *raj hada* of the Halrana had faded until the hand

and eye were hardly visible. He had soft white hair and a scruffy ginger beard, flecked like salt and pepper combined with hotspice. His eyes were intensely blue, and they were twinkling as he regarded her.

"No, I am not serious. You've been passed out in the back of my wagon for about an hour, and that's the truth. What were you doing, leaping hedges like that? One moment I'm peacefully plodding along, and the next moment a slight piece of sunlight comes crashing into my poor drudge. He's never going to feel the same way again."

The old man pointed at one of his constructs. Ella could almost swear it exhibited an injured pose as it hobbled along.

"Now, I'm supposing you live somewhere around here. Where to? Hope I haven't carried you too far."

Ella thought rapidly. The drudges were by no means fast, but they were definitely faster than her best walking speed. "It's quite far, actually." She cleared her throat. "I'm going," she pointed, "there."

The old man's eyes followed Ella's pointing finger to the distant peaks of the Elmas. "What in the Lord of the Earth's name for— don't you realize there's a war going on?"

"I have family. They live on the other side of Wondhip Pass."

"In Petrya? Dangerous place there for a girl like you."

"No it isn't," Ella chanced. "You just think that because you don't live there. If you grow up there it's fine."

He regarded her incredulously. "Whatever you say, it's no business of mine. It happens I'll be going in that direction for a time. Care for a ride?"

"Are you sure? That wouldn't be too much trouble? Are you certain that he"—she indicated the drudge—"won't mind?"

The old man laughed—a rich and hearty sound. "No, young lady. I don't think he will."

Ella felt quite comfortable perched next to the old man. She'd already been unconscious in his presence, and he'd shown she was safe from harm.

"I'm Ella," she said.

"I'm Evrin, Evrin Alistair."

"That doesn't sound like a Halrana name."

"Good! That means my father was telling the truth when he told my mother he was an outlander."

Ella chuckled. "So where was he from?"

"The curiosity of youth," Ervin grumbled, but Ella could tell he wasn't serious. "He was from . . . he was from . . . well, the fact is, I don't really know where he was from."

"But your mother was from Halaran?"

"Well," Evrin scratched at his beard, "in a way she was. But they didn't call it Halaran back then."

A little confused, Ella was silent for a moment. "You're a merchant?"

"Well, you could say that."

"What's your cargo?"

"A little of this, a little of that. It's wartime, and almost anything can be a valuable cargo now, if you're brave enough to make the journey. Tell me, how did an Alturan girl come to have family in Petrya?"

Ella thought quickly. "I'm from the last village, Rowen. My mother's sister met a man from across the pass. He'd come to look for . . . trading opportunities." Ella stopped at a harrumph from Evrin. Was he laughing? "What?"

"Nothing, nothing," he said. "Just got something caught in my throat, that's all. Please continue."

"So she went back with him, and they were married. I spent a lot of time there as a child, so I'm going back there now."

"Ahh, I see," said Evrin. "What town was it, this town across the pass?"

"It was a small village, just a collection of buildings really. In the middle of nowhere. You wouldn't have heard of it." Ella paused, thinking furiously. "Mintown, I think it was called."

There was another harrumphing sound from Evrin. "Sorry, sorry," he said. "I'm in need of a little liquid, that's all. Is that beer I see in your bag?"

"Should we share some?"

Evrin turned slowly, a twinkle in his blue eyes. He looked like some kind of grizzly animal, with his ginger beard and shaggy eyebrows. "Oh, yes. We should indeed."

Ella and Evrin shared one of the large bottles of dark beer. Then, at Evrin's suggestion, they followed it up with the second. It made Ella feel slightly warm and light in the head. Evrin grew jovial and began to sing—rather than speak—the activation runes to control the drudges.

"I have a secret to tell you," he confided to Ella. "I'm a drudge-singer. It's like a bladesinger, but more powerful."

Ella snorted and shared out some of her food as the drudges continued their ground-eating pace.

"How does it work?" she asked, unable to hide her curiosity. "Is it a difficult thing, controlling them?"

"Controlling them? Of course. It's because they don't want to be controlled. The left one is called Tortoise because he's always slower, which makes the cart veer to the left. The right one is called Geezer. It's because his joints creak like an old man's."

Ella laughed. "No, really. How does it work?"

She glanced over at the old man. He had a stone tablet on his lap, glowing softly, lit up with the runes. Ella could name a few, but others were unknown to her. The arrangements were complex, but she was sure that with time she could figure some of them out.

"Well, here goes then. This tablet is the controller. A controller is linked to a construct or to multiple constructs. These small symbols are the runes, and the groups of runes are called matrices. You'll see them both on the tablet and on the drudges. Understand?"

Ella nodded and Evrin continued. "The runes that are lit up are the ones that have been activated. Activated means they are doing something, or they are prepared to do something. To activate a matrix, we speak its activation sequence. Watch."

He gestured to the left construct, Tortoise. *"Forahl-an-ahmala."*

A series of runes on the tablet began to glow silver.

At the same moment the construct kicked out with its front legs. It snapped forward with its head, lunging from side to side. If it had been an animal, it would have snarled. It would be devastating to anything in front of the drudge.

Evrin shrugged. "A useful trick to use against anyone with an eye to stealing cargo. Now. Some of the sequences are based on touch, others on a spoken activation sequence. Others yet use a combination. Some don't require the controller at all. I've heard that an incredibly skillful animator can control an iron golem with voice alone. I haven't seen anything like that myself, of course, but I imagine it would be something like the song of your bladesingers. Only perhaps even more complex."

Ella felt a new respect for the animator's art.

"What about the rate of loredrain? How long will a single essence charge last?"

"Loredrain?"

Ella hesitated. She was a village girl from Rowen, she reminded herself. "It's just a term I picked up somewhere. It means how long it can last before the runes need to be renewed, doesn't it?"

"Yes, it does. It depends on the construct. It actually has little to do with the strength of the creature and more with the agility and complexity. So a big lumbering drudge doesn't use much, while an iron golem, a complex fighting machine, uses a lot."

Ella nodded.

Evrin turned. "Do you have friends at the Academy of Enchanters, Ella?"

At the mention of the Academy, Ella started. "No, no. Nothing like that."

Evrin shrugged his shoulders and settled back in his seat. Ella decided to wait awhile before asking any more questions about animating.

38

Open your eyes, and all is revealed.
—*The Evermen Cycles*, 18:29

"Bladesinger Miro. Please take a seat." Blademaster Rogan indicated a chair.

Nodding in acknowledgment, Miro sat down and faced the blademaster. Next to Rogan sat Marshal Sloan. Miro guessed the marshal had been apprised since his initial debriefing.

"Have you taken refreshment?" Rogan asked.

Miro nodded.

He'd gone straight to the blademaster with news of the Veznans' subversion to the Black Army's cause. It hadn't gained him the reception Miro had thought it would. He'd been told to say nothing to anyone and then been called to this clandestine meeting.

He still bore the scars of the experience, both inside and out. The cultivators' defenses had been formidable; he had been lucky to escape. It had come down to a pitched skirmish on the outskirts of Rosarva. Not one of his Veznan pursuers had lived to tell the tale of the black-clad bladesinger with the ghostly blue sword.

Most of all, Miro couldn't believe the truth of the war they were fighting. Men were dying every day. Towns and cities were burning, and across Halaran bodies were piled up and buried in mass graves. Yet they were all nothing but pawns.

Miro seethed inside. Now that he knew the culprit, he wanted nothing more than to lay the truth out to the lords and commanders and point the swords of their armies in the right direction. He knew it wouldn't be simple, though—not with the houses all allied against them. With the cultivators joining the cause of the Black Army, there were now four houses against two. Altura and Halaran didn't stand a chance.

"So the primate has discovered a new secret. It's something to do with essence. Is that correct, Miro? And he's using it to turn the high lords to his cause?" Marshal Sloan said.

Miro frowned. "As I said to Blademaster Rogan, he has created some new substance from essence. He calls it elixir. Where essence creates magic, elixir destroys it. And where essence is a deadly poison, elixir gives powers of rejuvenation. The primate is giving the high lords a simple choice: to join his cause and gain these powers, or else he will conquer their houses and use this substance to permanently destroy their Lexicons and all their lore with it. I saw him give this elixir to the son of the Veznan high lord. It drove him mad, mad enough to kill his own father. And this substance does give regenerative abilities. I saw the primate slice Moragon's hand, only to see it heal in front of my eyes."

"Hmm. It sounds a little far-fetched," Marshal Sloan said, watching Miro carefully.

Miro sighed. "At least, that's what you think Prince Leopold will say, isn't it?'

"Well grasped," Sloan said. "That's the truth of it. Don't worry—I believe you, Miro, though the Skylord knows how we're going to get out of this mess."

There was one piece of information that Miro hadn't dared to mention. He couldn't believe it himself; he didn't see how it could be possible.

For his whole life he'd had the same dream. A man held him. Miro was powerless to stop him; there was no strength in his arms. The man held a knife to Miro's throat, its razor-sharp blade glistening. Miro felt terrified. He could never forget the man's face.

And now he'd seen the man in the flesh.

Primate Melovar Aspen.

Miro looked from one man to the other. "The high lords are trapped: promised eternal life and then twisted by the addiction of the substance the primate gives them. They cannot escape the cycle. The primate is their only source of the stuff."

"Yes, yes. But practically speaking, from a military sense, we have four houses allied against us and the Halrana high lord is obsessed with taking back Ralanast. To be honest, we won't hold Halaran itself for more than a month."

Miro was shocked to hear the commanders talk in this way.

"The enemy soldiers, though," Miro said, "some of them are just following orders. If they knew . . ."

"Yes, we've thought of that. But we don't know how far it spreads, how deep the taint runs. Does it run to the lords? The officers? We know enough now that we can protect ourselves from the templars. But to eradicate this poison from the other houses could be a task that is simply beyond us."

"What are we planning to do, then?"

"Prince Leopold and High Lord Legasa have ordered a full frontal assault on Ralanast."

Miro scowled. "But you know the Veznans will start pushing from the north at any moment. The Black Army in the east grows larger every day. If they push us hard enough, any force attacking

Ralanast will be cut off from the Ring Forts. It would be a massacre. We would lose everything."

Blademaster Rogan sighed. "You always had an excellent grasp of tactics, Miro. Since your return I've tried speaking with Prince Leopold and High Lord Legasa, but . . ."

Miro could see the defeat in the blademaster's eyes. He remembered how relentless Rogan had been in the Pens. The training had honed him like a fine weapon, both his body and his mind. Yet it seemed his teacher had given up.

"Miro," Marshal Sloan said. He looked equally tired, his skin gray with fatigue. "You were at Seranthia when we discovered that the Halrana Lexicon had been stolen. We're hiding it from the men, but many of the constructs' runes have completely faded. Half of the ironmen, a third of the woodmen, even many of the golems and the colossi . . . are now useless. Barring some miracle, the Halrana will cease to be effective as a force in another week. For the Halrana, it's now or never."

Miro put his whole being into the conviction in his voice, "I understand that; I really do. But please don't throw away Altura's best as well. Our runes are still bright, and our armies are strong. If you attack Ralanast now, you'll weaken our flank. If we hold the flank, our chances are next to nothing. If we don't, there is no chance at all."

Marshal Sloan looked at Miro intently. "That's where you come in."

Miro looked from one man to the other. "I don't understand."

"Miro, I've seen the way you handle yourself. You're a good leader, and the men trust you. I'm offering you a position in the army."

"In the army?"

Blademaster Rogan spoke, "It wouldn't be the first time a bladesinger has become a leader of men. We're free agents, Miro.

Perhaps it is your destiny. It will mean following orders, though. Just because you're a bladesinger doesn't mean you don't have to listen to a man who outranks you."

"Your name has good standing among the men, Miro; you have earned their respect in your own right." Marshal Sloan looked away and then gazed directly into Miro's eyes. "When we tell them who your father was, they will only love you more."

"My father?" Miro was confused.

"Miro," said Rogan. "It's not for me to tell you the full story, or to tell you why the truth was hidden from you, but your father wasn't an anonymous soldier, as I know you believe."

"What are you saying?"

"Do you know the name Serosa the Dark, Miro?"

Miro frowned. "Of course. He was the Alturan high lord who fought the emperor during the Rebellion. They say he was a warmonger."

"I know they say that—it's a distortion of the truth put out by Tessolar, the man who replaced Serosa. I remember him, Miro," said Blademaster Rogan. "He was a good man and a strong leader."

"I remember him too," said Marshal Sloan. "His full name was Serosa Torresante. I don't know how to say this, so I'm just going to come out with it. He was your father."

Miro looked from one man to the next. "How is that possible? I was told my father was killed in the Rebellion and that my mother died of grief. Is that a lie?"

"It's close to the truth, but the full story is not mine to tell," said Blademaster Rogan. "The important thing is that the men will follow you. They remember the name Torresante. They remember who stood on the walls of Sark and defied the legion all those years ago."

Miro thought about the taunts at the Pens, taunts about his heritage. He was pensive for a long moment. The blademaster's revelation had opened up more questions than answers.

"I want you to tell me . . ."

Blademaster Rogan held up his hand, "No, Miro. It isn't for me to say, nor is it for Marshal Sloan. Listen to the truth behind my words. If you take this path, I promise you that the truth will follow."

Miro's father had been high lord of Altura. He had led these same men against this same foe. "I accept," he said.

Miro's mouth set in resolve. He would find out the truth.

"Excellent," said Marshal Sloan. "Understand—this isn't a reward. We're giving you perhaps the most difficult task of the coming battle. Your task is to hold our flank. When the attack on Ralanast begins, the Black Army is going to surge through here, aiming to cut off our main force. Miro, you must do everything in your power to hold."

Miro nodded. "I understand."

Marshal Sloan spoke, "You are to serve under Lord Devon's son, Lord Rorelan."

"Rorelan?" Miro remembered the name of the man who had relinquished leadership to Prince Leopold. "He's here?"

"He's a changed man since his father died, but yes, he's here."

The marshal and the blademaster expounded on their plans. Miro listened in growing horror, hiding his feelings behind a blank façade.

It was a pitched effort—they were throwing their best men, their best weapons, into a doomed attempt to liberate Ralanast.

Miro knew. He knew it better than anyone. If the liberation of Halaran's capital failed, holding the flank would be vital to an army falling back.

Miro would hold.

He had to.

39

And the Lord of the Sky said, "Look up, but not to look at me.
For I shall be there with you, and we will be looking up together."
—*The Evermen Cycles*, 15:38

"Well, this is as far as we go together, my dear," Evrin said, drawing the drudge-pulled wagon to a halt. "Wondhip Pass awaits you." The old animator gazed up at the mountains and shook his head. "Just be careful now, you hear me?"

"I'll do my best," Ella said. "Thank you." She sighed; she'd enjoyed the old man's company.

"Glad I could help. You'd better get going. You've got a tough journey ahead."

"How about you?" Ella said as she slipped off the wagon. "Where are you bound next?"

"A few quick stops, and then I'm off to Salvation."

"All the way to Aynar? I know the templars are supposed to be neutral, but is it safe?"

Evrin smiled. "You don't need to worry about me." The way he said it made Ella wonder about Evrin, not for the first time. He appeared very confident for someone traveling around in the middle of a war. "There's someone I'm looking for, and all signs point to either Salvation or perhaps Stonewater, home of the primate."

"Well, I hope you find him."

Evrin gave a casual salute. "Me too. Farewell!" he called out, and the two drudges spurred into motion.

Ella waved until the wagon was out of sight, finally turning away and fixing her gaze on the mountain range separating Altura from Petrya as she hoisted her satchel to her shoulder and began to walk.

She reflected on her journey with the old animator. Evrin had taken her a great deal of the way she needed to go. They'd traveled together for nearly a week, sharing food and conversation even as Ella knew she would be gaining on Killian. During their journey, Ella had learned more about the animator's arts than she ever would have thought possible. Evrin was a patient teacher, and with such a quick pupil—too quick, he observed on numerous occasions—she was soon taking her turn controlling the drudges. He even showed her more of their defense mechanisms—kicks and lunges, ducks and rolls.

Behind it all were the runes themselves. An animator's real skill was in creating the constructs, and Ella put effort into learning the structures and discovering how life was breathed into a collection of carved pieces. She learned much more than she let on, and vowed to try her hand at creating a simple construct when the next opportunity presented itself.

Evrin also had a wealth of fantastical stories he'd shared. Tales of people with strange powers who could stave off death itself, of evil lords and proud slaves who challenged their masters. His most vivid story was about a man whose wife was torn open by his enemy's sword, and how her husband, in his grief, tried to use runes of strength on her body. Miraculously, the lore had saved the woman's life. Ella liked the story, such a change from what she knew essence was capable of.

With the increase in journey speed, Ella felt confident she'd gained at least a day on Killian. She was now forced to think about what she would do when she caught him.

Ella's greatest advantage lay in the fact that Killian wouldn't be expecting her. He would be on the lookout for the high enchantress or perhaps a bladesinger—anyone but the young girl he'd used to further his own ends.

She needed to use that advantage somehow. Perhaps she could get a disguise when she arrived in Petrya and appear to be one of the locals. Then when she accosted Killian, she could use his surprise to her advantage. She had her green silk enchantress's dress with her, and she could enchant more weapons. She was hardly defenseless.

Ella kept repeating this to herself as she walked.

The air was drier, and a little warmer, here in the south. The road was far less traveled, and much of the land was unoccupied, little more than rocky desert. A thin trail left the road, barely a walking track, winding its way around huge boulders toward the peaks of the Elmas. Evrin had said Ella wanted to take this road. He'd also reminded her that bandits lived in these parts.

Ella felt exposed as she entered a region of sheer cliffs and narrow canyons. The great mountains loomed over her, blotting out the light of the sun so that she was in perpetual shade. The Elmas had long formed the natural border between Alturan lands and Petryan lands. Except for the treacherous Wondhip Pass, there was no way across.

The trail inclined sharply, and Ella bent down, walking with her hands on her knees as her strength flagged. Loose stones and dust-covered rubble littered the ground.

Ella hoped she could catch up with Killian before she encountered any Petryans.

The Petryans and their elementalists were always discussed in hushed tones in Altura, as if discussing a dark spirit would bring it out of the shadows. They were considered strange, even sinister, keeping largely to themselves and rarely traveling except for physical and lore-based contests, which they participated in wholeheartedly. As a house they fiercely asserted their independence, and if they fought with another house as an ally, they would still fight in their own way, on their own terms.

They'd fought with the emperor against Altura and Halaran in the Rebellion, and High Lord Tessolar still refused to communicate with the Petryan high lord, Haptut Alwar. Terrible atrocities had been committed in the last war of the houses, especially by the Petryans. Rumor had it that they had no pity for weakness and no sympathy for the sick, the old, or the infirm.

The majority of elementalists lived in their great tiered city, Tlaxor. It was perhaps the most well known and least traveled city in the world. As if to defy their chosen deity, the Lord of Fire, the Petryans had built their capital on an island in the middle of a lake. This lake, Lake Halapusa, was in the caldera of an active volcano.

The water of Lake Halapusa was constantly at near-boiling temperature. It was said one of the Petryan high lord's favorite methods of execution was to throw dissidents into the lake and watch a man's skin turn bright red as his flesh boiled away. If the high lord was particularly angry, the man would dangle from a rope, lowered by a hand's breadth every day.

Ella felt these might just be stories. At any rate she didn't plan on spending time in Petrya; she just wanted to catch up with Killian and get back to Altura with the Lexicon.

She stopped and caught her breath, looking back the way she had come, at the road down below, a ribbon of dusty brown. The barren ground stretched on and on until some poor farmland could be seen at the limits of vision.

Ella now looked ahead, upward. The rough path twisted and turned as it wound its way up the mountainside. It was steep enough here that she would be forced to follow the path as it doubled back on itself, intentionally curving first one way, then another. It was either that or climb up the nearly vertical face.

She tilted her head back and looked farther up still. Above her the imposing mountain range frowned down, dark and foreboding. Ella couldn't see how a crossing could be possible; the jagged crags and sheer walls appeared completely impassable. She scanned the series of peaks to either side, following them with her eyes, looking for an indication of where she would cross. Shaking her head, Ella continued on her way.

It was a grueling climb, dangerously steep, with loose scree threatening to knock her down with every step. Ella knew that if she hurt herself, there would be no help; a sprained ankle meant death up here in the mountains. She simply concentrated on placing one foot in front of the other.

At some point she stopped and ate, sipping at her water, careful to ration her supplies. Even so, she was down to her last two bottles.

Partway through the afternoon, Ella looked up to see she was heading for a narrow defile between two of the peaks, a thin split in the rock.

Wondhip Pass.

Ella camped that night with the pass in view, choosing a protected spot with a clear view of the approaches from above and below and the defense of a natural cleft in the rock. Fighting her exhaustion, she gathered some rocks of various shapes and sizes and prepared herself. Whether by creature or by man, she wouldn't be taken unaware.

———————◆———————

The next morning, Ella entered the pass.

Presently, she'd entered deep enough into the narrow gully for her way back to be easily barred.

Ella saw the bandits soon after.

They were eight men, dressed in a motley collection of leather and armor. Two carried swords, one gripped a dull spear, and another tossed a rusty dagger from hand to hand. The rest were unarmed, but their size was enough.

They sprang out suddenly from a place where Ella would have sworn there was no one.

Her heart in her throat, Ella continued to walk steadily along the walled defile that was Wondhip Pass.

She'd put on her green silk dress. Anyone who knew something about lore would know the runes on her dress weren't there for decoration, but she hoped these men had no idea.

As Ella drew closer, she saw a few of the men were injured. One of them had his arm in a makeshift sling, and another had a red lump the size of an egg on his temple.

Killian, Ella thought. He would have had to come this way, and in his priest's garb these bandits would have considered him an easy target. Ella wondered if he'd taken any wounds in return.

For the first time Ella wished that the silk of the dress wasn't so sheer, so figure hugging. It was the last impression she wished to create.

One of the swordsmen, a young man with a hooked nose and thin face, whistled as she approached. He circled Ella, looking her up and down as he did. "My, my, my," he said. "Lovely, very lovely indeed. You make a fine change from the usual sort we get up here, Princess."

The other swordsman stepped forward. He was much older, and everything about him was big. His hair was long and shaggy, like an animal's pelt, and his head sat squarely on his wide shoulders, while his legs were each the size of Ella's waist. "Enough, Rostram. Let's see what she's got first."

"Can't you see what she's got?" the young swordsman responded, his eyes still on Ella's body. "Did you want to ask her, and maybe she'll tell you?"

The other bandits laughed.

The big man's expression blackened. "You think we'll be able to buy food with what you're talking about? What will that give us to get through the winter?"

"Maybe she's got both gilden and pleasure for us, hey Blackall?" the man with the dagger called out.

The big man grunted. "Maybe." He turned to Ella. "Well? Got money?"

Ella probably had enough gilden to buy each man a small piece of cheese, with none for herself.

"No . . . no, I don't." She tried to keep her voice steady. Killian had come through these men; she could too.

Blackall came closer to her. His breath stank as he spoke for her ears alone. "Listen, girl. These men, if you can give them a bit of money, I might be able to stop them doing what it is they want to do to you."

Hearing it spoken about so openly made Ella feel sick. Her heart hammered in her chest, and her throat closed up so it was difficult to breathe and even harder to speak. Every instinct told her to run. But Ella's wits told her the pass would be closed behind her, the way blocked by these men, and that to run was to die.

She had to confront them.

Rostram spoke from behind her, making her jump. "Whatever she's got, it's either in that bag or in that dress. How about you search the bag, Blackall, while I search the dress?" He chuckled.

The bandits began to crowd in, eager to see her body revealed. Rostram reached in to rip Ella's dress from her body.

Ella whispered an activation sequence. Instantly, the runes on her dress lit up, bright flashes scattering across the fabric like lightning.

"Argh!" Rostram screamed in pain. He pulled his hand away, the fingers badly burned.

"That dress, it's enchanted!" yelled Blackall, raising his sword. "Kill her—it's worth a fortune to every man here."

Ella lifted the hood of the dress, pulling it around her head. She continued to chant, the words coming in staccato syllables as she spoke one activation after another. The brightness of the dress increased until it was as bright as the sun and projected a scorching, fierce heat. Ella was protected from it, yet even so, she could feel the radiating fire. The bandits cried out as blisters popped on their skin. Two ran, their screams fading into the distance.

Blackall swung at Ella's head, but as his sword made contact with the dress a fountain of sparks sprayed out as the fabric protected her.

Ella increased her chant still further.

She vanished.

Then, with a flash of green silk, a bandit went down. A pale face hovered next to a hulking man, and he collapsed, hands covering his crotch. One by one the bandits turned and fled. Blackall simply stood, wide-eyed and gaping.

Ella dodged and struck out until finally she was past the last of the bandits. She chanted until she'd left the bandits far behind.

Panting as she ran, Ella resisted the urge to slow until the pass opened up again. Eventually the narrow gully became a gorge, and then the walls of the gorge spread themselves apart to show what they truly were—the sides of mountains. Ella slowed, constantly looking behind her, only deactivating the runes when she was sure she wasn't being followed.

Ella was now the same as she had always been—a young woman wearing a green silk dress.

The knowledge that she was now beginning the descent into Petrya spurred Ella on. There was just as much rubble and loose gravel as there had been on her ascent, but her steps were now more determined than ever. Perhaps it had something to do with her supplies of food and water, which were running dangerously low, the benefit being that her satchel was the lightest it had ever been.

One thing was for sure: Ella felt warmer than she had in a long time. Although the Alturan side of the range had been cast in perpetual shade, on the Petryan side the late morning rays warmed the dry air.

The bright light of day revealed the land below in a panoramic vista. Looking to the east, Ella's eyes followed the Elmas as the range curved toward where the mountains became hills at the Gap of Garl. The land of Petrya was a great plain surrounded by mountains on all sides but one, for to the south was the Hazara Desert.

Ella's main viewpoint was ahead of her, at the path leading into the rust-colored land of Petrya. It was a harsh land, barren and littered with stones and boulders.

Suddenly, Ella stopped. There, at the base of the mountain, still a great distance in front of her, was a man. He was clothed in white, and his hair was long and fiery red.

Then, as quickly as she had seen him, he vanished into a copse of trees.

Ella ran through the possibilities one more time. Killian was perhaps half a day's march in front of her.

He couldn't know she was behind him.

Her steps more careful now, Ella prepared to hunt down her quarry.

40

*The Lexicons may not even be the greatest works of the
Evermen. Who knows what other wonders reside deep in the
bowels of Stonewater?*
—Diary of High Enchantress Maya Pallandor,
page 680, 411 Y.E.

Primate Melovar Aspen could remember the time before the elixir.
It was hazy, like a remembrance of childhood.

He could recall feeling tired. Sitting at his desk in Stonewater, high up in the hollowed-out shell of the mountain. The aching
cold, deep in his bones. His pen scratching endlessly. The feeling of
impotence, of being trapped by his position.

Why had he felt impotent? A memory came to him of a conversation he'd had with an Imperial ambassador. A money-grubbing
peddler from Tingara, with jewels on his fingers and rich dark
clothes of velvet.

The meeting had followed the usual pattern, and then Melovar
remembered standing up at his desk, his joints cracking. He had
walked to the large window. Without a word he'd opened it, his thin
arms encountering resistance, grunting with effort.

Instantly, a stiff breeze gusted into the room. It was always windy at Stonewater—something to do with the mountain's height.

The primate leaned against the window frame, gazing out at the city of Salvation below. He beckoned the ambassador forward. After a moment, the man hesitantly joined him.

"Do you see?" the primate pointed.

The ambassador seemed giddy for a moment, made breathless by the height and the sheer drop below the window. The stone face fell for thousands of paces.

"What is it, Your Grace?"

"On the edge of Salvation, outside the city walls."

The ambassador's brow furrowed. "Some kind of camp."

"The dispossessed," Melovar said, looking at the ambassador to make his point. "Vagrants. They come from all over, but most of all, they come from Seranthia."

"Really? From the Imperial capital? But these are just rabble—what trouble can they cause? They probably aren't even Tingaran citizens."

"Most are not."

"Then what is the problem? Your templars can't control them?"

The primate shook his head. "They are too weak to be unruly. The system is corrupt, Ambassador. That is the problem. The non-citizens are multiplying faster than the Tingarans. The citizens force them out of work, and the emperor leaves them to starve. The Wall shuts them out of Seranthia, so they come here, to Aynar, to Salvation, because as templars we can at least give them order. We can feed them and give them work hauling the raw materials for essence manufacture."

"Scum." The ambassador spat out the word. "I'm sorry, Your Grace, but in Seranthia we give short thrift to non-citizens."

"But don't you see, Ambassador?" Primate Melovar was desperate for him to understand. "Isn't that going against the very tenets of what the Tingaran Empire stands for? What we here at the Assembly of Templars stand for? The Evermen gave us the relics for a reason. They gave us the Lexicons and the ability to create works of lore, but for what? I'm beginning to believe that perhaps lore is more of a cause than a solution to our problems. Lore is driving our greed—our constant striving for more wealth, more power. We aren't helping people; we're using them. And when they're all used up, we discard them."

"Without lore there would be no Assembly," said the ambassador. "No templars."

"Ah, you are referring to our role as custodians of the relics that produce the essence. But, Ambassador, you are forgetting our original purpose," said the primate. "To guide the people, and teach them of the Evermen. To help them lead lives free from sin. I am the spiritual head of the empire. My job is to help. Somehow, with the constant demand for essence, that has become lost."

Melovar waited for a reply. The Tingaran ambassador opened his mouth to speak, then closed it, frowning.

Melovar gripped the man's shoulders. "Look, Ambassador, look when you are home again. Look deep within. Then, let us talk more."

The ambassador shook his head. "Your Grace, what can I do? There will always be those who help themselves, and those who don't. I bid your leave."

The ambassador left Melovar standing at the window, staring out at Salvation and the camp outside.

The ground suddenly heaved and the boom of an explosion made the earth tremble. The primate put his hand to his head, shaking off the fugue, bringing himself back to the present. The conversation had taken place some time ago; it was just a memory. How long had it been? He'd been several minutes without the elixir, and he quickly sipped from a golden goblet.

Instantly, he felt rejuvenated. Where was he? He looked around him, at the fitted stones that made up the walls. The parade-ground voices of soldiers called somewhere outside.

Ah, yes. He was far from Stonewater, in Torakon. He was encamped with his army, in the middle of the Azure Plains, standing in the command center the builders had constructed at his request.

The last vestiges of the remembered conversation left him. The elixir had been having a strange effect of late.

Primate Melovar banished such thoughts and looked at the map spread on the wall. Half of the Tingaran Empire was now under his direct control. Soon the black sun would fly from every building in every city of the world.

Moragon entered the room. "Your Grace, the Halrana attempted a sneak attack from the Ring Forts. We've repelled them, but some men were killed."

"Ah, Moragon. I was just about to summon you."

The primate had long known Moragon in his former position as the emperor's executioner, but only recently had Moragon been persuaded to join the primate's cause. Not an intimidating man by nature, the primate had enjoyed the fear Moragon inspired in others. Primate Melovar now took great pleasure in seeing people react the same way to himself.

"Our opportunity is coming," the primate said. "The last resisters are attempting to liberate Ralanast, and their flank will be exposed. I want you to lead the attack."

"Me, Your Grace? The Tingaran lord marshal . . ."

"Bah! The lord marshal can hardly keep his wits about him. The addiction is killing him."

"And you?"

"Don't presume to worry about me. I have the Evermen on my side."

Moragon frowned. "I'll lead the attack, if it's your command. But still, the Alturan Lexicon . . ."

"I know," Primate Melovar snapped. "Yes, we need it, and I don't know how far the thief can be trusted. Send for Saryah. Instruct her to find the thief."

Moragon's face turned grim. "Saryah? Are you sure?"

Primate Melovar simply regarded Moragon for a time. Moragon finally nodded. "I'll see to it. When do you plan to destroy the Halrana Lexicon?"

The primate licked his lips. "For now, we need drudges or our war machine grinds to a halt. Lore can be useful, but never fear, my friend. When the time comes, we will permanently eradicate it from the world."

Moragon bowed and left. Primate Melovar Aspen's eyes closed as he sipped from his goblet, thinking about lore and about a bold new future with no wars among houses and with one man to rule them all.

41

Have you no wish for others to be saved?
Then you are not saved yourself, be sure of that.
—Sermons of Primate Melovar Aspen, 537 Y.E.

Ella entered the town of Hatlatu with a terrible feeling of foreboding sending a chill through every bone in her body.

She'd changed into her most neutral garment, a gray dress with white and blue stripes on the hem. It was still perhaps too revealing, if she compared herself to the Petryans she was seeing, but it would have to do.

She felt out of her depth. When she'd finally made it to the base of the mountain, she'd thought it would be easy to follow Killian's path, but there was no path to follow. It was as if he'd vanished into the dark forest.

Not for the first time, Ella wished Layla were with her.

She'd finally found a game trail leading through the forest. The sounds of this forest were completely new to her, eerie shrieks and sighing sounds coming from all directions.

Ella spent the night huddled under a tree and woke sore and weary, fatigued from short snatches of fitful sleep. Half a day saw the game trail turn into a fully fledged path. The trees grew thinner, and she had emerged onto a dusty field, spotted with outbuildings. She'd followed the edge of the field until she'd come upon this small town.

The land was sparsely populated; Ella knew that much. There was a high chance Killian had passed through here. The town was an opportunity she couldn't afford to miss.

Now she was having second thoughts. The sun was harsh in Petrya, and the people had sun-darkened skin and swarthy features. Women frowned at her; she was obviously different. Some wore scarves tied over their hair, whereas Ella's long pale hair fell loose and straight. Some of the men frowned too, and others stared. Many of the men had curled moustaches or sported neatly trimmed beards. Ella was surprised to see that both men and women wore a charcoal paste around their eyes. It gave them a strange, exotic look.

Ella walked along what she thought was the town's main street. The buildings were constructed of dark slate with beams of red wood. Some appeared to be taverns, and the noise from inside indicated it must be mealtime. Ella could smell spicy aromas and saw the local men and women drinking from bowls held in two hands while they conversed.

Ella decided she needed to ask her questions and quickly leave before she got herself into trouble.

She walked up to a moustached Petryan who looked like his face was less severe than the others'. He backed away slightly when she approached, keeping a few paces between them.

"Excuse me," Ella said. "Have you seen a young man, a priest, pass through here? He has red hair and blue eyes."

"Where are you from?" the Petryan frowned.

"I . . . I was raised in Altura, but my father . . ."

"Altura?" The Petryan half-turned and called out a name. "Putahnmet!"

Another man popped his head out of an official-looking structure with painted gold trim on its wooden beams. He wore a flat red hat on his head, and the *raj hada* of Petrya—a teardrop and flame—presented on the breast of his red coat. "What is it?"

"Look at this girl. She asks about the priest, the one who sleeps at your house. She says she's from Altura."

The official looked hard at Ella for a moment. "Altura? Wait there. I'm coming over."

Ella sensed something menacing in his tone. She glanced to the left and the right. "I need to be going."

The moustached man grabbed Ella by the arm. She began to panic.

"Nothing to fear," the moustached man said in soothing tones. "We just want to ask you a few questions."

With her free arm, Ella reached into a pocket of her dress and withdrew a small stone, the size of her palm, inscribed with runes.

"*Tuk-talour,*" she whispered. She threw the stone into the middle of the street, then put her hand over her eyes and looked away.

There was a sudden flash of white light. People screamed. Removing her hand, Ella saw both the moustached man and the official clutching at their eyes.

"I'm blind! I can't see!" she heard someone shriek.

Freed from the moustached man's grip, Ella began to run.

"I can still see. Should I stop her?" someone yelled.

"Yes, she might be a spy. Stop her!"

Ella put her head down and sped down the main street. She weaved to the side and ducked through a market, the sound of pounding feet behind her spurring her on. Colliding into a woman holding a gauzy roll of cloth, Ella yelled an apology and kept running.

She ducked into another narrow street, and then turned again. Soon, Ella left the commotion behind her and reached the outskirts of the town. Dashing over a bridge, she made a quick decision and dropped down to the riverbank below, rather than continuing on the road. She followed the bank away from the bridge, slowing to a walk now. When she was sure she'd lost all pursuers, she sank down to her knees.

Ella couldn't believe what a disaster it had been. She should have chosen to make her encounter somewhere quiet, where she could have been more prepared to deal with any opposition, where she could have tested the reactions of just one person instead of many.

She considered her options. What should she do now? The man with the moustache had said something about a priest staying with the official. Perhaps Killian was even still there, and she'd gone walking in, bold as brass.

Ella cursed herself while she watched the shallow waterway flow slowly by.

After a while it occurred to her that there was only one option left to her. She had to leave the town, following the road farther into Petrya. Once she'd gone far enough, she would wait.

———————

It was the third day of waiting.

Ella sat on a crest of rock, high above the road, where she could see for a great distance in each direction. It was difficult business, waiting.

Beside her, the slope dropped down to the shore of a small lake, and Ella looked at the water hungrily. She could feel the buildup of dirt and dust on every part of her body. Her eyes were grimy and her cheeks stained with the signs of her travels.

It was the middle of the day. The winter that was so cold in the north seemed almost nonexistent here in Petrya, and Ella felt uncomfortably hot. Sweat ran down the skin between her breasts, adding to the buildup of grime. She imagined how she would look to Killian. Not that she cared of course; her priority was to get back what he had stolen.

Sunlight sparkled off the water. There was a tapered tree leaning out over the pool. She could see its rust-colored leaves reflected in the water.

Ella sighed and continued to watch the road, just as she had for the last three days. Looking as far as she could from the peak, she wondered how long it would take for a man to walk the distance of road her viewpoint covered. After some thought she estimated three hours.

Three hours. And that was if he came as soon as she left her perch. Most likely she would come back and find nothing had changed. In a worst-case scenario, she would come back and see him walking along the road with plenty of time to prepare.

Three hours, and all she needed was a moment.

The cool water beckoned.

42

Just be glad the Veznans never joined the Rebellion. I hear they were close. Ever seen what happens when a building is abandoned for a while? Nature beats civilization every time.

—Torak soldier, date unknown

Killian grimaced as his face pushed through a spiderweb. He peeled the web off, wiping his hands on his once-white cassock. He crept forward, pulling the branches to the sides, keeping his body low and under the cover of the trees. His feet were silent on the soft dirt, moving forward slowly.

The cloth of his acolyte's robe caught on a thorn. His movements even and careful, he untangled the garment and continued his stealthy approach.

Not for the first time he thanked the Sunlord for the providence that had given him a priest's outfit. It was a part he could play to perfection, having grown up around priests on the streets of Salvation and seen how they spoke and acted his whole life. People always assumed the best of a priest. They thought he was a gentle, nonviolent man, with little interest in worldly possessions, consumed with worship of the Evermen.

If they'd known some of the templars Killian had been acquainted with, people would swiftly revise their opinions.

His acolyte's robe meant the locals didn't look twice when, disheveled and stinking, he'd passed through the country towns of Altura's south. He was a priest, he lived on another plane, what more could be expected? Still, Killian needed to pay his way somehow and felt guilty about stealing from the innkeeper at The Steady Hand.

The garb had also been of major benefit when he'd been accosted by the bandits at Wondhip Pass. They'd snickered and called him weak. He'd played his part, pleading for them to let him on his way, before he'd withdrawn the cudgel he'd pocketed inside his robe and let at them.

He'd let his anger flow freely then, and even though he only fought one or two at a time as they got in each other's way, he bore bruises from the encounter. At least the bandits were another hazard between him and any pursuers.

It was a haven to be in Petrya. Killian wasn't especially fond of the passionate Petryans, but a priest of the Evermen was always welcome in their lands. He'd simply said he was on pilgrimage—on his way to Stonewater—and they'd taken him in, feeding him and giving him time to bathe and repair himself. Knowing that Petryans had a history of enmity with Altura, he'd also asked his hosts to be on the look out for Alturan bandits who'd been trailing him on the journey.

Killian had a good idea he was being followed. He knew the Alturans would stop at nothing to get back their Lexicon, and the high enchantress appeared to be a woman who possessed an extraordinary determination. He'd prepared his way both into and out of Altura with care, cutting across country to make himself harder to follow and covering his tracks with every bit of forest lore he knew. His acrobatic experience enabled him to climb down the cliff face, and unless his pursuers could fly, that would surely slow them down. The rope bridge across the Sarsen had been more difficult to cut, but he'd wrecked that completely.

It had been much easier the last time, when he'd escaped from Halaran. He'd only had to get to the Azure Plains to be in friendly lands.

Killian had come clean away then; there hadn't been the loose end of Ella left behind. Not that she knew anything about him, of course, but a physical description could be enough. He found he still thought about her, though he tried not to.

He'd left the town of Hatlatu with caution. The townsfolk said there was only been one Alturan, a woman. It had to be the high enchantress. With every sense on high alert, Killian ducked straight into the forest and shadowed the trail, still heading east.

And then he'd spotted her.

She'd chosen her position well. It was covered on two sides, and had a magnificent perspective on the road. It was sheer luck that Killian was on the approach that afforded him the opportunity to see her in the far distance. At first he'd stopped and stared; her form was so still it could have been part of the cliff, but then he saw her move.

Killian took a deep breath as he crawled under an arch of branches and drew closer to the peak.

If only he'd managed to keep some essence! Killian still had his necklace; all he needed was to copy the runes from it onto his body, and once again he would have been invisible.

There was no use worrying about what could have been. He only had his cudgel; it would have to be enough.

Killian approached slowly, without sound. She hadn't seem him coming—he knew that much. Her attention was focused on the road.

He thought about his strategy. He needed to catch her without her apparatus—the green dress, the orbs and knives, and other unknown weapons she undoubtedly carried.

Killian looked ever so carefully around a corner of the rock.

She was gone.

His heart suddenly hammering, Killian twisted, expecting to feel the scorching heat of an enchanted knife slipping through his ribs.

He looked wildly about, his cudgel out and ready. She was good, he realized. He had thought it all seemed too easy. Wouldn't she have bladesingers with her? Soldiers, trackers? He cursed himself for a fool for expecting her to be out here by herself.

His breath coming fast and shallow, Killian raced along, shadowing the bottom of the peak. He kept a sharp eye out for a flash of green, any indication of Alturans or anyone at all. He stopped and listened intently.

He heard a soft splashing sound from the direction of the lake.

As silently as he could Killian crept along the bed of undergrowth and brush. A twig snapped under his feet, and he stopped, ears pricked. There was another splash. Sweat dripped from his forehead, running into his eyes. He blinked it away and silently continued forward.

Killian looked through the bushes out into the rippling water of the pool.

His mouth dropped open.

Killian wondered if what he was seeing was an apparition, mere paces away.

It was a female figure with milk-white skin. Her back was to him, and her arms were busy at some task. She was knee deep in the water. Killian involuntarily caught his breath.

Her body rose out of the water like a water spirit. The water ran down her skin like beams of light caressing a piece of silk. Her shoulders tapered to a narrow waist from which her hips flared. She was beautiful.

She hummed a simple tune to herself, completely oblivious. The scene was so incongruous to what Killian had expected that he kept telling himself to look away—it must be a trap, some trick—but he couldn't tear his eyes off her.

She turned slightly, washing her stomach. He could see one of her breasts in profile, small but firm, crowned with a pointed pink nipple.

She turned all the way around. He looked up at her face, this image of beauty.

It was Ella.

Killian gasped. She glanced up, frowning at the bushes, before continuing to wash herself.

Her pale blonde hair cascaded in a long train, framing her heart-shaped face. Green eyes caught flecks of sunlight. She licked her rosy lips in concentration as she washed her arms.

Killian had to take this opportunity. She was without her enchanted dress, her tools. She was naked.

She turned again. Killian licked his dry lips as he drank in her body. With a great amount of difficulty, he tore his eyes away.

Ella was defenseless, and he had to take this chance.

43

The Imperial Legion is remarkable, is it not? The strongest, fittest, most lethal force in the world. They fight wherever I send them and are loyal unto death. How do I maintain such loyalty? The question is easier to answer than you may think. You see, most soldiers' greatest fear isn't death. It's being maimed. Spending life as a cripple. But you won't see cripples in Tingara. If one of our legionnaires loses an arm, or a leg, we replace it with a limb twice as strong. Scattered throughout the legion are meldings. And occasionally, we reward special loyalty by saving the direst cases. I'm sure you've heard of avengers.
—Emperor Xenovere V to Primate Melovar Aspen, 524 Y.E.

Ella quickly finished and left the lake, walking toward the grassy bank where she'd left her clothes. She'd been gone from her post for moments only.

Ella looked up to where her clothes should have been, and screamed.

Killian sat with his back to her, holding everything of hers on his lap: her clothes, her tools, her bag—everything.

"Here, put this on," he said, his voice strangely gruff. He flung a dress out with his arm. It landed a few paces behind him.

One arm covering her breasts, Ella scurried over to the gray dress and put it on. While he wasn't looking, she felt in the secret pocket.

"I've taken the liberty of collecting all of your little tools and tricks and throwing them in the lake," he said. His voice was still strange, as if tense with emotion.

"You threw them into the lake?"

"Your little bottle of black liquid. Essence, I suppose. Your long, thin, metal quill-thing."

He turned around. He had changed from the Killian she'd met. This man was weary; Ella could see it in his eyes. They were still just as blue, though. His long tousled hair was still a fiery red.

He regarded her seriously.

Ella faltered under his gaze. Her mouth went dry.

"Now, what are you doing here? The truth."

Ella thought about simply running. Then she looked at Killian. He was tall, and his legs were strong. Here she stood, barefoot, dripping wet. She wouldn't get far.

"I asked you a question," he said.

Ella glanced up at his face again. His eyes were different, she realized. Where before there had been a mischievous twinkle, a reckless daring, he now seemed more serious. Killian looked at her with a more steady expression, as if really seeing her.

"I came to retrieve our Lexicon. My brother is fighting out there. People are dying. Please, Killian, I want it back."

Ella waited for him to burst out laughing. Instead, he simply shook his head. "You need to understand. Lore shouldn't be used to wage war. It shouldn't define a group of people, causing them to identify with it and raise arms against anyone who is different. When the houses are one, we can finally work at making this world a better place."

This was the real Killian. Ella knew she was seeing him for the first time. "What are you talking about? Are those your words or the words of someone who put them in your mouth?"

Killian sighed. "It doesn't matter. If you could see the things we have already accomplished . . . But no mind." He shook his head sadly. "I believe you, but I can't believe you would be so bold. Who else is with you?"

"No one."

"Who else!"

Seeing Killian angry suddenly made Ella aware of just how vulnerable she was. If he were going to hurt her, if he were going to do anything to her, he would have done it, wouldn't he?

"No one," she said softly.

Killian visibly calmed. He gathered himself for a moment, appearing less confident, more unsettled than the Killian she had known before. "I should kill you now, but that's not my way. The bladesinger was an accident. Perhaps you'll be useful in case your high enchantress shows up. Here." He handed Ella her boots. "Put these on."

Killian seemed strangely afraid to touch her skin, and the few moments his hands touched hers, his breath caught.

"Here's your shoulder bag," he said. "I'm taking you with me."

Killian tied Ella's wrists with a length of twine and led her back onto the road. He said there wasn't much point in keeping to the backcountry now; they would make better time on the road. Besides, he now had a bargaining piece in case any pursuers caught up to him.

Ella still couldn't believe what had happened to her. To come all this way, only to get caught so easily. She should have known better than to let down her guard, even for an instant.

Worst of all she'd lost her essence and her tools. She was in a strange land, being taken the-Skylord-knew-where by a man she knew nothing about. She only prayed that the high enchantress would catch them before Killian took her to whomever it was he worked for.

Killian was silent for a long time, a silence Ella didn't want to break. He seemed lost in thought. His breathing was heavy. She noticed that he occasionally winced when he took a step.

"Are you in pain?" Ella murmured.

He grunted in reply, "It's nothing."

They continued as the afternoon wore on. The sun cast its setting rays from behind them, illuminating the barren land. Rocks and boulders were strewn everywhere, and a haze of dust rose from the earth in all directions. The colors of rust and tan were prevalent, with every shade in between. Even the occasional copse of trees or distant forest was tinged red.

It seemed the Petryans' chosen color of red meant more to them than elemental fire. It was the color of their land.

"How about you—are your hands tied too tightly?" Killian said suddenly.

Ella started; they'd last spoken so long ago.

"A little," she said.

"I'll take a look when we make camp for the night," Killian said.

The earth turned a deeper shade of red as the sky darkened. The moon rose above the horizon, tainted crimson by the dusty haze in the sky. Stars began to show, first one, then another, until there were hundreds of pinpricks visible in the twilight.

"So many stars," Ella said.

"Your people use too many nightlamps in Sarostar, with your Crystal Palace radiating colors and all your enchantments. You miss the stars. You should see . . ." Killian trailed off.

"Should see what?"

"Nothing," Killian said.

"You don't give much away, do you?" Ella said.

"We'll turn off now and find a place to camp for the night. We won't use any nightlamps. A heatplate would be welcome, though. Did I see one in your satchel?"

Ella had renewed the simple stone device since the disaster at the waterfall. "Yes." She sighed.

They made camp in a clearing under the stars. Killian eased the bonds on Ella's hands but wouldn't free them, making all of the preparations for the camp and meal himself. He rested a small pot on the glowing runes and filled it with water, then added a few teaspoons of powder to the pot.

Ella smelled the aroma. "Cherl!" she exclaimed with a smile. It reminded her of home.

Killian smiled slightly. "One of a few Alturan foods I can't do without."

While the water was heating, he stretched and placed his travel bag against a tree. The edge parted slightly, and Ella could see part of a green cover.

As Ella saw the Lexicon, her breath caught. Killian's back was to her, and she wondered if she had the strength to . . .

He turned and saw her gaze. "Don't even think about it," he said in a grim voice. "You touch me or steal from me or try to escape, and I'll tie you up here and leave you for dead."

It was spoken so matter-of-factly that Ella felt a chill. She wondered again about this strange man with his peculiar name and distinctive looks. She supposed he worked for the emperor.

Killian handed her a mug of cherl, deactivating the heatplate. They drank together in darkness.

Then he came over to her, breathing heavily, and for a moment Ella felt a qualm in her chest, but he just had another length of twine in his hands.

"Get comfortable," he said gruffly. "I'm tying your legs, so don't expect to be able to move much."

He was surprisingly gentle as he tied Ella's legs, before he went to sleep himself.

Ella lay still, listening to his breathing. He tossed and turned, trying to get comfortable. She heard him moan in pain several times as he rolled onto his back.

It serves him right, she thought.

Any day now the runes on the Alturan Lexicon could fade. Ella didn't know if she had days or weeks, but she knew that renewing the Lexicon required essence and special knowledge. Perhaps if Ella read the book, she could understand how to renew it, but even so she had no essence.

Ella sighed.

She thought about Miro, so far away, fighting for his life. There had to be something she could do to get the Lexicon back to Altura. She thought about Amber and her marriage to Igor Samson. Was Amber happy? Layla's drowned eyes came to her mind, looking at her reproachfully, her skin wrinkled. Last of all Ella thought about Brandon.

Then she slept.

———◆———

Ella woke in the morning, feeling cramped but refreshed. Killian was asleep, with the heatplate separating the two of them.

Ella tested the twine carefully. It held her hands tightly bound together, the wrists facing opposite directions. There was no chance of escape.

Feeling like she'd lost all circulation in her hands and feet, she started rubbing her hands against her body.

"I know how to tie a knot. You won't break through it."

Ella quickly glanced up. Killian was sitting up, watching her. Ella glared at him.

"I wasn't trying to escape. My hands are completely numb. I'm probably going to lose them to gangrene."

He snorted. "You're not going to lose them to gangrene. Here."

He came over and, watching her carefully, loosened the twine around her hands, leaving her feet tied. He rubbed her hands gently between his own, the color slowly returning.

His touch was gentle.

"Please,"—Ella spoke so low, she almost whispered—"can't you let me go?"

"Without the Lexicon?" he said.

"No, not without the Lexicon." Ella pulled her hands away in anger.

Killian shrugged and tied her hands back up again. He then unbound her feet, working on them in silence and then leaving them untied.

He stood up. "We're leaving."

———◆———

This was not the clear day the previous one had been. Winter came back for a time—not in the way it chilled the air, but in the clouds that turned the sky a sullen gray.

Ella felt rested, but Killian looked as if he'd been through a night of complete misery. His blue eyes were bloodshot, and his back obviously pained him. He set a determined pace, though, the dust kicking up from his boots under the white priest's robe. Ella had no choice but to keep up.

He caught her gaze. "Did you hear it last night?"

"Hear what?"

"The screams." He looked back over his shoulder. "There's something following us, I can feel it. I don't know if it's your high enchantress, but there have been noises at night, sounds that chill my blood."

Ella recalled hearing eerie sounds in the night. "I think I know what you mean. Shrieks."

He looked at her quickly. "Yes, that's it. Do you know what it is?"

"No." Ella looked at him in return. "Do you?"

"No."

They walked along in silence.

If anything, the sky grew darker as the day progressed. Ella couldn't even tell where in the sky the sun was. It was all the color of smoke.

"Tell me then," Ella said suddenly.

"What?"

"Tell me. Tell me the part you play in this, why you think it's so necessary to attack my people."

Killian paused for a long moment, and she thought he wasn't going to reply. When she was about to open her mouth, he spoke.

"Let me ask you some questions first. What are the houses?"

"The houses? They are peoples, nations. Governed by a high lord and with individual customs, attitudes, and culture."

"And lore?"

"Yes, and with their own lore."

"What's the emperor's role?"

Ella felt like she was in class at the Academy again. "The emperor's role is to govern the realm and facilitate commerce and trade. He is supposed to keep the peace and prevent war."

"And how about the Assembly of Templars?"

"The priesthood? Well, as well as teaching us about the Evermen and the origin of lore, the primate oversees the distribution of essence. With no need or use for it themselves, the templars are

405

trusted to help produce and guard the essence. If one house, even the Imperial House, were to try to take essence by guile or force, the wrath of not just the houses, but the templars too, would rise against the offending house."

"Good, good," Killian said. "That pretty much sums it up. Do you think it's a good system?"

"Good? It's not perfect, but it works—to a greater or lesser extent."

"Do you think it could be better?"

"There are probably things I'd like to improve—but I'm not a high lord, so I'm not really in a position to do so."

"So you think a high lord is the best person to make improvements?"

"Only for his house. The emperor should be able to make changes that improve conditions for everyone. Limit the power of the high lords, perhaps. Or set out a universal system of rights."

Killian's eyes lit up. "See? You think it too. Don't you think it's terrible that some people have wealth while others starve? Or that here in Petrya the high lord can execute a law-abiding citizen for no greater reason than that he wants to?"

"Yes I do," Ella said. "The emperor—"

"The emperor!" Killian spat. "Seranthia is a cesspit of corruption."

Ella nodded. "My brother Miro said the same thing."

Killian scowled, making Ella wonder who he worked for, if not the emperor.

Ella took a breath. "So what do you think the solution is then? To steal Altura and Halaran's Lexicons and kill their young men in battle?"

"It's regrettable, but . . ."

"Regrettable? My brother is there!"

Killian fended off Ella's arm as she moved to strike him. "Listen to me!" he said heatedly. "The time of the houses is over. It's time for a new start, a change. One nation, with no corrupt emperor, no random executions, no wars, no essence rationing. Don't you see, Ella? My master . . ."

"Your master? Who is your master?"

Killian suddenly stopped talking.

"Listen to *me*," Ella said with venom, "and you listen well. I don't care about your ridiculous ideals. My people are being forced to submit. We are being warred upon. Your thievery will see the end of everything I hold dear. Noble ends don't justify vicious means. Remember that, Killian."

There was silence for the rest of the day.

That night they went through the same routine of food and camp, speaking only when necessary. Ella felt uncertain and adrift. Killian seemed equally confused, as if wrestling with inner turmoil.

After they ate, they both sat in stillness.

Killian looked up. "It says so, in the book, you know."

"What do you mean?"

"The Lexicons are just different chapters in a greater work. The houses were never meant to be separate. They all say it."

"Show me." Ella held her breath.

Killian went to his bag, gently taking out the green-covered book. He held it in both arms; it was a precious thing. He took Ella's nightlamp and activated it at the lowest setting, then squatted down next to her. She could feel his closeness, and his smell came to her.

Ella couldn't believe she was next to the Lexicon of House Altura. She had dreamt about seeing it her whole life. She longed to touch it, but she knew he would never let her.

"See?" Killian said. "The number one." He pointed at the rune on the cover.

Ella looked intently at the number rune. It glowed softly, and she tried to judge it. The rune would fade in perhaps a few weeks. At that point, every seeker, every nightlamp, and every zenblade would fail. Back in Sarostar, the invisible arch of the Runebridge would disappear. The Crystal Palace would cease its display of colors.

And when that happened, the Alturan army was doomed.

Unaware of the desperation in Ella's eyes, Killian opened the cover. The pages were made of a strange metallic fabric, remarkably thin. The book contained a great deal more pages than seemed possible from its girth.

There was a message on the first page, written in a graceful flowing script.

To the common people of Merralya, one and all, I give you this, the first volume in my Tomes of Lore. Evrin Evenstar.

"Evrin Evenstar," Ella started.

"Does that name mean anything to you?"

"No, no. I just met someone with a similar name. Evrin Alistair. He was a little strange, but I doubt he's hundreds of years old," Ella said wryly. She thought of the old man.

Killian turned the page. A title was embossed, the colors leaping from the page with incredible beauty: *The Lore of the Enchanter.*

Ella felt goose bumps rise on her skin. She couldn't believe she was here, seeing this book. She wished she held it herself.

"That's it," Killian said. He closed the book. "They're all numbered, as if they're made to follow a series. Perhaps there were never supposed to be separate houses, each with its own lore. Perhaps we were all supposed to be one."

"Please, may I see some more?" Ella couldn't believe she was begging.

"No." He saw her crestfallen expression. "I'm sorry."

"Well, what does it say?"

"I don't really understand any of it. I only know one matrix, and that I have to copy."

Ella's interest was piqued. "What is it?"

He grinned. "I'll tell you another time. *Tish-toklur.*" He deactivated the nightlamp.

Ella could only just make out his figure against the black sky. There were no stars tonight. No moon to light their camp.

"I'm not going to tie your legs. I didn't like those strange shrieking sounds last night, whatever they were, and I'm not going to risk some animal taking you while you lie there helpless."

Ella shuddered at his description. She was still helpless enough with her hands tied. With some beast out there in the dark, she knew she wasn't going anywhere.

"What was that?"

"Quick, get the nightlamp on! Lord of the Sun, can you hear it?"

"*Tish-tassine.*"

The camp was suddenly bright with warm light. Ella blinked, her eyes wide with fright.

Killian stood shirtless, cudgel in hand. The snarling sound came again, from a different direction this time.

"It's not far away."

"What do we do?" Ella asked. "Do we stay here, or do we leave?"

"We stay here," Killian said. "Once we leave, it can herd us or pick us off, whatever it is."

Something black passed among some trees, only paces away. Ella screamed.

"Here!" Killian threw Ella something. It was one of her enchanted stones. It fell to the ground beside her. Ella realized with a start that he hadn't thrown them all into the river after all.

"I can't move my hands!"

"Oh."

The snarling sound came from the trees in front of them. Killian knelt at Ella's back, cutting through the bonds in seconds.

She picked up the stone. "*Tuk-talour,*" she said and activated the runes, throwing the stone in the direction of the sound.

"Look away!" she cried.

A sudden bright flash came out of the trees. Stars sparkled across Ella's vision. There was a sound of crashing through the trees.

Then there was silence.

Ella and Killian were both panting, faces pale in the light of the nightlamp. Finally, Killian spoke.

"Are you all right?"

"Yes. Yes, I'm fine. But if it's all right with you, I don't want to sleep with my arms bound anymore."

Killian chuckled. Ella laughed too; it had a slightly hysterical edge to it.

"Here," Killian said. "I'll come and sit next to you. You catch some sleep."

"We'll take turns keeping watch."

Killian nodded. "We'll take turns."

***

Ella watched Killian's chest rising and falling as he slept. He tossed fitfully, his skin clammy. Perhaps his wound was infected. She decided to have a look when morning came.

Ella caught herself. What was she doing? She should be smashing his head in with a rock and running off in the morning with the Lexicon.

There appeared to be a change coming over him, though. Ella didn't know what it was, but she could hope. And it was no time for her to be in the wilds alone.

Watching Killian sleep, Ella saw a small amulet on a chain around his neck. Ella had seen it before, when he'd been half-drowned in the Sarsen and the high enchantress had removed his shirt.

Ella leaned forward, carefully watching his eyes and listening closely for a change in his breathing. The front of the amulet was plain, simply decorated. She could just make out the back. There were runes there.

Ella leaned her arm over him and, as carefully as she could, lifted the hanging pendant. She turned it over, her arm precarious over his body. There were definitely runes inscribed on the back. She read the matrix; it wasn't a common sequence, but it wasn't uncommon either.

Ella frowned in puzzlement. When activated, the sequence would cause the amulet to disappear. It was a novelty trick, used for lovers to mysteriously cause their gift to appear out of thin air.

To add even more to Ella's perplexity, the runes were dead. The essence had drained long ago. The amulet wasn't even functional.

Killian sighed deeply and Ella froze, her arm still across his body. She let go of the amulet just as he moved his body, nestling in to her. Her arm now lay across his chest.

Ella stayed motionless for a long time, then relaxed. She could feel his heartbeat under her arm. Her head was nestled in the crook of his body. Killian's breath came softly as he relaxed.

She would wait until he was deep in sleep again, and then she would move. She would wait just a moment . . .

44

*Reputation is the shell a man discards when he leaves life
for immortality. His character he takes with him.*
—Sermons of Primate Melovar Aspen, 540 Y.E.

Ella and Killian both woke at the same instant. It was sometime before dawn. He looked about in confusion, noticing her cuddled up to his body. She couldn't read the expression he gave her.

"I . . . I don't know what happened. I guess I fell asleep."

"Shh!"

At the edge of hearing, Ella heard a man's scream. It was suddenly followed by a roar, a wild cry of triumph. A wailing sound rose and fell, as if a man were in deathly pain. "Do you hear that?" she said to Killian.

"It sounds like the beast found other prey," Killian said.

The screaming continued for hours until it was suddenly cut short. Ella trembled.

The first vestiges of gray tinged the black sky as the sun rose to another dismal day. When it was light enough to see, they gathered the camp together and began the day's journey, neither mentioning the fact of Ella's unbound hands.

The sky above rumbled softly, as if perpetually on the edge of a mighty storm. Ella stayed close to Killian, the memory of the man's scream still fresh in her mind. Killian set a brisk pace.

"We'll need to cover a great deal of distance today," he said. "We need to get to a town. I worry we might not survive another night with whatever it is that's stalking us. The nearest town is Torlac, most of the way to Tlaxor, the Petryan capital. Torlac is a common way-stop for the merchants bold enough to trade with the Petryans. It's on the edge of the great volcano Halapusa."

"Can't we just turn back?"

He shook his head. "No, it's behind us, whatever it is. Besides, we would never make it to another town before nightfall. It must be Torlac." He looked at her sharply. "You'll have to be very careful. They bear no love for Alturans in these parts. That blonde hair is a dead giveaway."

He smiled at her expression. "I like it, though."

They managed to find a clear stream where they could refill their water bottles—they'd been running dangerously low. Killian teasingly asked Ella if she would like to take a bath, receiving a sharp blow and a heated blush in return. She still didn't know how much he'd seen that day; even thinking about it was embarrassing.

The sun came out for a moment, and it was with lighter hearts that they marched along the dusty road, the fears of the night temporarily banished.

The road began to incline, rising steadily. The pair passed through gullies and ravines, the rust-colored rock jagged and unyielding.

"We're already on it, you know."

"On what?"

"Mount Halapusa."

"We're on a mountain?"

He grinned. "Yes. It's huge, isn't it? I can't imagine how big it must have been before it blew, to leave behind such an immense crater. It must have been the biggest mountain in the world."

"Do you have big mountains in your land?"

He smiled at her. "Not too subtle. We have one mountain. It isn't very big, but it's very famous."

"Stonewater! You're from Aynar?"

He smiled. "From Salvation, to be specific."

Ella decided to keep the tone light. He was finally talking.

"What's it like there?"

"You've never been on pilgrimage?"

"No. Are you a priest?"

"No, no. Nothing like that. I was a . . . an acrobat actually."

"An acrobat?" Ella couldn't believe it. Then, seeing how lean and strong his body was, how nimble he was on his feet, she suddenly could.

"Well, I wasn't always an acrobat." His eyes grew distant. "I lived in Salvation. I have no memories of my parents. The first thing I remember is the queue at the temple shelter. The boys used to hurt each other, badly, so that they would be first in line. The food always ran out, you see."

Ella stayed quiet. She thought about her own childhood. At least she had some happy memories. She'd been loved by someone. At least she'd been clothed, fed, and protected by Brandon and Miro.

"I saw one boy, they burned his eyes out. He just screamed pitifully for food. The priests tried to help him, but there were so many to help. They tried hard to do good deeds, but Aynar isn't a wealthy place. With no lore, cities like Salvation have nothing to trade with the houses. We saw the lords on pilgrimage sometimes, with their rich clothing and bright jewelry. The priests always said these were the ones who should be paying to feed and clothe us."

"They do," Ella said softly. "In lands like Altura and Halaran, at least. Were you educated? Were you taught skills?"

Killian shook his head. "The priests did their best. Some were accepted into the Assembly of Templars. They were the lucky ones. Others became sick and died." He looked at her. "The rest became beggars or thieves. I was one of the latter."

Ella nodded, not willing to speak for fear he would stop.

He smiled. "I was a good thief. The best. I was quicker than anyone, quieter than a falling feather. Then one day I met my match. I stole a jeweled timepiece from a tall, black-haired man, a Halrana. He had a ferocious temper. I taunted him." He chuckled ruefully. "I suppose that would do it."

Ella pictured the scene and smiled. She supposed being stolen from and mocked would have that effect.

"I ran across the rooftops, up the steep sides of one of the temples. He came right after me. I have never seen someone so agile. He leapt from building to building with no fear. This was my city, I knew it by heart, and here was a stranger, gaining on me. I ran faster and tripped on a rail. The next thing I knew I woke up with a knife to my throat.

"'You lost my timepiece,' he growled—he had this rolling voice. 'It fell into the sewer when you tripped. Now you owe me a great deal of money.'

"There was nothing I could do. He could kill me with no questions asked—I was a problem to the priests as it was. One of the templars stood nearby, nodding, waiting for him to stick me.

"I began to thrash around. If I was going to die, it wasn't going to be quick and easy. The templar kicked me, but the man made him back away.

"'He's my problem now,' the Halrana said.

"He made me go with him to a great tent erected on the outskirts of town, where they'd set up a traveling show in hope of making money from the wealthy pilgrims. There was an acrobat, an animal trainer, a juggler, and an escape artist. The Halrana was an acrobat, but he was also the leader of the troupe. He made me work there, to do everything he told me." Killian's voice continued expressively, he gave the story richness with his voice. "I loved that man."

"What was his name?" Ella asked.

"Marney. His name was Marney Beldara. He was the best acrobat I have ever seen. He taught me every day. He fed me and clothed me. I soon became good, very good." Killian gestured with his hands.

"Then I met a woman. Her name was Carla. She wasn't beautiful, but she was clever, and she made me laugh. She joined the troupe as we traveled around Tingara."

Killian took a deep breath. "I didn't like Tingara. It was worse than Aynar, much worse. I could see the urchins lurking around the big tent, picking pockets in the crowd. The beggars there had it worse than I ever did. They say the streetclans in Seranthia teach the children sweet songs and then cripple them, sending them out to beg."

Ella put her hand to her mouth.

Killian continued. "Carla and I became lovers. One night, we left the camp and stole into Seranthia to be alone together. To see the night shows. When we returned, the camp was gone. The big tent was no more."

Ella held her breath.

"It had all been burned to the ground. I asked everyone in the area what had happened, but no one would talk to me. Finally an old woman told me they'd been taken by the legion. Someone from the crowd had reported that the troupe was spreading sedition against the emperor. All I could remember was Marney saying something about helping the street children."

Killian's voice began to shake with emotion. "We arrived in Seranthia just as they were lined up along the top of the Wall, along with a bunch of other 'seditionists.' We could see the blood on their skin; they'd been cut to pieces by the whip. They were all there. They were my family. We watched as they were pushed off the Wall, their bodies broken beyond recognition when they hit the bottom. Carla left me then. I didn't blame her. Marney was her father."

Tears slid silently down Ella's face, but Killian didn't notice. He seemed to be living the events all over again.

"I buried them all, as best as I could. I dug their graves in the forest with my hands, carrying their poor, destroyed bodies one by one. Then I went back to the ruins of the camp, where nothing but the corpses of the stage animals in their blackened cages remained. I don't know how long I stayed there.

"Eventually, I made my way back to Salvation. I started to steal again, but this time I don't think I cared whether I was caught or not. I got into trouble a few times, and I broke some bones. Then I stole from a templar, but my body gave up on me." Killian shrugged. "They put me into a cell in Stonewater, and one day they gave me something to drink, some kind of black potion. The templars watched me carefully. It tasted strange but it didn't affect me, and they were excited."

"What do you think it was?" Ella asked.

"I really don't know. Then one day I felt a hand on my shoulder. I turned, and there he was. He asked me my name, and I told him. He said, 'Do not fear, Killian, for all your troubles are now over.'

"I asked him who he was, but I think I already knew. He took me in, cared for me. He gave me a small house in Salvation, with my own guards and everything. I call him my master."

"Who was it?" Ella said.

"Primate Melovar Aspen, leader of the Assembly of Templars."

Killian looked away, and they continued their long march.

Ella digested the information as if worrying at a piece of meat. Something strange was occurring. The templars had no lore, no knowledge about runes or matrices or activation sequences. However, they possessed essence in abundance.

Somewhere in Stonewater, the primate's mountain home, the templars kept the relics for producing essence. Only they could operate the machinery of the Evermen that created the black liquid.

Ella needed to figure out how the primate fit into everything that was happening. She had been so focused on the emperor. Was stealing the Lexicons simply a way of weakening the houses? Was it the primate's plan to seize the Lexicons and eradicate lore from the world? But Lexicons weren't made by human hands and couldn't be easily destroyed, and without lore there would be no need for essence—how would he control the houses, those who would do anything to get their Lexicons back? The primate couldn't expect to conquer all of Merralya, even with every templar warrior at his disposal.

Yet something was happening. They were at war. People were dying. The Halrana were fighting for their very existence, and soon it would be Altura's turn. If the primate had a plan, where did the emperor stand in all of this?

Killian appeared lost in thought too. He had obviously brought up memories he'd thought long buried. Ella's feelings toward him had changed too; she knew him better now. She understood his purpose. She'd shared herself with him back in Altura, and he'd now shared himself. Yet he was still distant. What would happen when they reached the Petryan trade town of Torlac? Would he decide to help her rather than crippling her people? Or would he trick her and leave her behind, as he'd done last time?

The sun burst through a hole in the clouds. The horizon rose in an unbroken line, dropping off suddenly in the distance, as if they were walking toward a cliff.

"We're walking to the rim of the crater," said Killian. "There is a small canyon just on the edge. That's where Torlac is located."

"When will we arrive?"

Killian looked at the sky. "Before sundown, if we're lucky. After sundown, if we're not."

"Killian?"

"What?" He frowned at her.

"Thank you for telling me. About your life, I mean. It must have been hard."

He shrugged. "There are people who've had it worse, I should know."

"Still," Ella said, struggling to find the words. "I . . ."

"Come with me," he said.

He took her by the hand, his palm warm and dry. Ella followed him to a crest in the rock—a random peak—tall and with a shallow enough slope to be easily ascended.

He laughed as he half-led, half-dragged her up the hill. Soon she stood with him at the summit, panting.

"Look!" he said.

Ella's gaze followed his arm, and she gasped.

Ella looked over the rim of the cliff and into the bowl of the crater itself. It was immense. A road wound down from the rim, twisting first one way, then another, to eventually reach the shore of the sky-blue volcanic lake. An island occupied the center of the lake, and a tiered city perched atop the landmass, rising level upon level to a turreted palace on the very summit. Flags and pennants fluttered in the wind, visible even from this distance, the *raj hada* of the elementalists a red-and-blue blur.

419

"There's something rising from the water. What's that haze?"

"It's steam," Killian said. "The water is hot, almost boiling."

"It's true then. How do they cross it?"

"See that small square halfway across the lake? There's another one, passing it."

"I see it."

"That's the Halapusa Ferry."

"It's definitely a secure city."

"That it is, Ella. Look over to the far right now—see that cleft in the crater's rim? That's where we're headed: the trade town of Torlac. We'd best be going if we're going to get there before nightfall."

45

Choose your ground well. War is a game of geography.
—Memoirs of Emperor Xenovere I, page 218, 381 Y.E.

High Enchantress Evora Guinestor blanched when she saw the body. Her scout had been torn to pieces, completely dismembered, viscera spread across several hundred paces. The man's head was finally found by one of the trackers, an expression of horror still readable on what was left of his face.

"There's still one more scout missing," Captain Joram said soberly.

Evora composed herself. "Thank you, Captain. How many does that make in total?"

"Five. Two trackers and three scouts. Whatever it is, it'll be onto the sentries next. High Enchantress, may I have a word alone?"

"Of course, Captain."

Evora walked away from the other men. The four ever-present bladesingers came along unbidden.

They had left Alturan lands some time ago. Moving such a large group of soldiers—nearly forty encumbered men—through the Wondhip Pass had been a difficult task, but they had come through with only a few cuts and scrapes. Her trackers said the thief had come this way, as had Ella. They'd also found evidence of two separate struggles in the pass. Apparently, the thief had been accosted by bandits, but escaped. The second struggle was a different story—Evora could see the scorching marks left on the stone, burn marks that only powerful runes could make.

The young enchantress was learning.

One of the men said he could pass for a Petryan. He'd scouted the town of Hatlatu, learning that there had been a struggle between some officials and a young woman with pale blonde hair who had asked about a priest.

Then the trackers came back and reported that Ella had been captured. Evora only hoped the girl came out alive, unharmed by the hands of the thief.

Their entire journey had been plagued by cliffs, rivers, and treacherous passes. Now there was some evil creature out in the wild.

Evora could tell when she was being hunted.

Her guards couldn't keep up a fast pace and still be fully prepared for whatever was out there. Something was toying with them, slowing them.

High Enchantress Evora Guinestor had a fury now, a pent-up rage that needed releasing. The trackers now told her they were only a day behind the thief and his captive. She would see him pay.

Joram waited until they were a short distance from the men. He crossed his arms in front of his chest. "Those wounds—they weren't made by any beast. It was a man."

"A man?" Evora raised an eyebrow.

He nodded.

"It's true," one of the bladesingers said. Captain Joram frowned at him. The bladesinger looked away, unperturbed.

"How do you know?"

Joram continued. "The weapon used was a sword or perhaps a knife. The slashes were made by an edged weapon, not claws or teeth."

"But the sounds—the snarls, the roars?"

"I can't hazard a guess, High Enchantress."

Evora nodded. "You did well by telling me this away from the men. How are they holding up?"

"Fearful, but determined."

Evora decided she was beginning to like Captain Joram. He may have been thorough and rigorous, but he was also truthful.

"Good. Speed is our ally in this chase, but we mustn't neglect our defenses."

"High Enchantress, let me find this creature," one of the blade-singers said.

"No."

"I could wait . . ."

"I said no!" Evora turned the full weight of her glare on the bladesinger. He backed down.

Silently, they rejoined the company. The men's faces were grim—they knew they were far from home. It was unlikely in this barren land, but if a party of Petryans caught them out here, it would be impossible to explain their presence. They would be considered a war party, and treated as such.

Captain Joram spoke. "Remember men, House Petrya are thus far neutral in this conflict, but our presence here is far from welcome. Stay alert. Scouts, I want you to stay in sight at all times. Trackers, continue to read the signs, but always stay between the scouts and the main body. Move out."

The bladesingers stayed close to the high enchantress as they moved. Every rock was a potential enemy. Every tree could contain a foe. It was tough going, and it wore on everyone's nerves. The men had been up since before dawn and continued long past sunset. It was the only way they could keep pace with their light-traveling quarry while still maintaining an effective defensive formation.

All the while, there wasn't a man who didn't know the high enchantress was burning up inside. Calling always for more speed. Longer marches. Her countenance was so fearsome that the men relied on Captain Joram to communicate with her on their behalf.

They ate on the march. The sky was so darkened with clouds that Evora's glowing timepiece was the only way to know it was midday. The men felt the presence of some unseen evil. The darkening of the sky only echoed the feeling.

Suddenly one of the scouts sprinted down the hillside, yelling as he ran.

"Pull yourself together, man!" Captain Joram said.

The scout spoke between gasps. "Sir, I saw it. Gayal, he was on the ridge, not far from me. One moment he was there, the next he was gone. It was so quick I couldn't believe my eyes. The blood, it gushed out of his body."

Evora could see the men exchange fearful glances. She wished the scout would be quiet, hold his tongue and give his message elsewhere.

Joram pressed him for more information. "Yes, yes. But what exactly did you see?"

"It was a shape in white robes. It walked on two legs—it must have been a man. I thought I saw steel."

They all heard it then, a great snarling sound reverberating from the hills. Even Evora jumped when it was followed a heartbeat later by a piercing shriek.

The bladesinger looked at the high enchantress, one eyebrow raised. Sighing, she nodded. He loosened the zenblade at his side, a wicked grin on his face.

They posted half the already exhausted men as sentries, and the other half caught what little sleep they could. The bladesinger had left at dusk, and there wasn't a man or woman among them who didn't watch his departure, a prayer to the Skylord on their lips.

They lit up every nightlamp and all the soldiers checked their weapons and then checked them again. These weren't common Alturan soldiers; they were elite infantry, with enchanted metal armor of overlapping scales and the best single-activation swords the enchanters knew how to make.

Yet whatever was out there had scared battle-hardened soldiers who had faced the Imperial Legion during the Rebellion without a qualm.

From far away came a sudden snarling.

"Look!" a soldier said.

A piercing bright light flared somewhere in the night. Even through trees and other obstructions, it still lit half the night sky.

"That's one of ours," said the high enchantress. The men looked at her. "It must be the young enchantress. We're close."

There was silence for a time. Every face showed a soldier on edge.

A man's scream sounded in the night, somewhere not far away, the note one of extreme pain. Evora held her breath. The scream was suddenly cut off.

The roar was ear-splitting, so loud Evora gritted her teeth in pain. It was a cry of triumph.

Silence again.

Then the screaming began. It was the bladesinger's voice, a rising and falling cry of utter pain and torment.

The bladesinger's screams continued throughout the rest of the night. At times the sound would stop, only to start again.

One of the bladesingers stood, his face white. "I'm going to help him."

"You'll do no such thing," Evora snapped. "Remember your duty. There is nothing you can do for him."

Not a man among them had any sleep that night. They stayed silent, rigid with tension, until the dawn saw the cries ended, and the clouded sky signaled the start of a new day.

Evora had wondered when it would be coming. She looked down her nose at Captain Joram, her face like stone.

"We need to turn back," he said.

"I will be giving the orders around here, Captain. And I'll remind you of that, this once, before I have you removed from service and find a replacement."

He nodded. He wasn't a fool. He knew he was speaking out of turn.

Evora softened a little. "Listen, Captain. A hard day's march will see us in Torlac. You saw the display from the girl last night—the thief is facing the same problem we are. He will seek safety in Torlac. One more day, Captain. One more day and we will have him."

Captain Joram nodded, turning away.

Evora sighed. It wouldn't be long before she faced open mutiny. She was so close she could feel it. Let them be unhappy; let them continue for one day more, and she would reward them when they arrived back in Altura.

Torlac lay ahead. And with it, the Lexicon.

46

If you chase two lovers, you will not catch either one.

—Alturan saying

Killian threw off his shirt and collapsed into the bed, groaning with exhaustion.

Ella headed directly for the tub, sighing with pleasure when she saw the steaming buckets of water resting beside it. She looked at Killian; he seemed fast asleep, but she wasn't about to disrobe just because she thought he was sleeping.

Ella strode briskly to the bed. "Roll over," she said.

"What?" he said, his eyes bleary.

"Roll over. I want to use that blanket to shield the bath."

Killian rolled over, and Ella took the blanket away from him, but she couldn't help looking at his body, and suddenly all thoughts of a bath fled. The red scar down his back was puffed and angry, a line that started between his shoulder blades and stretched nearly to his waist.

"Your back! How can you keep going? Doesn't it hurt?"

"It does," he admitted.

Ella strode to the door leading from their room and opened it, poking her head out to scan the hallway. A maid stood holding some towels, a surprised look on her face.

"Blessings," said Ella, putting on the accent in the way Killian had shown her. "Do you have honey and wine?" The maid nodded. "And some clean linen we could purchase? Here." Ella handed her a coin. "Please bring them up immediately."

The maid nodded.

"I think you need a bath more than me," Ella said, entering the room again and closing the door.

"I just want to sleep," Killian said.

"I mean it. Get in. Do you want to get bad blood, reaching from your back to your heart?"

"Bad blood?"

Ella hoped it sounded official. "Yes, bad blood. Now, get in the bath."

Killian slowly sat up on the bed. There was a knock on the door as the maid brought up the requested items.

"Thank you," Ella said.

"Blessings," the maid replied.

Ella closed the door, and turning, she saw Killian was already in the bath.

"Trying to avoid making it even, are you?"

"What are you talking about?"

"You saw me. I know you did," she said.

"Saw you?"

"You know. In the lake. Bathing."

"I did not."

"It doesn't bother me," Ella said airily. "I would often dance naked in Altura. For men."

He snorted. "I doubt that."

"Why wouldn't I?"

"First, they don't do that kind of thing in Altura. Second, you'd hardly had a night out drinking before I met you, let alone dancing naked."

"Don't you think men would pay to see me? Is that it? I've heard it's quite common in Seranthia for women to dance naked for money."

"Trust me," Killian said. "It's not a profession you would enjoy."

"Don't you think I'm beautiful enough?"

Killian looked at her seriously. "I think you are the most beautiful woman I have ever seen."

Ella blushed and looked away. The atmosphere in the room became uncomfortable. She was suddenly incredibly conscious that there was only one bed and that they would most likely be sharing it. Her heart started to race.

Taking a slow breath, Ella moved to crouch by the bath and fixed her attention on Killian's wounds. She took a rough piece of caustic soap and lathered it up in the water. Without warning she began to rub the lather against the wound in Killian's back with a wet cloth.

"Aaah!" Killian cried in pain.

"Don't be a baby," Ella said, smiling. She was starting to enjoy herself.

Some yellow pus and small bits of dirt came from the wound. It started to bleed again, first the dark black blood of infection, but then followed by fresh red liquid that finally stopped flowing altogether.

"Good," Ella said. "I think I've cleaned it. Can I trust you to keep it clean?"

"Yes, mother," he smiled.

Ella prepared the bandages while Killian finished washing. She turned her back while he dried himself and pulled on some trousers, and then she dressed the wound on his back.

Ella emptied and refilled the bath and hung up the blanket while she bathed, seeing the water turn from clear to dark brown as the grime of the hard march came away. Lord of the Sky, it felt good to be clean again. She spent a long time brushing her hair, running a comb through the tangled knots. She dressed and removed her protective curtain.

Killian lay on his stomach on the bed, wearing only trousers, his legs and arms sprawled in all directions. Ella had heard him lock the door and put the key in his pocket, but he was now fast asleep.

She looked down at him. The creases of care were smoothed from his face in sleep, and he seemed younger, his fiery red hair shining in the soft shifting light of a candle.

Ella walked to the corner of the room to replace her comb in her satchel. She stopped, pausing. Next to her bag was Killian's.

Ella again looked over at him. He appeared fast asleep, his chest rising and falling evenly. Ever so gently she opened the bag, unfastening the buckle and withdrawing the tongue. It was right in front of her, the green cover reflecting the light: The Alturan Lexicon.

Ella withdrew the book. It was strangely light. She opened the cover and began to read.

The light flickered and dimmed. Ella looked up. She'd lost all track of time, and the candle had burnt down to a stub.

Killian lay on his side, his head propped up on his elbow. He regarded her seriously.

"I . . . I just wanted to read it," Ella stammered.

"I know," he said. "I was watching you. Your eyes were lit up. You seemed so intent. I didn't want to disturb you."

Ella stared into the distance. She had only just begun, but she knew there was knowledge in this book beyond anything she'd learned at the Academy. She was also starting to believe that Killian must be right, that the Lexicon wasn't an isolated text, it was meant to be part of a greater whole.

Ella had always experienced leaps of intuition during her studies at the Academy. With time, she was sure she could develop her ability further than she'd ever imagined before. Her intuition—the things she understood without quite knowing why—was explained and expanded in the Lexicon. Here was the power to unlock her potential.

Ella closed the book. Uncertain for a moment, she left it sitting on her lap. There were still so many questions in need of answers.

"How did you do it?" she suddenly asked.

"Do what?"

"All of it. The essence, it didn't harm you at all, did it? The Crystal Palace—you got through every defense the high enchantress had made, and I know how good she is. You went through the palace, holding this book, yet not one guard saw you."

Killian sighed, "Do we have to talk about it?"

"Yes. First, the essence—why didn't it hurt you?"

He shrugged. "The fact is, I don't know. The templars discovered it when I was in Stonewater. My body works differently."

"It's amazing, do you realize that?"

"I guess."

"The Crystal Palace, though. How could you walk right past so many people? I heard them say you were naked, that you were like a ghost. How is that possible?"

"Stealth and invisibility are nothing new."

431

Ella nodded. "We enchant our bladesingers' armorsilk with something called shadow. When they activate the sequence, the armorsilk bends the light around their bodies. It's not perfect, though; you can still see the runes glowing slightly, and you can see their faces and hands—anything that's not covered by the armorsilk. I've never heard of perfect invisibility, and I know you weren't wearing a suit of some kind."

Killian shrugged. "It's my secret, isn't it?"

Ella could tell he was withdrawing again. She noticed his hand go to the amulet around his neck.

"It's not anything to do with that amulet, I know that much."

His eyes widened. "You've been . . ."

Ella was surprised. "Why are you upset? The runes on that amulet simply give it an ability similar to shadow. A novelty—now you see it, now you don't. Unlike armorsilk, which is a complex fabric, it's simple to cloak a pendant. And your pendant doesn't even work. The runes drained a long time ago."

"What? That's not true."

"How much do you know about lore?"

Killian shrugged. "I don't know. People draw runes with essence, that's about it."

"Where did you get it?"

Ella held her breath. Killian took a long time to answer. "The primate. He gave it to me and said that if I copied the runes onto my skin and said the words, the pendant would turn me . . . well . . . invisible."

"Killian," Ella said softly. "Lore doesn't work like that. The runes on the amulet simply give you something to copy."

"What do you mean? That I could copy any runes onto my skin, any at all?"

"I think so. I don't know what this power you have is, but it's completely new to me."

432

"Why wouldn't the primate tell me that?"

Ella knew she was in dangerous territory. "I don't know. Perhaps he thought that was how it worked. The templars don't have any lore, after all."

Killian shook his head while lines of anger came to his forehead. "No, he's smart. He knows."

Ella could only see one answer. The primate didn't want his prize thief to understand too much about the power he possessed.

"Does essence ever hurt you?" Ella asked.

"No. It gives me a strange feeling, a tingling sensation, but that's all."

"What about when you activate the runes, when you say the words?"

"I don't feel anything. I simply look down at my skin, and I can see through it."

Ella breathed in awe. "Incredible. Have you ever tried any other runes?"

"No, I don't know any runes."

For a time there was silence. Ella moved to sit next to Killian on the bed but Killian's eyes were far away, a pensive expression on his face. Finally, Ella broke the stillness.

"Killian," Ella whispered, "what are you going to do?"

The silence stretched out, and then Killian's shoulders slumped and he looked down. He sighed before he met Ella's gaze.

In his blue eyes Ella saw a soul adrift.

It was the moment that Ella knew he would never harm her. She didn't know what he would do next, but he had changed.

"The Halrana Lexicon. You stole it, didn't you?"

He hesitated. "Yes."

"Where is it?"

"It's at Stonewater. The primate intends to destroy it."

"Can you save it?"

Killian opened his mouth and then closed it. He frowned, and then he smiled and straightened, as if a weight had been removed from his shoulders. "I can try," he said.

"There's one more thing I have to know," she said. "Why did you choose me?"

Killian took a deep breath. "Are you sure you want to know?"

"Of course I want to know. Is it because I'm an enchantress, and you thought I was an easy target?"

"No. There's much more to it than that. The primate knows who you are, Ella. He made me study you. The primate said you might be able to help me find the Alturan Lexicon."

Ella felt a chill in her breast. "How would I know? Only the high lord and the high enchantress know where it's kept."

Killian stayed silent. Ella took Killian by the hands. "Tell me."

"I'll tell you," Killian said, regarding her with grave eyes. "You deserve to know." He gripped her hands in return.

"Nearly twenty years ago, there was a war between your house and Tingara. The Halrana fought also, and the Petryans."

"The Rebellion," Ella said.

Killian nodded. "The Alturan high lord, Serosa, was captured by the emperor at the end of the war. He was given up by the man closest to him, Tessolar."

Ella frowned. "They say Tessolar wanted to end the war, but Serosa wouldn't listen."

"Whatever happened, the Alturan high lord was going to be killed by the emperor's executioner. In an attempt to save her husband's life, High Lord Serosa's wife visited the primate to see if he could intervene on her behalf."

Ella looked up. This was a part of the history she'd never heard. "I didn't know that. What happened? Did the primate help her?"

"The primate said he would only help if she helped him in return. He made her agree to spy for him, and help him find secrets he'd long been searching for. But there was a condition she would also have to accept before he would speak with the emperor. The primate had no use for the wife of the ousted high lord of Altura, a woman with little access to the circles of power. He made her pledge herself to the new high lord, Tessolar, before he would agree to help Serosa, which she did."

Ella's brow furrowed.

"Even so, the attempt was in vain. Serosa was executed. They hanged him at Mornhaven while his wife looked on."

Ella gasped.

Killian took a deep breath. "Why did she still go ahead with the marriage to Tessolar? Because the primate gave her a choice. She was beautiful, you see. He told her that she had to marry Tessolar and get the primate what he needed, or he would kill her two children."

The pieces finally connected in Ella's mind. "Lady Katherine," she whispered. She remembered the day Katherine died as clearly as yesterday. The cost of betraying her house and being kept from her children must have been too great. Katherine had cast her body into the Sarsen, drowning in her slippers.

"She was Serosa's wife, and then she was Tessolar's. She did what she had to do to save her children. Those two children were you, Ella, and your brother Miro."

Ella's breath caught, and her knuckles were suddenly white as she grasped Killian's hands.

"Tessolar didn't want anything to do with Serosa's children, but Katherine only assented to Tessolar's demands because of the primate's threat—she knew she had to remain useful to the primate. Tessolar gave Katherine's children to the rearing of a soldier."

"Brandon." Tears ran down Ella's face.

"I'm sure your mother loved you, Ella. It must have torn her apart."

Ella remembered the day Lady Katherine had come to her, fearful, saying good-bye. She remembered the connection she had seen in Katherine's eyes.

Ella cried at her loss, at what could have been.

"Just remember that what she did, she did to protect you. She probably gave information to the primate in bits and pieces, believing that if she gave him everything he needed, he would kill you. In the end it must have been too hard."

"I . . . I can't believe it."

"It's true, Ella. I learned the tale from the primate, though not in those words. I suppose he thought it might be useful to my purpose. Your father was Serosa Torresante, High Lord of House Altura. Your mother was Lady Katherine. I'm sorry that you had to find out this way."

Killian suddenly stood up and walked over to his bag. Ignoring the Lexicon that still rested on the floor, he rummaged around and finally took out a shirt, swiftly pulling it on. "I'm going to go downstairs."

"It's late."

"I know, but I need to think. I'll get some food sent up. I might be awhile." Opening the door, he turned and smiled sadly. "I'm sorry, Ella. The primate . . . Don't feel bad. I think he's using us all."

Killian left without another word, closing the door behind him.

Ella sat still for some time, thinking about all he'd said. She eventually wiped her eyes and straightened.

Then Ella realized Killian had left her alone with the Lexicon. She was in a foreign city, a strange place where she had difficulty fitting in, despite the hooded cloak Killian had bought to cover her skin and hair. Yet she finally had what she came for.

Ella waited for hours, but Killian never returned, and then remembering the look on his face, she finally she knew in her heart that whatever his plan, he wasn't coming back. She didn't know where he'd gone, but with the creature still out there somewhere, she would wait for morning and then she would flee Torlac, Lexicon in hand.

***

That night, Ella slept a sleep of pure exhaustion.

Just before dawn, the door to the room burst open.

As Ella's eyes shot open, she was suddenly blinded by a white light. She cried out as stars burst in her vision.

Then the light vanished, and Ella heard a man's voice. "It's just the enchantress. You heard what the maid said. The thief is long gone."

"We have what we came for. Well done, bladesingers. Let us not stay a moment longer in this place."

Ella knew that voice—she would know that voice anywhere.

It was the voice of High Enchantress Evora Guinestor.

47

People of Merralya, I will be sad to leave you. I fear for the fate of the world when I leave it in hands that do not keep at arms length the gifts that have been offered to me. I hope the Tingaran Empire will long be known as a state of benevolence.
—Memoirs of Emperor Xenovere I, page 368, 381 Y.E.

"And then?"

"And then he left the room."

The high enchantress gripped Ella firmly by the elbow as the bladesingers—their green armorsilk covered with gray travel cloaks—cleared the way.

Evora looked from side to side as she walked, her strides betraying her haste. "You truly believe he had a change in heart, and that this is why he left you with the Lexicon?"

Ella hesitated. "I suppose I do. That doesn't mean I know where he's gone, though."

"Ella," the high enchantress said. She looked Ella in the eye, squeezing her arm. "You did well. You did very well. To catch up with him, and to turn him from this path . . . The promise I saw in you was no lie."

The small group pressed themselves against a wall as a throng of Petryans ran past to join the crowd piling into the town square ahead of them.

"Trouble ahead," one of the bladesingers said.

Ella saw squares of armed men formed up, red and black colors decorating their heavy armor.

"We need to get through the square," another said.

"Find another way," the high enchantress hissed.

The bladesinger nodded to his two fellows and darted away. The other two pressed Ella and the high enchantress behind them. Ella still carried the Lexicon in her shoulder bag. Part of her wished the high enchantress would take it from her; another part wanted to keep learning, to find out what she could from within the book's metallic pages.

"Is it us?" Ella said.

"No, I don't think so, Enchantress," the high enchantress said.

Ella looked out into the square. Someone was addressing the files of soldiers and milling townsfolk, a man dressed in the red robes of an elementalist. On his robe was an emblem, the teardrop and flame *raj hada*. Voices suddenly rose up from the crowd, cheers and shouts. At first there was such a din that the words were indistinguishable. Then they became clear.

"War! Death to House Halaran! Death to House Altura!"

The two remaining bladesingers exchanged glances.

"Nothing changes," the high enchantress said sternly.

The other bladesinger returned. "There is a way—follow me."

They followed the bladesinger, almost running now in their haste. He led them through several alleys and finally to a small gate in the wall.

Ella wrinkled her nose at the stench.

"Refuse gate," said the bladesinger with a grin.

The group passed swiftly through the gate, seeing Petryans running in from the countryside to hear the news, and long queues of drudge-pulled wagons lined up outside the main gate.

Darting among the wagons, they soon left the trade town of Torlac behind, and eventually the group entered a hidden canyon. Ella saw at least three dozen soldiers in Alturan green waiting for them. Seeing the soldiers, Evora let out a breath of relief.

A worried-looking soldier ran up, a captain by his *raj hada*. "High Enchantress, what news?"

The high enchantress looked about the camp. Sensing an announcement, the soldiers began to gather. Evora waited, the tension building until they all stood arrayed in front of her.

"Soldiers, hear this. You have come far from home. You have experienced trial and fear. But listen to me, and listen to me well. All has not been in vain." Evora murmured to Ella, "Show them."

The high enchantress turned back to the men. "We have it!"

Ella raised up the Lexicon.

The cheer was deafening. Ella could see broad smiles across the men's faces as they slapped each other on the back.

"The news isn't all good, however," Evora continued. "We are now officially at war with House Petrya."

The soldiers sobered.

"Well done, all of you, but our journey is far from over. Now, Captain Joram," Evora said, "we need to talk."

Captain Joram nodded and instructed the men to prepare for departure, before turning to Evora. "Are we making all haste for Altura?

The high enchantress dropped her voice. "I will need some days to renew the Lexicon. Time we do not have, not exposed as we are here. There is an army behind us and a strange beast dogging our steps. I fear now even more than I did before, for now that we have what we were looking for, it is even more imperative that we return safely. We head south."

"South?" he said incredulously.

"Yes," she said firmly. "We'll head south into the Hazara Desert. We'll find water on the way there."

"And the tribes?"

"The tribes are the lesser of the evils. You heard. We are officially at war with House Petrya. The soldiers will be out in force, and people will be on the alert for anything suspicious, let alone a group of foreign soldiers. We stand the best chance skirting Petrya and traveling a short way into the desert. The Lexicon must make it back to Altura safely. That is our priority."

Captain Joram quickly moved the men out, every soldier thinking of the comforts of home. The touch of a missed woman. They marched south.

———◆———

The sun rose across the land, revealing a desolate landscape of tan and dark brown. The red in the rock was absent now. The boulders were not so massive.

Marching through the day and night, Evora's party had left the trees behind not long ago, and no more could be seen ahead. As the sun rose, Ella felt the intense heat of it, though the day had barely begun. She could hear the groans and gasps of the already weary soldiers. The only people who seemed unaffected were the bladesingers—as unperturbed as always—and the high enchantress herself.

Ella still hadn't relinquished her burden, the high enchantress appearing content to let her carry the Lexicon. Ella still wore her gray dress, but she didn't have her green silk dress anymore—it was deep in a lake somewhere in Petrya.

Ella wrestled with thoughts and ideas. There was something about Killian's ability that resonated with her, something that had its place deep in the fabric of the history she had been taught, in the tales of the Evermen and the myths of the past.

She thought of Evrin Alistair's story about the man who healed the broken body of his love by drawing runes on her skin. Perhaps there was more truth to that tale than the old man realized.

The high enchantress had now quizzed Ella on every aspect of her time away from Altura. Left with her thoughts, Ella wondered about how she felt about Killian.

How could he have left her like that? He'd simply fled, again, and Ella didn't know what to think. Where had he gone?

The high enchantress was anxious to get back to Sarostar and tell the high lord of the primate's role in the theft of the Lexicons. Ella wondered if Evora also knew about her. Ella would be surprised if Lady Katherine hadn't asked some of her closest friends to keep an eye on them—perhaps Rogan Jarvish or even the high enchantress herself. Ella would ask her when the right moment came.

There was complete silence now except for the wheezing breath of the soldiers and the stamping of their boots. The hours passed in a daze. Marching for a whole night and the entire next day seemed too much to ask, but the men pushed on without complaint.

Finally the scouts came across an isolated wall of rock, providing some shade from the burning sun. The fiery orb beat down mercilessly. Ella hadn't known the sun could even grow so hot; it felt as if she were in a furnace. The heat radiated from the pebbled yellow sand, and she knew that without the thick soles of her boots she would never be able to walk on it.

The party halted when they reached the rock wall, and one moment Ella was in the sun's direct gaze; the next she was in blessed shade. She fell thankfully to her knees, simply content to be breathing out of the scorching heat.

A soldier passed over a water bottle, and Ella drank deeply, letting some of the water run down her neck and trickle between her breasts. She handed the bottle back.

The gray dress was hideously hot, seeming to soak up all of the heat and hold onto it. Not for the first time Ella wished she were wearing white.

***

"Move out!" a voice called. Ella's eyes jerked open with a start. She'd fallen asleep. It couldn't have been more than a few moments. The soldiers around her groaned but shot up with alacrity—these were trained veterans after all.

"Here," a soldier said. He handed Ella a hardened piece of bread and some dried meat. She nodded her thanks.

They'd left the shelter of the rock wall and traveled for only a few hundred paces when they heard it: a great noise in the distance, a terrible shrieking, snarling sound.

It was the creature.

"Quickly! Form up!" Captain Joram called.

The soldiers of Altura moved into rigid formation, the scouts on the fringes, the bladesingers in the center, flanking the high enchantress and Ella. Ella felt safer having them around her, but she'd heard the soldiers' stories, spoken in hushed tones on the march. Whatever the thing was, it had faced a bladesinger and won.

They resumed the march, and the pace grew even faster now. Even the high enchantress began to look weary, unable to hold up her implacable exterior. The bladesingers still seemed calm, but their mouths were set in grim lines. They had a score to settle with the creature producing those cries.

Ella concentrated on placing one foot in front of the other. Rocks were becoming scarcer now, being replaced with dark yellow sand. Rather than remaining flat, the ground began to rise and fall like the waves of the sea, forming dunes that had to be climbed and then descended, uphill and then downhill, over and over. Looking ahead, all Ella could see were dunes, one after the other, like a great sandy ocean as far as the eye could see.

The heat finally began to slacken as the sun began to fall toward the horizon.

"We're on the edge of the Hazara now," Captain Joram said to the high enchantress.

Evora nodded. "Take us in. The creature may fear the open ground."

It was nearly sundown when one of the scouts ran forward, panting. Everyone heard him report. "Men, armed men."

"Petryans?" Captain Joram frowned.

"No. They're not Petryans. The creature . . . I think it's with them."

"Who are they then?" said the high enchantress.

"I think they're . . . Templars."

"Templars? Here? How many?" Captain Joram demanded.

"Perhaps twice our number. The creature. It seems a part of their group."

"The creature must serve the primate," Evora said. "They're after the Lexicon."

Ella's heart began to palpitate in her chest. The primate's men. They were here. She looked around and saw many of the soldiers muttering, prayers on their lips.

Looking around, Ella felt incredibly exposed here in the open desert. She longed for the rivers and forests of Altura like never before.

The high enchantress paused to think for a moment.

"At last," one of the bladesingers said, "we can face it on open ground."

"Quiet," said Evora Guinestor.

The high enchantress turned to Ella. "Enchantress Ella, your work is not yet done. There is one more thing I have to ask of you."

Ella swallowed but nodded. "What is it?"

"Be strong, Ella."

Without another word the high enchantress removed her shimmering green silk robe, standing only in a light underdress. Embarrassed, the soldiers turned away, while the bladesingers looked on, interested.

"High Enchantress, that's your . . ."

"It's my gift to you for as long as you need it. I have enchanted this with the most powerful runes of concealment and protection that are within my ability to construct. Now, put it on, and place the hood over your head."

Ella did as she was told.

"You have the Lexicon. That is what is important. Contained within its pages are the instructions for renewal. We face an unknown enemy here, but with three bladesingers and my skill we may yet prevail. One must make plans for undesirable outcomes, however, so you are to stay hidden, Ella. I will activate the runes of concealment, and you will stay here. Do you understand?"

"I do, High Enchantress."

Evora Guinestor met Ella's eyes. Ella saw compassion there, and understanding.

"You opened the book, didn't you?"

Ella nodded.

"Good. I am glad. Remember, all schools of lore are different facets of the same jewel. The one who understands this and applies it is the one who holds the world in her hands. Now kneel. Cover your head with your arms."

Ella sank to the sand, ignoring its blistering heat.

"*Su-nam! Al-turak-astour!*" the high enchantress chanted activation sequences, one after the other, in short, staccato syllables.

Ella knew the shimmering robe would be growing translucent. She knelt on the ground, completely still, her satchel inside the folds of the robe. Her head was covered; she could see nothing.

Ella heard the sound of the men grouping into a battle formation. They moved away from her, still audible through the crisp desert air.

A roar sounded, as loud and sinister as Ella had ever heard.

A glimmer of light shone through a tiny gap in the robe, and Ella looked out. She could see a crest of the desert, a long line of sand outlined against the setting sun. Figures suddenly rose from the summit like spikes from a barricade. Men. Many men. They were all dressed in white, a black sun on their breasts. The templars drew swords.

"Men, draw swords!" Captain Joram commanded.

The templars ran down the hill, gaining momentum as their numbers pushed forward.

One other figure ran at the forefront of the templars, a long dagger brandished in either fist. It was a woman wearing a billowing white dress. Her hair was a wild mess, and she ran with a disconcerting gate that reminded Ella of nothing so much as a bounding wolf.

The woman opened her lips and screamed, and the sound was the cry of the beast, the shriek of the night creature. Ella pulled the robe closer about her body. All she could see now was darkness.

Ella could hear the high enchantress chanting. The Alturans cried together as they ran to meet their foe. There was a horrible crunching, rending sound as sword chewed into bone. Men screamed. A liquid squelching told of a man's disembowelment. Explosions boomed, and Ella imagined she could feel the searing heat of prismatic orbs. Above it all the sound of the bladesingers' voices rose as they called forth the power in their armorsilk, their swords becoming blades of flame.

There was a hideous grunting sound, and then Ella could only make out two of the bladesingers' voices.

Then, moments later, just one.

Remembering the high enchantress's activation sequence for the cloaking effect, Ella chanted under her breath, frightened and alone in the darkness.

Ella listened for Evora's voice. It was gone. She listened for the last bladesinger, but his voice was also gone. Ella stopped her chant, lest someone hear her.

There was one final clash of swords.

And then there was silence.

Ella heard a soft, crunching sound, and a sniffing came from directly beside her. Tears ran down Ella's face as she trembled and smelled something terrible, a fetid odor of corruption.

Suddenly, the air split with a mighty roar, a terrible scream of power and triumph. Ella nearly screamed in fright.

"I sssmell sssomething . . ." a sibilant voice hissed.

"Saryah, some Alturans fled over that hill. Hunt them down," a deep voice said.

"Yes . . ." the voice responded.

The presence was gone.

Ella stayed perfectly motionless, her breath still, listening to the templars as they searched the dead and dispatched the wounded. A man sobbed softly for help, and Ella recognized the voice of the soldier who had handed her the water bottle. His voice was quickly cut off.

Ella wanted the earth to swallow her, to take her out of this terrible place.

"The Petryans wanted the body of the high enchantress."

"I'll see to it."

"Did you save one?" the deep voice said.

"Yes, Templar. Here, their captain."

There was a heavy sound that could only be a body being dropped. Captain Joram! Ella held her breath. Was he alive?

"Please." His voice was almost indistinguishable. He spoke with a strange gurgling sound.

"Listen, man. You've got no legs. They've cut your arms off too. Next we'll take your eyes. Why not tell me, where is the thing we seek? Where can I find your Lexicon?"

"No," Joram said in a voice of indescribable pain.

"Take his eyes."

Ella was forced to listen as the templars tortured poor Captain Joram. He knew exactly where she was.

He lasted through to the very end.

For her.

48

*The emperor's menagerie held all manner of creature. The lengths that
had been gone to and the expense incurred—well, it astonished me.
I saw birds with plumes of feathers ten times as long as their bodies.
Large furred creatures with tails and pitiful expressions on their
round faces, and translucent fish that were born, lived, and died
in the span of a day. What madness enabled the emperor to possess
animals from farther than I had ever traveled, yet none of these
places were rendered on our maps?*
—Toro Marossa, "Explorations," page 38, 423 Y.E.

The bulk of the combined forces of Altura and Halaran left together,
the soldiers' faces grim. All knew the coming battle for Ralanast
would decide the fate of Halaran once and for all.

As the horde of men and constructs departed, leaving behind
perhaps a tenth of their number, Miro prayed for their success as
he watched them pass: dirigibles without number, Alturan heavy
infantry, mortar teams, Halrana pikemen, and all of the bladesingers but Miro. He looked on, stone-faced, as the still-functioning
ironmen and woodmen, and finally three of the massive colossi

stormed off, the animator cages atop their huge heads looking tiny by comparison.

It was like witnessing some great exodus.

Lord Rorelan and Miro then led their smaller force in the opposite direction. A week after the split, Miro found himself wearing a different *raj hada* on his green armorsilk. It proclaimed him a captain of the Alturan army.

He and those with him had decided to make their stand, to hold the flank, at a place called Bald Ridge. The morning sky was dark, the color of smoke, and it started to rain, a cold drizzle that pooled in the freshly dug earthworks to form puddles of mud. Miro ignored the rain as he gazed back along the line of men.

"Would fighting two deep be more suitable, Captain?" Lord Rorelan said.

It still felt strange hearing his rank on the lord's lips. Rorelan was a young man, perhaps three years older than Miro. The late Lord Devon's son was officious, with a beaked nose and small eyes, but he appeared much more reasonable than many of the other lords Miro had met. He thought carefully through decisions regarding their deployment and even made some useful suggestions of his own.

At their first meeting, Rorelan had looked the battle-hardened bladesinger up and down and then instantly deferred to Miro.

"No, my Lord," Miro said. "We occupy a long ridge, which gives us the advantage of high ground. We want to hold the entire face, so it is better for us to have a long thin line than a short deep one. The enemy will be seeking to overrun one of our positions and then come at us from behind. Men who will face an enemy down from a hill balk at being attacked from behind. If we allow the enemy to outflank us, we're dead in moments."

"Ahem," Lord Rorelan said. "Hence the flying brigade then?"

"Yes, my Lord. If there is a breach, we need to stop it up immediately."

Miro and Rorelan gazed down at the plain below, where the soldiers of the Black Army scurried about like ants. Miro's lips thinned as he saw mortar teams forming up under the cover of dirigibles. If the enemy commander was clever, he would concentrate his bombardment in one area and then hit that same area with his troops.

It was what Miro would do.

There were five Imperial avengers at the forefront of the mass of enemy soldiers. The darkest meldings produced by the lore of Tingara, these creatures were once men but were now something else altogether, a mixture of flesh and lore-enhanced weaponry, bodies enclosed by metal and cloth and one arm grafted with a black sword. They were obvious by the way the human soldiers stood apart from them, fearful of the monsters in their midst. Miro could just make out their barbed flails. There was a great danger here, he knew.

A man ran up to Miro. "Everything is ready, Captain."

Miro nodded. "Thank you."

He looked again along the line of men. Miro and Rorelan's holding force was a motley collection of Alturans and Halrana, the best units having been sent to the liberation of Ralanast. Miro could see heavy Alturan infantry, their scaled metal armor glowing silver, drawn swords ready to be activated. These men would stop all but the strongest of the enemy. He saw Halrana pikemen, mouths set in thin lines, eyes steely with determination. But Miro's line was mostly made up of regulars, soldiers with ordinary swords and spears, some with armor of metal, some with armor of leather, and some with no armor at all.

Miro stood with Lord Rorelan at the center of the line. A short way behind them was Miro's carefully assembled flying brigade, men he had worked with, men he knew. When the time came, Miro would fight with them. And most likely, he would die with them.

Miro locked eyes with Rorelan, finding a surprisingly determined gaze meeting his own. The young lord wore his *raj hada* on his cloak, underneath which he wore heavy enchanted armor. The sword at Rorelan's side was bright—it had probably never been used. Miro hoped he would stand. Nothing took away men's courage like seeing one of their leaders run.

Scanning the line, Miro saw a man in a gray cloak, working his way through the defenders toward him. Miro frowned; the last thing he wanted was unexpected bad news. Then the man reached Miro.

"Excuse me, Captain." The man in gray grinned, looking up. "I thought perhaps I might join you here."

Miro laughed and reached out his hand, seeing the curly dark locks and tiny moustache as the man threw off his cloak, revealing bright green armorsilk below. Bartolo laughed as well, clasping Miro's hand in a firm grip.

"Happy to have you. Very happy indeed. Lord Rorelan, this is Bladesinger Bartolo."

"Always a pleasure to fight beside a bladesinger."

"My Lord," Bartolo acknowledged.

Bartolo stood beside Miro and watched the Black Army's preparations below. He looked along the line and whispered to Miro. "What have we got, three thousand?"

"Something like that," Miro murmured.

"Against, what, thirty? Lord of the Sky help us."

"It's nothing our young lord can't handle," a grizzled soldier said. He grinned, coming up and taking a sip from a flask.

"Tuok." Miro gripped the man's hand, smiling broadly.

"Listen well to Captain Miro, men," Tuok called loudly. "If anyone can beat this scum, it's him."

Miro frowned when he saw a tall man with a shaved head and arm of metal come out to stand in front of the Black Army.

Miro recognized Moragon from the Borlag in Vezna. Moragon pointed up at the hills, directly at where Miro stood. He made a sweeping gesture across the line of his throat.

A horn sounded—three powerful blasts.

The first wave of attackers surged forward.

Lights flared along the line of defenders as they activated their armor, and there was a hissing sound as men drew weapons from scabbards. Bartolo and Miro both stayed silent, knowing they would save their song for the battle itself.

"Tulak-mahour," Lord Rorelan murmured. His scaled armor began to glow. Rorelan then activated his sword.

Miro looked down at the running attackers. He could see this was a testing push, a thin line of men meant to draw out any surprises the defenders had in store. Many of the running soldiers carried long wooden planks. Miro waited until they reached the spiked trenches, halfway to the ridge.

"Mortars!" he cried.

The air crackled as the mortars released their charges, and the volley of prismatic orbs vanished into the night sky. There was a moment of silence, and then the explosions began. Detonations of flame and earth blew into the air, followed by pieces of men. Some of the attackers still managed to get their planks down before the second round of orbs took its toll. Then the first wave was no more.

Moragon ran out in front of the army again. He shouted something and pointed his arm in the air.

The horn sounded again, a long drawn-out blast followed by a short note.

Ten thousand legionnaires stepped forward. At their front were two of the Imperial avengers.

"Here it comes," Miro heard Tuok mutter.

Miro signaled the two enchanters he'd managed to recruit. "It's time for the devastators. Are you ready?"

The two men in green robes stepped forward. "Yes, Captain. The gaps in the line of trenches?"

"The gaps are there. Just release them at the places I've indicated, and they'll get through."

The enchanters nodded and withdrew.

Moragon dropped his arm, and the legionnaires surged forward. Miro watched one of the avengers. It ran like a grotesque puppet, lurching first one way, then another. The tendrils of its flail made it appear to be a many-armed creature.

The mass of attacking men swarmed up the hill, covering its surface.

"Release!" Miro cried.

He looked back along the line. It was taking too long. What was happening? He watched as the mortars took their toll on the attackers. These were legionnaires, though—their glowing armor prevented much of the orbs' devastating effect. They added more planks as they crossed the defensive trenches.

Finally, evenly spaced along the ridge, five great metal balls began to roll down the hill, their runes glowing fiery red, each twice the length of a man in size. They gathered momentum as they rolled, and Miro prayed they would find the correct gaps in the trenches.

Miro held his breath as the devastators approached. Some had worried that seeing them approaching, many of the enemy would panic and flee, reducing the devastators' effect. But these were Imperial Legionnaires. They wouldn't panic.

One of the spheres fell into a trench. Another found a gradient in the hill and started to drift to the side, missing the line of trenches completely. A groan went up from the defenders.

The other three devastators made it through the trenches and into the mass of legionnaires who had yet to cross.

The devastator in the trench exploded first, as a score of attacking soldiers were crossing. Miro saw it an instant before he heard it. The hillside simply exploded. Earth and rock shot in all directions, flying into the air in a huge cloud, obscuring Miro's view. The boom of the explosion was deafening, the sound rolling around the hills like thunder.

Miro watched as the wayward sphere followed the line of the hill, rolling steadily toward the main army encampment below. His heart racing, he willed it to roll closer to the main body of men. First rolling away from the Black Army, the sphere then hit a bump and turned back toward the enemy. Seeing its approach, men began to scatter. The devastator stopped near the edge of the enemy force, where a group of artificers operated the Black Army's dirigibles and mortars.

Then within moments of each other, all of the remaining spheres detonated. Even Miro had to put his hands to his ears. Nothing could be seen through the smoke and dust, and he peered anxiously as it cleared.

Miro now saw that half of the hillside had been blown away. Perhaps two-thirds of the wave of legionnaires had been wiped out, but it meant the loss of their defensive trenches. Miro hoped it had been worth it.

Looking at the main body of the enemy, he saw they'd lost scores of Louan artificers along with a multitude of mortars and dirigibles.

But twenty thousand of the enemy still remained. Twenty to their three.

With a roar, the remaining legionnaires from the attacking wave came pouring out of the smoke, rushing toward the defenders. One of the Imperial avengers came on, at the head of their wedge formation, like the point of a spear. It was missing an arm, the thin slit of its eyes glaring with menace.

The initial testing over, the battle began in earnest.

The legion smashed into the front of the line like a wave breaking on the shore. There was instant chaos, all sense of order lost.

Miro and Bartolo fought in the middle of the fray, the flying reserve unexpectedly embroiled when the legionnaires hit the center of the line. If anything, Miro was glad they'd hit him where he was strongest, but he hoped the reserve would save some of its strength.

The song of the two bladesingers held the men together, the glare of their armorsilk and sparking zenblades a beacon to guide them. To Miro's surprise, Lord Rorelan was in the thick of the fighting, parrying and lunging with a formal style that gave away his training.

"Hold for me!" Bartolo cried. Miro braced himself.

Bartolo leapt into the air, his feet hitting Miro's shoulders and using Miro to propel himself an incredible height above the fighting soldiers. He landed next to the Imperial avenger.

"Altura!" Bartolo cried, His voice echoed by the soldiers.

The defenders began to surge forward.

"Hold!" Miro called. "Hold the line!"

Looking over the heads of the enemy, Miro could see another wave coming behind.

Most of Miro's men pulled back; those who didn't soon found themselves alone. They didn't last long.

Miro ducked the swing of a legionnaire's sword and thrust his fiery zenblade at the man's stomach. Blood sprayed out into his face. He quickly wiped his eyes with the back of his hand and then blocked a vicious overhand cut from a half-moon axe blade. Miro kicked out at the man, lunging into the space he created. His song reached a crescendo as he spun on his heel, the length of the glowing sword arcing through the air. Miro's zenblade cut through two spears and a shield. Three men went down.

Panting, Miro regained the height of the crest and looked along the line. They were holding—just.

Then the next wave of the enemy hit, and Miro concentrated on staying alive.

The day became a blur of swinging swords and grunting men. The corpses piled high all along the front of the ridge, impairing the efforts of attackers and defenders alike. Sticky red blood formed pools on the ground, combining with the mud. As many men died from the treacherous ground as from being genuinely bested. The rain continued.

There was a brief respite during the middle of the day. Suddenly, all Miro could hear were the wheezing gasps of the men. He looked down onto the plain. Moragon stood alone in front of the army, his fists clenched as he exhorted his soldiers to greater efforts.

Once more scanning the line, Miro saw it was patchy now. He could see where the men had closed up, inadvertently creating weaknesses.

He looked down at the enemy. Their numbers seemed as vast as ever.

"Water the men, Captain," came the panting voice of Lord Rorelan from somewhere nearby.

"Water!" Miro called.

He walked along the ridge as young boys ran forward with buckets of water. The men drank thirstily, and Miro spoke softly to them as he walked, patting an arm here, congratulating a soldier there. They stood taller as he approached, their resolve as firm as ever.

Miro bent down and sat with a young Alturan for a moment. The boy was perhaps five years younger than Miro. His face was gray, blood frothed at his lips.

"You did well, son of House Altura," Miro said as he knelt.

"I did . . . well?"

Miro took the boy's hand. "We fight to protect our people, your family. They are safe because we are here."

"My mother . . . she is safe?"

"Yes, she is safe."

The boy struggled to breathe. Miro bowed his head and then closed his eyes for a moment, praying. He thought about his sister. He prayed for her safety and that he would see her again. He thought of Amber, her warm smile and her infectious laughter.

It seemed so far away, that world of love and sunlight. Miro wondered if he would ever see Sarostar again, if he would ever again ride one of the pleasure boats on the Sarsen on a warm summer's day.

Miro opened his eyes. The boy was dead, his eyes glazing over. The rain fell on his grimy face, forming rivulets like tears.

Miro stood. He could see the men around him, looking at him, wondering. Without knowing what came over him, Miro jumped down from the crest and started to pace the front of the line.

"Soldiers of Altura, fighting men of Halaran. Some of you know me. I am your captain."

There was a cheer from the men.

"My name is Miro Torresante. If you know that name, then you know the name of my father. His name was Serosa Torresante, and he was the lord marshal of the combined forces of our two houses during the Rebellion, during that great war when we faced the same enemy we face here today."

Miro's expression blackened. He spoke with a force that came from somewhere within him. He was fighting with these men—they were putting their lives in his hands. He wanted them to understand.

"Some in Altura say my father was a warmonger. That he gave up the lives of our children for some petty political gain. I challenge anyone to stand here and say that to me today. Today, when our two houses stand against the same foe. When we give our hearts and minds to this cause, to protect those who cannot protect themselves, to fight tyranny. I am proud to be here. I would be nowhere else."

Miro paused for emphasis. "When I was just a small child, my father led Alturan and Halrana against this dark enemy because I needed protection. Now I am a man, a warrior, and I am here to give that same protection. To anyone. Anyone! Any man, woman, or child who needs it. And I call on you to join me!"

The men roared—a mighty sound of defiance.

Miro rejoined Lord Rorelan, who gave him an enigmatic look but said nothing.

Bartolo simply pointed and said, "Here they come."

Two hours into the fighting, the enemy broke through the line.

Miro had never believed such continuous fighting was possible. His face and hands were covered in blood. He had a wound on his left ankle where a lucky spear had found part of his body unprotected. He had to concentrate on his song now; the chant of a bladesinger no longer came without thinking. He was no longer able to use shadow—the complexity was just too great for his tired mind.

Miro heard a despairing cry followed by a bellow and, dispatching an opponent, he looked up. The attackers were pouring through a gap in the line, countless numbers of them. At the point of their wedge formation, two Imperial avengers lumbered ahead. As men along the line suddenly found they had an enemy at their back, they turned to defend themselves. In turn, this put too much pressure on the front of the line. It wavered. They were being overrun. In moments the battle would be lost.

Miro looked frantically around. He saw green, somewhere in the distance. "Bartolo!" he cried. "Breach! Breach!"

Without seeing whether he'd been heard, he looked around him. "To me!" Miro gathered the men to him and ran to attack the ravaging horde.

Sensing their opportunity, the enemy's commanders threw everything they had at the defenders, and the final wave came surging up the hill. Miro drew on his last reserves of strength as he ran, calling the men to him as he approached the breach.

Then suddenly Miro was in it. The avengers were tossing men around like leaves before a wind. Miro knew he had to stop them before anything could be done about the legionnaires.

Miro signaled to a group of Alturan heavy infantry, their armor slick with blood but still glowing silver. "Go for the legs, get it on the upswing."

The soldier in front nodded, though Miro could see the fear in his eyes.

"I'll lead the way," a voice came from behind Miro. Bartolo swept forward, his armorsilk a bright star among the chaos. Heartened, the infantry followed him in.

This left the other avenger for Miro.

Miro's zenblade flared yellow. The avenger turned to watch him, malevolent, its flail twitching one way, then the other. Freed from its rampages, the soldiers swarmed to push back the assaulting legionnaires, leaving Miro alone with the creature.

Miro entered that state he had only found once before, during his testing. He now tried to go further, to add the same strength of purpose to his armorsilk. Fatigue made the effort more than twice as difficult, and his song faltered. Taking a deep breath, he tried again, pushing through the fatigue.

The zenblade turned an ethereal blue. The armorsilk took on the luster of crystal.

Miro rolled in under the flail. The avenger's arm punched down where he'd been a heartbeat before, the sword impaling the empty ground. Miro stabbed at the creature's leg but the avenger was quicker. It twisted and the flail came back around, hitting Miro squarely in the chest. His body flew up in the air.

The point of the avenger's great sword waited for Miro's body to fall, to impale itself on the blade. Instead, Miro twisted in the air, his zenblade crashing into the sword. Sparks sprayed out, accompanied by a noise like lightning.

The avenger's sword sheared off halfway.

Far from dead, the avenger's flail caught Miro again, the spiked ball throwing Miro's body to the ground, slamming the breath out of him.

Miro's song was lost as he choked and gasped in vain for air to fill his lungs. The broken sword thrust at the ground, and Miro rolled to one side and then the other as it thrust again.

Finally, he gathered enough air to shout.

"Hul-ta-unmar-al-ran!" With the single activation sequence, the zenblade flared red. Miro leapt up into the avenger's backswing, his sword held in two hands.

The blade pierced the creature's skull with a terrible crunching sound. Miro fell back to the ground, coughing and wheezing. With a mighty crash, the Imperial avenger fell to the earth beside him.

"Here, Captain," a voice said.

Miro turned; a soldier was offering him his hand. He lurched to his feet, his breath finally returning.

"Thank you, soldier," he said.

Miro looked around. Bartolo was struggling. Half of the heavy infantry had been mauled by the second avenger.

Miro chanted as he ran, his armorsilk becoming comfortably bright. "Hold for me!" he cried.

461

Without waiting to see if Bartolo heard him, he leapt atop Batrolo's back and jumped. Miro's leap was impossibly high, taking him over the avenger's head, past its field of vision. He thrust his zenblade down at its neck as he flew past, landing heavily on the avenger's other side. He turned just as the creature fell to the ground, to see Bartolo follow with a sweeping cut, taking the Imperial avenger's head clean off.

Bartolo grinned at Miro, rubbing his back theatrically. "I didn't hear you. You're not that light, you know."

Miro smiled back.

<hr/>

After the great attack, the enemy finally withdrew, leaving the defenders to lick their wounds.

Miro had traversed the full length of the line several times during the fighting. Sweat and blood covered him from head to toe. He'd picked up a small, but deep, cut on his neck when a prismatic orb had exploded near him, sending splinters of blood and bone in all directions.

Miro looked about him. There were perhaps a thousand men left. Corpses littered the battlefield in all directions, friend and foe alike. The men had given everything they had on this day, everything and more.

Miro saw Tuok standing on the ridge. The one-eyed soldier grinned down at him, as indestructible as ever. Remembering when Tuok had taught him about Seranthia and the way of the world, Miro grinned in return.

It was then that Miro noticed a spreading red stain above Tuok's waist. Seeing his gaze, Tuok nodded before lifting his sword up in the air.

"Is that all you've got?" Tuok shouted down from the ridge. Miro raised his zenblade in salute. The wound was a death sentence. They both knew it.

"Captain?" a soldier said, standing at Miro's elbow.

"Yes?"

"Lord Rorelan, he is asking for you."

"Of course," Miro said. He felt dazed. He had no idea what time it was. Staring upward, he saw the sun was low in the sky, making it some time in the afternoon. Had it really been only one day?

The defenders nodded their heads as Miro walked past. There wasn't a soldier among them who didn't have some kind of wound. Most had seen their comrades die on this day. Yet they stood proudly. They had held against the storm.

Lord Rorelan was seated, leaning against a mound of earth, a strange expression of contentment on his face.

"My Lord, what is it?"

"I want to talk to you, Captain Torresante."

Miro's eyes moved down as he realized why Rorelan was so awkwardly prone. A spear was embedded in his thigh. As he watched, Miro could see blood pooling under the lord's body.

"You need attention," Miro began.

Rorelan waved his hand. "They're on their way. I have a request, Miro. I would ask something of you."

"Of course, my Lord."

"Miro. Seeing you today. It showed me what being a lord was about."

"You've fought valiantly, Lord Rorelan. I mean that."

"Thank you, Miro, thank you for indulging my vanity," he chuckled. "However, my request has to do with your family."

"I don't understand."

"Your father was high lord of Altura. Whatever Tessolar's motivations are, you have the right to call yourself a lord. I want you to talk to him, Miro. Make him give you your right."

Miro's face grew bitter. "No . . ."

"Miro! That is my request. Now promise me." Lord Rorelan sank down further onto the ground.

"I . . . I promise, Lord Rorelan." Miro kissed the man's bloody brow. "I will talk to High Lord Tessolar."

Lord Rorelan didn't hear him. He had passed into unconsciousness.

"Who is in command here?" a voice shouted.

Miro stood. "I suppose I am."

An Alturan messenger ran forward, his green and yellow uniform so clean it seemed absurd in the surroundings. "I have a message for the commander."

"What is it?"

The messenger handed Miro a scroll. Miro unfurled it; his brow furrowed.

A moment later he looked up, seeing the men watching him expectantly.

"Soldiers, our work here is done. We have accomplished our mission, against all odds. Remember this day. And if anyone asks you what happened at Bald Ridge, simply tell them: We held!"

The defenders cheered, shouting their approval.

Miro concealed his expression. They all had a difficult journey ahead of them. He thought again about the message he held in his hands.

Army in rout. Ralanast remains in enemy hands. High Lord Legasa killed in action. Marshal Sloan killed in action. Blademaster Rogan killed in action. Request immediate support defensive action to Mornhaven. Signed, Prince Leopold Mandragore, Lord Marshal of the Armies of Altura and Halaran.

49

Artists make for terrible enchanters. They seek to imbue the symbols with personality, to describe some state of being with the whorls and bridges. However, the converse can be infinitely true.
The best enchanters are artists.
—Diary of High Enchantress Maya Pallandor,
page 224, 411 Y.E.

"This one, she is alive," a voice said.

Ella woke to intense heat. She opened her eyes.

The first thing she saw was two sets of legs, both wearing high dark boots. Black cloth was wound around the legs in a crisscross pattern.

The high enchantress's robe must have finally exhausted itself. It had so far filtered out the worst of the sun's rays. Filled with despair and exhausted beyond belief, Ella had slipped into unconsciousness.

She realized she could be seen. These men were looking at her.

"It is strange, that garment," said a second voice. "We should take it to the prince."

"She bears the same features as the ones we killed earlier. See? That hair, the light skin."

"From the north, I think she is."

"Kill her then, and let us get away from this place before the carrion birds arrive. I have rarely seen so much blood in one place; it will draw them like flies."

Ella looked up. The two men wore dark trousers of silk, with a length of soft black cloth wound around their body, billowing in the light wind. Their skin was dark, their mouths cruel. At their hips they carried curved daggers, and each casually leaned on a wicked scimitar. The man on the left was slim, with long black hair and eyes like coal. His companion had a larger build and wore a jewel in one ear.

"Please don't kill me," Ella whispered.

She looked about her. The first thing she saw was the mutilated corpse of Captain Joram. His screams had continued for an impossibly long time. Now she could see what they had done to the poor man.

Ella was suddenly sick, falling to the ground and heaving up the contents of her stomach. The bile fell to the sand, sliding away in a sluggish rivulet.

"Whatever she is, she's disgusting," the slim man said.

"Watch me take her head from her shoulders with one blow," said the man with the earring.

"You said that last time. 'Half off' isn't the same as 'off.' I told you, your saber is too blunt."

"It is not. I had it sharpened by Alhaf last week."

"Alhaf does a terrible job. You should sharpen it yourself. I do."

Ella lay still, incapable of movement. She could still hear Captain Joram's tortured cries. The sun was merciless. She felt sick to her core.

"Ready?"

"Yes, yes. I'm ready. Hurry up."

The big man stood beside Ella. He marked his sword and then lifted his arms above her head.

"If you swing like that, you'll more likely hit her shoulder."

"I will not!"

"You will."

"Watch."

The big man took a deep breath and with a shout he hacked down at Ella's body. Ella didn't want to die. She tried to move, but exhaustion had her in a relentless grip, and aside from the high enchantress's robe, she had no weapons.

"Salut!" there was a shout in the distance.

The curved sword stopped mid-swing. The big man looked up.

Her eyes closed, Ella uncertainly opened them when she heard a strange noise, a rolling sound of thunder like many men running on the sand.

Four more men approached. They were dressed in the same dark billowing clothing and high boots as the first two. Three of the newcomers had beards and unruly hair; another was beardless and wore a circlet that held back his shoulder-length black hair. He appeared to be the leader.

Ella's eyes opened wide. The men were astride tall animals—four-legged creatures with wide nostrils and elegantly arched necks. The steeds were a range of colors, from mottled white to an almost complete black. The sun shone from their coats, and they snorted as they pounded through the sand. They were graced with a sense of nobility. Man belonged with this creature.

The slim man put his hand on the big man's arm and called out to one of the newcomers. "Salut, Jehral! What news?"

The four men reined in their mounts. "We rode down some of the armored men in green," the leader, Jehral, said. "It was like they almost wanted to be killed. Not much sport."

"What of the men in white?"

"Long gone. The same goes for that creature. Whatever it was, we heard no more of its cries. Where are your horses? What do you here?"

Ella prayed that perhaps this leader would save her.

"We hobbled them a short way away; the blood was making them restless. Rashine here was just showing me his swordsmanship."

Jehral laughed. "This should be good. Continue."

The big man harrumphed and lifted his arms above his head again. Ella closed her eyes, fighting to regain her senses, willing it to be over quickly. She thought it was sad to be ending it here, like this, in the middle of the desert. No one would ever know what had come of her.

Rashine grunted as the sword swung down. The scimitar hit the green silk of the high enchantress's robe and bounced off like it had smashed into stone. A noise like the crack of a whip resounded through the hills and Rashine howled in pain, nursing his wrist.

"Interesting," said Jehral. "It is a strange garment she wears. Who are you, woman?" he addressed Ella.

"I . . . I am . . ." Ella thought furiously. How could she convince them to spare her life?

"No matter. Rashine, remove the garment, and we will give it to the prince as a gift. I will wager your sword will be sharp enough then."

Ella slowly rose to a standing position. It took all her strength and courage. She looked Jehral in the eye and summoned her most commanding voice. "I am High Enchantress Evora Guinestor of House Altura. I demand you release me, lest the might of my nation fall upon you and your people."

Jehral simply looked at her in interest. "High enchantress? Interesting. The prince may have use for you."

Rashine growled, "But . . ."

Jehral held up his hand, "No, Rashine. We will see what the prince has to say about this one."

Ella weaved as she fought to remain standing, but Jehral reached out a hand. Not knowing what to do, Ella took it. With an iron grip he swung her up behind him onto the back of his mount. The animal snorted and stirred, but Jehral patted the horse's neck, calming it.

From her new height, Ella could see the gruesome scene that had once been the soldiers of Altura. She saw a bladesinger, his neck sliced open and a horrified expression on his face. The body of Evora Guinestor couldn't be seen; the templars had lived up to their promise of giving her body to the Petryans.

Ella apologized silently for using the woman's name. She vowed to get revenge on those who had wreaked such carnage on her people.

As the strange men rode away from Petrya and into the emptiness of the desert, Ella took stock of herself. She carried her shoulder bag still; she had the Lexicon.

But for how long?

As they rode and Ella's strength returned, she realized how the high enchantress had managed to keep much of her composure in the stifling desert heat—there was some property of the runes on her robe that tempered the scorching sun. Even so, it was with pain and thirst that she bumped along on the horse behind the silent desert warrior.

A few hours into their journey, Jehral handed Ella a water bottle. She drank greedily, feeling strength return with every gulp, then handed the bottle back to him. Jehral shook the bottle and chuckled, shaking his head. Taking a tiny sip, he returned the bottle to his saddlebags.

Ella decided she needed to act with strength and determination to pass herself off as the high enchantress. As she revived, she straightened her back and finally found the rhythm of the horse's motion, raising and lowering her hips with its body. Jehral grunted an acknowledgment; she thought it might have been approval.

"Who is this prince?" she asked.

"He is the leader of our group. His father is a great noble. We are *shalaran*, fighting men, unmarried warriors. We protect the borders of our lands from the other tribes and from people like your green soldiers, like the warriors in white."

"How long do we travel?"

"Half of the sun's passage across the sky."

"Your prince, will he let me go?"

Jehral laughed. "No," he said.

There was no further conversation.

The horses plowed through the dunes, the sand tossed into the air like foam. Ella could now see nothing but white sand in all directions. She felt like she was adrift on an endless white sea, the sandy crests and troughs frozen in time, the waves perpetually on the point of breaking.

She wondered how they managed to find their way—the desert warriors didn't appear to use anything like a seeker. Then Ella saw Jehral look at the sun's position in the sky and take a bearing from a stony peak in the far distance. He altered their course slightly.

The heat was oppressive, and Ella longed for more water. Any moisture that might once have been in her mouth was long gone. A wind started to blow, the air hot and dry. It took the tops off the dunes in a line of white spray, blowing the fine sand through the air. Ella was forced to cover her mouth with a corner of silk after the sand kept entering her mouth, getting into her eyes. She raised the robe's green hood over her head and used it to protect herself.

After a time, they began to encounter strange formations of rock, sprouting out of the desert like bizarre plants from soil. Some of the shapes reminded her of mushrooms, others of animals or trees. One had an incredible mass balanced on a tiny stem. Ella couldn't believe it hadn't broken.

Jehral handed her the bottle again. "Finish it," he said. "We are almost there. If the prince orders you killed, you might as well be well watered."

Ella eagerly accepted the bottle and drained its contents. There were only about two mouthfuls, but she instantly felt rejuvenated.

They rounded a long formation of stratified rock, and suddenly Ella could see signs of settlement.

There were perhaps a score of black tents, each nearly indistinguishable from the other. Ella could make out the figures of men moving about. One of the tents in the middle was perhaps twice the size of any other, with gold cord entwined about its ropes, and was fronted with what appeared to be a carpet.

Surely this couldn't be the residence of a prince? Perhaps they were at a way-stop to gather water?

"We have arrived," Jehral said.

The six warriors straightened in their saddles and slowed their pace to a prancing trot. The desert men in the camp looked up as the newcomers approached. Ella saw that some had dark eyes, but others' eyes were blue or green. Their skin was a universal dark bronze, smooth and unlined, and they all wore billowing black clothing above high boots. They were all men.

The other riders peeled off to the sides as they rode in, answering greetings from their friends. Rashine stayed with them.

Jehral came to a halt outside the central tent. He leapt lightly to the ground and then lifted Ella from the waist, setting her down with surprising gentleness.

"Wait here," Jehral said. "I will see the prince now."

"I will guard her," said Rashine.

"That won't be necessary," said Jehral. "Where can she go?"

Rashine scowled. "She has powers. I will guard her."

Jehral sighed but didn't argue. Rashine took Ella by the arm, gripping her hard. She kept a smooth face, not showing any sign of discomfort.

Two guards at the door of the tent moved the sides apart as Jehral approached. He nodded at them and entered.

Ella waited outside, doing her best to ignore Rashine. He appeared to have some kind of vendetta against her. Perhaps he'd been slighted when she hadn't gracefully allowed him to remove her head from her shoulders.

Ella tried to listen intently, but the tent muffled any sound. Looking around, she saw the camp had been carefully chosen, situated away from the wind in a position where it would receive the most shade from the sun's rays.

Some of the warriors looked at her curiously as they passed, Ella's shimmering green silk garment covered with silver runes drawing their attention. She felt an unfamiliar tugging, and turning, she found Rashine rubbing her pale blonde hair between his fingers, looking at it curiously.

"Remove your touch," Ella said in an ominous voice.

Rashine jumped and plucked his hand away, then frowned when he realized he'd shown weakness.

"What's in here?" He pointed to her satchel.

Ella shrugged. "The tools of my trade."

Finally Jehral strode out of the tent, looking at Rashine and then at Ella. "The prince, he will see you now."

"She is dangerous," said Rashine.

"Are you saying the prince cannot take care of himself?" Jehral said.

Rashine grunted. "Take her bag."

Ella held her breath. The Alturan Lexicon was in her satchel. So much had been lost to recover it, and with Evora's words fresh in her mind, Ella still desperately needed to see whether she could learn

472

to renew it. Her thoughts constantly turned to Miro, imagining his armorsilk fading as an enemy impaled him with a sword.

"I'll make sure the prince gets it," Jehral finally said. He looked at Ella expectantly.

Ella gave Jehral the bag, at the same time pulling away from the big man's grip and walking toward the tent on her own. As she stepped onto the carpet, she looked down. Ella saw that what she'd taken for yellow in the weave was actually gold thread. It had been woven with the highest quality silk, shimmering and luxurious. Ella realized it was the finest carpet, better than any she had ever seen. The material lining the ropes of the tent was also gold, lending a strange combination of opulence and austerity to the surroundings.

The guards made way for Ella as she entered the tent.

It was surprisingly spacious. Ella could have lifted her arms above her head and still not touched the ceiling. The interior had been divided into smaller areas and where she stood was the largest, with more private chambers to the sides and the rear. Cushions littered the corners of the room, along with low tables. The carpets lining the floor were even finer than those outside. With a start Ella saw the light came from nightlamps, the best quality, made by Alturan enchanters.

Ella breathed in through her nose. It was cool and comfortable, and there was a pleasant odor to the air, sweet and pungent Ahead of her, she heard a gurgling sound. As her eyes adjusted to the soft light, Ella saw the form of a man leaning against some cushions, holding a piece of flexible hose to his lips. As she watched, he removed the hose and exhaled a stream of blue smoke, an expression of pleasure on his face.

His face was beardless, his skin smooth and unblemished. He wore his hair very long, past his shoulders, pulled back behind his head with a golden clasp. He wore an earring of amber and gold in his left ear, and around his neck was a chain of gold with a curved turquoise triangle. With a shock, Ella realized he was her age, perhaps only a year older.

In front of the man was a low table, with cushions on the opposite side. He gestured. "Please take a seat."

Ella wasn't sure how to respond. He was a prince, after all. She touched her fingers to her lips and forehead in the Alturan manner, bowing her head.

"It is my pleasure to meet you, Your Highness. I am Evora Guinestor, High Enchantress of Altura."

"Yes, yes. So Jehral tells me. Will you not sit down, young lady? Or are you preparing to enchant me?" he smiled.

Blushing, Ella sank to her knees, unfamiliar with how to seat herself on the cushions. She eventually settled. The prince simply smiled.

He took another long draw on the hose, the bubbling sound coming from a glass vessel on the ground. He blew the smoke into the air.

"If you were a man, I would offer you the waterpipe," he said. He then shrugged. "But you are not a man."

Ella didn't know how to respond.

He looked up at her, suddenly revealing a steady, intelligent gaze and piercing eyes, half green and half brown. Contrasting with his smooth dark skin, it gave him an exotic appearance. He was undeniably handsome.

"You see, women in our lands are not allowed to ride horses. They do not smoke or curse or fight."

"What are they allowed to do then?"

"They raise the family and teach the young ones. They feed and clothe us."

"Why are you telling me this? Will you let me go?"

The prince simply raised a finger. He did it with such aplomb, so accustomed to authority was he, that Ella fell silent.

"Your people, we know they are very quick to talk. Quick to anger. My people prefer to think long and hard before we follow a particular path. Be patient, High Enchantress Evora; there is purpose to my dialogue."

He took another draw on the waterpipe. His chest rose and then fell as he exhaled. He looked at her.

"Before the decay of our culture, our women had another role. They were the custodians of our lore." He looked into the distance. "We raised storms to confuse our enemies. We led them over cliffs. Our horses came thundering out of nowhere. One moment, there would be nothing. The next, a thousand, ten thousand riders would rise out of the dust." He sighed. "But that is no more. The in-fighting among the tribes has seen to that. Only a few women remember, and their knowledge is fragmented. Do you understand, High Enchantress Evora?"

"I . . . I think I do."

"That is good. Your coming here, it is a sign." His eyes gleamed. His voice was compelling. "It has always been my dream to see my people united, to see us come once more to our former glory. It is no chance that brought you here. Will you help us?"

Ella felt she was in unfamiliar waters. She had urgent business, yet this man expected her to somehow rediscover his people's lost lore. Ella clenched her fists. There was a war going on. Her people were dying. She needed to renew the Lexicon. She needed to get away!

"If I help you, will you let me go? Will you guide me back to my homeland?"

"Yes, yes. Of course. So you will help us. Good. I am glad."

The prince called out. "Haruth!"

One of the guards poked his head inside the opening. "Yes, my Prince?"

"I need a messenger. Someone fast. Marhaba. Send him in— quickly now."

The prince turned back to Ella. She had no idea what was happening. "Now, tell me of your people."

"What do you want to know?"

"Is it true you are ruled by one man, a high lord?"

"Yes. He administers our realm, along with our lords. He works closely with our high . . . with me. We trade our produce with other houses, and oversee the training and deployment of our armies."

"Salut! May I enter, my Prince?" a voice came from outside the tent.

"Enter," said the prince.

A small, wiry man entered. He had a leather thong over his head, and a patch covered one eye. It gave him a rakish appearance.

"Marhaba, I need you to go to my father. Tell him, I need the prize. Can you remember that?"

"Yes, my Prince. You need the prize."

"Excellent. Thank you, Marhaba."

The desert man bowed and left the tent.

"Now, where were we?"

The prince continued to ask Ella question after question about Altura and the other houses. She answered him as best she could, finding that although he knew little of life outside the desert, he had a quick intelligence. He probed her about intricate elements of court life, and she found herself having to think hard in order to respond. His voice was warm, and despite her situation, Ella decided she liked him. He saw things in simple terms. He was candid and expected others to be open in turn.

Eventually, he asked her to leave.

"Jehral will see you are given a dwelling. It will be humble compared to what you are used to, I am afraid."

He had become quite impressed when she'd told him of the high enchantress's role in Altura. He appeared to think it was a form of nobility.

"I will summon you again, Evora Guinestor."

Ella nodded and stood, then went to the entrance of the tent, where one of the guards was holding the fabric open for her.

"Oh, and High Enchantress?" Ella turned. "My name is Ilathor Shanti. Prince Ilathor Shanti of Tarn Teharan."

Ella nodded again and left the tent.

50

With a guiding light, all obstacles can be overcome.
The Evermen Cycles, 16:18

Amber picked up a withered apple and turned it over. She thought about its juicy flesh. The sweet taste. There were two on the wooden table.

An old woman hobbled up to the table and picked up the second apple. She chomped on her gums and handed a coin to the vendor.

The same coin would have bought a dozen apples not too long ago.

Amber reached into her apron for a coin. She felt a tugging at her elbow. A young boy, no older than seven, stood looking at her forlornly. He held a coin in his hand.

Sighing, Amber handed the boy the apple and moved on through the markets of the Poloplats.

As she did so, she looked at her hands. They were blistered and calloused. Worn like her heart. Like her spirit.

Amber worked as an enchantress from an hour before dawn until sunset, and then she had a short break before she began work at the collective. This gave her just enough time to get some food for her and Igor's supper. As a master, he was even busier than she was.

"Amber Samson!" called a voice. Turning, she saw Lorna Donwright, Enchanter Corlen's wife, standing with her two young boys. Amber frowned when she heard the name. She still wasn't used to the change. Amber's expression darkened even further when she saw that Lorna carried a bag of fresh vegetables. She even had a piece of meat.

"Lorna," she said.

"Well, how are you? You aren't looking too well. Are you eating properly? You and Igor are always welcome at our table—you know that."

"I'm fine, Lorna. Just worried, that's all."

Lorna nodded with sympathy. Somehow the gesture served to further irritate Amber.

"My Corlen, he said Igor left early today."

"He did?" Amber said.

"He said it was strange."

Amber shrugged. "I have to go, Lorna," she said. She didn't have the energy to be polite.

She turned and left, hurrying from stall to stall, finally settling on some cabbages and two small rabbits some boys had caught.

Amber knew Igor would need a meal. Married life wasn't what she'd expected it to be. She didn't know how she could hate him on one hand, and on the other she tried to do her duty by him. There was also one other unresolved matter. Something she needed to talk to him about.

Trepidation like a stone in her stomach, Amber headed for home.

———————

He was already there when she arrived. Still working on the sword, she saw. He moved back and forth along it, examining the runes, making a touch here, a touch there.

The immense sword was like a wall between them. Rather than their shared knowledge of enchantment bringing them together, it simply pushed them apart. He would allow no involvement with anything he was working on, instead treating her always like a simple student. Amber's brow darkened when she saw him.

Igor Samson, Master of the Academy, didn't even acknowledge his wife when she entered; he was so wrapped up in his work. She put her heavy bags onto the counter and activated the fading heatplate with a word.

When she added the meat to the pan he looked up. "Amber, you're here. I didn't even realize."

"What's new," she muttered to herself.

"What was that?"

"Nothing, Igor. Nothing."

"That smells good."

"Don't expect much. You have no idea what the level of food is getting like at the market now."

He grunted. "I can imagine. I've had my essence curtailed again."

"It's not the same thing," she muttered.

"What?"

"I said it's not the same thing," she said. "Those people . . . they're struggling to feed their children. Your essence allocation would buy enough to feed entire families."

"I don't feel like arguing, Amber. Not today."

Amber stirred the pot. Lord of the Sky, she was tired.

"I take it you heard about the defeat, then?" he said.

She grunted.

"They're falling back to Mornhaven. A conference has been called. A war conference. High Lord Tessolar himself left today."

"Good. Perhaps someone else will do a better job at running things here in Sarostar."

"Amber, listen to yourself. Are you well?"

She whirled. "No, I'm not well!"

He took a deep breath. "What is it?"

"I don't know!" Amber kept mindlessly stirring the pot. "Everything." Tears welled in her eyes. "I just want everything to be back the way it was. I want my friends."

"You can't mean Ella? She ran away. She showed promise, but her reckless nature told, didn't it? People like you and I have to work that much harder because she left. Everyone here does their part, but where is she now? We're better off without people like her. It's war. We all need to support our soldiers in the front." He paused, clearing his throat. "Speaking of which . . ."

"I wish I were at the front," Amber said. She thought of Miro. Was he even still alive?

"No you don't."

"At least I wouldn't be here."

Igor sighed. "High Lord Tessolar asked the Dunfolk if they would help us. Did you know?"

Amber looked up. "No. What did they say?"

"They said no, what else? Stupid creatures."

"They aren't stupid. I met their leader, the Tartana."

"That's right. I forgot. Well, perhaps 'stupid' isn't the right word. 'Ignorant,' perhaps. What would they understand of war? They'd rather keep to themselves. I will tell you something, though: if Altura falls, so do the Dunfolk. They wouldn't last a moment without our protection."

Amber thought about the vicious steel pointed arrows, propelled with unerring accuracy by the bows of the Dunfolk hunters.

"I wouldn't be so sure of that."

"Bah," Igor said. There was silence.

Amber dished up the food, and they sat. Eventually, she broke the silence.

"Why did you leave the Academy early today?"

Igor stopped for a moment. He took a deep breath. "I've been summoned to the front."

"What? You must be joking."

"It's true. It's that desperate, Amber. They're calling up every man without white in his hair."

Amber didn't say anything as they ate in silence, not tasting the food, but simply fueling their bodies.

"Well?" Igor finally said.

"Well what?"

"Aren't you going to say anything?"

"What do you want me to say? You're leaving me just like everyone else."

Igor sighed. "I leave tonight. I've finished my sword and I'm taking it with me."

"You're no bladesinger, Igor."

"I know. But I've been around warriors in the Pens. I know a thing or two."

Amber snorted. She didn't know why she was being so cruel to him. He was leaving her. The emotions swirled around her head, leaving her drained and empty until she felt nothing, nothing at all.

She knew it then. She wanted him to die. She wanted to be free of this marriage, to find Miro, wherever he was, and tell him how she felt.

Igor sighed again and left the table. Amber stayed motionless, her head in her hands. She stayed silent while he packed, then he came up to her and kissed her head. She looked up at him, the feelings of guilt wracking her body. He stood in the doorway and looked back at her. Then he was gone.

Amber put her hand to her belly.

"I'm sorry," she said to the unborn child inside her.

Then she broke down and cried.

51

*I would give anything to see what our house is capable
of given unlimited essence. Can you imagine what we could build?
I'm not talking about fortresses. I'm speaking of public buildings,
such as you might find in any of Merralya's great cities.
Schools could float in the clouds, and libraries could be housed
deep underwater. We could build up, rather than out. Or in many
directions all at once. Why would we build such things?
Why, simply to show that it could be done.*

—High Lord Koraku Rolan to
Primate Melovar Aspen, 541 Y.E.

Ella felt the wind in her hair, the great power of the noble creature beneath her. The sensation was complete exhilaration. She had
never felt anything like it.

"Keep your back straight. Hold onto the horse with your knees,
not your hands. Yes, that's it."

Watching her, Jehral grinned at her enjoyment. She rode away
from his standing figure, then turned in a wide circle, heading
straight for him before pulling up and trotting along a line.

"Well done, High Enchantress. Remember, though, if the prince finds out, he will cut out my tongue."

Ella's status had risen with the prince's approval, but it had still taken days since her arrival to convince Jehral to take her out. Women simply did not ride horses, nor did they want to. It was this simple supposition that had enabled Ella to take this step in the first place. The prince was often busy with his men and Jehral had been charged with her protection. The pace of life was slow in the tents, and when Ella had asked the prince if Jehral could show her the desert, he had agreed easily enough.

Ella's motives were more than simple enjoyment. After leaving Torlac, Evora had said they had less than two weeks before the Lexicon would fade. A horse was Ella's way out of the desert. Away from these men, she would make renewal her primary objective.

Ella realized that, after her conversation with the prince, there had been a shift in the men's attitude toward her. The prince had acknowledged that she was a woman of high rank, and obviously intended her for some purpose. Even Rashine left her alone now, although Ella sometimes saw him frown as he watched her from a distance.

Prince Ilathor had summoned her twice more to talk about the lands outside the Hazara Desert, showing a dedicated desire to learn everything she could teach him. He had sat close to her, leisurely smoking the waterpipe, his intense eyes watching her every move. Ella eventually grew comfortable in his presence as he asked her about the lands in the north, but the talk made her desperately worried for her homeland.

"Rise and fall with the horse, cushion yourself with the stirrups. You should feel you are one. Good."

Ella spoke to the horse as she rode—simple words of encouragement and affection. She patted his neck. His name was Sundhep, which Jehral told her meant "dark storm." He was a very dark brown, almost black, with a white blaze on his forehead.

"That's enough, High Enchantress. We should be heading back now."

"Please, Jehral? Just a moment more?" Ella wanted to make sure she was comfortable with the horse. When the right moment came, this was how she planned to make her escape.

"No, that's enough. The prince returns soon. He will want to see you."

Ella sighed and dismounted while Jehral held the reins. He mounted up and then pulled her up behind him.

"What would my mother think of me, teaching a woman to ride?" he muttered to himself.

He spurred the horse to a gallop, its hooves pounding through the sand.

***

Ella could tell something had changed in the camp. Jehral gave Sundhep to another man and led her to the prince's tent.

Prince Ilathor Shanti burst from his tent before anything could be said. "Here you are. Come in immediately."

For a moment, Ella wondered if he'd found out about her learning to ride. She exchanged glances with Jehral, who remained impassive, and then she entered the tent.

"Please be seated," Ilathor Shanti said.

Ella lowered herself onto some cushions. There was something to his manner; he seemed excited.

"I have something for you," he said. "A gift."

Ella's expression grew even more puzzled.

"Before I give it to you, though, I must tell you that this gift cannot be taken from my tent. It is to be used in my presence only. Do you agree?"

"Yes," said Ella.

"Good." He smiled. Surprising her, he casually rested his hand on her arm for a moment. The prince touched her blonde hair briefly. Ella felt uncertain. Was he attracted to her?

Ilathor moved to the back of the tent, entering a smaller room. He returned a moment later, holding something in his hands.

He placed an item down on the low table. It was a scrill, made of solid gold and beautifully worked. He then followed it with a flask the size of a large water bottle, sloshing it a bit as he set it down.

"Essence," he said, smiling down at her, gauging her reaction.

Ella couldn't believe her eyes. She had never seen—never even heard of—so much essence in one place before. Here it was, in a simple water flask, enough essence to enchant a hundred sets of armorsilk!

"Are you pleased?" Ilathor said.

"I . . . I am surprised, Your Highness. How did you come by . . . ?"

"No, wait. I have one more thing. The final surprise."

The prince left again while Ella stared at the assembly on the low table. They were actually giving her essence!

He returned and set something down on the table in front of Ella. Her heart nearly stopped. Her jaw dropped open.

It was a book with a yellow cover. The pages were of a familiar metallic fabric. A rune was on the cover, the number five.

It was a Lexicon.

The prince laughed when he saw her expression. "You are pleased."

"Where did you find this?"

He sat next to her, leaning in, his leg almost touching hers. "My father."

Ella reverently opened the cover as Ilathor watched her closely. She saw the same message, in the same flowing script:

To the common people of Merralya, one and all, I give you this, the fifth volume in my Tomes of Lore. Evrin Evenstar.

Ella turned the next page. An embossed title leapt out: *The Lore of the Illusionist.*

Ella's hands moved of their own accord as, one by one, she turned the pages. It was a whole new set of principles, completely different from anything she'd ever seen. Ella soon lost herself in the book. Ilathor seemed content to simply watch her as she worked.

After some time, Ella looked up. "Do you realize what this is?"

"Tell me."

"Well, what do you know of your people's lore?"

"It is said our people would come from the storms, striking from the shadows. I do not understand this, though."

"Illusion," Ella said.

"What?"

"Your lore, it is the power of illusion."

"I still do not understand."

"If you give me enough time with this book, I'll show you."

Ilathor smiled. "Then, Evora Guinestor, time is what you shall have."

Ella knew that the prince had her satchel somewhere in this tent. Their agreement for the prince to let her go remained unspoken.

◆━━━◆

It took three days before Ella was ready; she'd worked harder and faster than at any other time in her life.

In this new Lexicon were its instructions for renewal. The process required essence being carefully inscribed into the cover rune over a number of days, with complex chanting at regular intervals. Ella only hoped that, armed with this knowledge, renewing the Alturan Lexicon would be simpler than might otherwise have been the case.

Ella's head was filled with runes and matrices—terribly complex combinations. Her existing knowledge of enchantment and animation was expanded, fitting neatly in with this new lore. She .was beginning to see the pieces of the puzzle come together in a way she never could have imagined, in a way none of the masters at the Academy came close to realizing.

The desert warriors stood lined up at the foot of a dune, blank expressions on their faces, arms crossed in front of their chests. Ella saw Rashine scowling. Many appeared to think this was a waste of time. What could essence do that a good sword could not?

The prince stood apart from the men, his demeanor serious, his clothing of black and gold billowing in the gentle breeze. He looked suddenly imposing, and like what he was: the commander of a lethal force of fighting men.

Taking a deep breath, Ella reached out, and Jehral handed her the scrill and flask before returning to stand beside the prince.

Ella was determined to construct the runes without reference to the Lexicon. She hoped she wouldn't regret the decision. In many ways this new lore was very different from enchantment. It was both simpler and more complex.

The runes had fewer whorls and bridges, but a great degree of skill was required to minimize the amount of essence that was used. With enchantment, one could use a small amount of the shiny liquid to write on almost any surface. With illusion, the surface was first prepared by moistening with essence, and then the runes were written on top. It made illusion most suitable to cloth or sand—surfaces that to some extent could absorb the moisture.

Some experiments with sand had taught Ella that it was actually easier than it appeared. Several large drops of essence could be carefully spaced, each drop leaving a patch of moist sand ready for a rune to be drawn.

Ella opened the flask of essence and dipped the scrill in the bottle. Without waiting further, she allowed a drop of the oily liquid to fall onto the sand. She placed another drop above it, and then another. When she had a row of the wet patches, she started on the next row. Soon, row upon row of dark patches covered the sand.

Ella began to draw. The scrill made small sweeping strokes on the sand, smoke rising as she moved her hand. The men behind Ella began muttering.

She pictured Master Goss watching her draw on such a poor surface—he would have had a fit. This was where the lore of illusion was different. The strokes of these symbols were broader. Less precise.

Ella covered a huge amount of ground, using up perhaps a tenth of the bottle. She realized she would never have been able to make the matrix without such a large supply of essence. Her little crystal vial would have been exhausted long ago.

Finally, she was done. She walked back to the line of men and regarded her work. Ella prayed that it would work as the muttering increased in volume.

"Well?" the prince said.

"Shu-tala-nara! Tuhr-alhambra!" Ella called.

The runes came to life.

The patch of desert sand instantly disappeared in a cloud of yellow dust. It spread faster than the eye could follow, left, right, and high above.

"Khamsin!" one of Ilathor's men cried, turning and running. "Sandstorm!" He was soon followed by the rest of the warriors as they fled in panic. Only Jehral and the prince remained.

Ella smiled, walking forward. Ilathor and Jehral watched as she vanished into the storm. She knew that to them she was lost for a long moment before she materialized again, walking out of the dust.

Prince Ilathor took a deep breath, looking sideways at Jehral. He walked forward and entered the illusion. Several heartbeats later he emerged, a broad smile on his face.

"There is nothing there. I can even see you, Jehral. It is incredible! Come, enter."

Jehral entered the seemingly impenetrable barrier, followed closely by Ella and the prince.

Jehral walked about in amazement. "You could hide five hundred horses in here!"

Prince Ilathor laughed—a bright sound of joy. "You could indeed. Come, I want to see it from the outside again."

They exited and watched the storm with awe. Some of the men had trickled back, bashful expressions on their faces.

Ella watched as two of Ilathor's men walked up to the illusion, followed by a third man, Rashine. Ella then decided to activate the last sequence.

"Assan-shulanti!" she called.

An outline appeared in the storm—a huge face bearing a formidable scowl.

"Ahhh!" the two warriors jumped and ran away, their eyes wide with terror. Rashine was close on their heels.

The prince and Jehral laughed uproariously. After a moment, Ella joined in too.

<hr />

"Tarn Fasala did this," Jehral said, looking down at the body.

There were six other bodies on the ground. All Prince Ilathor's men.

The prince swore. "The enemies of my father. We cannot let this stand."

"Will you exclude them from your gathering of the tribes?" Ella said.

The prince frowned. "Exclude them? I plan on murdering them. Every last man, woman, and child."

"How will you ever unite the tribes if these things continue?"

Jehral touched Ella on the arm. "High Enchantress Evora, you do not understand."

"What's not to understand? You kill them. They kill you."

"This was a message, High Enchantress," Jehral said. "They are saying that Prince Ilathor does not have the power to call the tribes together. It is an insult. The other tribes will be waiting to see how we respond."

After Ella's demonstration the prince had sent messengers to all of the tribes, calling them to a great gathering in the deep desert. He had hinted to Ella that only a powerful leader could call the tribes together. Ella hadn't realized it would elicit this type of response.

Prince Ilathor was kneeling down, stroking the cheek of one of the men. "Setara, the son of my mother's cousin."

"Should I call the men together, my Prince?"

The regal figure raised himself up, an expression of determination on his face. "Call the men. We ride to battle."

Tarn Fasala could muster twice as many warriors as Tarn Teharan. With half of Ilathor's men hidden by an illusion, the remaining warriors of Tarn Teharan would provide a tempting target.

Rather than a sandstorm, Ella created the illusion of a great mound of rock. The hidden warriors waited impatiently within its confines as their brothers departed to draw the enemy to their position. Meanwhile, Ella climbed to the top of a far-off formation where she could watch the battle unfold.

The riders of Tarn Teharan came into view at the crest of a mighty dune, Prince Ilathor leading them, clearly recognizable in his gold trim. Their enemy followed closely, and as one the warriors of Tarn Fasala lifted their sabers into the air and spurred their horses forward.

The prince rode swiftly away from the charging riders, his men forming a ragged formation of fleeing warriors. Seeing their prey trying to escape, the enemy surged ahead, their leader losing control as bloodlust took over his men.

As the prince passed the illusion, he turned in a tight circle to face the charging riders. He raised his saber into the air and charged directly at them, the horses quickly gathering momentum.

They met in a mighty clash of beasts and men. Ella saw blood spurt into the air as the sabers cut into flesh. Horses fell to the ground, crushing their riders beneath them.

Once the two groups had passed each other, they both wheeled again in preparation for another charge. Tarn Fasala had lost scores of men, and Prince Ilathor had lost even more. They built their speed up again like two fighting bucks about to meet head on.

Jehral timed it perfectly. One moment there was nothing, and the next, his riders came flying out of the illusion to crash into the side of the enemy. Instantly, it was chaos as their leader was unable to regroup his men for another charge. Bodies were entangled in a fighting mess.

Ella could see Prince Ilathor quickly gain the advantage. Some of the enemy tried to run but were cut down from behind. She waited for the prince to offer quarter to the men of Tarn Fasala.

The offer never came. She watched in horror as the enemy was slaughtered to a man, and the sand became drenched with blood.

Ella thought about her brother, involved in battles of this kind, fighting an unyielding foe.

She had helped the prince enough, and she didn't know when or if he would honor their agreement.

With or without his permission, she had to get away.

52

*The world is a truly marvelous place. But the most wondrous
thing of all is the human spirit.*
—Toro Marossa, "Explorations," page 18, 423 Y.E.

Amber looked over the empty shelves at the food market. No apples
today, not even an onion. She sighed and looked around. There
must be something.

She saw Lorna Donwright. The woman's eyes were red; she'd
obviously been weeping. Her husband had also been called away
to war, and it seemed there was nobody left in Altura but women,
children, and the elderly. The vitality had gone from Sarostar.

A woman suddenly came up to Lorna, a shocked expression
on her face. It was Hollie Ronson. When she spoke, Lorna's face
drained of all color. Another woman joined them.

Amber walked over.

"What is it?" Amber said.

"Did you hear? A soldier arrived during the night, terribly
wounded. He'd been in the south—he was with the high enchantress's
party. They're dead, Amber. The high enchantress has been killed."

"No." Amber couldn't believe it. "Lord of the Sky, save us."

"I can't believe it," Lorna was saying over and over, shaking her head.

Hollie continued. "I hear the army is being pushed back all the way through Halaran. They don't even expect to hold Mornhaven much longer. They'll be on our doorstep soon."

Amber suddenly spoke. "Ella. Did they say anything about Ella?"

"Yes. I . . . I'm sorry, Amber. She was with them when they were attacked. Ella didn't make it."

Amber didn't move. Ella was dead.

"I'm sorry, Amber," Lorna said.

"You were her friend, weren't you?" said Hollie.

"Thank you, Lorna, Hollie," Amber said woodenly.

Amber turned and started walking. She thought of Ella's vitality and her smile. She cast her mind back to the day of their graduation, when she had sat in the sunshine with Ella and Miro, the joy of one another's company warming their hearts. She couldn't believe her friend was dead.

Amber only realized where she was going when she arrived: the Temple of the Sky in the city's heart. She pushed open the heavy doors and instantly felt the calm of the place. Soothing, tinkling music came from somewhere hidden. A great circle shone in the ceiling, entirely of crystal, artfully made to scatter sunlight throughout the temple in a gentle glow.

Rows of marble benches were tiered back from the podium, and Amber saw quite a few other people scattered about the room, their heads bowed in prayer.

Amber picked a place at random and sat down. She felt tired, so tired. The words of prayer didn't cross her lips, and her thoughts weren't on the Skylord. She just took the time to remember Ella. With the loss of her friend, Amber had lost the last hold on her youth. All she had now were her memories.

"May the Lord of the Sky bless you, my child," a voice came from beside her. It was the priest, Father Morten. Amber hadn't much liked his sermons about wickedness and morality when she had been a child. Now, with his kind face looking down at her, she suddenly felt the warmth of his presence like a fire in her heart.

"Would you like to talk?" Father Morten said.

Amber nodded. He took a seat beside her.

"I learned today that I have lost a friend," she said. Her voice cracked slightly as she said it.

"I offer you my sympathy. Wherever she is now, she has gone to a better place."

"My husband has gone to war."

"I will pray for him. It is hard—to fear for one you love."

"But I don't love him. I should never have married him." Amber found herself opening up to the priest. Before she knew it, she had told him everything. About Miro and Ella. About Igor and her pregnancy.

The priest said little. He simply listened and offered words of encouragement.

"It's the nature of war, I suppose," Amber said finally. She felt tired now. "I'm so tired, but I wish I could do more. Thank you for talking to me, Father. I am sorry I didn't come before."

"We all have our own way of expressing faith. It doesn't have to be within these walls. Even the Dunfolk have their Eternal."

Amber looked up. "Father, could you tell me something?"

"What is it, my child?"

"The Dunfolk—why do they hate us so much?"

Father Morten sighed. "It is a sad story. I fear not all men of the cloth have hearts as pure as the Evermen."

"Would you tell me?"

"It was long ago, but the Dunfolk have long memories. There used to be a shrine, on the edge of Dunholme, what they call

496

Loralayalana. They built it to their god, the Eternal. It was a deep well, lined with stones, a simple structure, but quite beautiful, they say. A circle of trees had been planted around the well. It symbolized what the Eternal meant to them."

"What happened?"

"Many years ago, some priests and townsfolk decided that the Dunfolk were wrong to worship the Eternal. They tried to convert them to worship of the Evermen. A large group of men entered the forest with picks and shovels, and they destroyed the shrine."

"Did the Dunfolk ever rebuild it?"

He shook his head. "They never did. Not one of our finest moments, I must say."

There was silence for a moment. Amber sighed.

"Are you eating well?"

"Yes, Father."

"How about sleep?"

"I don't know. I'm exhausted, but I can't seem to sleep."

He stood and put his fingers to Amber's forehead. She closed her eyes.

"Rest will come. Your future will be bright. Go with my blessings, my child."

Father Morten left her.

———————

Amber walked through the doorway of her home. Home. How many times had she called it that? It was more Igor's house than her own. His signs were everywhere.

Her mind was too busy for sleep, and she decided to tidy up. She put away all of Igor's tools. Clothes lay scattered about the floor. She couldn't even tell which were clean and which were dirty.

There was a tear in one of Amber's dresses, so she opened her desk drawer, looking for a needle. When she didn't find it, she tried Igor's desk. Odds and ends were piled in the drawers, and she wondered how he could ever find anything.

Amber saw a piece of paper underneath a set of scrills, at the very bottom of the last drawer. It had her name on it.

She removed the paper. It was a letter, folded in half.

Her heart hammering, Amber unfolded it. The note was from Igor to her. To be read in the event of his death.

Amber read it through and sank to her knees. It was a message of such love, it hurt her heart to read the words. The letter fell out of her hands.

She thought about the war and about the words of the priest.

She pictured Igor, his worried face set in determination as he faced a horde of Imperial Legionnaires.

The father of her child.

Amber stood up, catching herself in a mirror. She looked at her tired face, her disheveled hair. Her mouth set in a line of determination.

She had to do something to help.

Amber left the house and started to walk.

"The Tartana is busy. He is in a meeting."

"In a meeting?"

"Yes," the hunter said. He hadn't fitted an arrow and didn't seem to think Amber was much of a threat—all she carried was a spade. Three other hunters watched her in interest. She was sure there were more of them hidden in the trees.

"In a meeting with whom?"

"With what."

"What?"

"In a meeting with *what.*"

Amber scowled. "In a meeting with what?"

"With a leg of venison. I saw him enter his hut. He had a whole leg on a plate. I told him it looked like a good piece of meat. He said not to be disturbed, he would be in a meeting with some meat. Meeting meat," the hunter chuckled.

"Take me to him," Amber said.

"No. You have not been invited. Do you even bring a gift?"

"I don't care about your gifts! Listen, where is the shrine—the one that was destroyed?"

He frowned. The hunter's answer was a long time coming. "We do not speak of it."

"I will give you a gift—whatever you want—if you take me there."

"No."

"Listen to me," Amber said. "Your people are in as much danger as ours, yet you sit here doing nothing. We are dying so that you can sit here safe in your forest, making stupid jokes. Now, take me to the shrine."

The hunter smiled. "Your face is red. I did not know your people could change color like that."

One of the other hunters spoke. "It is a gift."

"I suppose it is," the hunter said. "Come, we will show you."

The hunters led Amber to a place in the forest, on the edge of Dunholme. It seemed no different from any other place, but the air was fresh, the grass below her feet soft and green.

Amber couldn't see any sign of a well. She hunted around for a long time, until she kicked a stone with her toe. She went down on her knees and parted the thick grass. She could see them now, smooth stones, chosen rather than cut to fit together.

The hunters watched her curiously.

After several minutes searching, Amber finally made out the circle of stones that had surrounded the well. It was roughly three paces in diameter.

Taking a deep breath, Amber put the spade against the earth, and began to dig.

———————

"There you are," a voice said.

Amber looked up, breathing heavily as she leaned on the spade.

It was Lorna Donwright. She stood on the edge of the wide hole, gazing down at Amber, an expression of puzzlement on her face.

"I grew worried about you when I didn't see you at the market. Yesterday you didn't show up for work. Today I went to your house and you weren't there. I told Father Morten, and for some reason he thought you might be here. Amber, what in the Skylord's name are you doing?"

Amber sighed, "It doesn't matter, Lorna."

"No, I want to know."

Amber looked over at the watching Dunfolk hunters. There were more of them now; they just stood and watched her dig.

"I'm rebuilding this shrine."

"But why?"

"For the Dunfolk."

Amber returned to her work. There was still an impossibly long way to dig; she had barely scratched the surface. The water would be very deep, and she knew nothing about laying stones. If it wasn't done properly, the water would be muddy and undrinkable.

After some time Amber looked up. Lorna was gone.

———————

She slept beside the hole in the forest, having eaten some hard bread she brought with her. One of the hunters had left a deerskin that Amber assumed was for her. It stopped her from freezing at night.

In the morning Amber returned to her digging. The hunters were back again; this time there were nearly ten of them. She ignored them and continued as the sun rose higher in the sky.

Suddenly, a man dropped to the ground beside her: Father Morten. He had a shovel in his hand. He said nothing, simply started to dig. Amber looked up and saw Lorna standing at the edge of the hole, holding a basket in her hands. She began taking the dirt away in loads.

Amber felt a lightening of her heart. Father Morten smiled at her.

Later in the day two boys appeared, young lads with boundless energy, who made a game out of the digging. Amber left them to dig while she helped Lorna remove the soil and rock as it piled up beside the hole.

"Mind if I help?" It was Hollie Ronson. She stood awkwardly with her father, Tod Ronson. "My father, he was a stonemason."

"Of course," Amber said.

Hollie began to collect the stones that were littered around the ground, arranging them by size. Her father, an ancient man with thinning white hair, grinned and started to examine the area, using a marked rope.

There were more of the Dunfolk watching now. Some women had joined the group. They didn't say anything, nor did they laugh or smile. They simply looked on as the townsfolk worked.

More people began to arrive, mainly women from the town. Amber recognized one of the market vendors, the one who never had any fruit. The woman gave her a broad smile and started to help cart the dirt away.

The well was a flurry of activity now, and Amber could see it begin to take form. Tod Ronson gestured wildly, enjoying himself thoroughly, directing the women and boys as they lined up the stones and dug deeper, ever deeper.

There were now hundreds of the townsfolk around the well, too many to perform the work. Many just watched, smiling and holding hands. They formed a large crowd around the workers, pitching in wherever possible.

A short distance away, the Dunfolk formed their own crowd. Their faces were very serious, almost grave. Amber glanced at them occasionally, but they just stood off to the side, watching.

Suddenly there was a cheer from the diggers. "Water! We've hit water!"

The townsfolk all cheered along, hugging each other, beaming. Amber had never felt such a part of the people around her.

Without warning, Tod Ronson jumped down into the hole. He started calling for more stones. People passed them along in a chain, each stone passing through a score of hands on its way into the well.

The sun moved through the sky and started to fall. It sent slanted light through the trees, the rays diffused by the lush greenery, casting a golden glow on the clearing. Amber could now see why the Dunfolk had chosen it. It was a special place.

Buckets started to come out of the hole as the muddy water was drained out. Amber and two other women worked on the well's rim, creating a low wall around the entire circumference.

As the sun began to set, people started to jump out of the hole, leaving just Tod Ronson behind. He busied himself for a while longer and then called out, "Get me up!"

Two big lads leaned down, each taking an arm, and lifted the old man out of the hole. He was drenched to the waist, but

Amber had never seen a smile so broad. He beamed out at the onlookers.

He sat on the low wall and gazed into the well, a look of pride on his face.

"Mr. Ronson!" one of the boys called. He threw a wooden pail to the old man, who caught it deftly. A long rope was tied to the handle. "Give it a go."

He shook his head and turned, looking directly at Amber.

Suddenly, all eyes were on her.

"Here," Tod Ronson said, holding out the bucket.

Amber walked over to the well and took the handle of the bucket. She drew in a deep breath.

She threw the bucket into the well, holding the rope. Everyone heard the slap it made as it hit the water.

Amber waited a moment and then lifted the now heavy bucket, looking inside. The water was crystal clear. Amber reached into the bucket with her hand, and lifting her hand to her lips, took a sip.

It was the sweetest water she had ever tasted.

"It's good," she said. She looked up at the townspeople, smiling, the first time she had smiled in days. "It's good."

Everyone wanted to taste the water. The bucket was tossed into the well again and again, passed from person to person, with broad grins.

There was a sudden commotion from the Dunfolk.

The townsfolk stepped back from the well. Amber looked up as she saw the Tartana approaching, while behind him, through the trees, stretching for as far as the eye could see, were the Dunfolk. There was a sea of people: men, women, and children—all come to see.

The townsfolk stepped back farther, leaving Amber alone at the edge of the well.

The Tartana stepped forward, his eyes on Amber, his wizened features inscrutable. He waved one of his arms forward.

Ten young Dunfolk women came out of the crowd, each carrying a small sapling in her arms.

Amber stepped back, and as she looked on, the Dunfolk women planted the saplings around the well. The women then withdrew.

The Tartana moved closer to Amber. He was so small that he had to look up to meet her eyes. Without knowing why, Amber sank to her knees, and he placed a wreath of flowers around her neck.

Then all of the Dunfolk cheered, the Alturans joining them.

The Tartana threw the bucket into the well. Still on her knees, Amber could only look up in astonishment as the Tartana withdrew the bucket, and grinning mischievously, upended it over her head.

53

The greatest test of courage is to bear defeat without losing heart.
—*The Evermen Cycles*, 19:9

Miro paced the balcony outside the great hall, looking out over the town of Mornhaven. His hands were clenched in fists at his sides. He fumed.

"What did you expect?" a voice said.

He looked up. Bartolo had followed him out, leaving the lords inside to bicker. Behind Bartolo, Miro could see Captain Beorn, a survivor of the terrible defeat at Ralanast.

"You should do something, Marshal," Captain Beorn said. He was a scarred soldier with a gray beard, a veteran who had risen his way through the ranks after years of service. Miro still couldn't believe he had such men serving under him. "Most of the officers will back you."

After the doomed battle for Ralanast, matters had gone from bad to worse. The army was in complete disarray, the men fleeing for their lives, running for the safety of the Ring Forts. With many of the officers killed or wounded, Miro had been forced to assume command with the aid of the thousand men who had stood with him at Bald Ridge. Miro's men had passed through fire and come out tempered like strong steel. They contrasted with the terrified soldiers who'd fought at Ralanast.

When he'd finally reached Mornhaven, the force Miro had assembled on the way was more than twenty thousand strong. He'd had no choice but to promote men from the ranks and create a leadership structure. To his complete shock, he realized on arrival at Mornhaven that his men were the only intact force to make it. The rest of the lords, captains, and marshals were either dead, lost, or in despair. It had broken Miro's heart to see brave soldiers with such weak leadership.

To his surprise, he'd been included in the hasty conference that had been called at Mornhaven Town Hall. Great things were expected to come out of it, and even Miro had hoped some cohesion and decisiveness would finally come about. High Lord Tessolar would be coming from Sarostar—perhaps he would give the army the strong leadership that Prince Leopold had so far denied them.

Miro had been given chambers in the east wing of the majestic town hall. When he had taken his bath, he'd found the *raj hada* of a marshal lying on his bed linen. It was a strange way to give a promotion. Even the captains who'd shown up requesting orders seemed confused.

Bartolo and Beorn now stood silently, watching him.

"What are you suggesting? That I somehow have Prince Leopold removed from command?"

"The high lord certainly isn't going to do it—not to his nephew," Bartolo said.

"The men will support you. They will follow a Torresante. They've had enough of Leopold," Captain Beorn said.

For a time Miro was silent as thoughts ran through his head.

"Come on, Marshal. Are you saying you think their plan is a good one?"

"No," Miro said, shaking his head. "I am not."

The news had recently arrived that the Petryans had joined the war. The primate's taint was spreading. With five houses allied against them and the back of the army broken, they didn't stand a chance.

"What about Wondhip Pass? The Petryans could be in Sarostar in a week!"

"I know," Miro said.

"Yet they want to hole up in Sark. Marshal, you know it as well as I do, Sark is lost. Halaran is lost. We need to worry about Altura now."

The Black Army had pushed them constantly. The horde of ravaging legionnaires, macemen, pikemen, axemen, mortar teams, and dirigibles was bad enough—but that was before the Veznans joined the effort.

They had come out of the forest, a wall of wood and thorn. The trees had come alive. It was simply too much for the exhausted soldiers of Altura and Halaran, who still talked about them with wide eyes. Seeing a man cut down with a sword was one thing, but seeing his limbs casually torn off one by one was quite another.

And now the elementalists of Petrya would come, their balls of fire would fly through the sky, and they would use the waters of the Sarsen to sweep Sarostar off the face of Merralya.

"Miro," Bartolo said. "Altura needs you. You've seen the looks on the lords' faces. They've already given up. I've even heard them talk about surrender. We don't want a repeat of the Rebellion. What would your father have done?"

"I don't know!" Miro said. "What would you have me do?"

"You know what to do."

Miro saw a commotion coming from inside the hall as the conference drew to a close. Looking out from the wide terrace, he could see the lords talking together, dressed in their finery. Catching movement from the corner of his eye, he looked up.

High Lord Tessolar stood high above on a small balcony. He gazed out over the town of Mornhaven, looking older and weaker than ever. He was alone.

Taking a deep breath, Miro knew it was time to speak with the high lord.

———◆———

"You are throwing away the lives of our people."

The high lord turned. "Ah, the son of the late Lord Serosa Torresante. Somehow, I knew you would seek me out."

"Don't you realize that the Petryans are on their way to Sarostar even as we speak? We still have a great force here. We need to pull back."

"It's too late for that, Bladesinger, or Marshal or whatever it is you prefer. We've sent a missive to the emperor. We'll discuss terms."

"You did what?"

"We'll surrender, salvage whatever we can from the situation, and then . . ."

"You do realize who we're dealing with, don't you, High Lord?"

"Face it, Miro: We've lost. We fought well. You fought well—your father would have been proud. But you're young. You haven't seen the things I've seen."

"How can you say that? Don't you even realize what we're up against? You think it's the emperor? It's Primate Melovar—he's the one behind it all. He has twisted the minds of the high lords and probably many of the lords too. I've seen it with my own eyes. If we can save Altura, we can try to find the allies we need.

There will be dissenters within the houses, lords or commanders who have seen the change in their high lords, who can feel the weight of the primate's yoke. There is hope, High Lord. There is hope."

High Lord Tessolar laughed—a dry chuckle. It was one of the worst sounds Miro had ever heard, symbolizing everything that was futile and without optimism. "There is no hope, young warrior. They want our Lexicon." He laughed again. "We couldn't give up our Lexicon even if we wanted to. It was stolen weeks ago. We've kept it as secret as we can, but at any moment the runes on your armorsilk are going to fade, and then you'll know. You'll be sending ordinary soldiers against Imperial avengers, Miro. There is no hope."

"Listen, High Lord," Miro said, unwilling to give up, even as fear clutched at his chest at the thought of the runes fading. "You are wrong. I am sorry to speak so plainly, but it is the truth. Wondhip Pass can be blocked, preventing the elementalists from taking an easy route into Altura, but it must be done quickly. We need to pull the army back to the Sarsen, to the edge of Halaran, where the river is wide and there is no ford to be had. The Black Army will follow us—they will have to if they want the decisive battle they are looking for. They cannot leave an army of this size at their back. We can cross our men over to Altura, and we can save the soldiers and refugees of Halaran. We can then destroy the Bridge of Sutanesta behind us."

"You would destroy the Sutanesta? It is an insane plan."

"It is our only chance."

"You would isolate Altura. We would be completely cut off."

"We would be protected. It would give us the time we need."

"Time for what?"

"To regain the initiative. To eradicate this plague of the primate's creation."

509

"Bah. Our men would be pinned between the Sarsen and the Black Army like ants beneath a boot."

"Yes, there is that chance. But it would be better than surrendering here. They surrendered at Ralanast, and the Black Army put the soldiers' heads on pikes. Do you expect any better? The emperor's executioner killed my father—what do you think they would do to you?"

High Lord Tessolar looked away. "I have been given assurances."

Miro's blood ran cold. He couldn't believe what he was hearing. "Then you are a traitor."

Tessolar spoke with spite. "You dare question my right, Miro Torresante? Watch your words. Who do you think gave your father to the emperor all those years ago? He was destroying our house, and I did what I had to do."

"Yes, you killed him. And you might as well have killed my mother. Seeing my father executed killed her too."

"That's what you believe?" Tessolar laughed. "Listen to me, Miro. Serosa persisted in his belief we could win the war, the Rebellion. I believed him at first, but there was no sign of imminent victory. All I could see was our reserve of essence drying up. We had answered Halaran's call, but it was time to end it. Altura could not be seen to break the treaty, but your father gave me the perfect opportunity. He gave me a chance to end the war, and then Katherine was mine."

Miro was confused. "What are you saying?"

"Your father and I, we were once close. Your mother was a great beauty. We both courted her, and we became rivals. But because he was high lord, she chose him."

"So, how did she die then? Did you have my mother killed just like you had my father killed?"

"Don't you realize, you fool? Your father was the only one who died in the Rebellion. As soon as he was dead, your mother was mine. She never died of grief. You've seen your mother by my side. Miro, your mother was my wife, Katherine."

Miro felt his world crashing down around him.

"All that stood in the way was two children, you and your sister. A permanent reminder of Serosa. I forbade Katherine to see you or even speak of you, and gave you into the care of a soldier."

"Brandon," Miro mouthed. He put his hand to his head.

"I don't think Katherine even cared that she didn't know you."

"Did you kill her?" Miro's tone was like ice. "My mother . . . Katherine . . . when she died . . . did you drown her?"

"No, Miro. She did that to herself. And with your sister dead, you are the only legacy of that family left."

The words hit Miro like a punch in the gut.

"What did you say about my sister?"

"Your sister, Ella. She was killed in Petrya, on the edge of the Hazara Desert. The high enchantress died also. They were trying to recover our Lexicon. Only one soldier survived."

"Why are you telling me all this?" Miro whispered.

High Lord Tessolar shrugged. The pain was openly displayed on his ravaged face. "Why not? There is no hope now. You seem to think everything will be fine. I am simply telling you that it won't. Wherever the Alturan Lexicon is, its power is fading. Don't tell me you don't know what I'm talking about. You've seen what it did to the Halrana, seeing their lore weaken and fade. Our enchantments won't last another week."

"You are not fit to be high lord of Altura. You are not fit to call yourself a man, let alone a lord," Miro said with venom.

"We'll see what the Black Army's leaders have to say about that. I meet with them tonight."

Miro reached for his zenblade, but someone grabbed him from behind, and his hand was caught in an iron grip. Turning, he saw two bladesingers standing behind him. The one holding his hand—Torathon, Tessolar's personal guard—shook his head. The other was Ronell, eyes glaring out of his disfigured face.

"Take him to the dungeons under Sark," High Lord Tessolar said. "Be careful with him. I hear he can fight."

They led Miro away.

54

I sometimes wonder if we're too dependent on lore. Look at the Dunfolk. We may think them primitive, but they have learned more about the use of medicinal herbs and plants than any of our battlefield surgeons. The bows and arrows they carry can be as lethal as an elementalist's fireball, yet we disdain them as barbaric. Yes, a heatplate is a highly advanced technology compared with rubbing sticks together. But if there were ever a dearth of essence, how soon would it be before we were reaching back to these methods of the past?

—Diary of High Enchantress Maya Pallandor,

page 219, 411 Y.E.

Some of the warriors snickered as Ella walked toward Prince Ilathor's tent. She'd heard whisperings among them—she knew they thought there was more to her relationship with Prince Ilathor than was proper. He was certainly handsome, but he had never acted other than as a perfect gentleman to her.

"Ah, High Enchantress, I want you to meet someone," he said as she entered. "This is Hermen Tosch, from Castlemere, in the west. Hermen, this is High Enchantress Evora Guinestor." Ella touched her lips and her forehead in greeting. "High Enchantress," the prince continued, "you wondered where we obtained the essence. Well, here he is."

Hermen frowned at the prince as Ilathor simply laughed. "Do not worry, Hermen," Ilathor said. "She can be trusted."

There was one other person in the room, an ancient crone in a black silk shawl, her skin wrinkled and limbs like sticks.

"And this is Elder Shal Hamsa. She still remembers the old ways. She is here to learn from you, and perhaps to teach you as well."

"It is a pleasure, Elder," Ella said.

The woman looked up. Her eyes were a piercing blue. "You are young, to be loremistress to an entire house."

Ella swallowed. "Yes, I am."

She felt the woman's piercing eyes on her for a moment. Ilathor simply watched in interest, sipping a hot drink.

"You are from the north?"

"From Altura."

"Ah. The enchanters.'

"Yes."

The old woman grunted and turned back to the prince.

Ilathor spoke, "Hermen was just catching us up with the latest events around the world. Merralya is much in turmoil of late. You were saying, Hermen?"

The man from Castlemere spoke with the guttural voice of the free cities. "The Petryans have assembled a great army of soldiers and elementalists. They will march for Wondhip Pass. They aim to attack Altura from the south."

The prince watched Ella as she struggled to remain impassive. She thought of the high enchantress and her perfect composure.

Hermen continued, "The Alturans and Halrana were crushed at Ralanast. Most of their leaders are dead. I have heard the Alturans have only a score of bladesingers left."

Miro! Ella breathed in and out, slowly and evenly.

"What comes next?" asked Ilathor.

"Well, if the enchanters don't surrender, my guess is they will pull back to Altura. Halaran is lost—that much is clear. Refugees are crossing the Sarsen into Altura, countless numbers of them. They will be lucky to make it out before the Black Army catches up with them."

Ella listened in horror. She fought to keep her face carefully smooth. The prince looked at her again and then looked back to Hermen.

"What do you make of this Black Army?" Ilathor probed.

"I have heard it is the biggest army the world has ever seen. Four houses, united. Who would have ever thought to see it?"

"Five with the elementalists—Tingara, Torakon, Loua Louna, Vezna, and Petrya. I cannot believe it myself. Nothing good can come of it."

"I agree," said Hermen. "Nothing stops this army. Independent cities like Castlemere, we will be next."

"I will think on it." The prince frowned.

"This gathering of the tribes, when is it?"

"In seven days, on the full moon."

"You will never unite them," Hermen said. "Too many long hatreds. Old habits are hard to break."

Ella thought the prince might react badly, but he merely smiled. "We shall see, my friend. We shall see."

Prince Ilathor watched as Ella worked with Elder Shal Hamsa throughout the day and long into the night.

The trader from Castlemere was long gone. Before he left, the prince asked Ella and the elder for a quick demonstration for Hermen.

Ella thought long and hard, before creating the illusion of a pile of gold coins on the low table. Hermen had laughed with pleasure, attempting to scoop them up but finding his fingers touching only air.

With interest Ella had watched as the elder removed a small statue of a horse from a pocket.

"I know only a few tricks, taught to me by my mother. There are few of us left now who know the old ways. This is one of my tricks."

The old woman spoke the activation sequence, and the horse began to glow with spidery silver lines. Instantly, a full-sized horse appeared in the open space of the tent, its chest heaving, nostrils widening with each breath.

Ella could see how it was constructed. It was a simple but effective creation—she could already see how it could be improved. For one thing, the eyes were merely pinpricks of light, and the coat was a dull gray.

"Excellent," Prince Ilathor had said.

Ella now rubbed at her eyes. She'd been working for hours, but even as she worked, she considered her plan to escape. Every moment was critical, but the prince and his people watched her constantly.

The old woman was surprisingly quick and determined. Ella had always had an excellent memory for the runes, and she could now work without referencing the Lexicon for all but the most complex creations. Most of her time was actually spent in showing the elder how to use the Lexicon—it required a framework of lore to even begin.

Ella found she had a much greater knowledge than the elder, but the Elder knew some useful tricks for short-cutting the runes, something Ella had never thought of doing before. By connecting simple structures, the end result was less detailed but also easier to create and required less essence. She filed it away in her memory.

The work temporarily took Ella away from thinking about Altura, but whenever she paused, she again pictured Miro or Amber. She tried to remember them smiling, but their faces became washed with blood.

Ella felt a touch on her shoulder and jerked, startled. It was Prince Ilathor. She must have fallen asleep. He put his fingers to his lips and gestured with his head. Elder Shal was lying back on the cushions, snoring softly. Ilathor smiled and took Ella's hand, helping her up.

The prince led Ella outside the tent. As she walked, Ella looked up at the night sky, once again amazed at the number of stars, a shimmering curtain that spread its way over the darkness.

She had begun to get a feeling for the desert. It seemed so empty at first, barren and desolate, but it had more character and expression than was first apparent. There were many different winds—they blew soft and gentle, or strong and fierce. The sand had different textures as well—from fine, like dust, to coarse, like grain. The dunes changed constantly, moving and reforming day after day.

Prince Ilathor led Ella away from the camp to stand on the crest of a dune, overlooking the motionless waves of the desert. He took her by the hand.

"It is beautiful, is it not?" he said.

"It is," Ella said.

"That you say that gladdens my heart," he said. He turned to her with a smile. "The desert is more beautiful for the single rose that stands within it. You are that rose, Evora, and a more beautiful woman I have never seen."

He reached up and took her head in his hands, cupping her chin. Before Ella knew what was happening, Prince Ilathor kissed her.

Ella broke away. "Your Highness . . ."

"Call me Ilathor."

"Ilathor . . . I barely know you."

"I feel as if I have known you my whole life," he said.

"I'm just not sure we . . ."

"I am certain."

The prince moved to kiss her again, his arm going around the back of her green dress. Ella pushed him away.

"Well, I am not!"

He frowned. "Do you not feel something, as I do?"

Ella thought. He was handsome and gentle. She thought about Miro and Amber, needing her help.

Ilathor's eyes sparkled. "Think of what we could accomplish together, Evora. You and I. We could change the face of the world. Bring peace to all nations. Restore my people to their former glory."

For a moment Ella was lost in his vision.

"No," she said. "Prince Ilathor, we don't belong together. I . . . I don't know what you speak of." She spoke in the harshest tone she could. "I feel nothing for you. Nothing at all."

Ella could see pain in the widening of his eyes. *Please forgive me,* she thought. *My friend needs me. My brother needs me.*

The prince whirled and walked out into the night, leaving the encampment behind. He fled into the darkness of the desert.

Ella saw her opportunity.

She knew she had little time. As Ella ran back to the prince's tent, the guards frowned at her, seeing her alone and unguarded. "The prince, he wants me to bring him something," she said.

They let her in.

Searching the tent while the elder slept, Ella finally found her satchel. She put her scrills into the bag, along with the Alturan Lexicon, but left the yellow-covered Lexicon of the desert people.

Ella looked at the large flask of essence, and with a feeling of guilt, she took it also.

She ran out of the tent, and the guards didn't say a word. Ella looked for Jehral's tent, and walked over to it, purposefully, as if she knew what she was doing.

A man grabbed her tightly by the arm of the high enchantress's green silk robe. "Where are you going?" a harsh voice asked. It was Rashine.

"*Ala-tut-ha,*" Ella muttered.

The robe flared as the runes came alive in searing blue. Rashine screamed as he pulled away, his flesh sizzling. Ella was glad she'd taken the time to decipher some of the capabilities of the high enchantress's garment.

The desert men called out to each other, wondering what was happening. Ella reached Jehral's tent, where his horse was a black shape against the night sky. Sundhep—dark storm. Ella was glad for his dark color on this night.

The saddlebags were full. There was water in them. The desert warriors were always ready to ride at a moment's notice.

Ella removed the hobble from the horse. It whinnied as she jumped up and onto its back. Hoping that her lesser weight would give her enough speed to get away from the prince's men, Ella took a deep breath.

She dug in her heels and galloped away, into the night.

55

*And so you can see the core units of the houses represented
on the simulator, from bladesingers to avengers.
The colossi, obviously, are not to scale.*
— Enchanter Saimon Bower to Marshal Timor Lewin, 412 Y.E.

Miro woke to the sensation of having a bucket of cold water thrown squarely in his face. He blinked in confusion and then moaned in extreme pain, unable to hold it in.

His body was paces above the ground, arms manacled to the wall, well above his head, his ankles likewise immobilized with metal loops. All his weight rested on his wrists.

He could feel a trickle of blood running down his left side. The scar running from under his left eye had opened when they had thrown him face down to the hard stone floor.

Miro opened his eyes. He had no idea where he was but guessed he was somewhere deep in the bowels of the fortress Sark. The roughly cut walls dripped with moisture. Fissures showed in the rock.

Standing in front of him was Torathon, High Lord Tessolar's personal bladesinger guard. Torathon had stayed in Sarostar while the rest of them fought and died.

Bladesinger Torathon smiled when he saw Miro's eyes open. Miro couldn't stop another moan from escaping his lips.

Next to Torathon was Ronell. The former recruit had given up trying to hide the disfigurement of his face, and his eyes glared from a scarred and deformed visage. Ronell's one arm rested on the hilt of his zenblade; the other ended in a stump.

"New orders from the high lord," said Torathon. "You're to be killed."

"Torathon . . . don't . . . do it. The high lord is a traitor. Save Altura. Ronell, please . . ."

Torathon simply grinned and looked up, and for the first time Miro noticed his eyes. The irises were yellow. He was already under the primate's spell.

There was a hiss as Torathon drew his zenblade, and with a few words he activated the runes. Miro watched the glowing steel with horror, and the weapon grew brighter with Torathon's song. Miro felt more blood running down his arms as the manacles cut into his wrists. He prayed for it to be over quickly.

Torathon's zenblade became filled with a searing, scorching heat. Miro could already feel his skin begin to burn. The grinning bladesinger slowly approached, the fire growing. He paused in his song.

"I'm going to slice you open from your nose to your navel," he said. "I'll open your ribs like wings and see if you can fly off the walls of Sark. Serosa the Dark died near here, didn't he? How fitting."

Torathon added more to his song, and the zenblade flared. Miro was forced to close his eyes. He felt as if his head were in a furnace.

Suddenly, there was a second hiss. Miro heard Ronell's voice, activating rune after rune in quick succession. There was a sickening crunching sound. Miro flinched and Torathon's song cut off.

Then there was silence.

Miro felt the heat slowly fade away, and he opened his eyes. Ronell stood silently, his zenblade in his hands, its runes already fading. There was an unreadable look on his face, but his eyes were clear of the yellow taint.

Torathon's body lay on the ground, staring into nothing. Blood formed a pool around the bladesinger's body.

Ronell looked at Miro, the zenblade still wavering. Then he sheathed his weapon.

"It wasn't your fault I was injured." Ronell paused. "I know you tried to help me. Let's get you down."

The two men ran through the endless corridors and chambers beneath the fortress. Miro knew he had limited time to act. It was now or never.

The two bladesingers stumbled into an infirmary. Miro recognized many of the men. They had fought with him from one end of Halaran to another.

A Halrana in an officer's uniform stood in front of them, his hand on his sword. There were two other guards with him. Every eye was on them, and Miro held his breath.

Suddenly, every man in the infirmary who was able to stand did so. Hundreds of men, young and old, rose to their feet. They said nothing, only stood.

The Halrana officer looked behind him and then looked at Miro.

"What orders, Marshal?" the officer said.

Miro nodded, releasing his breath.

"Find Captain Beorn. Tell him to gather the men outside Mornhaven Town Hall."

"At once, Marshal."

"What about us?" Ronell asked.

"We need to get to Mornhaven before Tessolar surrenders to the primate."

"It's this way, Marshal," the Halrana said.

"Thank you," Miro said.

Miro gathered men with him on the way. At one stage Ronell disappeared without a word, returning with Miro's armorsilk and zenblade.

The men followed Miro's orders without question. Their silent approval gave him confidence. He finally knew that what he was doing was the right thing.

They formed into a column with Miro at the head. The march down the long winding road from Sark to Mornhaven began as the moon rose above the town below.

Miro's heart filled with pride when the column reached the marble façade of Mornhaven Town Hall. Behind him stood an army of two nations. These weren't men for whom hope was lost. These men were willing to stand up and be counted.

"Marshal, Bladesingers—look," said Captain Beorn, pointing.

Bartolo lounged against a pillar near the entrance to the hall. With him were the rest of the bladesingers. Miro felt a moment's concern, and then he saw the smile on Bartolo's face.

"Saw you coming down from Sark," said Bartolo. "You should get that face looked at. We're all behind you. The lords—they're in there." He gestured inside the hall. "They're waiting for you."

Miro entered the hall, flanked by the bladesingers.

Prince Leopold and the lords of Altura and Halaran were seated at a glass-topped table. In front of them were the trappings of a feast—stuffed game birds, crystal decanters, and artfully constructed nightlamps.

"What's the meaning of this?" Prince Leopold said.

"High Lord Tessolar. Where is he?" Miro demanded.

"He . . . he isn't here."

"Where is he?"

"I don't know!" the flaxen-haired prince cried.

Miro drew his zenblade. Behind him, his brother bladesingers followed suit. Prince Leopold blanched.

"Where is he? Say it loud and clear so that we all may hear."

"He's meeting with the primate and the emperor," Prince Leopold whispered. The lords exchanged glances, expressions of shock on their faces.

"Say it louder!"

"He's discussing surrender."

Miro pointed his sword at the lords. "Did you know about this?"

"No, we didn't," a lord gasped. "It's treason."

"Did you hear that, Prince Leopold?" said Miro. "Treason."

"Marshal, I . . ."

The sight of the bladesingers with swords drawn was too much for Prince Leopold. He slumped. "What do you want from me?"

"Address the men," said Miro. "Tell them what you've told me now."

They escorted Prince Leopold from the room and onto the terrace. Leopold gasped when he saw the number of soldiers waiting below. When they saw Miro, the men roared, a mighty sound of approval.

"Loyal fighting men of Altura and Halaran!" Miro cried. "We have been betrayed." A shout of rage came from the men. "High Lord Tessolar is at this very moment meeting with the enemy. He wants to surrender. He's looking to save his own skin. Isn't that true?"

Bartolo shoved Prince Leopold forward. "It's true," the prince gasped.

The soldiers roared in anger.

"Where was High Lord Tessolar at the Battle for Ralanast?" Miro pointed to the north. "Where was High Lord Tessolar at the Battle of Bald Ridge? You've seen what the Black Army does to those who surrender. Has he?"

"No!" the men cried as one.

"I tell you now, as long as we are one, we can win this war! We are strong. Our enemy uses tricks and treachery to win battles. We use our hearts and our minds."

The lords filed out of the Town Hall. They stood uncertainly behind Miro. One of them stepped forward, saying something to Bartolo.

The bladesinger gestured. "Don't say it to me, say it to them."

The lord walked to stand beside Miro. His face was gray, and he walked with a limp. With a shock, Miro recognized him.

It was Lord Rorelan.

Rorelan took a deep breath, "We wish to appoint a new lord marshal of the combined forces of Altura and Halaran. Miro Torresante, will you take up this duty?"

Miro suddenly realized the responsibility being placed on his shoulders. He looked steadily at Lord Rorelan. "I will."

The shout of approval rolled like thunder. "Torresante! Torresante!"

But Miro was already looking into the distance. There was much to do.

56

Your first responsibility is to the path that lies before you.
The Evermen will give you a duty, and this is what you must do.
Be content that if you Follow the way, and
Serve with all your heart, then Salvation will follow.
                                    —*The Evermen Cycles*, 19:15

Killian stumbled into Salvation shortly before midday. He'd walked throughout the night.

The journey was a barely remembered blur. He'd pushed himself harder than he ever had before, even when he'd fled Altura with their Lexicon in his arms. One night ran into another in his memory—nights sleeping under hedges, nights in barns, and nights in the freezing open with a rock for a pillow. He'd used every trick at his disposal—stealing, lying, and conning his way into rides with Petryan merchants or food from humble villagers.

Now he was finally here, in Salvation, with the mountain of Stonewater looking down. His objective was never far from view, yet all he wanted to do was collapse.

Killian was going to enter Stonewater, venture into the primate's mountain home, and recover the Halrana Lexicon.

Killian looked about him at the ordered streets and the hordes of the poor queuing outside the bread shops. He'd been gone for what seemed like an age, and now he couldn't believe he'd once called Salvation home.

His first mission for the primate had been to Halaran, when he'd stolen the animators' Lexicon. He'd journeyed through Torakon and Loua Louna before reaching Halaran, and he'd seen sights that had opened his eyes to how big the world really was. Famed throughout the world, Stonewater was still an incredible place—a great temple, carved into a mountain! But cities like Seranthia and Ralanast were also incredible in their own way.

Killian tried to define it in his mind. Stonewater was a place of worship of the Evermen. Essence was created at Stonewater. The Evermen lived in Stonewater. Whereas in Sarostar—well, people lived there.

Killian had been lifted up by the primate, higher than he'd ever thought possible, but he now knew that it wasn't difficult when he'd had such simple goals: a soft bed, a full stomach, safety, and most of all, a chance to bring down the emperor.

He looked around him. The streets of Salvation seemed so much smaller now.

The buildings were all of the same uniform gray stone—squat, ugly structures of one or two levels. It was a small city for how many people there were in Salvation, hordes of them, all fighting for space.

There were no soldiers of the houses in the land of Aynar. In Aynar everything was run by the Assembly of Templars. The priests took care of the souls of the people. The templars took care of the more secular aspects of life.

Gazing around, considering his options, Killian saw there were more templars than ever before. The white uniforms were everywhere. Killian caught the eyes of a solidly built templar with his hand on his sword, and quickly looked away. Those yellowed eyes looked menacing.

Killian stopped in the street and looked up at the solitary mountain that was the destination of so many pilgrims: Stonewater, the home of the greatest relics of the Evermen, residence of Primate Melovar Aspen.

He'd only ever entered Stonewater at a summons from the primate. Now, with the primate away with the Black Army, he had to find another way to get inside.

Killian only hoped he wasn't too late.

He'd returned the Alturan Lexicon to Ella, but the Halrana Lexicon had been in the primate's possession for many weeks. If the primate destroyed it, the Halrana animators would be no more. They would cease to exist as people and would be absorbed by the primate's motley forces.

And it would be Killian's fault.

He cursed his strange ability. He felt dirty, used, lied to. What did the primate really know about his abilities? Who was he? He was an orphan, but who were his parents? All Killian knew was they were dead.

With a heavy heart, Killian rounded a corner and crashed into a templar in the process of tearing a poster from the wall.

The man in white turned his strangely yellow eyes on Killian. "Stop right there."

Without quite knowing why, Killian ran.

He felt the pattern of the streets come back to him and quickly lost the templar. He dashed through an alley and entered an area of taverns and eating houses. Slowing, Killian's breath returned.

A plan finally came to him, and he stopped. He would accost a templar and clothe himself in the white uniform. Once he was inside the mountain, he would figure the rest out as he went.

A group of three templars approached, too many for Killian's plan, and he turned away, but stopped when he saw their attention was taken with another poster. They gestured to each other and shook their heads. Finally, a templar stepped forward and tore the announcement away, but not before Killian read the words.

"True tales of the Evermen, told by the famed storyteller Evrin Alistair. Daily at the Tawny Tavern."

Killian frowned. Evrin Alistair. Evrin Evenstar. The name was too familiar. The templars began to walk with bold strides, and Killian decided to follow.

Sure enough, Killian saw the templars halt outside the Tawny Tavern as if waiting. Passing them, Killian walked in and opened the heavy doors, casting a final look over his shoulder.

People threw stern glances at the commotion when Killian entered the open tavern room. Wooden benches and tables were filled with townsfolk, all intently looking at the raised dais.

An old man sat on a high-backed wooden chair, his arms gesturing wildly. He looked at Killian but continued to speak. Killian found himself a seat and ordered a tankard of beer.

Killian regarded the man. He wore a faded white priest's cassock, the sun of the Assembly barely visible. His hair was white, but it must have once had color, as there were flecks of ginger in his scraggly beard. His eyes were his most noticeable feature, piercing blue, like Killian's own.

The voice was rich and deep. "Lorelei had killed his enemy, but Suhlan had been grievously wounded. Her body lay crumpled on the stair. Lorelei ran to her, screaming her name.

"He threw away the accursed sword that had caused him so much trouble." The old man made a throwing motion. Some children giggled and then were hushed by their parents.

"Lorelei fell down beside Suhlan's body, watching the life-blood flow from her veins. Her eyes fluttered, and she opened them to say her last words." The storyteller paused, looking out over the crowd. They hung on his every word, entranced. "She touched her finger to the blood on the ground while the tears flowed down Lorelei's face. Suhlan whispered something, but Lorelei could not hear, and with every moment that passed the breath was leaving her body." Killian found himself becoming caught up in the story.

"Suhlan's finger moved to the wound on her neck. She drew a symbol there, in her own blood. Lorelei's fists clenched with frustration, for he could not understand what she was trying to say."

"What was it?" one of the women said. She was hushed by the other patrons.

"Then Lorelei looked at the symbol. It was a rune, a simple rune of mending. Suddenly Lorelei understood. He knew she was different, and there was only one thing for him to do. He took the crystal bottle and ivory scrill from his pouch and he traced over the rune she had drawn in blood, this time with essence."

"But it would have killed her!" the woman called. She was instantly hushed.

"That's what Lorelei thought. But as he watched, she spoke the rune with the last of her breath. It lit up with silver, and in front of Lorelei's eyes the terrible wound sealed itself. Color returned to her cheeks. Lorelei had saved his love."

"That's magic," one of the children said.

The old storyteller smiled. "It is indeed. I will continue the story after a short break."

He rose and bowed. The audience clapped, and he left the stage.

Killian couldn't believe what he'd just heard; it was as if the message were intended for him. He looked around him. The people in the tavern spoke quietly, some hefting large jugs of wine to refill empty glasses. None seemed to be giving him any special attention. The old man was gone, and from what Killian had seen, at any moment the templars would be on him.

Killian stood abruptly, attracting some sideways glances from the other patrons. He left the table and walked to the bar.

"The storyteller, where is he?"

The barman jerked his head toward the back of the room. Killian pushed open a heavy door and entered the kitchen. He was greeted by warm smells of roasting meat, but there was no sign of the old man. Finding a second door at the back, Killian opened it and blinked in the glare of daylight. He was back onto the street, in a dusty alley.

Then Killian saw three men in white uniforms on the street; it was the group of templars he'd seen earlier.

"Stop right there," a deep voice said. Killian flattened himself against the wall.

"What is it?" It was the voice of the storyteller.

"We've told you about your posters, old man. We've asked you to stop peddling blasphemous stories in the taverns. We're not going to be polite this time."

"Peddling stories? Well, I haven't asked anyone to pay for them yet. More's the pity."

"You're coming with us."

Killian crept forward and poked his head around the corner. He could see that the three templars had started to encircle the storyteller. Killian couldn't let them take the old man. He knelt down for a moment.

Without dwelling on what he was about to do, Killian darted forward and grabbed the storyteller by the hand. He thrust out his other hand and threw a handful of dust at the templars, aiming for the eyes.

"Wha—?" the old man said.

Killian pulled him along. "Come with me. You don't want to know what they have in store for you."

"Argh!" one of the templars cried. "The Evermen curse you! Stop right there!"

Killian led the storyteller back through the door and into the kitchen, hearing the door thud a second time behind him as the chase began. The old man was surprisingly spry, and Killian pulled down the shelves of pots and pans behind him, ignoring the shrieks and calls that followed. He grabbed the handle of a huge bubbling pot and pulled it onto the ground, barely avoiding being scalded himself.

Killian had to find out about the old man's story—and no one was going to get in his way.

The old man in tow, Killian pushed open the door leading into the dining hall. The patrons were looking at the kitchen with wide eyes, but Killian pushed away their clutching hands as he ran, whisking the storyteller through the crowd.

"Stop him!" he heard from behind him.

Killian pushed open the tavern's front door. He was back onto the street, the door swinging closed behind him. Killian looked left and then right.

"What are you doing?" the old man panted.

"Saving your hide!"

The old man looked Killian up and down. "Head left—I know a safe place."

Without pausing to question, Killian started to run, the storyteller beside him. A large crash from inside the tavern spurred his steps.

"Turn left again here," said the old man.

They dashed into a side street. It was a plush quarter, where visiting nobles lodged and spent their leisure time.

Killian felt resistance and turned to see the old man had stopped outside an ornate wooden door, unmarked and unsigned.

"What is this place?"

"The finest guesthouse in Salvation."

"We can't go in there! Look at you . . ."

Then Killian looked once more at the old man. Gone was the faded white priest's cassock; it had been replaced with a flowing red coat. He now wore a ruby earring with a matching ring. Below the waist the old man wore leggings of a rich brown material, and his boots were high, with a steel buckle. He looked every inch the wealthy merchant.

"How did you do that?"

"Illusion," the old man grinned.

"Illusion?"

"It's a long story. Wait a moment." He took out a white kerchief and dusted off Killian's shirt. "That will have to do. They'll think you're my servant. My badly treated servant." He chuckled. "Come."

The old man pushed open the door.

Killian's jaw dropped at the opulence of the entry hall. A thin man in black silk strode up to them, bowing low. "Welcome. Welcome to the Wrenly."

"Thank you," said the old man in a pompous voice.

"Do you require lodging, or will you be enjoying your lunch with us today?"

"Lunch for a start, and as for enjoying it, my stomach will be the judge of that." The old man chuckled again.

The thin man smiled politely. He looked at Killian but quickly disregarded him. "Please come this way." He cleared his throat. "How many should I set the table for?"

"For two. I am in a generous mood. My servant will be joining me."

"Very good."

Killian stayed silent. There were too many mysteries here. He had thought only to prevent the templars from taking the old man away before he could find out about the story. Now the initiative seemed to have been taken from him. He'd lost his control of events.

The thin man handed them over to a stately woman. They were seated at a glass table and given two elegant cards to read. Killian couldn't understand the strange descriptions of food.

"Would you like me to order for you?" the old man said.

Killian nodded.

The old man waved, and the woman came to their table. "My servant will have the braised wood hen. I will have the rare fillet. Please choose a suitable wine. I trust your judgment."

The woman left. "I always find it best to let them choose the wine," the storyteller whispered.

"What's happening?" Killian said. "What are we doing here?"

The old man gestured around the empty room. "Isn't it obvious? Privacy and security. The templars would never look in here."

"That's not what I . . ."

"I know what you meant," he said. The old man was silent as two glasses were placed beside them and filled with a rose-colored wine. Killian could smell the rich aroma from where he sat. The woman withdrew.

"Try it," the old man said.

Killian took a sip. "It's delicious. Your story . . ."

"Yes, my story." He put the glass to his lips. "Ah, Louan wine." He looked up at Killian's frown. "Do you have any idea how many times I have told that story?"

"No."

"Too many times, with absolutely no sign of success."

"I don't understand."

"First, I need to know. Why did you come to me?"

"The story."

"What about the story?"

Killian took a deep breath. "The part about the essence drawn on the woman's skin."

A glow came to the old man's face. He gave a long, drawn-out sigh as his gaze ran over Killian's features and his fiery red hair. A smile spread, becoming a broad grin. "You? It's you?"

"I don't understand."

"What's your name?"

"Killian."

"Killian. I am Evrin Alistair. Once I was called Evrin Evenstar. I've been looking for you for a very long time. But now that I've found you, we have all the time in the world."

Killian frowned. He opened his mouth and then closed it. Finally he started to rise from his seat. "I don't have all the time in the world. You may call yourself Evrin Evenstar, but I know that's not possible. There's something I have to do, and you can either tell me what you know and help me, or I'm leaving."

Evrin raised placating hands. "Killian, please sit," he said soothingly.

Killian slowly sat back down.

"I am who I say I am. Tell me, what is this quest of yours?"

Killian wondered if he should dissemble, but his heart told him to tell the truth. "I'm here to recover the Halrana Lexicon from Stonewater. I'm here to stop the primate's evil in whatever way I can."

Evrin sighed, and his eyes took on a faraway look. "This war . . ." he whispered. "I always said I would stay away from the affairs of the common people."

"It's too late not to take sides," Killian said.

Evrin sat pensive for a long moment, and then he nodded. "You're right." He sighed again. "Perhaps sometimes inaction is the worst evil of all. But if you want to stop the primate, you're going to need my help. Recovering the Halrana Lexicon is important, but there's something more we can do."

"What?"

The old man told him.

57

Essence is the embodiment of life. A mighty tree grows from a seed.
The tree gives shelter to birds and shade to animals. It grows old,
withers, and dies. As it decays, the life force of the tree sinks into
the earth. The life force of a thousand trees comes together to form
lignite. The relics of the Evermen process the lignite, forming essence.
Understanding of the holy relics is beyond us, but one thing is clear:
The power of lore is the power of life itself.
—Sermons of Primate Melovar Aspen, 535 Y.E.

"Sir, I think you had better see this for yourself," the scout said.

Miro raised an eyebrow at Bladesinger Huron, who shrugged. He glanced at Marshal Beorn and Lord Rorelan. "Come with me," he said to the two men, newly made commanders.

It had been hard going since Mornhaven, but it was with a new sense of purpose that the army abandoned the Ring Forts for the promised safety of Altura. The men poured down from Sark first, and finally the other four fortresses emptied themselves. Miro formed them up quickly. There was no use delaying.

Halaran's strongest defenses would soon be occupied by the enemy.

There had been the inevitable departure of some Halrana who refused to leave their homeland. Miro let them go. He could understand what they were feeling. Even so, it was still an immense army he led, perhaps four-fifths Alturan and one-fifth Halrana.

The constructs' power had long faded completely, and there were no drudges to pull the great carts, yet the Halrana valiantly struggled to pull the wagons by hand. One day, if the Halrana Lexicon could be found and renewed, the ironmen, woodmen, colossi, and golems would fight again.

Miro didn't have the heart to tell the Halrana about the primate's plan to destroy the Lexicons permanently.

For the enchanted swords and armor, the nightlamps and heatplates, it was now impossible to hide the gradual fading of the runes. When he was alone, Miro had activated his armorsilk and zenblade. The light was still fierce, the armor supple yet strong—but for how long?

Miro kept telling himself that if he could get them to Alturan lands, they would live to fight another day.

The scout led the commanders up a hillside and over some rubble. Miro followed the scout as he climbed an abutment and stood on a high crest.

"Lord of the Sky," Marshal Beorn breathed.

The Sarsen curled in a ribbon below them, wide and turbulent in these parts. The mighty river formed the border between Altura and Halaran, a wild place of cliffs and canyons. There was one place only where the land lay low enough on either side to allow passage. This was the site of the Bridge of Sutanesta, a great stone arch supported by immense columns.

It was a relic of the elder days, the Sutanesta. There was no lore holding it together; it was an example of ancient ingenuity. Each gray block was the size of a house. How the stones had been put together and assembled was still a mystery.

In the lowland on their side was a sea of people. More people than Miro had ever seen in one place, and he had seen mighty battles. They weren't numbered in the thousands. They were numbered in the tens of thousands. These people were the refugees of a defeated nation: the men, women, and children of Halaran.

Their numbers were so great that they were packed together side by side. Children screamed and babies bawled. Fathers jostled for room with their arms in a circle around their families. The crowd surged and fell back, then surged again.

"Skylord save us," said Lord Rorelan.

The Bridge of Sutanesta had been destroyed.

Where it had existed was now an immense empty space. The columns at the beginning and end of the bridge were still intact, but the great blocks that had formed the arch could be seen here and there in the current of the river.

"It's the work of the enemy," the scout said. "You can see where they laid the runebombs. Massive, they must have been."

Miro took a deep, shaky breath. He had to be strong. He was the leader. He'd brought them to this place. Now only a river stood between his army and the security of Altura. A wide, surging river—and an innumerable mass of refugees.

"What do we do?" said Marshal Beorn.

A cry came from behind them. Miro turned. Prince Leopold stood transfixed, his face drained of color.

"We should never have come to this place. We had safety in Sark. My uncle—"

"Your uncle deserted us, all of us, and that includes you," said Miro.

"He will be back," said the prince.

"Not as long as I'm here," said Miro. He waved to one of his captains. "Take him back to the army, and keep him away from the men."

"At once, sir."

"You can't do this," Prince Leopold said.

"It's done." Miro turned back to the refugees as the captain led Leopold away.

"He will hate you for that," said Marshal Beorn, scratching at his beard.

"Let him," said Miro. "We need to plan."

"You know what this means," said Lord Rorelan. His smooth face was creased with worry. "We need to get this army across that river. The soldiers have to take priority."

"I know, I know," said Miro. "There has to be a way. If only we had more dirigibles."

"The task would require hundreds, and we have a handful, each only able to carry a couple of men. We need to begin clearing the refugees so that our men can start rebuilding the bridge," said Marshal Beorn. "I have to warn you, it will take days."

Miro cursed. "We don't have days."

Lord Rorelan laid a hand on his shoulder. "We also need to think about our defenses."

Sighing, Miro nodded. "Get the men to start digging trenches. I want them ready before sunset, but don't stop digging until the end. Detail some of the Halrana soldiers to take care of those refugees. We need them to allow space for our engineers to get through to the remains of the bridge. Send some enchanters with them. In two hours I want a report on what we can do to cross that river. We'll put the bladesingers and two colossi on that ridge there. The colossi aren't functional, but the enemy may not know that. The mortar teams and dirigibles can go up on the hill to the side there. We want the heavy units up the front. When the Black Army comes, it will be with everything they've got."

Men ran in all directions. Miro looked down at the refugees again. They were so helpless, milling around in confusion. The task of getting so many people across the Sarsen appeared insurmountable.

Miro closed his eyes. He remembered Layla's talk about the Eternal. It was time to pray.

58

The constructs of House Halaran disgust me. Gross mechanical creatures—who could love such things?
—High Lord Vladimir Corizon to
High Cultivator Draco Brasov, 538 Y.E.

Killian trudged up the hill, his back bowed under the weight of his pack. He glanced at Evrin beside him. The old man had changed his clothing back to the faded priestly garb. From all outward appearances they were pilgrims on their way to Stonewater.

He sighed. He was still ignorant as to his past. What he really was and why he was different. The old man had explained his plan, and now here Killian was.

Not for the first time, Killian wondered if he was yet again the pawn of another's grand scheme. It was the thought of Ella that kept him going. She knew who she was—she didn't need to be told. She'd made it clear to Killian whose side she thought he should be on. He wondered where she was. He hoped she'd found her way safely back to Altura.

Evrin gave Killian a significant look. They were getting close to the peak of the mountain now. They rounded a bend in the rock, and Evrin drew to the side, pretending to be out of breath. Killian stepped forward as if offering his aid. Then, when there was a break in the line of pilgrims, they ducked around the rock and scuttled over the scree to a protected cleft in the side of the mountain.

Killian took a moment to gather his breath. He thought about what Evrin had told him. "This substance the primate has made from essence, this . . . technique he uses to turn people to his will, I don't see how you are to blame," Killian said.

Evrin's blue eyes studied him. "It is a long tale, too long for today. But there are some pieces of knowledge that are better kept hidden. This is one of them."

"What do you need me for? Why don't you do this yourself?"

The old man ignored him. He was busy rummaging through his bag. He turned to Killian, a small brown bottle and a scrill in his hands. "Take off your shirt. This won't take long."

Killian noticed Evrin didn't bother with gloves. "Aren't you worried about the poison?"

"No, I am not. Off. Take your shirt off completely."

Killian removed his shirt.

Evrin deftly dipped the scrill and began to draw runes with a quick, sure hand. The smoke rose from the bare skin of Killian's chest. He felt nothing but a slight tingling.

Killian had seen Ella draw the symbols, but this was something else. Evrin drew rune after rune without pausing, without thinking. Killian's chest was soon covered in the matrices, followed by his neck. His arms followed. Finally Evrin drew the runes on Killian's back.

"There," he said. Evrin drew away to regard his work.

It had taken only minutes. Killian hadn't seen many runes, but he had the feeling that this was lore of a level beyond anything, beyond even the loremasters of the houses.

"*Shak-lan,*" said Evrin.

Some of the matrices came alive, glowing with silver light.

"What have you done to me?" Killian said.

"It is a rushed effort, but I have enhanced your body."

"Enhanced? What do you mean? Why don't you enhance yourself?"

Evrin sighed. He seemed to lose some of his strength. "I cannot. It was my final punishment. They took it away from me. Now, I am just like the common people. I can create lore on items such as my clothing here. Essence does not harm me. But the abilities you have, I no longer possess." Evrin activated some more sequences, naming the runes one after another.

Killian felt his body . . . change. His skin firmed, his weight grew lighter. He bunched his fists. His arms felt like steel.

"If you only had the knowledge, we could do more. Much more. Your dreams could only half-describe the things that could be done." Evrin regarded Killian's glowing body. "I have kept it simple. You will not need to name any runes yourself. Wait a moment." He drew a quick succession of symbols on Killian's trousers.

"*Sur-an-ahman,*" Evrin said.

Killian felt no change. Then he looked at his hand. There was nothing there. He looked down at his body. He was invisible.

"Are you ready?" Evrin said.

Killian nodded. Evrin just looked at him, his eyes slightly unfocused. Then Killian realized the old man couldn't see him. "I'm ready," he said.

Evrin pointed. "There is a special entrance, guarded by templars. It leads to the first in a series of chambers. They store the lignite ore here—essence in its raw, unrefined form. Each small block of lignite contains the life force of a thousand trees or a million blades of grass. Are you listening?"

"Yes, I understand," Killian said. "The first chambers contain the ore. Is this really the right thing to do? What about the Halrana Lexicon? That's what I came here for."

"Listen to me, Killian. Imagine every person you have ever cared about being held above a flame. You have a choice. To free them or to have another taste of the tainted essence and watch them burn in front of you, their screams haunting your nightmares for the rest of your days. Killian, if you were in its thrall, you would choose to watch them burn."

"But to destroy the relics . . ."

"We're destroying the primate's methods of production. The primate uses essence to produce his elixir. If he can no longer produce essence, his supplies of *raj nilas* will soon run dry."

"But the houses . . ."

"The houses have their essence stockpiles. And Killian?"

"What?"

"The knowledge—how to produce essence"—Evrin tapped the side of his head—"right here."

"What about the Halrana Lexicon?"

"It may have already been destroyed. If it has, there's nothing we can do. First destroy the relics the primate uses to produce essence, and then you can worry about the Halrana Lexicon. Now listen: Stonewater has a wide shaft running vertically through the mountain's core. The most secure place is at the foot of the shaft. This is where the refinery is housed and where essence comes into being. It would stand to reason that the essence is further refined into elixir, *raj nilas*, here. When your mission is complete, look for the animators' Lexicon somewhere near the refinery.'

Killian closed his eyes, breathing in, and then slowly opened them. He was filled with a new determination. If the primate didn't have any more of the tainted essence, he could no longer bend the houses to his will. This was Killian's chance to save lives, the lives of people like Ella. "So what's after the ore chambers?"

The old man gave Killian a further set of instructions and then handed him three small cubes, each covered in tiny runes. Killian could see the cubes were numbered from one to three. "These will destroy the relics. To activate them, say, *'Lot-har'* followed by the number. They will explode ten seconds after you activate them."

Killian put them into the pocket of his trousers.

"Each has great destructive power. Make sure you are far away when they detonate."

The old man suddenly looked his age. He held out his palm, and Killian gripped it, although it looked like Evrin's hand gripped nothing. "Be careful. When you return, we will talk. And Killian?"

"Yes?"

"The yellow eyes. Be careful of the yellow eyes."

59

You can't fall off the floor.

—Louan saying

Miro had pushed the men hard, and himself harder. They had accomplished miracles in the two days they had been in the borderlands. Somehow, though, it hadn't been enough.

From his command at the summit of the tallest hill, he gazed out over the incessant activity below. He studied the wide loop in the river. They had cut the loop, forming a half circle. Their defenses now formed a ragged line from one point in the river above the bridge to another point lower down. The treacherous ground rose and fell, making a straight line impossible. Miro had taken advantage of the terrain wherever possible, deploying his strongest units on the crested hills and natural rises.

The earthworks now stood high above the spiked trenches below. The men permanently lined the long embankment, waiting for the inevitable.

Inside the defenses were the refugees.

Their needs for food and attention grew daily. Miro had asked them to form a council to oversee their needs. Some people had soon come forward, priests and administrators mostly. Even then their numbers had been too great to deal with. They bickered among themselves and came to Miro to resolve the most mundane details. Finally, in a fit of rage, he asked for just one leader to be nominated to look after the refugees' needs. That was when Pamela had come forward. The widowed wife of a Halrana commander who'd died in the battle for Ralanast, she'd formed a bridge between the nobility and the common people. Her gray hair reminded Miro of steel, as did her personality.

Under her command, the refugees soon ordered themselves. She had even sent Miro hundreds of stonemasons and other workers from within their numbers, freeing up the valuable soldiers for the important role of protection. Work on the bridge had started to see some progress.

But not enough. The blocks were simply too big.

With the aid of the army's engineers, the workers had started to unravel some of the techniques of the ancients. They said the Bridge of Sutanesta's construction had relied on an elaborate system of levers and pulleys. A rough gantry had been put together with some success, but it was crushed while moving the fifth block.

There were hundreds of the great blocks. At this rate, Miro would be here for months. It was time he simply didn't have.

Miro looked over his forces. At least they were ready—as ready as they could be. He stroked his chin; he hadn't shaved in days. He couldn't even remember when he'd last slept.

Miro remembered the words of Tessolar. Ella was dead. The Alturan Lexicon had been stolen.

Miro almost prayed for the enemy to come soon, while their enchantments still held. It would be bitter irony if they were given more time to complete their fortifications, but in that time the symbols on Miro's armorsilk faded altogether.

A uniformed man with the *raj hada* of a dirigible pilot ran forward, seeking the lord marshal. The pilot looked from side to side, a harried expression on his face.

"Speak, man," Miro said.

"Perhaps, away from the . . ."

Miro took the pilot by the arm and led him away from the command post. "What is it?"

"The Black Army, we've sighted them."

Miro sighed. "How far?"

"Perhaps a day."

"Can you take me up?"

"Sir?"

"Your dirigible. Can you take me up?"

The pilot stared at the ground and then looked up. "Now?"

"Yes."

The pilot's eyes met Miro's. "Yes, sir. Sorry sir, but no one has ever asked me that."

"Lord of the Sky, why not?"

"The height, sir."

Miro frowned but didn't reply. He followed the pilot down the hill to the dirigible post.

He hadn't thought about the height.

The soldiers looked surprised to see Miro's arrival, but they swiftly drew back as the airship pilot gestured to where a man held a ladder. Seeing the dirigible floating high above, Miro gulped. He took hold of the ladder and began to climb, feeling his weight cause the airship above him to dip slightly.

"One foot after the other," he muttered to himself.

"Sir!" the pilot called from below him.

"What is it?" Miro called, turning to look down at the pilot.

"Don't look down!"

Miro's vision swam. He breathed in and then out, slowly releasing the air. "Thank you, pilot," he called.

He finally reached the top of the ladder, tumbling over the side of the wooden tub. "Not too graceful," he muttered.

The pilot soon followed him over. "I meant for you to not look down, sir," the pilot said.

Miro grinned wryly. "I know you did, pilot. What's your name?"

"Pilot Varoun, sir."

"Varoun. That's a Louan name isn't it?"

"Yes, sir. My father was an artificer, sir. I was born in Altura."

Miro smiled. "Good to have you with us, Pilot Varoun. Now, how about you show me the whereabouts of our enemy."

"Yes, sir," said the pilot.

Pilot Varoun called a series of runes as the men below released the rope. The dirigible began to rise into the air while Varoun went to the side and brought up the ladder. "Wouldn't do for the enemy to climb up, sir."

"I'm sure."

There was barely room in the dirigible for the two of them. Miro looked over the land below. He couldn't believe how high he was. "Lord of the Sky, it's incredible," he said. "Every commander should spend time up here."

The pilot nodded. "I have often thought so myself, sir."

Looking ahead, Miro could see far into the rugged land of Halaran. He turned around. Behind him the Sarsen wound through deep canyons. Far in the distance it plunged inland, to be lost in the beloved forests of Altura.

The dirigible moved slowly, the runes lighting up as the pilot activated them. Miro felt the freshening wind on his face.

"There, sir." Varoun pointed. "We probably shouldn't go any closer."

At first Miro couldn't see what the man was referring to. Then he realized. That long line on the horizon, stretching across the entire land. It wasn't a forest. It was the Black Army.

Miro peered forward. He could make out the haze of dirigibles in the air. There must be hundreds of thousands of men down there. "Are you sure? A better knowledge of their numbers would be invaluable."

The pilot simply tilted his neck, revealing a deep scorch mark. "The elementalists. They've got a few with them now."

Miro held the man's gaze. "I understand."

Miro gauged the distance as best as he could. Their numbers would slow them down, but he knew this enemy well. They had pushed him across half of Halaran, from east of Ralanast all the way to Mornhaven, and now they had pushed him here.

A day was the upper limit.

"We can return now, Varoun. Thank you."

"My pleasure, sir."

Miro fought to keep his face impassive. They were out of time.

60

And the Lord of the Sky said, "Anyone who thinks the sky is the limit, has limited imagination."

—*The Evermen Cycles*, 14:14

Killian slipped past the templar. He was so close that he held his breath, afraid the sound of it would reach the man in white.

"What is that?" the templar suddenly said. Killian didn't slow. He dropped and rolled, straightening behind a column.

"Did you feel it too?" another warrior said.

It wasn't the first time. Somehow the templars were able to sense him. Killian knew he had to keep absolutely silent.

The harvesting plant was just ahead, and reaching it, Killian gazed at the height of the great machine. Evrin had said this was where they brought the lignite ore. The priests said the harvesting plant was a relic of the Evermen, a sanctified gift to the people of Merralya.

Killian saw an awesome construction, made of the same strange metal as the Lexicons. It was covered with runes and glowed with an array of colors. Pipes and vats whistled and bubbled. Steam suddenly shot out in a hissing cloud. As Killian drew closer, he could see the intake, a massive doorway the size of a house.

The instinct that had seen Killian survive the streets of Salvation on his wits alone suddenly told him to drop. As he hit the floor, a sword whistled over his head. The templar swung overhead at Killian's body, but Killian rolled away from the blade. The man swung again; this time Killian wasn't quick enough. He vainly raised his arm in front of his face in protection. The sword crashed into his arm, bouncing off it like stone. The templar howled.

"What is it?" a voice called.

"It's here, there's something here!"

Killian leapt to his feet and saw the feverish yellow eyes of the templar look first one way, then the other. There was something in the essence taint that enabled them to sense him.

Killian threw a fist at the templar. The man ducked to the side, his movement a blur, and the templar's sword came at Killian's chest. Killian punched into the man's sword arm. Time slowed. He watched, sickened, as his fist went straight through the templar's skin like a burning rod. Blood spurted out, and the sword fell out of useless fingers.

The templar screamed. Killian looked at his fist, then turned as he heard the sound of running footsteps. The room was filling with warriors in white uniform.

Killian took out the first cube. He activated it by speaking the sequence Evrin told him and then took a slow breath. The templars crowded in, heading straight for him as he counted to five. Then he threw the glowing cube into the intake of the harvesting plant before leaping back between the swords of two of the running soldiers. The whistling of their swords followed him. Running at full speed now, Killian leapt again.

His body flew through the air. The vaulted airway that ran the height of the mountain sucked him in.

The harvester detonated as Killian grabbed hold of a rail. The air was forced out of the chamber, and then blew back with the force of a hurricane, heat like a furnace tossing Killian's body around like a feather in a storm. He held onto the bar, his eyes shut tight. His body slammed again and again into the wall of the vertical chamber. He didn't know where the strength to hold on came from—it must have been the protection of the runes. Killian opened his eyes.

High above him, easily hundreds of paces away, smoke poured out in a billowing cloud. Below him was nothing but the depth of the mountain. Killian held up a hand, looking through it to make sure he was still invisible. Then he took a deep breath.

It was time to find the extraction system.

Pulling himself up onto a ledge, Killian rolled onto the cold stone floor. He stood up and tried to get his bearings. He was somewhere in the living quarters of the upper echelon of priests—which meant that the extraction system was on a level below him. He could hear shouts and cries. A priest suddenly ran past him, his cassock billowing around his bare ankles.

One direction was as good as another. Killian began to run.

He passed innumerable priests; it was strange to see them away from their temples and sermons. Finding a staircase cut into the mountain, Killian began to descend but stopped. A templar was ahead of him, frowning, his hand on his sword.

Killian charged into the templar, knocking him from his feet. Hearing the whisper of steel being drawn, he turned and struck out with the flat of his hand, catching the templar on the skull. The templar grunted in pain, a red mark appearing on his skin. He turned yellowed eyes in all directions, searching for his adversary. As Killian watched, the red mark began to dissipate.

To Killian's shock, the mark subsided. The man's skin healed in front of his eyes.

The templar suddenly thrust out with his sword, faster than Killian could react. The sword sparked against Killian's side, but the pain was minimal, like a pinprick. Killian swung again into the templar's backswing and caught the man's head on the side with the full force of his fist. The templar's head exploded and his body crumpled to the ground.

Killian's skin tingled and he felt strange, like he was in another man's body. He reached the bottom of the stairway and looked out.

Murals decorated the walls, depicting scenes from the Evermen Cycles. Incense rose from a golden brazier, the smoke curling and twisting. The ceiling was vaulted here, rising from columns that had been cut into the rock of the mountain.

As Killian walked, he could feel the history of the place. He passed niches cut into the walls, realizing he was in something like a museum. The first niche contained a strange bracelet covered with runes. Next was a silver dagger, curved wickedly. Killian saw a lock of long red hair, tied with a ribbon. A sound came from behind him—templars pouring out of the stairway, swords drawn.

"This way!" one of them said. "I can feel it. Pure evil."

Killian ran to the back of the chamber and found a second set of stairs, carved in intricate patterns. Making out runes on the wall, he knew he was getting closer.

The priest knelt at an altar. A stylized depiction of the Lord of the Sun scowled down at him from above. The priest mumbled to himself, the words endless and repetitive.

He started at the sound of Killian's breathing directly behind him.

Killian grabbed him around the neck. "Make a sound and you're dead. Understand?" The priest nodded, his eyes wide. "Where is the extraction system?"

Killian loosened his grip on the priest's neck slightly so he could speak. "Three floors down," the priest gasped. "You'll never get there. It's protected—"

"Never mind that it's protected." Killian slowly turned the man's head from side to side. The eyes were clear. "Priest, I would leave Stonewater if I were you. There is darkness here. Perhaps you have felt it. If you have, you already know you should leave. If you haven't, perhaps you deserve whatever comes to you."

Killian pushed the man away. The priest coughed, placing his hands on his neck.

Killian looked for the next set of stairs.

61

*One of the weaknesses of our age is our apparent inability
to distinguish our need from our greed.*
—Memoirs of Emperor Xenovere I, page III, 381 Y.E.

Primate Melovar Aspen stood at the summit of a jagged hill. He assessed this final front of resistance.

"Peace." He smiled. "Emperor Xenovere, we are so close now, I can taste it."

Melovar looked over to gauge the man's reaction. Emperor Xenovere V shivered in the brisk air. His shoulders were slumped in his full-length purple coat. The immense collar simply made his head look small in comparison to his body. His purple *raj hada* was stained with the signs of travel.

A fitting sign—the Imperial *raj hada* tarnished with mud. *How far the mighty fall,* the primate thought. He smiled again.

"Well?" Primate Melovar said. "Here we are. About to crush the enemy who rebelled against your rule not so long ago. Are you pleased, Xenovere?"

"Just kill them and get it over with." The emperor sighed.

"What? You are unhappy? Your legionnaires form the heart of my army. I would have thought there would be some pride there. Are you not proud of your people, Xenovere?"

"Proud?" Xenovere said. Some fire rose to the emperor's eyes. "Yes, they rebelled. We fought and won, while they lost. But at least they knew what they were fighting for. We knew what we were fighting for."

The smile left the primate's face. "Peace," he snarled. "Something you were never able to give them. I promise peace in this life and salvation in the next. What did you ever offer them? I promise to never let men like you think you have the right to abuse your responsibilities. I promise universal law, Xenovere. That is what we are fighting for."

"Then why are they here?" The emperor pointed at the mass of Halrana refugees, the lined fortifications of the defenders. "They don't appear too interested in the peace you offer."

"You heard the Alturan high lord; they are led by a rebel. Now that Tessolar has been converted to our cause, we simply need to remove this rebel, and the last elements of resistance will crumble."

"Who is this man, this rebel?"

The smile returned to the primate's face. "You would know him, actually. As a babe he watched as his father, Serosa, was killed at Mornhaven."

"You convicted him, as I recall," the emperor growled.

"At your orders," the primate returned with a nod. "The child was Miro. Bad coins always turn up, eh?"

"I fought him at Bald Ridge," said Moragon. "He fought well."

The emperor suddenly struggled to control a spasm, his back arching. The regal face grew contorted. Melovar nodded to Moragon.

Moragon held the emperor's head, dribbling a small amount of black liquid between his lips. The seizure began to subside. Soon only the emperor's facial muscles were twitching.

"It is killing him," Moragon murmured to the primate.

The emaciated figure shrugged. "He was one of the first. There were refinements I still needed to make. The new ones will last longer. Think of Saryah."

"She is different. Perhaps she was lucky, or perhaps she was unlucky, but the elixir worked differently on her. What will you do when the Tingaran Empire has no emperor? Xenovere won't last much longer."

"I won't have need for him after this day."

Moragon turned away, his face like stone.

Emperor Xenovere wiped at the corner of his mouth. "Give me a sword," he said in a hoarse voice. "At least let me die like a man."

The primate chuckled. "So you can try to kill me? Come now, Xenovere, I am not that stupid." He resumed his survey of the battlefield. The defenders were outnumbered twenty to one. "Stupid," he murmured. "They should have removed the refugees long ago."

"What would you do if you were in command?" the emperor said. "Kill them all and throw their bodies into the river? In the name of the Evermen, you are a priest!"

"Xenovere, you have military sense. You can see it. We simply need to break through their line and start killing refugees, and we'll start a stampede. The Halrana refugees will overrun their own protectors in their desperation to get away."

The emperor started to twitch again, his limbs shaking in agitation. The primate nodded to Moragon, who dribbled more liquid into the emperor's lips. Xenovere was beginning to outlive his usefulness. The charade was becoming too difficult to keep up.

"We'll crush them against the Sarsen," Moragon said, once again surveying the battlefield.

Primate Melovar smiled. "We'll probably drown more than we'll kill with the sword. I'm always pleased when we can do things without reliance on lore."

"You should be pleased, then," Moragon grinned, sweeping his arm grandiosely.

The Black Army stretched to the horizon in all directions, an unstoppable force. The catapults and trebuchets were lined up. A surprise lay in store for the defenders, for the stones were covered in runes—a trick Moragon copied from the Battle of Bald Ridge.

Forty Imperial avengers led the advance elements of the legion. Behind the elite troops would be the full weight of the army. Dirigibles and mortar teams were ready to rain destruction on the embankment. Pikemen and a motley collection of swordsmen formed the bulk of the men in the rear.

It was a glorious sight. The defenders looked pitiful in comparison.

"Is that their command?" said the primate, pointing.

Moragon nodded. "Do you want to offer them terms?"

The primate barked a laugh. "Terms? At this point? Let us offer them unconditional surrender. Who knows—they may take us up on it. If they do, that river is going to be very handy when it comes to disposing of so many."

Moragon spoke briefly to a herald as Melovar continued to survey the field.

"And the status of the bridge?" the primate asked.

"They weren't able to rebuild it. They've constructed rafts. They're ferrying the refugees across the river, a score at a time."

The primate tilted his head back as he laughed. "They'll be there until the end of the world—which it probably is for them. Every beautiful garden has its weeds. It's time to remove the last bunch."

62

Without fear, there can be no courage.

—Alturan saying

Miro had feared it would come to this, but he'd always held out hope. The Lord of the Sky had turned his back on them this day.

"How many are still functioning?"

Marshal Beorn's face was as still as the grave, "None, Lord Marshal. Some hours ago, the runes faded on our last functioning zenblade. None of our enchantments will activate. It's been too long since the Lexicon has been renewed."

"Let's not focus on what we don't have," Miro said. "We still have the tools of the artificers—prismatic orbs, dirigibles, mortars."

"I'm sorry, Lord Marshal," said Lord Rorelan. "We did our best. I expect we'll get little mercy from the primate, but perhaps we should consider surrendering."

"No," said Miro. "I would rather fight and die here today than see our people butchered out of hand. You know we can't expect any mercy, not after what happened at Ralanast."

"Miro," said Rorelan, "we tried. But even if our bladesingers were able to fight, even if the iron golems and the other animators' constructs were fully functional, we can't last against an army of this size."

For the first time, Miro accepted the chance of defeat. He'd tried so hard! The despair clutched at his chest; he felt he couldn't breathe.

"There must be a way!"

"I'm sorry, Miro," said Marshal Beorn. "Ordinary soldiers just won't last against Imperial avengers and elementalists. With no enchanted armor, the prismatic orbs—both ours and the enemies'—will devastate our men. Our entire battle plan relies on our enchantments."

A strident trumpet blared out. A courier came running, his breath coming in gasps.

"The emperor is giving us a chance to discuss terms," the courier said.

Miro looked at Marshal Beorn and then at Lord Rorelan.

Miro sighed. It was over. "Tell the primate I'll discuss our terms of surrender."

———————◆———————

Miro walked alone through the masses of the enemy. Lord Rorelan had begged him to take an escort, but he didn't want to risk more lives as well as his own. He felt naked without his zenblade—he'd left it behind, even though its runes had faded over a day before. He still wore his green armorsilk but wore a covering cloak; it looked strange without the spidery symbols covering every inch of its fabric.

Surrounding Miro on all sides were armored templars with white tabards, escorting him to his meeting with the primate. The soldiers of the Black Army drew back from them fearfully. Templars were well-trained soldiers, but this was something else. With a start, Miro noticed their yellow eyes and remembered what he'd seen in the Borlag. These men had the taint.

For the first time in his life, Miro saw the emperor. The man was still far enough away that it was difficult to distinguish his features, but the purple robe and the Tingaran *raj hada* were unmistakable, particularly against the black and white of the soldiers around him.

Miro passed through an inner circle of templars. They stood guard around a hill, where Miro could now see a thin man in white—Primate Melovar Aspen—standing beside the emperor. Moragon also stood with the primate. The melding's eyes gleamed as he watched Miro approach.

Miro fought to keep his breath steady and even. He was coming face to face with Melovar Aspen. This was the man he'd had nightmares about his whole life. Miro would also be mere paces from Moragon, the emperor's executioner, the man who'd killed his father.

"You come alone, Lord Marshal. How brave," said the primate.

Miro stared into the man's yellow eyes. More than at any other time in his life, Miro wished he had his fully functioning zenblade with him. He would gladly have given his life for a chance at destroying this man.

"I've come to discuss our terms of surrender," Miro said stiffly. The words caught in his throat; he couldn't believe he was speaking them. He spat them out as if choking.

Miro glanced at the emperor. Drool ran from the man's chin. He would offer no help.

"You and I have met before, Miro. Do you know where?"

Miro wasn't sure if he wanted to know. "No."

"You were only a small child. Much as you are now." The primate smiled. "I needed your mother to spy for me, but she wouldn't cooperate. A knife at your throat soon changed her mind. She married Tessolar and did what I asked. You see, none of this would have been possible without her. She gave me the information I needed to develop the elixir. Your mother was the ultimate betrayer, Miro."

The pieces finally fit together for Miro. He understood it now—why his mother had married Tessolar. Even Tessolar himself hadn't known. This man was the reason he'd grown up without parents. He was the reason Katherine had been forced to pretend to love her husband's betrayer, to stay away from her children, even though they must have constantly been on her mind.

Primate Melovar Aspen smiled when he saw the look in Miro's eyes. "You understand, don't you, Miro? I have you to thank for all this. In a way, the destruction of your house will be entirely your fault."

Miro's eyes burned. He forced himself to speak. "I am here to discuss terms of surrender."

"Ah yes, terms. You will enjoy hearing them. First . . ."

Miro didn't hear the primate's next words. Out of the corner of his eye, just below the edge of his cloak, he saw a line of silver appear on his armorsilk. Another line appeared. One symbol after another came to life. How could it be possible?

The only explanation was that someone had renewed the Alturan Lexicon.

Moragon was looking at the primate. Neither had noticed the return of the runes. Miro fought not to look and draw attention to them.

"And finally, Miro, I want you personally. This is not negotiable. You could be very useful to me if Tessolar gives us trouble. It doesn't matter how much willpower you think you have. I can still turn you. In fact, nothing would give me greater pleasure than to see you lead your people, under my control. You can be my puppet, Miro." The primate gestured toward the emperor. "Just think of the illustrious figures you'll be joining."

Miro looked up at the primate.

The man started at the menace in Miro's gaze.

"I take back my offer of surrender, Primate. I hope you've enjoyed your moment. The next time we meet, it will be at your demise."

The primate laughed and signaled. Some templars came forward. "Take this man somewhere out of the way, and give him the elixir. Force it down his throat if you have to."

Miro allowed himself to be led away. Even with his armorsilk functional, he had no chance of killing the primate or even escaping alive. He needed to wait until there were fewer of the enemy to guard him.

He had to make it back to his men.

Somehow, they had been given a chance.

The Alturan Lexicon had been renewed.

———◆———

Six templars forcefully led Miro to a tent set aside from the main force. He carefully kept his bearings, taking note of the hills and valleys, places where the enemy's numbers were thin.

He tried his best to appear to be docile, despondent, a defeated man. He could feel the strength in the wrists of the templar who held him.

But Miro was a bladesinger. And when they reached the tent, and two templars moved to open it wide, Miro took action.

He smashed down his wrists and at the same time butted back with his head, feeling a satisfying crunch as he crushed an opponent's nose. While the man behind him fell back, three templars came in, and Miro activated his armorsilk with gasping breaths.

His advantage lay in the fact they wanted him alive.

As Miro's armorsilk tightened, settling around his shoulders, its protective strength warded off the savage blows of the templars. They moved with incredible speed, the taint giving them speed close to that of a bladesinger.

But not close enough.

Miro's fist crashed into the jaw of the closest templar, and he put everything he had into the blow, all of the rage and frustration he'd felt at facing the primate and walking away. It was a killing strike, and the templar fell down as Miro's next opponent met the heel of Miro's other hand, flinching back from a direct hit on the throat and falling back with a cry.

They came in fast now, and Miro chanted activation sequences as he fought. When a templar grabbed at Miro's cloak, he spun, freeing himself of its encumbrance.

Miro chanted for shadow, and he weaved through his opponents with all the skill he'd learned at Blademaster Rogan's hands and from fighting in a violent war.

After mere moments, six templars lay on the ground, but more were rushing in.

Calling on more shadow from his song, Miro tried to remember the best route back to his army.

He had a battle to win.

Some time later, Miro stumbled but righted himself. Blood matted his hair and his knuckles were scratched and raw. Without the armorsilk he would never have escaped.

"Miro! You made it." Marshal Beorn embarrassed Miro by giving him a rough hug.

"It's a miracle," said Lord Rorelan, gesturing at Miro's armorsilk, which glowed fiercely with power.

Miro smiled wearily. "The runes . . . ?" He held his breath.

"All of the enchantments are functional."

Miro began to feel hope again. "Spread the word . . ."

"Already done," said Marshal Beorn.

"All we can do now is wait. They'll attack at any moment."

They all sobered. Miro looked over at the rafts ferrying the refugees across the Sarsen.

Every time he saw another group of refugees unload at the Alturan side, Miro thanked the Lord of the Sky.

At mid-morning, the Black Army attacked.

———◆———

Forty Imperial avengers led the way. Behind them, a horde of legionnaires formed the front of a relentless tide of screaming men.

Miro watched as the Black Army drew closer to the first of the white marker stones. As the enemy passed the line, Miro's eight dirigibles blinked into existence as their charge of essence was depleted and the shadow wore off. Miro released his breath. He hadn't even realized he was holding it. The effect had lasted.

Miro's dirigibles dropped their loads of orbs in a black rain. Soldiers and dirt flew in all directions as the prismatic orbs exploded in blue fire. The airships then turned to fly back to the protection of the defenders, enemy mortars shooting up at them in a fiery stream. Five of the dirigibles were hit and began to plummet to the ground. Three escaped.

Miro looked on, his chest squeezing his heart like a vise, as the five stricken pilots activated the other new sequence that had been built into their vessels. Miro had hoped it wouldn't come to this. Pilot Varoun was in their number.

As they struck the ground, the dirigibles self-destructed, taking their pilots with them, along with vast numbers of the enemy.

Still, the Black Army came on.

The enemy reached the second of the white markers. Miro's four catapults released their loads—hundreds of smooth stones from the river. Without the essence to enchant the stones, it had been Marshal Beorn's idea to instead enchant heatplates and bring the stones to an incredible temperature. Miro almost felt sorry for the soldiers of the Black Army.

The flying boulders whistled in the air. The catapult strike hit the enemy like a giant squashing thousands of men with his foot. The attacking soldiers simply went down.

Those who fell were soon replaced. The weight of their numbers pushing them forward was simply too great.

The enemy now began their own catapult bombardment. The tall earthworks had been roughly enchanted to the strength of iron, and Miro now watched to see if it would hold. He saw a mighty boulder sail through the air. It flew over the barricade to crash into an Alturan mortar team, exploding on impact, tearing them to pieces.

Miro caught the ashen faces of the commanders around him. His own face stayed impassive.

The Black Army reached the third of the white markers. The Alturan and Halrana mortar teams began their bombardment. Orbs fell down from the sky, and Miro watched an avenger go down in a haze of blue fire. He saw the bodies of legionnaires scorched black and then trodden into ash by the surging men behind them.

The men in green and brown roared their defiance.

Still, the Black Army came on.

An Imperial avenger ran ahead with its strange gait, the point of a wedge of countless soldiers. It passed the fourth white marker, and a dozen bladesingers suddenly materialized, high on a hill, their armorsilk flaring like the sun. Miro could almost hear their eerie song from where he stood, and part of him longed to be with them in that fierce charge. The bladesingers smashed into the side of the attackers, blood spurting like a fountain in their wake. Miro could see Bartolo rampaging through the enemy, his zenblade like a purple flame. An avenger went down, followed by a second.

Their advance momentarily halted, the enemy began to pile up against the extreme force of the world's finest swordsmen. But from his vantage point, Miro could see the enemy's momentum building, unstoppable as the tide.

Miro watched as one bladesinger went down, followed by a second. Then Miro saw Bladesinger Huron go down as another avenger was destroyed.

"Pull out," Miro muttered. "Pull out!"

As though they heard his command, eight bladesingers left the fray to regroup behind friendly lines.

The Black Army continued their assault, an avalanche of men. The fifth white stone was reached.

The bottoms dropped out of a camouflaged series of ditches, as deep as the height of two men, lined with sharpened wooden spikes. As Lord Rorelan had said, "Forget about essence for a moment; the old tricks are often the best."

An avenger fell and was impaled, roaring like thunder. Miro saw hundreds, thousands of men fall to their deaths, unable to stop because of the weight of the men pushing them from behind. It was sickening, a massacre. Legionnaires ran over the bodies of their comrades. The corpses became bridges over the trenches.

Miro watched as a group of soldiers in the orange of Vezna threw something into a ditch. Suddenly a coiled vine bloomed out, forming a platform over which the men advanced. Behind them, Miro could see the tops of the Veznan nightshades, huge tree warriors, scores of them preparing to wreak havoc on the defenders.

And then the Black Army reached the embankment.

The avalanche rolled over the wall, men clambering on top of each other to spill over the raised earthworks. Steel points and flailing limbs were everywhere in a massed confusion as the defenders fought to hold back the tide.

"Send in the reinforcements," Miro said.

"But, sir . . ."

"Now!"

Miro watched the Alturan heavy infantry pour into several gaps opening up in the line. They reformed the line, barely holding the Black Army back.

Miro looked behind the defenders, past the panicking refugees and at the Sarsen. The makeshift rafts crossed the turbulent water at a snail's pace. The refugees crowded near the broken bridge, wailing and screaming, terrorized beyond belief. Barely a tenth had crossed. Miro had given orders that in the event of their being overrun, the rafts were to be destroyed, along with all of the construction work on the bridge. Pamela, the refugees' leader, had sworn an oath that she would see to it.

The bladesingers reentered the battle. There were only half a dozen now. Miro saw Ronell leap impossibly high, landing next to two avengers. His zenblade flashed upward in a spray of sparks to tear the closest monster open at the waist. The second avenger's flail curled around Ronell's torso and tore him into two pieces.

Miro thought of the recruit who had faced his fears. He hoped Ronell was now at peace. He forced himself to avoid looking for Bartolo among the remaining warriors.

One of the soldiers, an Alturan by the green of his *raj hada*, ran flying ahead into the massed enemy forces. Carrying a huge glowing sword, he fought like a man possessed. The enemy fell back from his furious assault, giving the line another chance to reform. The gaps were stopped. They were safe for the moment.

"Who is that?" Miro said.

"I don't know," Beorn replied.

63

It pays to be brave.
—Memoirs of Emperor Xenovere I, page 181, 381 Y.E.

Igor Samson, Master of the Academy, threw himself into the battle. He snarled and thrust at a legionnaire. The man raised his glowing sword to block, a shocked expression on his face as the enchanter's enhanced blade cut through it as if it wasn't there. The legionnaire went down.

Igor turned and whirled, wielding the long, fiery weapon with two hands. Even the Alturan heavy infantry around him gave him room.

Igor was fighting for Amber.

He muttered the runes like curse words, biting them off with each blow. He activated the sequence for the prismatic spray. A dozen of the enemy went down as the rainbow of sparks flew from his sword, burning out their eyes.

The lessons learned from his brief spell of training at the Pens as a younger man were coming back to him. Igor cut a legionnaire in half and then turned on his heel to reverse his blade into a black soldier holding a long spear. A space opened up in front of him, and Igor ran into it, screaming his rage.

A monster of flesh and grafted weaponry stood in front of him, its flail twisting and lashing against the ground like the tail of an agitated beast. Its other arm had been grafted into an immense black sword. The head was nothing but a steel mask showing a menacing red slit.

The avenger waited while Igor activated the full strength of his enchanted armor. It would drain swiftly at this rate, but he knew he would need its protection. He strode forward, his great sword throbbing in his hands, and activated another sequence. A high-pitched buzzing came from the blade, and Igor could feel the heat washing off it, even from within the protection of his armor. All of the men around him fell back from the phenomenal temperature, leaving just Igor and the avenger.

The flail flickered. Igor ducked and then leapt forward, sweeping his sword high above his head. He caught two of the steel chains, shearing them off. He ran forward and thrust at the creature's rune-covered chest. His sword scored a line along it while sparks fountained off.

Then the avenger's black sword hit his armor, cutting through his back and into his flesh. Igor cried out.

Igor swung his sword against the creature again and again, each time blocked by the black sword. A dark shadow passed overhead. The whip of the flail.

Igor activated the final sequence in his specially crafted sword. The buzzing whine grew louder, until it was all that could be heard, the crash of steel inaudible. A bolt of pure energy left the sword. The runes dimmed by half as the power of the blade was projected forward.

The bolt struck the avenger, leaving a hole where the monster's chest had been. The avenger pitched forward and fell, dead.

The cataclysmic confrontation left a gap in the enemy's ranks. Igor surged into the empty space, his mind filled with determination.

He cut down three legionnaires, one after the other, as the rest fell back from his fury.

Igor reached a small rise from which he could see above the heads of the sea of enemy soldiers. There, ahead of him, was a tall prominence, a broken outcrop. He saw a man in a full-length coat of imperial purple. The immense collar framing the man's head identified him as one man, and one man only: the emperor. Next to the emperor was a thin man in white robes.

Igor caught movement from the corner of his eye, a blinding light speeding from another hill, directed right at him. He ducked and rolled just as the ball of flame smashed into where he'd stood a moment before. Looking up, he saw a man in the red robe of an elementalist throw a second fireball at him.

Igor ignored the danger. He began to run. He would end this, once and for all.

For Amber.

64

We will find only what we look for,
nothing more and nothing less.
—*The Evermen Cycles*, 26:12

The piercing shriek came again. It sounded like a terrible beast was lost in the hollows of Stonewater, restless and searching for food. Killian put it to the back of his mind and pondered the extraction system.

He paced the length of the endless tubes and bubbling vats. Runes glowed with eerie power. Hoses connected transparent flasks to great drums. At the heart of it all was a pumping machine the size of a house. It rumbled and throbbed, symbols changing colors constantly. Killian decided this was where to place the second cube.

A mighty roar echoed through the huge chamber. There was something he recognized in its sound.

Then Killian remembered.

The trail from Sarostar to Torlac in Petrya. Ella huddled in fear. The dark forest. The screams of a man in extreme agony.

The beast. It was here.

Killian quickly withdrew the cube and spoke the activation sequence. He placed it on the ground next to the pulsing machine and began to count as he turned away.

One.

There was a sound from behind him, almost lost in the thumping of the machine. A heaving, as of a panting creature.

The blow snapped his head back, and Killian's vision went dark. He held up his arms in front of his face. A second blow smashed into his forearm, tearing his skin away. Some of the runes on his arm went dark.

Two.

Killian opened his eyes and ducked. The creature was faster, and a shifting blow caught him under the chin. He flew through the air, smashing into one of the vats. It burst open, scalding liquid covering his torso. Killian screamed.

Three.

The beast came toward him. With a shock Killian realized it was a woman. She may have once been beautiful, but any beauty she once possessed was lost in the twisted snarl, the wild hair. She wore a billowing white dress, torn and bedraggled. The symbol of the priesthood could still be discerned on her breast. Her eyes were a complete, solid yellow.

Four.

Killian came to his feet. He felt the strength of the runes flowing through him. His arms had the strength of steel, the lightness of air. He crouched and then jumped. His arms caught the thin steel of some tubing overhead. In a single movement he flicked his body into a spin. He dropped to land behind the woman and spun his elbow into her head, crushing her skull, following it with two hard blows to her torso that stove in her ribs.

Five.

She fell.

As Killian watched, her body started to writhe, somehow reforming itself in front of his eyes. A rasping, wheezing sound came from the creature. He realized she was laughing.

Six.

She stood, holding her distorted arms out at her sides. She was unarmed, but her hands were like claws, curled and tipped with black fingernails.

Seven.

One moment she was in front of him, the next she was behind him. She moved so fast Killian couldn't follow her. She went for his throat, scratching and gouging at any piece of flesh she could find, and Killian's body became visible as the runes sparked again and again. She shrieked in triumph as she found the weakness in his left arm. He felt her clutch it in a grip of unbelievable strength, her fingers cutting into his skin as she began to tear his arm from its socket.

Eight.

Killian cried out in pain. He writhed and swung his head from side to side. He looked down and saw a rune, one among so many drawn all over his body. He remembered Evrin's story: a rune for mending. It was the same rune. He knew it.

Killian named it. The skin on his arm began to reform, and he felt the strength flow back into him with the lessening of the pain.

Nine.

Killian smashed his head backward and simultaneously lashed out behind him with his elbow, throwing the woman off him. She fell to the ground.

He ran.

Ten.

The extraction plant blew in a series of explosions, each greater than the last. Killian's body was thrown across the chamber to smash against a wall. He picked himself up and ran for the vertical shaft. The mountain thundered as flame and superheated air tore Killian from his feet.

And then he fell.

65

A real leader faces the music, even when he doesn't like the tune.
　　　　　　　—Memoirs of Emperor Xenovere I, page 150, 381 Y.E.

Miro's gaze left the lone warrior as he watched his weakening line begin to crumble. There were simply too many of the enemy. They pushed against each other with endless momentum, pressing forward.

The defenders were about to be crushed against the Sarsen.

Miro saw an overcrowded raft topple, sending dozens of women and children plunging into the icy water. They were swept away, never to be seen again.

He cast his mind over what he'd done to bring them here. He knew events couldn't have turned out better if they'd surrendered. The Black Army's past actions proved that.

Two more rafts safely landed their precious cargos on the shore of the opposite bank. Miro sighed. At least some had made it. Even if they landed all of the refugees now, he still had the army to pull back. There was no hope.

"Hold that line!" Marshal Beorn called, as a group of legionnaires burst through the defenses, opening the floodgate that held back the horde of bloodthirsty warriors. The gap opened to become a surging tide of men.

Miro watched, sickened, as they went straight for the refugees. He saw children trampled beneath heavy boots, women vainly trying to run, cut down from behind. The panic began, and the refugees began to surge. There was nowhere for them to go. The rampaging attackers surged through the gap as the slaughter began in earnest.

"You cowards!" Lord Rorelan screamed. There were tears streaming down his face.

Miro spied a sudden commotion on the opposite bank. The trees began to move, and a group of men emerged from the forest. They were small men, with light-colored hair and ruddy complexions. More men came out. They were followed by a multitude of others. They continued to advance all the way to the riverbank. More men kept coming all the time. They held weapons in their hands: bows, curved pieces of wood with feathered spears fitted to a string.

"It's the Dunfolk," Marshal Beorn whispered. "As I live and breathe, I cannot believe it."

There was a woman at their head. She wore an enchantress's green silk dress, auburn hair flowing down her shoulders. At her side were a tiny man and a white-robed priest.

"Amber," Miro said when he saw her.

The Dunfolk formed a line along the bank. As one, they leaned back, pulling on the strings of their bows until their arms must have been bursting with the pain of it. They released.

The sky darkened with the flight of the arrows speeding over the Sarsen. Miro held his breath as he watched the arc of their flight. The sharpened heads of the shafts weighed down their flight as they reached their apex. Then they fell.

The wave of arrows decimated the rampaging legionnaires. A second flight was already on its way. The attack faltered.

"Plug that gap! Every third man to the top of the line!" Miro cried. "Hold them back!"

The leading wave of attackers was cut down to a man. The Dunfolk released another flight of arrows, this time into the rear of the enemies' lines.

Miro held his breath. They had gained some time. But for how long?

"Sir, look!" Marshal Beorn pointed.

Miro gasped as he saw the lone warrior. He had crested the peak of the enemy command point, his sword blazing like the sun.

He was still unopposed.

66

Love starts with a smile, grows with a kiss, and ends with a tear.
—Torak proverb

Amber immediately grasped the situation as the Dunfolk released yet another flight of arrows. She had never realized the devastating potential of the weapons. Used in a group, they were deadly.

Father Morten helped some of the refugees. The priest looked exhausted. He and Amber had led the Dunfolk for two days without stopping. She only prayed they were in time.

"I'm going to get to a higher vantage to see what's happening on the other side," she called. The priest nodded without looking up.

Amber ran to the crest of a hill, breathing heavily by the time she arrived. The sight that greeted her was like nothing she could have imagined.

There was a mass of refugees on the opposite bank, their numbers uncountable. Protecting them from the horde of attacking forces was an incredibly long line of Alturan and Halrana soldiers.

They were only barely holding. In moments they would be overrun.

The refugees were coming across in rafts. Where the great span of the Sutanesta Bridge had once stood was an empty space.

The massive blocks were scattered across the river, their tops poking above the water. There was no way the refugees would make it across before the defenders were overrun.

Like a surging ocean the enemy threw themselves against the defenders again and again. The Alturan commander was skilled indeed to have made it this long, surviving by the barest margin. Amber could see him outlined against the sky, gesturing as he gave orders.

The enemy had chosen a similar vantage for their command of the battlefield. Amber could just make out an imposing man in imperial purple, another man in white at his side. She frowned.

A lone warrior, an Alturan by his colors, was rushing up the side of the hill, throwing enemy warriors to the left and right with sheer determination. He carried an immense two-handed sword, shimmering with a rainbow of colors. Amber knew that sword. She knew that figure.

Her eyes opened wide. Her breath caught in her throat. It was Igor.

As Amber looked on, her husband cut into a legionnaire, tearing the man open in a burst of blood. He caught a blow in return on his neck but ignored it. He threw another warrior from the summit of the hill.

Amber couldn't watch. This was the father of her child. Her husband. But she couldn't look away.

He crested the hill. Ignoring the man in white, he went for the emperor. The sword turned blue with fire. Igor leapt forward.

People of all nations watched Igor Samson, Master of the Academy, plunge his enchanted blade into the chest of Xenovere V, Emperor of Tingara. He withdrew the blade. The man in purple crumpled to the ground and then keeled over.

Amber put her hand to her mouth in horror as Igor was in turn cut down from behind, a sword penetrating all the way through his chest.

As he fell to his knees, he looked out over the battle below, and Amber could swear he met her eyes. Then the light went out of his.

Amber cried out. Father Morten looked up at her in concern. She started to run. Down the steep hillside she ran, not knowing where she ran, or why, her legs just carrying her forward.

Shrubs tore at her ankles, gravel slipped under her boots, and Amber's breath came in and out of her chest in sobs and heaves.

Amber reached the rafts. An enchanter was hard at work, a rope in his hands as he pulled a raft in to shore. One glance told Amber he was holding the bits of wood together by lore alone; hastily scrawled runes glowed on the motley collection of planks.

"Take me across," Amber said.

"Are you crazy?"

"Now!" she screamed.

The enchanter looked at her green dress. "Get on."

The crests and troughs of the river surged in a turbulent fury. The raft threatened to tip with every wave, and that was with just the two of them. Amber could only imagine what it would be like crowded with a host of refugees.

Igor! He was wounded and needed her. She'd tried so hard. She'd done her best. The arrows of the Dunfolk hadn't been enough.

Now Amber raced to be with the only man who had ever loved her. Her husband was wounded. He'd battled through hordes of the enemy to protect her.

The raft smashed into the opposite bank. Amber fell out onto the bank, half in the river. She pulled herself up by her arms.

"Igor!" she cried.

Amber ran in the direction of the fiercest fighting.

67

Pain is inevitable.
                              —*The Evermen Cycles*, 8:11

Killian opened his eyes and panicked. He was blind!

No, not blind, but there was something obscuring his vision.

He tried to move, and winced in pain. He was pinned down, something heavy holding him in place. As his eyes adjusted to the lack of light, he realized it was a massive piece of rock. Another boulder lay across one of his legs. Behind his head he could feel hard stone. He was covered in rubble.

Killian coughed; dust filled the air. The last thing he remembered was the beast. He'd set the explosion and the woman had nearly killed him. With sudden force the memories returned. The refinery. Evrin had said he needed to destroy the refinery above all else.

With a surge of strength, Killian kicked forward with his free leg. Stars sparkled in his vision, and he nearly passed out again from the pain, but something moved. He kicked out again. The rubble shifted, and wriggling his knees, he finally managed to free enough space to kick out with the full strength of his legs. He heard the crunching sound of rolling rocks as a spot of light showed near the lower half of his body.

Killian next tried to move his arms. His left arm screamed in pain, and he cried out aloud.

Then he stilled, his breath coming ragged. Had he heard something? Then it came again. A shriek, followed by a beastly roar. Somewhere in the distance. The creature. Even with the explosion, she was still alive.

Killian imagined her finding him trapped in this way. He remembered the screams of the man in the woods of Petrya. The cries had lasted until dawn. There was some twisted streak in the woman—she enjoyed seeing pain. He imagined her looking at him, laughing in her rasping croak as she clicked her fingers together and prepared to watch him squirm.

Panicking in earnest now, Killian ignored the pain in his body and kicked out with his arms and legs. He pushed his head upward, feeling the weight of the rock above move slightly. He took a deep breath. He pushed again, with every bit of strength he possessed.

His head burst free of the pile of rock. He reached out with his arms and freed his body. Scrabbling over the rubble, an eye out for the figure in the ragged white dress, he crawled and pulled his way out. Killian stood panting, the massive rocks littering the floor in all directions.

He was at the very base of the shaft. He looked up. He had fallen the entire height of the mountain and then been crushed by the immense weight of boulders.

Killian then looked down at himself. He felt pain all over his body, yet he didn't even have any broken limbs. Half of the runes on his skin had faded; the rest glowed faintly silver.

The muscles of Killian's bare chest were now clearly visible. He could see the cuts and slices on his body. He was no longer cloaked by the runes.

Killian felt in the pocket of his trousers. The last cube was still there. There was work to do.

The scream of the woman sounded again, closer. Killian looked around. There was only one direction he could take.

A bright light came from a glowing archway, its stones covered in the flowing letters of an ancient script. Evrin had described this chamber. Killian had reached the home of the refinery, where the most precious substance in Merralya came into being.

Killian limped into the chamber. At one end of the vaulted room was a strange, pointed cylinder. A beam of light shone from the cylinder and onto a great crystal that buzzed and hummed. Light shone from its glittering facets and focused on a single point underneath. The light at that point was too bright to look at.

Killian stared in awe at the ancient relic of the Evermen. The energy in the room raised the hair on his arms, the air fairly crackling with power. It seemed a shame to destroy such a wondrous creation.

Entering the room almost reluctantly, Killian reached into his pocket for the cube.

Then he noticed it, a small pedestal in the corner of the room, a brown-covered book resting on it.

The Halrana Lexicon.

Killian turned as he heard a noise behind him, and a figure in white stepped into view.

"It was no difficulty to determine where your next target would be," she said in a sibilant voice.

This time, she carried a silver dagger in each fist.

Killian looked about for a weapon. The floor was white marble. The walls were bare.

He felt fear course through him.

"Who are you?" he asked.

"My name is Saryah. I am the High Templar. You are standing on hallowed ground. Your presence here disturbs the Evermen."

Killian fingered the cube in his pocket. It would kill both of them. If it came to it, could he do it?

Saryah raised her weapons. Her yellow eyes glinted murderously.

Killian's skin tingled, but with nothing like the power of before. So many of the runes were dark. He had lost the advantage of invisibility. "Would you face an unarmed man?" he asked.

"A blasphemer like you? I would remove your head from your shoulders with pleasure." Saryah crept slowly forward, her daggers held in front of her. "And you survived a fight with me. I think you are the first. I would hardly call you defenseless."

Saryah charged. Killian weaved, attempting to move outside the whirling blades. His adversary responded too quickly, twirling and thrusting at Killian's chest. A dagger stabbed a short way into his body before Killian managed to twist away. His skin sizzled. The sensation was agonizing.

Killian tried to lash out with his elbow. Saryah ducked and swung at Killian's legs. Killian jumped the stroke but fell heavily as one of his ankles gave out. He rolled out of the way just as a blow came crashing into the ground.

Killian stood. He gingerly put weight on his ankle, and his face contorted with pain. He was forced to put most of his weight on the other foot.

Saryah wasn't even out of breath. Her gaze was venomous as she charged again. She feinted at Killian's head. As Killian tried to duck, she changed her stroke to stab at his stomach. Bright sparks sprayed off as the blow was turned by the runes.

Killian took the opportunity to back away, moving around the jewel. He needed time. Time he didn't have.

There was no other choice. He had to activate the cube while he still could.

Killian withdrew it and spoke the final activation sequence. The cube came alive in his hand.

Saryah frowned.

"We will both die here together," Killian said. "The primate will no longer be able to control the people he has turned to his will. It will all come down. One day we will reconstruct the machines. But never again will we give them to the control of a madman."

Saryah threw herself at Killian. A blade bit into his thigh and another into his shoulder. The room crackled and roared with the blows. Blood started running down from Killian's body. Saryah was in a frenzy to retrieve the cube.

In the throes of pain, Killian was pushed backward, away from the jewel. He needed to get closer. If he didn't destroy it, he would be throwing his life away for nothing.

He was almost to the wall at the back of the chamber when he sensed something behind him. Risking a look, he realized it was the pointed cylinder, its beam of light continuously energizing the crystal.

He suddenly had an idea.

Killian tossed the cube past the book on its pedestal, seeing Saryah rush to retrieve it. Then, running to the cylinder, he grasped it in both hands.

The pain was excruciating. It felt like his hands were melting. Killian gritted his teeth and tensed his arms, the beam of light moving away from the jewel. Killian summoned all of the power in his limbs.

Saryah recovered the cube at the same instant that Killian pointed the intense ray of light at the woman in white.

The beam was wide, and Saryah had no way of avoiding it. She raised something in her arms, between her face and the light.

It was the Halrana Lexicon. The brown-covered book had a rune on the cover—the number six.

As Killian looked on, the rune lit up with power. The Lexicon began to glow, brighter and brighter, until it was too bright to look on.

Saryah screamed, dropping the book.

The beam hit her in the face. For an instant, her twisted, contorted face turned white. In a sudden flash, her head exploded in a burst of energy.

Killian didn't wait. He released the cylinder and ducked under its beam. Scooping up the Halrana Lexicon, he tucked it under his arm, threw the cube at the jewel, and stumbled out of the chamber.

Killian fled, ducking into a narrow stairway, cut into the wall. He began to climb.

The refinery exploded.

Killian fell into darkness, terrible and absolute.

68

The fewer people who know of our Lexicon's location,
the safer we will be.
— Diary of High Enchantress Maya Pallandor,
page 868, 411 Y.E.

The death of the emperor gave the defenders new hope. The ragged line reformed, and a defiant group of Alturan infantry, supported by Halrana pikemen, even began to push back. Miro wondered who the heroic soldier had been. His sacrifice had given them the respite they needed. He was directly responsible for saving the lives of thousands of refugees.

Yet the reprieve was brief.

After an entire day's fighting, the defenders' strength was beginning to give out. Miro could see their weariness in every aspect as swords became impossibly heavy, and rather than protecting them, armor trapped the men in its heavy grip.

The soldiers of Altura and Halaran had fought beyond every call of duty. Nearly half of the refugees had been taken across the river. The defenders had lasted hour after hour, holding back the implacable tide.

"Sir." A man pointed.

Miro saw it then. The Veznan nightshades were coming in force. His heart lurched in his chest.

As tall as two men, with green limbs like clubs and skin of the toughest bark, the nightshades hardly paused as they smashed into the line. The soldiers—mostly Halrana—fled in terror. Behind the Halrana were the wooden carts containing row after row of idle constructs, but the nightshades were as opposite to Halrana constructs as night and day. A colossus or iron golem glowed fiercely and announced its presence with every footstep. Tangled vines covered the nightshades so that it seemed nature itself had come to destroy all in its path.

Two bladesingers fought a nightshade, vainly looking for an opening in the moss and vines. The creature picked one of the bladesingers up and, almost casually, tore the man into two pieces. The living tree then reached for the second bladesinger.

"Dear Skylord . . ." Miro whispered. He hung his head; he could watch no more.

"Lord Marshal!"

From through the ranks a glowing Halrana colossus lumbered forward to smash into the nightshade's side. Dwarfing the nightshade by an order of magnitude, the gigantic construct plucked it out of the ground and stamped down on its torso.

The animator in his controller cage then moved the colossus further into the battle. With great strides the colossus took the fight to the enemy, tossing nightshades through the air.

Simultaneously, the doors of a wooden cart crashed open, and row after row of woodmen poured out. Another wagon trembled under the weight of the ironmen marching out of its belly. Six iron golems hurled into four Imperial avengers.

Somehow, unbelievably, the Halrana were back in the battle.

Miro looked back at the river. Over half of the refugees had crossed now.

The ground suddenly shook, a thunderous crash coming from the battlefield as the colossus went down, the animator trapped in his controller cage. As Miro watched, a tree warrior smashed down on the cage, and the man was no more.

With the added support of the constructs, the defenders reformed the line. But the field was filled with the enemy, and even as the front line of the attackers fell, those next in line were pushed ahead by the weight of their numbers.

The Black Army's relentless momentum was impossible to stop.

———◆———

Miro watched as another bladesinger fell, swamped by scores of legionnaires. He looked at Marshal Beorn. The scarred veteran nodded. He then looked at Lord Rorelan, who put his hand on Miro's shoulder.

"You did well, Lord Marshal Torresante," said Lord Rorelan.

Miro shook his head. "Please don't call me that."

"Miro," said Rorelan. He drew his sword, the afternoon sunlight glinting from the sharpened steel.

Miro heard the whisper of metal as Beorn in turn stood with weapon in hand, a grim expression on his face.

Miro reached over his shoulder and drew his zenblade. The rune-inscribed surface shone like a mirror. The two other commanders activated their armor. Miro began to sing, the sequences coming smooth and unhurried.

In a dreamlike state he began to walk down into the battle. The zenblade grew brighter and brighter. It moved through yellow and orange. The blade flared in a burst of red fire.

As he descended, a flicker of motion caught Miro's eye, and he saw a figure in a green dress running through the ranks of the defenders. Miro nearly stopped in his tracks. He knew that face.

The woman was Amber.

What in the Skylord's name was she doing here? Amber was heading directly into the battle!

Miro began to run, leaving behind the two commanders in their heavy armor. He saw Amber again, a flash of green through the intermingled bodies of friend and foe. Miro cut down a legionnaire in black, and then thrust his blade through the neck of another. The soldier put his hand to the gushing wound and fell down.

Miro cut left and right, following Amber, but always she was too far away. The intense light of a bladesinger drew the enemy from all quarters, and Miro fought like a demon, but they kept coming. His hands became covered in blood. The zenblade turned blue with the force of Miro's song. Each thrust, each swing, was death to one of the enemy.

It was never enough. Amber had disappeared from his sight.

The enemy pushed at him, their numbers too great to withstand. Looking to the left, he saw the line beginning to crumble, and this time there was nothing to stop the enemy's advance. The Alturan soldiers in the distance were simply swallowed by the Black Army, their bodies trampled into the dust.

It was over.

Miro's arms burned with fire as he weaved, parried, and slashed with furious determination. He was going to take as many of the enemy with him as possible.

There was a buzzing in his ears, but he ignored it in his bloodlust. He let the enemy come at him, one after another in an unending wave. The sound grew louder.

Miro could no longer ignore the tone, the single crystal note at the edge of his hearing. It grew louder, until it was clearly audible. It was a note of the sweetest silver, a clarion of hope. The sound increased in volume. It became so loud that soldiers stopped fighting, putting their hands to their ears. Still it grew.

Miro turned, looking frantically from side to side. Where was Amber? The defenders around him were, to a man, looking behind them, back toward the Sarsen. The warriors of the Black Army all looked above Miro's head in the same direction. An intense light shone from somewhere near the river.

There was a tall pointed rock nearby, barely wide enough for a man to stand on. Miro pushed aside the men in his way and leapt atop the rock with the agility that only a bladesinger possessed. Balancing on his toes, he gazed into the distance.

Miro gasped as the men began to whisper. It came from the Alturans first, their eyes wide with the first faces of hope that Miro had seen all day.

Miro had to believe the whispers; he could see with his own eyes. There was no mistaking the shimmering green and silver hooded robe. It shone like the sun, the runes coloring and rippling as it put forth the call. She was at the river crossing. Something was happening.

"It's the high enchantress," the voices said. "She's opening the way home."

Then the note stopped. Men shook their heads. With renewed vigor, the battle resumed.

69

One person can make a difference.
—The Evermen Cycles, 5:25

Ella leapt down from Sundhep's back and slapped the horse on the rump to send it away. People everywhere milled about in confusion.

She was on high ground, on the Alturan side of the river, and could see a raft swamp at the far side as too many of the refugees jumped on at once. A baby screamed as a woman tried to hand it to the enchanter guiding the raft. He shook his head in despair, barely able to keep control as it was.

"Stop!" Ella called across the river, to no effect.

She rummaged through her bag, swiftly finding what she was looking for. Holding the scrill in one hand and the flask of essence in the other, she called again.

"Get back!" Once again there was no response.

Ella looked down at the high enchantress's robe, realizing what she needed to do. She chanted the runes, her voice coming strong as the sequences built one on the other. The robe began to glow silver, growing brighter as she continued. She added further complexity, projecting the light like a beacon as the people around her quailed in confusion. The enchanter held his raft at the far bank, his eyes tightly closed.

The robe began to hum as Ella continued to name the runes. It quivered like a drum, the hum growing louder, becoming a single pure note that grew in intensity. All activity on both sides of the river stopped.

When the sound reached a crescendo, Ella let the runes subside, and the sound died away.

Ella looked across the river at the waiting refugees, massed where the jagged far bank plunged down to meet the water. All eyes were on her.

Ella had their attention.

"Stand back!" she shouted. "You!" she cried out to the enchanter on the far bank. "Get back onto high ground, and line everybody up."

To Ella's sudden surprise, they started to move. From her vantage, she quickly assessed the situation.

The huge blocks that had formed the wide span of the Sutanesta Bridge lay in the chaotic current of the river, with only a few tops poking above the surface. They were scattered about, impossibly heavy.

Across the river the battle raged. The defenders were being overrun, and soon the massacre would begin.

Ella stepped forward onto a place where the rocky ground was smooth and once more looked at the scrill and essence in her hands. She felt the power and the knowledge swell within her.

Her trials flashed before her eyes. She remembered her pride at the Academy and the day she showed Master Goss she understood the runes better than he did. She recalled the night she broke into Master Samson's laboratory, Talwin's death, his body ruined by the essence. The wracking. Being awarded the Academy's highest honors. Her part in the theft of her house's Lexicon. Climbing, falling, and nearly drowning in pursuit of Killian. Layla. Learning from Evrin. The bandits in Wondhip Pass. The creature, chasing her and Killian in Petrya. The knowledge from the Alturan Lexicon. The lore of illusion.

It was all in preparation for this moment.

Ella looked down at the stone she was standing on. She knew what she needed to do.

She cleared her mind and let her intuition guide her.

Ella set her mind free to find the runes that she needed. Animator's runes. Enchanter's runes. Illusionist's runes. She looked at the Halrana bank. The refugees were watching her, an expression of awe on their faces.

The river surged through the wide channel.

Ella crouched and started to draw on the rock's flat surface. Her hand worked deftly, the matrices soon covering a great portion of the stone.

She could see the opposite bank, where the fighting raged on. In the distance, a man tried to protect his family from the rampaging legionnaires. He was butchered mercilessly.

Her hand moved almost of its own accord as Ella inscribed rune after rune in quick succession. This was nothing she had ever seen before. She was combining the symbols into completely new arrangements.

As Ella worked, she activated the runes, but she never stopped exerting herself. Her lips moved constantly—this made a blade-singer's song look simple in comparison. She didn't look up to see the effect her activations were having—if she stopped, she would falter.

Ella was enchanting the very air.

Her mind cast back to a simpler time, when she had been walking with Killian, showing him the nine bridges of Sarostar. She remembered when she'd walked with him on the bridge that led to the Crystal Palace. He'd trusted her that day, taking hesitant steps into nothingness.

Ella was building a runebridge.

She felt her spirit soar as she drew on the memory.

Finally Ella looked up. Her ethereal bridge soared above her, connecting the solid stone to the Halrana side of the riverbank. Ella breathed in deeply as she took a step into nothingness, and then another. Her heart surged with joy as she took three more steps, and then more, until she was at the apex of the glowing bridge of light.

Hearing voices, Ella looked back behind her.

A tiny man stood with complete composure on the shimmering bridge. He had the light hair and ruddy features of one of the Dunfolk.

"You are Ella," he said.

Ella felt she was in a dream. "Yes," she said.

He nodded. "I am the Tartana."

Behind him, countless Dunfolk were lined up. The Tartana waved his arm forward, and their small forms ran past Ella, down the far side of the bridge. In moments they reached the scene of the battle and instantly their numbers started to tell.

As more Dunfolk continued to cross, Ella followed them over the formless bridge to the Halrana side. For a moment there was silence, then a cheer came from the refugees. Reaching them, Ella caught the eyes of the enchanter. "Cross them over," she said. "It will hold."

"What about you?"

"There's still more to be done."

Ella activated the runes on her dress, and it shimmered with each stride as she walked toward the battle. Colored lights flickered from her body, and men fell back around her. The fighting continued, but none were prepared to fight her.

Ella saw a man with the *raj hada* of a commander. Several scales of his armor had been torn away. His face was scarred and framed by gray eyebrows and a ragged beard.

"Marshal," Ella said.

He dispatched an enemy and turned. An expression of complete surprise crossed his face. "Who are you? You're not Evora Guinestor."

"Marshal, a way has been found across the river. A bridge has been created."

"How?"

"It doesn't matter. The refugees will soon finish crossing. I need you to tell your men to fall back."

He pointed to the terrible specter of the Black Army's countless numbers. "If we turn now we'll be slaughtered."

"Leave that to me, Marshal . . ." Ella said. "What is your name?"

"Beorn."

"Well, Marshal Beorn. We can still save your men."

He nodded decisively. "I'll call the men back."

70

You have only one life; therefore, it is a perfect life.
—*The Evermen Cycles*, 4:14

Miro cut down another legionnaire, only to face one more. He could still see no sign of Amber.

"Fall back!" the order came from behind.

Dispatching his opponent, Miro turned around in surprise. Who had issued the order? To turn back now would invite slaughter. Where would they go?

"Fall back!" the order came again. "Fall back!"

A shape hurled itself into the enemy, a bladesinger, whirling like a fiery demon, cutting down his opponents, doing anything he could to give the retreating men the space they needed.

The enemy backed away under the bladesingers' furious charge, but they quickly regained their strength as the great mass pushed forward. Soldiers everywhere behind were abandoning the defensive embankment.

Miro could now see the sheer number of enemy corpses. They lined the ground under the earthworks one on top of another.

Along with some brave soldiers, the bladesinger was almost single-handedly holding back the tide of the enemy. Miro caught the man's snarling face under curly dark locks, realizing who he was.

Bartolo.

Before he knew it Miro had added to his own song, shouting it with the full strength of his voice as he ran to help his friend. Bartolo thrust his sword into a legionnaire's side and turned at the sound of Miro's voice. He grinned wickedly.

Miro threw himself into the fray with renewed vigor. His zenblade turned purple, then blue. He tore into the enemy ranks with the ferocity of a storm, cutting down man after man. He could hear Bartolo singing, their two voices joined in an eerie battle cry.

The enemy ranks in front tried to flee, but the force of the men behind them pushed them forward, directly into the whirling swords.

"That's enough—we need to go now," Bartolo panted.

He grabbed Miro's arm, and the two men turned and headed for the river.

As they left, Miro looked over his shoulder. Amber. What had happened to her?

71

The greatest harm can come from the will to do the greatest good.
—*The Evermen Cycles*, 11:19

Primate Melovar Aspen smiled as the defenders broke, abandoning their defenses. Two stubborn bladesingers kept fighting, but the rest were running. There was nowhere for them to go. Victory was his.

The crumpled body of the emperor lay next to him. The primate let it stay there. It gave him pleasure to see the proud ruler brought to nothing but a pile of bones and flesh.

The primate took a sip of black liquid from a crystal glass. His face twisted and grimaced. It tasted awful. He kicked the emperor's body, and to his left, Moragon grinned. Melovar briefly wondered if there was something in the elixir that was taking away his humanity. Hadn't he once wondered this before? The thought quickly fled.

He looked at the second body—the enchanter with the special sword. Now that had been a scare. He had almost laughed out loud when the fanatic breasted the top of the hill, splattered with blood and gore, and then ignored him and killed the emperor.

The sword was interesting. He would have to have it studied. He had never seen or heard of such a powerful enchanted blade. Even now it still quivered and sparked.

The Alturan's body was headless now: the primate had asked for the man's head to be mounted on a pike. It took the place of the emperor, looking out over the battlefield at the primate's right hand. An expression of triumph was on the man's face. A surprisingly old face. Who was this man? The primate supposed he would never know.

The two bladesingers had finally given up, and like the others, they were running also. The defenders were in full rout.

The primate could see the seething mass of refugees pinned against the riverbank. There was something strange about them, the figures oddly uniform, but he quickly discounted it.

A commander ran forward. "We have them on the run. The refugees are trapped along the bank. What orders?"

"Full attack," said the primate. "Push them into the river or kill them outright."

Melovar looked on as his Black Army flowed over the pitiful defenses like the dam of a river being broken. Each man pushed against the man in front of him. And with no resistance now, there was nothing stopping them from smashing into the milling refugees with the force of a breaking wave. The primate wondered how many bodies would show up bloated on the shores of the Sarsen. It was a pleasant image.

The primate frowned and rubbed at his eyes as the image of the refugees wavered like a mirage in the desert.

The air shimmered and then solidified. Melovar rubbed once more at his eyes. There was something wrong. The image flickered again. Then the scene abruptly shifted.

Changed.

The refugees were gone. His great army was racing headlong toward an empty ridge, with nothing but a sheer drop between them and the raging Sarsen.

Melovar looked on in horror as the soldiers pressed on, meeting no resistance. The refugees simply weren't there anymore. Where they had been, the earth terminated abruptly in a jagged cliff. The men in front tried to stop, but their momentum was too great.

"Stop it! Stop them!" the primate cried.

Man after man of the Black Army plummeted into the icy waters of the Sarsen. They died by the thousands, trapped by the weight of their own numbers.

A great cheer sounded. Looking up, the primate saw an impossible sight. The defenders had somehow crossed the river. A bridge of rainbow light crossed the Sarsen.

As Melovar watched, the bridge faded. Soon, it was as if it had never been there.

72

Never fight to the bitter end. Either fight to win,
or live to fight another day.
—Memoirs of Emperor Xenovere I, 121:1, 381 Y.E.

Miro was the last to cross the bridge. He leapt lightly to the Alturan side and gazed upward at the forests of his homeland. He had never seen such a beautiful sight.

He wondered again at the ability of whoever had assembled the bridge. It must have been the high enchantress. He didn't see how it could have been anyone else.

Miro heard the screams and cries of terrified men. Looking across the river, he saw a commotion as a horde of enemy soldiers plunged over a cliff. Their bodies tumbled into the water, sinking instantly as their heavy armor weighed them down. It was another event that left Miro breathless. What had really happened here this day?

A hooded woman in a green robe strode to the bank. She raised her arms, chanting runes in a powerful voice. At her command the magical bridge faded away.

The woman turned and her arms dropped to her sides. Suddenly Miro couldn't breathe. He simply stopped and stared. The pale blonde hair, the bright green eyes.

It was Ella.

She looked exhausted. He could see dark circles under her eyes, as if she hadn't slept in weeks. A small woman walked up to her, one of the Dunfolk. Miro recognized the healer who had saved Ella's life, so long ago. Layla.

The small woman opened her arms. Ella bent down and hugged Layla. Tears started flowing down Ella's face. Layla whispered something, but Miro couldn't hear what it was.

73

You won't know who my people are, but they will know you,
and they will know your children.

—Primate Melovar Aspen to
Lady Katherine Torresante, 524 Y.E.

"The Lord Marshal wishes to see you," Layla whispered.

Ella composed herself. "Where is he?"

"Right behind you."

Ella whirled, and there he was.

He looked awful. He was covered in blood, and a new scar ran from below his left eye to his jaw line. His armorsilk was torn. He looked like a man twice his age.

"Miro!" Ella cried. She ran to him, and he enfolded her in his arms. Ella felt wetness against her cheek. Was he crying? She pulled back from him. He was!

Miro wiped at his eyes. "Ella. It was you?"

Color came to her cheeks; she nodded.

"But how?"

"It's a long story. And you? You're the lord marshal?"

"I suppose I am." He grinned ruefully. "We have a lot to talk about."

They both looked around at the smiling onlookers.

Miro's face suddenly clouded. He gripped his sister by the arms. "Amber! Have you seen her?"

"She's here? No, I haven't seen her. Where is she?"

A man walked over, his eyes sad. It was Father Morten from Sarostar. "Amber crossed the river," he said. "She didn't come back."

Miro looked back across the river, his fists clenched at his sides.

Ella took her brother by the arm, and together they followed the Dunfolk into the forests of Altura.

74

And so I bid you farewell. My second expedition to the Great Western Ocean is finally ready to depart—we leave with the tide. This time I feel that we are prepared. The Buchalanti have stayed silent, but I have seen too much on my travels to believe that the world of the Tingaran Empire is all there is. Wish me fortune. I hope to see you all soon.

—Toro Marossa, "Explorations," page 589, 423 Y.E.

The people of Salvation thought it must be a miracle. Perhaps it was an omen? The promised return of the Evermen had come at last.

The mountain of Stonewater billowed smoke like a volcano.

A lone man came shuffling and stumbling down from the primate's home. He was bare-chested, covered in blood and grime, his flesh scratched and torn. Perhaps once his trousers had been brown. He had unruly red hair that hung to his collar. When he looked up people remarked on his piercing blue eyes.

Killian limped along with the glowing Halrana Lexicon held in his arms. He felt pain all over his body, but he ignored the stares of the ordinary citizens of Salvation. Their eyes followed him as he headed for the Temple of the Sky and his rendezvous with Evrin Evenstar.

Killian coughed and lurched, holding onto a wall for support. He turned into a side street and hobbled past a group of staring girls. Turning another corner, he saw the crystal dome ahead.

He had done it. He had accomplished the impossible. He had the Halrana Lexicon, and the primate's perversion of essence would be no more.

Killian wiped his mouth and looked at the smear of red on his hand. He touched his tongue to the moisture on his lip and then wiggled a loose tooth.

Reaching the temple, he had to summon all of his strength to even push the doors apart, but finally he entered to soothing music. Row upon row of marble benches confronted him. A man sat with head bowed. A young woman's lips moved in prayer.

Evrin Evenstar was nowhere to be seen.

Killian sat down heavily and put his head in his hands.

EPILOGUE

Prince Ilathor Shanti rose as Jehral entered the huge tent. Jehral's body was covered in dust, his face weather beaten, and his eyes tired. "Come, come," Ilathor said. "I am anxious to hear your news."

Jehral nodded his thanks as the prince gestured to a space on the floor. He sank down gratefully. Ilathor offered him a goblet of water, and the desert warrior drank in huge gulps.

"Well?" Prince Ilathor uncharacteristically hurried him along. Jehral's eyes opened in surprise.

"We lost her some time before the Wondhip Pass. We tried to cross but discovered the pass blocked. We don't understand how. Blocks of stone had been moved to form an impassable wall. Symbols covered them . . ."

"She was the builder of this wall?" Ilathor shook his head in appreciation. "She was truly a mighty enchantress."

Jehral paused. "My Prince, I do not believe she was the builder."

"Why? What is it you are not telling me?"

"The Petryans were gathering in force below the pass; they have been neatly kept from Alturan lands. One of our men infiltrated their camp. There was word that a great battle was going to be fought at the Sutanesta Bridge. The Petryans were angry because they would miss the battle."

"Jehral, what about her? What about the high enchantress? Tell me what happened to Evora!"

Jehral flinched at the prince's anger. "I do not know how to say this, my Prince. The Petryans, they were full of this story. They said that . . . They said that they possessed the body of High Enchantress Evora Guinestor. She was killed in the desert. The Petryan high lord hung her body from the walls of his capital, Tlaxor."

Ilathor froze. He eyes unfocused and the color drained from his face. "Did you see?" he asked, his voice little more than a whisper.

"We journeyed to Tlaxor. We saw the body. It was pointed out to us."

"It was her?"

"It . . . It was in a terrible state. It was too hard to tell." The prince suddenly stood. "I am sorry, my Prince," Jehral said. "I cared for her too."

Prince Ilathor Shanti walked out of the tent. The guards saluted when he exited, but he was oblivious. He fixed his eyes onto the distant horizon, picturing pale blonde hair and a pair of shimmering green eyes.

He remembered the tales she had told him. The fabled cities of wealth and corruption. Seranthia, the capital of the world.

His eyes fell. He looked down from his perch and into the valley below. A strong wind billowed up.

Prince Ilathor Shanti gazed out at the sea of black tents. They filled the entire valley, endless numbers of fearless desert warriors. The tribes had gathered at his call.

Soon, they would ride.

ACKNOWLEDGMENTS

Writing this novel has been a grand adventure, and I've been fortunate enough to have met some wonderful people along the way.

Huge thanks must go to my editor, Emilie, and the team at 47North, for excellent guidance, support, and assistance with every aspect of development and publication.

Thank you also, David, for believing in me.

Thanks go to Mike for tireless efforts with the editorial development of the manuscript and for endless patience. Something tells me I should insert an exclamation mark at the end of the last sentence.

I'd also like to thank all of the supportive family, friends, and colleagues who have helped me along the way. In particular, I'd like to thank Marc F., Lyn W., Andy McB., and Mark M.

Thanks to all of you who've reached out to me and taken the time to post reviews of my books.

My final thanks I reserve for my wife, Alicia.

I will be ever grateful for your constant support.

ABOUT THE AUTHOR

 James Maxwell found inspiration growing up in the lush forests of New Zealand, and later in rugged Australia where he was educated. Devouring fantasy and science fiction classics at an early age, his love for books translated to a passion for writing, which he began at age 11.

He relocated to London at age 25, but continued to seek inspiration wherever he could find it, in the grand cities of the old world and the monuments of fallen empires. His travels influenced his writing as he spent varying amounts of time in forty countries on six continents.

He wrote his first full-length novel, *Enchantress*, while living on an isle in Thailand and its sequel, *The Hidden Relic*, from a coastal town on the Yucatán peninsula in Mexico.

The third book in the Evermen Saga, *The Path of the Storm*, was written in the Austrian Alps, and he completed the fourth, *The Lore of the Evermen*, in Malta.

When he isn't writing or traveling, James enjoys sailing, snowboarding, classical guitar, and French cooking.